The Cause

The Cause

Roderick Vincent

Winchester, UK
Washington, USA

First published by Roundfire Books, 2014
Roundfire Books is an imprint of John Hunt Publishing Ltd., Laurel House, Station Approach,
Alresford, Hants, SO24 9JH, UK
office1@jhpbooks.net
www.johnhuntpublishing.com
www.roundfire-books.com

For distributor details and how to order please visit the 'Ordering' section on our website.

Text copyright: Roderick Vincent 2013

ISBN: 978 1 78279 763 0

A CIP catalogue record for this book is available from the British Library.

Design: Stuart Davies

Printed in the USA by Edwards Brothers Malloy

We operate a distinctive and ethical publishing philosophy in all
areas of our business, from our global network of authors to
production and worldwide distribution.

CONTENTS

"When men take up arms to set other men free, there is something sacred and holy in the warfare."
—Woodrow Wilson

For my country.

May we avoid the destructive path this pen forebodes.

The Cause—a term used by the Sons of Liberty, a group formed in 1765 by the Loyal Nine

Part I

The Abattoir

Chapter 1

"Man cannot discover new oceans unless he has the courage to lose sight of the shore."
-André Gide

May 13th, 2026

There it is—a blue marble in the blackness of space, sweeps of white fuzzing the spherical surface, so small you can put your thumb over it and blip it out of existence. The Earth, suspended in the darkness, silent and fragile. But this is deception. It's moving very fast, and just because you can't see and feel it, doesn't mean it's not the truth.

The moon photo of the Earth was shot by astronaut Timothy Skies, who said if he could drag the world's politicians up into space, choke them by the necks and say, *take a look at that, you bastards*, perhaps there might be a way forward. I don't share his optimism, but it's a perspective few have had the luck to experience—witnessing another gravity—standing in greyish moon dust, kicking up clumps of it only to see it slowly float in a snowflake sprinkle back to your feet.

I liked the shot and kept it tucked underneath my SWAT uniform and flak jacket, pinned over my heart. A good luck charm through the bank heist gun battles, the crack house raids, and the L.A. riots that erupted in 2022. It was then, through the conflagration of 7th Street when I saved Timothy Skies and his wife from the Charleston Building under a hail of sniper fire.

The day before, nearly all of us were called in for riot duty. The National Guard had been called up, but hadn't arrived. We lined up outside L.A. Superior Court looking like helmeted centurions. We stood shoulder-to-shoulder uneasily with our full-length polycarbonate riot shields in front of us, black truncheons in hand. The crowd was massed in front of us on Erwin Street, an ocean of humanity boiling in a sea of anger over sweeping cuts to city pensions. L.A. was going bust, and the 6:00 news had carried the hard reality. Fissures of angst were like cracks in the pavement over promises that couldn't be kept.

Two DARPA BigDogs stood on each of our ends, machineguns mounted on their backs armed with rubber bullets. Taller than the old models, they stood head-high. Their strange, articulating black metal legs were in a standstill march, as if about to charge. They had attached heads to the things. As the red camera eyes within swiveled back and forth, the dogs glowered, showing their sharp, metallic teeth.

This was a mistake, I had told Sergeant Smith. You don't want to agitate the crowd. You don't want to antagonize. You want to play defense. Smith told me it was above his pay grade, that a level of curiosity above him was eager to know how they'd perform.

Even with my helmet capped over my ears, the crowd's yelling and shouting grew to a wave of stadium noise. The air vibrated with tension. The mob just in front of us hurled rocks, yelled out taunts. Then someone threw a Molotov cocktail at us and the guns atop the BigDogs started firing. The first row of instigators went down, but the second line had shields—some metallic, some like ours. Canisters of tear gas were lobbed into the crowd but many of the protesters had masks. Like insects, their rage pitched higher into a war cry. Then the line charged. We dug our back feet into the pavement anticipating their surge. A Peacekeeper drone flew over and dusted the crowd. Too late. A melee. Chaos. One of the BigDogs charged through the crowd. One of the last things I remembered was a severed arm inside its jaws. The wall of police split apart by the spears of arms and legs unafraid of the whacks of our clubs. I began clubbing people until the swarm fell upon me, kicking and beating me until I fell unconscious.

The day after, the city was still in flames. A gang had looted a gun store and targeted police and pedestrians not smart enough to flee for cover. Some of the wounded we pulled to safety, but a couple of people were already shot dead. Red pools of blood coagulated in the streets. Bloody boot prints led to the cement blockade four of us hid behind in a vacant lot. Crouched down and pinned by snipers firing from rooftops, we saw a group waving inside the Charleston. Fire licked the walls out of the windows of the second and third floors. Billowing plumes of toxic black smoke gusted into the air. Soot rained down on us cloaking our uniforms in black flakes and ash. It was snowing in L.A., a blizzard of flames spreading throughout the city.

Another spray of bullets cracked around us. "Hold your position," Sergeant Smith ordered. "The BigDogs are on their way." I smiled at him and took a big breath. He grabbed my arm, but I shook him off. He looked at me knowingly as I darted out into the fray. Many officers in the department were fooled by what I did. Some thought it a play against the robots. But it hadn't been so long since I had been declared fit for duty. The guys who knew me guessed the reason I jumped off the gangplank into a sea of gunfire had nothing to do with heroics or saving police jobs as much as it did about having nothing more to lose. It was a monster dare, diving at the jaws of the Kraken. A game of chicken I was willing to lose.

The ground lit up underneath me. Dodge-and-weave and run like hell. Automatic fire punctured the streets, the roads opening like spores from a seedpod. The Charleston puffed in little white mushroom clouds from M16 rounds as I ran toward the middle of the street. I hopped into the armor plated SWAT-H mobile and put it into drive. Gunfire pinged against the sides and roof. I threw it into reverse and drove ass-ended straight up to the Charleston's front door so Timothy Skies and the rest of the occupants could pile in.

Three months later, in the summer of 2022, Timothy Skies

invited me to one of those Apollo 15 nostalgia dinners in Tucson. A token of gratitude for what he called the *courageous officer*. A sentimental thing for me to do—to go to such an event. But as a boy, astronomy fascinated me. For my thirteenth birthday my father gave me an *Orion Dobsonian* telescope. On the weekends we could afford it, we'd drive away and camp, hike out into the darkness and set it up on an open field or weedy bluff and gaze at moon craters and the lumpy lunar landscape. Then we'd rotate it toward the rings on Saturn, watch the perfect geometry of water and ice in retrograde motion. Farther out into space the gassy clouds of the Orion Nebula hovered above us in a creamy light. Back then, the highway miles between the campsite and L.A., and the light years to Alpha Centauri seemed to be about the same.

What my father would never know was how such a small, seemingly innocuous gift, would shake history. How it would change not only my future, but turn the eyes of the world.

The Timothy Skies Space Benefit Dinner was a champagne affair, a five-thousand-dollar-a-plate kind of fundraiser to send a man to Mars. Hosted by Virgin Galactic, banners posted around the place read: *Let's Take the Next Step for Mankind*. The clutter of cross-table chitchat bounded over the clink of flutes and origami napkin swans. The penguined waiters answered to a nod, bustling around us with monogrammed white towels tucked over their sleeves, refilling our glasses the moment they hit half-empty. Mr. Skies and I sat next to one another. Presented as the hero, I found all of the fawning over the ordeal embarrassing. I wasn't there for glory or gratitude and became annoyed as the story heightened from basic fact to tall tale.

When the conversation switched to outer space, my neighbors at the table spoke with syrupy voices, imitated friendliness and love for their fellow mankind. They toasted one another with full flutes, bubbles gurgling over the rims. They showered compliments on each other as lavishly as lobbyists spending on senators. They orated the future of technology, its merits on the world and how it would transform Mars and the moon into clones of the Earth. There were speeches. A red carpet rolled right up to the dais. People cheered—standing ovations no matter how lousy or unrealistic the touted goal was. Everyone euphoric, wired into the same dogma with the delusion the event itself was some fiery rocket lift-off to wow you into their belief system. The yappy lot slavering they were on the cusp of a new millennium in human space travel.

I had a moment of enlightenment after Skies' bold speech on fusion and exploring Earth-like planets light years away. I saw delusional eyes, the need to believe, heavy gravity under teary lids. But the audience wasn't going anywhere—that was the reality of it. Still, they clung to the idea as a priest chases Paradise. Perhaps they saw the familiar world ending, or at least turning the wrong corner. Technology was the drug of deceit, saving us from ourselves. But with current technology, it would take 40,000 years to get to Alpha Centauri—200 times longer than the average lifespan of a civilization.

People don't like to see the truth in something until it's too late—then it becomes shocking. Human behavior is history's broken record. Perhaps with Mother Earth supporting eight billion humans, each wanting his own share of the pie, gobbling up every scarce non-renewable resource in sight, they scratched the itch of a sixth sense. Perhaps they sniffed an undefined new world order coming, one that would shake the trees of humanity. It wasn't what the myopic politicians were selling, not what you've been lead to believe, but nonetheless it was out there, a dormant cataclysm waiting at the end of a windy road.

A year later, deep in a tunnel where darkness reigned, the image of humanity's emptying tank would come back to me. Our leader, Seee, would say, "When a giant falls, expect the ground to shake as he gets up to chase you, not yet realizing he is already dead."

We got to talking, Mr. Skies and I. I admit there was an expectation corked in the back of my mind, that he might say something about his space experience that would be life-altering. But I left disappointed. I was the Neil Armstrong who hadn't taken a step forward, but instead took a leap back. It was July 20th 1969 in reverse, and I should have known better.

Beyond Mr. Skies' moon-trip experience, we spoke about current affairs. He was one of the technology zealots at the table who told me the pace of innovation is parabolic. "Yet we still don't have a man on Mars," I countered.

"Well, NASA hasn't helped, has it? Their budget has been squashed into oblivion."

"So you think fund raising will get you there?" I asked.

"It's what we're here for, isn't it?"

"Thank God for Richard Branson," I remarked, eying the man three tables down sitting next to CEO Blake Thompson and a throng of senators. "What will you have to give him in return?"

Skies smirked.

"He wants to be the first man stepping out, doesn't he?" I asked. "Isn't he pushing past seventy now?"

"Who cares? The man is an inspiration."

"Certainly a man who can buy a lot of inspiration." I smiled.

"Whatever gets us there."

Talk was swift and pointed. His wife Melanie was more pleasant and called me *the handsome gentleman*. "Would the handsome gentleman like another glass of red?" Perhaps a dynamic stretched between the two of them I wasn't catching, but Mr. Skies shook me off, jumping out of his seat and walking toward the Branson table. Gratitude had been paid.

Another gentleman at the table by the name of Bloom picked up the baton of the broken conversation. "You don't believe in technology then, Mr. Corvus?"

I looked at him seriously. "What has been the enabler of humanity's population explosion?"

He shrugged. "Medicine."

"True," I said. "Certainly longer life expectancies and finding cures to some of the most fatal diseases."

"The advancement of technology? Yes?"

"But what else?"

"I don't know," Mr. Bloom said, staring at me. "You tell me." I smiled at Mrs. Skies, who was listening in on the conversation. I saw youth stripped away by the stress of a husband's fame, premature fissures of age within the lines of her neck and forehead. "An abundant food supply which has only been possible with cheap and abundant energy."

Bloom nodded, seemingly pleased with this response. I allowed myself some time to take a better look at the man. He had soft brown skin, a sleek Middle Eastern look. His beaked nose fell off his face in a huge arc below his shifty eyes. He tickled his pencil mustache, twiddling the end of it between his finger and thumb. "Have you ever been hungry, Mr. Corvus? Haven't eaten in more than a couple of days?" He shifted in his seat, grabbed for his flute of champagne and twirled it in the glass. After drinking, he put it down and picked up his spoon, glaring at his reflection fastidiously.

"No," I said. "But you must be about to make a point."

He stabbed a piece of prime rib off his plate and thrust it into his mouth. He chewed with zest, shoving a lob of it in one side of his mouth so one of his cheeks ballooned.

"After about three days without eating, you get a bit antsy. You find yourself weakening, and suddenly those dormant animalistic tendencies encoded in your genes wake up and want to do something about it. Socialization skills vanish in a flash. Now imagine we have that problem on a grand scale."

"We do have that problem on a grand scale," I said.

Smiling with a twisted sense of playfulness, he seemed to weigh every word, measuring each response by a rub of the chin, or dropping it on a counterbalance with a tug of the ear, scrutinizing its content through the tines of his fork. "I guess that's a matter of opinion," he said, pointing the fork at me. "I would disagree."

"Africa is not a grand enough scale?"

"Yes, Africa is a tragedy, but I don't consider it grand scale. Perhaps you are sensitive about that being African-American? I'm talking about when the supermarkets have bare shelves."

"There'd be riots of course, but we have that now. We—"

"We have riots for differing, debatable reasons," he said. "But what about you? How long do you think you could last without food before succumbing to the primeval, before you might resort to cannibalism, for example?"

I laughed as he produced a lopsided smile. "I think I could last for a pretty good time," I said.

Bloom smiled again politely at the remark. Picking up his wine glass, he tipped it to me, an almost whimsical salute, or was it one of a challenge-accepted?

The rest of the conversation felt like an interview. His questions were laced with intent but then would suddenly veer off course. From peak oil to peak population to war and destruction, we talked about it. He seemed unconvinced. He told me we were living in a world where moral climates had no atmosphere. He seemed the type to mole up in a motel room and glue himself to the green glow of a computer screen. A hacker, subverting vital information, ruining lives, twiddling his pencil mustache in rhythm to the keys that were the preludes to the concertos to come. These sorts of men I was familiar with, and I had a strange sense I was talking to a kindred spirit even though our views were in discord.

He rested his hands on the table as if he were about to go into prayer. "Mr. Corvus, you seem to be a cynic."

"People have called me worse."

Bloom laughed. Then, after his high-pitched guffaw sputtered, he paused and his smile went cold. "Kill your father and a cynic is born, is that it, Mr. Corvus?" He watched my reaction as I stood up. I bumped the table, and the plates and glasses clattered. He leaned back abruptly in his seat and said, "Sit down, Mr. Corvus. The Company knows what really happened."

Perhaps even then Seee was watching, wondering, listening through the avatar Bloom, whom later I would find out was one of Basim Hassani's personas. By that time, Seee must have known I had been accepted to The Farm. Seee—breathing me in, probing me with cameras and the wandering-eyed henchman recruiter strategically seated opposite my side of the table, wondering if I'd make it through CIA camp. I never asked Seee whether pre-emptive surveillance from The Company was part of standard routine, or his own precise machinations before we even got there.

Chapter 2

"There are four types of men:
1. *One who knows and knows that he knows. His horse of wisdom will reach the skies.*
2. *One who knows, but doesn't know that he knows. He is fast asleep, so you should wake him up!*
3. *One who doesn't know, but knows that he doesn't know. His limping mule will eventually get him home.*
4. *One who doesn't know and doesn't know that he doesn't know. He will be eternally lost in his hopeless oblivion!"*
-Ibn Yami, 13th-century Persian-Tajik poet

The many-worlds interpretation of quantum mechanics states that for each possible outcome of a particular action, the world replicates itself into a copy such that each potential action is played out in a separate universe. The key to this is that these universes don't interact.

The computer is a similar system where the many-worlds theorem has great appeal. Such Black Hat hackers see the computer as simply a virtual world, split from this one, yet alike, able to learn and evolve, one with a myriad of potential outcomes, but different in that it can seek out and stretch the real world. If every outcome is known, or at least can be hypothesized, then one can inflict much damage onto the real world from the virtual one. Just because there is a screen in front of you, does that mean it should be believed? A particular example of duality in the real and virtual worlds took place on September 23rd of 2018 when an Anonymous hacker named Cerberus broke into CNN's Twitter account and claimed a dirty bomb had exploded in the Capitol only a few blocks away from the White House. After this bogus news hit the Internet, another hacked media site reported the same story and within the short span of a second, high-frequency trading programs reacted by yanking their bids. Liquidity went dry. The result was a flash-crash in all of the major equity market indices. The Dow Jones Industrial Average crashed 663 points in less than a second. Other markets followed. System triggers tripped. The market shut down.

One over-leveraged CEO running a high-frequency trading company whose algorithms had gone awry jumped off a bridge the same day—all because of a keypunch sent from a 5x5 StorQuest storage unit costing $70 a month that had access to the Wi-Fi of an OfficeMax across the street where the command was sent.

There it was—one machine fooling a host of others—opening Schrodinger's box and forcing an outcome—puncturing the superstate of the real system by that of the virtual. Quantum suicide in motion. What was the proof? The body of CEO Johann Jennings floating down the Hudson, a red stain on the chilly waters. The virtual world is a blaze that's difficult to backburn, even if you wish you could. Like the photon, it's moving in two directions at the same time, stuck in a coherent superposition, and when you observe it, it suddenly changes, morphs and adapts, such that the original state is lost by the observation itself.

So on the morning of September 23rd 2022, four years later and two days after graduating from The Farm, the notion of the multi-world would flick back on again and I would remember the work of Cerberus the Hellhound. The "what if I did, what if I didn't" sort of metaphorical fork in the road. It was another important day in my history, not a news-breaking headliner like the 2018 flash-crash.

It was a day that started by schlepping along after forty-eight hours of nephrotoxic celebration. I had a hangover after waking, and the only cure had been hair-of-the-dog, luke-warm beers and a vodka-weighted Bloody Mary. Now, standing at a bus stop heavy-headed and aspirin-filled after a dizzying Williamsburg pow-wow in colonial town, I thought about the previous night at

Franklin's Tavern—double-fisted with friends Samuel Adams and Jim Beam at a staff-only after party. Drinking with Bunker-the-Blinded, waitresses Darlene and Kay (William & Mary girls) were dressed in uniforms of cheap Rococo strapless dresses. They wrestled with keeping their mobcaps away from Bunker while guzzling rummers. After hours more of drinking, sometime pecking the edge of dawn, Bunker decided to name his M40 rifle euphemistically "Titty Licker" instead of Daniel Boone's "Tick Licker"—this while he undid the spiral laces of Darlene's stay and wet her nipples with the foam of a lager. And then panniers, undercoats, shifts, stockings, garters flew into the air, tossed along with brain and body. The two days had been a breakaway from habit and discipline, and there was a bit of shame in the whole charade, although my frown still seemed to be worn upside-down.

A line of Sunday drivers turtled by. I was somewhere near Market Square, the 10 bus nowhere in sight. I stood inside a bus shelter with a huge poster plastered to the inside wall that said, *Government For You—Putting People To Work One Job At A Time.* I drooped over the glass casing containing a bus schedule and squinted to find 9:35, the time for the next departure. I turned around and looked back at the road. There was a saltshaker tipped over in the middle of the street, the wind so light, sandy grains trailed along the asphalt to where it had come to rest. Up in the sky, a couple of old-model Predator drones flew overhead, tiny white contrails trailing behind. They were in the air nights and days now. The newer models were segmented into different classes of use: sound capture, video surveillance, kill machines, covert spy apparatuses that looked like living things. Now, there were quiet, battery-powered gliders that flew low to the ground called EEDs (eyes and ear drones). They were silent chameleons, verging on imperceptible. They had skins that morphed from cerulean blue to pale white, flying blurs with camouflaged bodies adapting to the color of the sky. Built for video and audio surveillance, a slew of them had been taken down by organized crime gangs who could afford guided missiles. These were the people who took offense at having their activity monitored. Other people seemed not to care. The latest designs they built smaller, sleeker, but the rumors said these were being shot down too by new, short-lived neutralizer rockets, the hottest-selling item on the black market. Evolution and adaptation were in play across cities in America. To the naked eye most were impossible to see, but if you looked through a telescope at the high-flyer UAVs, it seemed like the sky was a swarm of insects over the big cities.

At the bus stop, my thoughts idled, slowly drifting over the last three months in the CIA at The Farm—paramilitary training, jump school, tradecraft, explosives, tactical driving, engineering, telecom. Flashes of memory blurred with the posted bus times, and I found myself again focusing hard at the bus schedule blank-brained and wobbly. Then I heard Tomray Bunker over my shoulder. "We're C, fucking I, fucking A, man." I turned around to his wide-lipped grin. Dumb-faced and giddy, he was out in the morning chill bare-chested and sockless, dressed in black Nikes and a pair of knee-holed jeans. On top of his head was Darlene's mobcap fluttering in the wind.

"Yeah," I said. "CIA who's DOA." Each of us was a NOC (non-official cover), a field operative—deep undercover where your existence would be denied should you ever be caught. Somehow it hadn't dawned on me yet, the significance of it all.

"Not me. I feel great," Bunker said.

"The bipolar feel best when they're down."

"C fucking I, fucking AAAA," he droned on, sticking out his wine-stained tongue. I glanced around but the streets were bare. The whole world had gone to sleep. He sensed my agitation and stuck out his tongue at me, shaking his head.

"All I seem to remember was you fucking Dar fucking Kaaaay."

"Very funny, motherfucker," he said laughing, tying the straps of the mobcap into a bow under his chin. "But you was there too, if memory serves. Kay, Isse, and Dar. A dark-meat white-bread sandwich—a 'K'—'I'—'D'. A palindrome for DIK, which seems to describe you quite well."

I laughed—had to—it was Bunker's way, always one-upping you. A fiery-mouthed kid, smart as a whip with a comeback. IQ of 161. A Rice summa cum laude son-of-a-bitch.

"So, you give any thought to the camp?" he asked, referring to The Abattoir, this time with a bit more discretion to the volume of his voice.

I dodged his question. "Spring training is long over. No need to go back to camp." I pointed to the saltshaker in the middle of the road.

The previous night he had told Darlene and Kay we were ball players from the Tidewater Tides. I was the slugger, Dirk Harmon who was batting .321 with 40 homers and 151 RBIs, sure to soon go to the show. He was Dan Rollins, a pitcher with a hundred-mile-an-hour fastball. So adamant about it, he piled a heap of salt and pepper shakers in his shirt, and with a bottle of tequila in his other hand, stumbled outside to give us a demonstration.

Now I gazed back at the tumbled saltshaker dusting up the middle of the street and wondered when the bus would get here.

"You're avoiding the question," he said, referring back to The Abattoir with a more serious tone. "You know what I mean."

"I certainly haven't thought about it today."

The bus approached, lugged to a stop. The door folded inward with a swish and an old woman in a purple dress and milky-white pantyhose hobbled down the steps.

"What are you taking a bus for?" Bunker asked. "You could walk it."

"I need a ride."

"I'm going to the show," he said, meaning he was going to

The Abattoir. There was a pause, and finally I nodded. He looked at me for a sign, eyes in bloom for a tell. I gave him nothing, because that was what I had to give.

"You coming?"

"I'll jump later," he said, moving off through the patch of grass toward the sidewalk.

"Catch you later then."

He nodded with a pointed head-jerk and was off in a lope, mobcap blowing in the wind.

Before the ceremony, head of training Basim Hassani—aka Dr. Bloom, aka The Paki, aka The Overzealous Immigrant, aka The Trainer—offered each recruit who was chosen to be a field operative a choice to go to The Abattoir for hardcore training off the grid. Rumors amongst the trainees were plenty—the real deal, live situations. Not only off the grid, but not condoned by the Office of the General Council. It was an important program for the CIA, who was losing the budgetary war to the NSA. Signal Intelligence (SigInt) was killing HumInt, and The Company was tired of embarrassments.

The Abattoir remained off the books, off the records. It wore the same clothes as the NOC—the jacket of deniability. For those who wanted to go, a leave of absence was granted—off the payroll. A rumor circulated that an Abattoir graduate received the most dangerous jobs—the multiple passports, the hits, the black-ops with secret funding. These were the frontline men of the CIA, the HumInt guys who counted because they were the ones with the guts to hit the self-destruct button should they get caught. Most of the guys had already made up their minds before the offer was given. We had until that day to respond. In the end, sixty percent of the recruits would go. Pride and honor were at stake. The *pussy* word was used for those who abstained, and here I was in a hangover haze trying to make the biggest decision of my life.

I had more to contemplate than most. Three days ago, a man

up the ladder had asked me for an interview. Told me not to disclose the meeting to anyone. He was a station chief. Claimed his name was Pelletier. Didn't give a first name, as if it didn't matter. We met at a restaurant called The Shake and ordered steaks and chatted about the future. I was skeptical, but he had all the right credentials. Talked a smooth game, said he had heard I was going to The Abattoir.

"Perhaps," I said, "I haven't come to any definite decision yet."

"There's a person there we have an interest in."

"Like a 'Dear Friend' sort of interest?" I asked, referring to the letter a Clandestine would send.

"Not so much."

"That's what the ops guys are calling the guys working the diplomats, The Dear Friends. Did you know about that?"

"I have no idea what anyone calls anyone," Pelletier said.

"I hear a lot of good agents have come out of this camp."

"I admit, the agents coming out are high quality. It's why the tops secretly support this program. But that's not why I asked you here." Then Pelletier explained they received a message, something passed along from the NSA. Said they hadn't decoded it yet, but the communication itself was suspicious. The NSA hadn't broken it yet. They had a suspicion it was going to an unfriendly satellite. All of this is top secret he said, he shouldn't even be telling me. Telling me what, I said. Exactly, he said. Then, he asked what assignments I was keen on in six months. He explained the mission and said I would be doing a great service to my country should I accept.

"I won't kill a man without a good reason."

"Who do you think you are?" he asked bitterly. "You're green and untested. I'm giving you an opportunity here. I thought you wanted to play this game."

"I do, but that doesn't mean I'll take out one of our own without knowing why."

"He's a traitor to this country."

"How do you know that?" I asked, a bit suspicious of the accusation.

"We have it from a good source."

"What source?"

"The source has to be protected. You're going to have to trust me on that."

The problem was, I didn't. He had the slippery tongue and mannerisms of Bloom, Hassani's alter ego. In The Company, you never knew what to believe. Pelletier was a stocky man, a heavy-breather with a stomach that had eaten too many buttered sauces—a hungry girth that wasn't afraid to take an extra dollop of sour cream with his baked potato. He had a head of brown curly hair no man his age should have had the luck to keep. Hassani had joked never to trust a man with curls. If a man's hair wasn't straight, how could he speak the truth? Hassani, Pelletier—these guys were a cult, and trying to read them was like hacking a password—you never knew how many attempts it was going to take to get it right.

I thought about things for a minute. What would my dad, the Marine, have done? Would he have done this man's bidding for the sake of country? I came to the conclusion he'd be proud to do it. I thought about his Purple Heart framed and mounted in the hallway of the old house. I thought of when I was a boy and him polishing and oiling his M16, shining the black metal until it gleamed like the waters of a dark lake under a shining sun, keeping it clean even though he never shot it anymore. "I'll give it some thought," I concluded.

Pelletier told me he wouldn't forget it. On leaving, he tapped me on the shoulder with a meaty palm and called me a patriot. Left me a number to call and said I was to state an identifier and repeat a witty phrase he had come up with which I had to memorize.

Now, thinking about it all, I needed the bus ride for quiet

contemplation. As a cluster of woods swept past the window in a deluge of green, my father's whisper settled in my head, a voice rattling from years ago—*Do right by your country and right by your family and life should be okay.* The words were coming through garbled. Perhaps it was the booze talking. His face appeared in the window's reflection. Shadows of speeding trees whizzed by in a swirl of green, blurring together with the image of his face and then suddenly everything evaporated into my own reflection. Then my mother floated into the window lighting a candle—Christmas, New Year's, his third missed birthday, their anniversary. Days where an overwhelming absence filled an empty house. Days when a vaporous omnipotent presence swept through the hallways. Maybe the candle was for me—that possibility hadn't escaped me—the flame burning with photospheric intensity to signify her disapproval. Anger and betrayal. Two words made of ash smoked up in a flame, because how could a mother loathe a son for such an accident?

The bus came to a stop and several passengers stepped off. The bus driver's eyes in the mirror were blue. He was probably six feet tall and a south paw. I noticed I was sitting in the closest seat to the exit. I watched what buttons the driver pushed and thought CIA boot camp had taught me something.

I was the one forsaken by my mother, more so than my brother, the drug dealer. I was the son who mistakenly killed his own father responding to a 211—who failed to recognize him through a *Scream* mask and a gangster's baggy pants and a checkered green-yellow flannel shirt, who wasn't even supposed to be there, the neighborhood not part of his regular beat. I was the son who would hear the radio call and race to the scene only a couple of blocks away. Who didn't even bother flipping the switch of the siren. Who crept in like a SEAL on ambush, and saw a figure through the window waving a pistol at a clerk. This boy who would grow up in a minute, crouching down behind the door of his cruiser in a kneeling Weaver stance armed with a

Glock 19 pointing straight for the glass door, waiting for the cling of a bell. This son would watch a single man grab a paper bag and flee out of a dime store, would say *halt* but not really want it to happen, and would finally shoot when the figure turned around with weapon in hand.

And then the masked man would struggle to get up from the blast, so unlike a hero, sternum caved in like a mule kick to the chest. There's not any air left to breathe is there? The boy still there would kick the man's gun aside, point his weapon at the perp's head. *Go on*, pull the trigger on this lowlife. No witnesses, and who would fucking care?

The cynic creeping out, the new man being born from the boy.

The wound spurts blood in the air like a little blowhole. The perp coughs and blood flows out of the mouth behind the mask. The boy removes it so the perp doesn't drown—there's an ounce of humanity left in him still. But then, there he is. It's like staring in the mirror down there. *What the fuck*, you scream. *Holy fucking shit, Pop. What have you done?* You throw your gun across the parking lot like it's a curse. He coughs again. Blood drains out of his chest like a burst balloon. "It's not your fault," he says through a raspy cough, throwing blame far away into the parking space where you have tossed your gun. "I had to do something. No other way. Forgive me." And there you are, applying pressure to the chest wound, figuring out how bad it really is. *Why, Pop? Why?*

He grabs the shiny copper badge on the dark, navy-blue uniform, rubs it softly between his fingers, the blood on the tips already drying in the soft wind. "No time for talk," he says. "Listen. Tell your mother I'm sorry. Tell her I love her."

Pressing on the wound only makes him howl. Then he's slipping away. *Stay with me, Pop. Stay the fuck with me.* His eyes flutter, turn inward and gaze up at the sky. "I'm proud," he says. "You're a better man than me. That's all I hoped for." He gasps. "Remember," he says. And then he coughs out the words that would stay with me forever: "Do right by your country and right by your family and life should be okay." I bent down to grasp him in my arms, his head falling limp until I braced it under my arm. We couldn't have been closer right then, his blood painted all over me. Yet we were universes apart—him floating away, me wishing to vanish with him. With my mother it would be a distance too great to contemplate, a void of silence and space. Wailing sirens came blaring down the road, but by the time they got there he would already be dead, and it would only be the first set of tears the cynic would shed.

The diesel bus engine droned on, and the world refocused. The headache was back. A couple of kids nattered at each other in the back of the bus, and their mother was squawking at them to behave. I saw the derby-capped bus driver's yawn through the thick convex mirror, left hand moving to the mouth to cover it. The humming of the motor vibrated the window against my scalp, and I used this time for rest, for absorbing what had to be done. In the end, it was a chance for a rebirth, my Homeland the new father to fight for. I would go to The Abattoir.

Near the base, I used a payphone and called a secret number. "A-507 entering the Panopticon," I said. And because the moment burned within me, I added, "I'll do it for free," then hung up. I was back on The Farm by mid-morning and packed up my things. Later, as I was walking between the barracks and shooting range, I saw Hassani walking over to his car and ran to catch up to him.

"I've decided to go," I said.

"I never really had a doubt you wouldn't."

"Why's that?"

"Why would you want to be left behind now when you're out there giving it your all?"

"It might not be enough."

"It certainly won't be enough," he said.

"What's that supposed to mean?"

"It means The Abattoir will test you in more ways than you can imagine."

I smirked at him. "I think I can hack it."

Hassani took out his keys from his pocket. "Physically maybe."

"Mentally too, man."

"Maybe. But what you have to ask yourself is if Isse Corvus is going there for the right reasons." He looked at me as if he had just decoded my phone conversation to Pelletier. Missing the pencil mustache and the ridiculous cowlick he had going the night of the Timothy Skies dinner, the purposeful stare of interrogator Bloom appeared.

There was a Sentinel drone up in the sky, and involuntarily I took a quick glance at it before snapping my eyes back into his. "And what reasons do you think those should be?"

"Well, that's entirely up to you. But they shouldn't be anyone else's."

I shook a finger at him in jest. "Have you been digging into my psych profile?"

Hassani smiled. "A dog doesn't need to dig a hole to sniff shit if it's lying right there on the sidewalk."

I laughed. "As always, the Hassani snout sniffs one thing, but out of the mouth comes the bullshit of another."

Hassani opened his car door. "Think about it." He held out his hand and I grasped it.

"Thanks for everything you did for me out here. You were in my corner."

He shook my hand. "You're welcome. Good luck out there."

The next morning at 0400, we were taken from Camp Peary in tinted-windowed vans. Most of the guys I was tight with during training were in my vehicle—Brock, Split, Conroy, and Mir. Brock and I were the only brothers out of the thirty-eight going. Bunker was conspicuously missing. Did he have a change of heart?

We drove in the van quietly digesting talk-show chitchat

about Detroit from *The Sunday Morning Sun Show*. Rioting again, the city completely lawless, another day of a tick-tocking clock until the whole city would explode. Funny how quiet we were that day, lulled to sleep by smooth, rational radio voices telling us how well-contained the situation was, praising the National Guard for their forbearance, castigating the unruly crowd of looters, each sound bite of street chaos clipped of high-toned protest-whistles and low-toned rolling tanks. The squeaky voice of host Barry Winterburn rubbed in our ears. Mir, sitting next to me in the backseat, yawned while fingering a tattoo on his arm of Lisbeth Salander, the classic chick from *The Girl with the Dragon Tattoo*. Up front, Conroy was looking out of the window at the Department Of Citizens' freeway banners racing by — *Be On The Winning Side of Red, White, and Blue — Join Today* and many other adverts from President Donnelly's PR Tsar.

"Ten dollar gas," Mir said, pointing out the window at a gas-station billboard. "Do you believe this shit? It was nine dollars last week."

"I hear they're going to tap the rest of the SPR," Brock said.

We fidgeted in the leather upholstery, the itch of collapse on the fringe of our thoughts, how other cities seemed to be catching the cold. While the days of rioting passed through the media innocuously, Detroit had fallen deeper and deeper over the previous weeks. The mainstream news lurched away from it, averting the camera's eye to newly uncovered celebrity affairs. But the Internet told a different tale, one where a wall of immutability stood firm with static policy and deadlocked government. One blog wrote an article titled, *From Bankruptcy to Oblivion, A Hard Look at the Last 10 years of Detroit*. It received 13 million hits. But the politicians had written it off, sweeping the city out of the headlines as much as they could. The population seemed willing to go along. Save what can be saved. Amputate the rest.

The vans rolled on.

The low-browed Conroy sat picking a thumbnail. Sitting on the window side of the middle backseat, shoulders slumped and yawning, was Brock. Brock was a Brooklyn brother ex-Notre Dame linebacker. Then there was bushy-haired Stanford Mir, crooked-toothed like a British schoolboy growing out of baby teeth. Out of the alchemy of an ugly smile, he forged charisma. Outsiders would say he was charming—but none of them knew he was nicknamed the Peepshow Perv. He was a boy who loved his porn, kept it pinned up over his walls. Then there was me. Full-ride MS UCLA grad in neurology and computer science, studying neural nets and writing a thesis on neuromorphic processors. Would go to work in the Silicon Valley for a while afterwards. Those were the days when Cerberus had one head in his job, another in his Black Hat role in Anonymous, and the third playing in his off-time with the genetic algorithms that would make the core of Rose, an artificial intelligence program. All of us in the van had excelled with our college educations, all in different disciplines—but recruitment paths to The Company were all strangely different.

Conroy pointed through the windshield. "Take a look at that."

A sign on an overpass read, THIS IS THE ONLY COUNTRY WE'VE GOT.

On the next overpass, there was a woman dressed in rags dangling out over the ledge staring down at traffic. Her feet straddled over a CCTV cam and everyone in the car had a sense of what was coming next. Another sign next to her read, WHY WON'T OUR GOVERNMENT STOP PISSING ON IT. We were in the middle lane and our driver merged left. As we passed, I caught a glimpse of her. Eyes wide and scared, caught up in the river of passing cars.

"Did she jump? Did she jump?" Mir asked, peeling around to try and gaze behind us. I wasn't going to look back. Why look backward when you're moving forward?

"No," I said, "but she probably will, and you don't need to be looking."

This was the new form of protest. The papers called them the Windshield Bugs, a group of homeless who had formed a suicide pact to jump when traffic got the heaviest. The banners never lasted long. Before attending to any accident or crawling traffic around the corpse, the first thing the police would do would be to rip down the signs.

Looking back at that moment now, I remembered how those jumpers had disgusted me. I couldn't condone their method of protest. I thought their actions were destructive instead of constructive. The show of civil disobedience wasn't helping solve any sort of problem.

We arrived at a large hangar on the outskirts of the Norfolk airport. The vans unloaded, and we hopped out and made for the entrance. Bunker still wasn't there. No one had seen him.

Inside the hangar, a beaten-up F14 was stripped down to its dull metallic skin, stabilizers taken off, cylindrical like a dead barracuda with the tail chopped off. With all the drones in the air, who needed it? It looked like one of those birds destined to end up in the airplane graveyard out in Tucson. Looking at it reminded me of the little excursion I took after the astronaut Timothy Skies' launch dinner. Under the moonlight, the dead war birds scattered about the dusty desert, wings still boldly spread out under sparkling star glitter. But in reality they were unaware of history's juke, left behind to wilt under sandstorms and tumbleweed. It made me wonder about the manner in which we were going to be stripped down and disassembled, and whether any of us would come back feeling young and indestructible like we did now.

The guys were grouped into different circles talking. Many of the discussions at The Farm were themselves conversational exercises. Today, conversations crashed into one another, a traffic jam of voices in apprehension and excitement about what was coming. We were in jeans and tees, stripped of usual field gear. It loosened the atmosphere and everyone spoke freely. In my group, Split was speaking about the secretive leader of The Abattoir. Split called him The Conductor. Mir said his name was C.

"Like *A-B-C*?" Conroy asked.

"Who knows?" Split said. "But Burns told me the tag Conductor goes back to his asset days."

"Burns doesn't know shit," Conroy said.

"Heard it had to be clean," Brock said. "Couldn't just clip the target, so the guy walks around town posing as some retarded conductor dude. Tooled around the same office building for ten years until he could get a clean hit."

"Ten years?" I asked.

"Ten fucking years," Brock repeated.

"It's what I heard too," Split said. "Then he went off and formed The Abattoir."

"That's a long time to be sitting around beating your meat," Mir said. We shook our heads in agreement. We were knee-deep now, and a lot closer to being thrown out into the undefined. The buzz of it all had us feeling dizzy.

All of us knew the legends pertaining to The Conductor. Stories that grew like vines around the barracks of The Farm— how he stood circled against four men and kung-fu'd them into oblivion. Gladiator talk of him with swords and shields. They talked of his deeds as if he were Achilles—untouchable, unbreakable, lofted into the realm of great warrior beyond death. But legend is carcinogenic to truth. It takes ancient voices to spread it through miracle or churchlike indoctrination, poisoning real events with myth and improbability. A good legend lifts the realm of reality while maintaining a thin sense of realism, and this is what I thought was going on here. So while I listened, the cynic in me took it all in with sprouting seeds of doubt.

Split, the Spanish Monkey, bowed out of the circle. Split was a skinny, hirsute Hispanic, ex-Army second-generation Americana go-getter who could talk the ears off an elephant. He ended up being part of the EOD squad in Afghanistan—one of those guys putting on the eighty-pound dome of ignorance in one hundred and thirty degrees Fahrenheit, sniffing out suspicious backpacks and rigged-up cars. He played with wire cutters the way a mongoose played with fangs. Split had cojones of a torro. Bullet-spun eyes doing tangos with pliers, pupils pulsing with each clip, anticipating the burst of a fiery flash. The death faces he saw in the IEDs were snapping shots of him, holding him in the lens for a sticky instant, silent, ephemeral, like a wisp of breath before his internals would be rocketed over a block's radius. "Blood like dust," he used to say. "Smithereens." That's how the king of nicknames accrued another—Split Smithereens—a name ringing to one day be blood dust on a killing field.

The social animal of the crew, he made rounds between the huddled groups, popping in and out of circles like a fish-begging porpoise. He stopped to see Briana and Chloe, the two chicks who were accepted and had the nuts to come. Briana had an Indian look where Chloe was Arab-looking. Most of us figured they were being groomed to bait a Middle Eastern prince funding terrorists. Briana was the shorter one—five-foot-four and fast as hell. A chick whose fitness challenged the toughest of the men. She had run the Boston Marathon in two hours twenty-five minutes. She was a flat-chested, loud-mouthed, feisty woman, whom Mir jokingly nicknamed the Energizer Bunny, coming up with it when he said she would fuck like one if any of them got the chance. No one had, but the name stuck and everyone called her Bunny.

Outside the hangar, the sun was almost up. I walked out into the fresh air and took a deep breath, letting it fill my lungs until they throbbed. Out in the distance, a couple of Stealth drones were high up in the sky monitoring airport landings. I shook my head and turned my gaze and let my eyes chew up the speckled sky where the stars were bursting through. Through my shirt, I felt the cut-out photo of the Earth taped to my chest. It was wrapped up in a protective plastic covering, old and warn. Most of the times, I taped surrogate encyclopedia cut outs, but this time it was the real one, the one I had kept. It was coming along with me for the journey, and it made me recall the first time I saw it.

I was fourteen, a year after the first family camping trips where, proud-as-a-peacock, I took my new telescope out for my first moon viewings. I was in the library reading an encyclopedia, dreaming of the purity of distant worlds as I read about the Milky Way. A stack of books surrounded me, and I was reading about black holes and quasars.

Images of the dingy neighborhood floated into my mind—the graffiti on sides of 7-Elevens and squatter houses, trash and litter tossed about gutters and sidewalks, broken 40-ounce bottles like mortar rounds glassed up on pot-holed streets, the broken-down cars on front lawns jacked up, drawn-and-quartered with the tires pulled off. My young mind asked why we had to live there, which led to a simpler question—how could my father, a garbage man, afford a telescope when we barely had the green to make it out of the city? I had never questioned it before that moment.

He had found it in the bin of some rich house and wrapped it up for me. I thought back—no tag, no operating instructions, no fresh new box. He claimed it on the fruits of his labor, telling me how he penny-pinched for years. I imagined the moment, gazing through his eyes when he found it, a jump of surprise when he saw it poking out of a cellophane bag in a big green trash container. *A telescope*, he said with glee, eyes lighting up. He probably breathed a sigh of relief. Now he wouldn't have to scrounge enough money away for a birthday present. He wouldn't have to renege on promises of payment for good grades. He could stretch the enormity of it out and use it for a couple of years, which he did ("Now, if your grades slip, I'm gonna take it straight to the pawn shop."). Perhaps he had to scuffle with Charles, his partner. Perhaps he had to make some difficult promises. But one day, like any other when he would burst out of the house before the sun cracked the sky, before the traffic jams veined the city, the morning smog smoked up the atmosphere, he would find something. Later that day, he would bring it back home around mid-afternoon when I was at school. He would smell like banana peels and flat Dr. Pepper, reeking of week-old fish and a thousand other mixed-up smells all clinging to his tan uniform. Work gloves would be shoved in his back pocket, stiff like the tails of two cocks fighting. This gift he would bring back for me and only me. Not for my brother, who couldn't name another planet other than the one his two feet were standing on, and who hated being dragged away from his 'hood' on astronomical campouts.

That day in the library, when I was fourteen and growing like a weed, I cut out the Earth from the encyclopedia and shoved it in my pocket. I strutted out onto the sidewalk and held it high in the air in front of me. A crescent moon gleamed in the upper atmosphere. The sun-split blue horizon shimmered to a darker indigo over the black expanse. The sky was zipped open by a pair of parallel contrails, ribs holding the guts of the Earth inside. I held the picture over the toenail moon and imagined me up there, looking back at the me down here. In the picture, I saw the Earth as an iris peeking into the dark void, and was awed by the question of God and if there was ever an end.

Now I was standing outside a hangar watching the day come into focus, the sun crisping a sheet of clouds into a beautiful pink to welcome a new day. Somehow a fiery intuition burning inside me knew this life was over. My hand was still over my heart, feeling the rim of the photo strapped to my chest. The Earth beat under my palm, and I felt I was going to burn up into ashes as the sun crept into the horizon. I thought the moment could last forever, lingering as long as I didn't exhale.

Then, a woman's voice behind me asked, "So what are you

thinking?"

I turned around to see Briana staring at me. "I'm thinking it's going to be a long flight."

"Could be." She paused a moment. "But that's not all you're thinking about, is it?"

This was Bunny. She had a way of getting in your business. She had her Ph.D. in Clinical Psychology from Temple, and it was just her natural proclivity to be curious. I was silent. Finally, she threw up her arms in the air. "Okay. Keep it to yourself. I won't press you."

"What exactly do you want me to say and I'll say it."

"What's on your mind—it's the same as what's on everyone's mind."

"And that is?"

She scoffed, blowing air out of her lower lip. "We're all scared, man. You're not a wussy if you admit it."

I laughed. "Scared? I'm not scared. Save your shrink degree for The Abattoir, Bunny."

"You're all fine," she said. "Just like always."

I smiled and winked at her. Out in the distance, a half a mile down the road, came the faint flicker of headlights. A black van appeared. Someone trotted out of the hangar while Briana walked back in. The guy went and opened the chain-linked gate. The van pulled in and parked among the six others. Grus and Bunker jumped out with their driver, Bunker with a wide grin on his face. He bounced toward me and yelled out, "Thought I wasn't going to make it, didn't you?"

"It crossed my mind."

"I wouldn't miss this for the world." Striding past me towards the hangar he said, "Look at you trying to bag the Energizer Bunny while I'm away."

Grus walked past. "We had to wait for Elliot and Harold, both of whom didn't show."

"Pussies."

"Maybe," Grus said, "or just smarter than the rest of us."

Then it started in earnest. A guy in a dull-green camouflage jumpsuit walked up to us with a clipboard. "Sanders, Richards, O'Donnell, Davis, Pugs, Blanchard—you're out. You can go home."

"What the fuck?" Pugs said, losing his temper. "Why even bring us here if you're just going to boot our asses right back?"

"Decisions of who goes are made last minute by The Abattoir. You didn't make the cut."

"That's bullshit," Blanchard roared. "You got to give us a reason!"

"It doesn't say," the airman said, avoiding eye contact. "It never says. But that's the way it is. It's their plane, and without their approval, you don't get on."

The airman scribbled on his clipboard while the six drivers formed a tight wall around him. More argument, but the airman stood his ground, waiting for them to leave. When they were finally driven out, the airman asked if we knew what was going to happen next. A Japanese guy named Kumo stepped forward, ready to take us up in a plane. Words were brief. We were led into a large room inside the hangar, black-bagged, drugged, and then all thirty-two of us, one by one, slipped into dream and hallucination, time like a piston compressing and expanding until we reached our destination.

We rose dressed in medical robes, dry-mouthed and foggy from a drug-induced haze, Kumo nudging us awake with a dirty bare foot. We found ourselves spread out on cots inside a mildewed plywood barrack, trees punching through sawed-out holes in the roof. My clothes were piled next to a sports bag full of my personal belongings. I leafed through the pile of clothes to find my Earth photo still tucked in the pocket of my undershirt. Briana and Chloe were hastily putting on their clothes under the covers.

A case of water sat on the floor in the middle of the room.

Each of us rushed to get one, but something was off. I did a head count.

"Who's missing?" Conroy asked. He had noticed too. Three guys were missing. Guzzling his water, he broke off and said, "Who the fuck are you?"

Conroy stood in my vantage point, blocking my view. His dark, gun-barrel eyes danced in his head glaring at someone beyond his spiked-up jet-black hair. As he moved to the side, a figure emerged. We saw the grotesque form of a man appear. He sat furtively hunched over, the weight of his bulbous head pushing him into a coil. His lopsided jaw twisted sideways on his face, and his cheeks were severely sunken. His head was a fat club, body a stick, and eyes with round black pupils more animal than human. Around his neck, the skin was a splotchy café au lait.

"Where did you come from?" Bunker asked.

"The same place as you," the stranger said. "The womb."

"Not from my mother's," Bunker said with a laugh.

The man glared at him as if he were staring at an alien, reversing the look we were giving him.

"Are you military?" I asked.

"No," the stranger said. "My name is Uriah, and I have come to train, just as you."

"When did the entrance requirements drop?" Bunker said.

"I've earned my spot," the stranger said.

While the others looked on, Mir, the Peepshow Perv, shrugged and went back to pinning up centerfolds above his cot. "We're out here now," he said. "Expect the unexpected."

Bunker smirked at the comment, then began calling the man "Clubhead," to which the stranger replied, "You'll be the first one I make an example of."

As Bunker went at him, Kumo barged back inside, eyes aglow with the fresh morning heat. "Lineup outside. Now!"

As Kumo turned, Conroy called out, "What happened to the

others?"

"They were left. They never made it here. Now move your asses outside."

Chapter 3

"Nor ought we to believe that there is much difference between man and man, but to think that the superiority lies with him who is reared in the severest school."
-Archidamus, Spartan King

The humid land gave us no clues to where we might be. Perhaps Africa. Perhaps Central or South America. Perhaps India. Perhaps Thailand, Vietnam, or Cambodia. Somewhere with sticky terrain and boiling air. Our bodies were in constant drip. Shirts were damp and mottled with sweat, our faces waxy and glistening.

We were deep in a dense jungle surrounded by a rampart of trees. Animal, reptile, and insect sounds reached our ears—the howling of monkeys, the croaking of frogs, the layered screeching of a thousand different insects. Our voices thrummed strangely in tune to the cacophony in the midst of the bombed-size clearing we stood in. The whole jungle was a humungous breathing being, and we were stuck in the stomach of it. We were food, the prey for this place, and any sense of free will we must have had melted away when the clouds rolled in.

The rain trickled at first. We stood there silent in two rows of fifteen each. We stood stiff-backed and straight-shouldered waiting patiently under the light drizzle while Kumo sat on a tortoise-sized stone whittling a stick into an arrow with a shiny nine-inch Bowie. Occasionally, he gazed up at us, rotating his eyes over ours, staring into our souls. Then he would shake his head gravely and go back to shedding the stick.

We watched Kumo and wondered how much he knew, how important he was. His face was elongated and oblong. A skin-headed Japanese, gaunt and lank with wide, insect eyes. He was taller than he should have been for a Jap. My height, six-foot-two, minus the meat. His smile, boyish under a praying mantis face.

He wore a pair of fatigue shorts extending to the knee. Bare-chested and bare-footed, muddy with droplets of rain glistening off his face, he seemed animalistic, a jungle character, a Jap Tarzan with stretched out simian arms—arms that could throw a jab on the button of your nose from ten yards away. I glanced around at the others looking at him. Our thoughts brooded without conclusion.

After a while, whispers broke out through the lines. Kumo told us to be silent. We should stand and listen to what the jungle was telling us. And so we did. For four more long hours. It felt like we hadn't eaten in a day. None of us was sure of the amount of time that had passed, but this was a new day, and the day before it we had left early in the morning. We were still drowsy from the drugs. Thirst, once again, set in. One of the men on the front line, David Rigby, began to slouch, tilting his head, slowly drifting off. Kumo, whittling with his knife, glanced up and saw him. He bounced up from his seat with a stone in his hand, and in a flash threw it at Rigby. The stone had been the size of half a fist and hit Rigby hard on the forehead. Rigby crumbled to the ground. Kumo shouted for no man to move. We obeyed, standing more rigidly than before. Then he went up to Rigby with his nine-inch Bowie and bent down over him. Rigby's head bled into his closed eyes. Kumo traced the tip of the blade around Rigby's face, dug a bit into the skin of his cheek, perhaps to see if Rigby was really out cold. Then he stood up and grabbed some zip ties from his pocket. He hogtied the bleeding man and dragged him toward the woods. Then he opened a trap door to a hole in the earth and slid Rigby into it. It would be the last I saw of David Rigby.

By mid-afternoon, a thicker set of clouds moved in, grey and languid, as if they had all the patience in the world. Floaters rolling like tanks across the atmosphere from a strengthening squall. Kumo gazed up at the sky and spoke for the first time since we were silenced. "Lesson from the heavy rain," he said, snickering at us. "Now you will start to learn bushido."

The rain fell in heavy drops and plunked on our heads. Out in the distance we saw more thunderclouds, purplish giants, swirling in wind-sheared, dark-grey cylinders up into the stratosphere and moving fast. The sky split and lightning jolted out of the pregnant clouds, murderous rain pouring furiously, sheets of it like curtains in the distance. I peered down the line. There were others peeking about. Kumo stood there with his severe eyes bulging out at us. Slowly the group came to attention—feeling the purpose without words or communication. This was a test.

The thunderclouds swept in on us. Lightning lit up the sky, cracking into the forest, the storm coming to humble us as its weight sunk us deep into the mud. Wind slapped our faces. The sideways rain needled our bodies as hot as stinging fire ants. Kumo sat there, sometimes peering at us with madman eyes while taking a pause from whittling sticks and fitting them with arrowheads.

After an hour, the rain lightened and finally the showers subsided and the jungle once more came alive with insect noise. Then he appeared like a phantom out of the woods, stepping out from the steam wafting off the forest. None of us laid an eye on him until he was right in front of us. He was shorter than I had imagined—five-foot-ten or -eleven, no more. He could have been Goliath the way the men had spoken about him. I imagined a Leviathan. And while I had heard only small stories and anecdotes—how he was called The Conductor for his legendary patience, how in his best days, if you were in his radius, you were a living corpse—I didn't put much belief in the small bits of chatter. Knowing we were drugged and brought here, I sensed an inflation of the truth. Stories of voodoo. Stories to psych you out. Tall tales.

Now that he was here, Kumo stood up. He was rugged-looking, dressed in fatigues with muddied boots. He seemed to carry the jungle with him. Moss and mud caked his face. Hair was slathered and damp, stringy and dripping, melting from his head. He walked over to Kumo, greeting him by placing a hand on Kumo's heart. Kumo did the same. A beetle scurried over his neck and he simply let it roam.

Three others slithered out of the forest. Those whom, with Kumo, would later be known as the Sons of Liberty, Ahanu the Native American, Des, and straggle-bearded Merrill. The leader craned his neck watching them, gave them a little nod and tipped them a smile, one laced with brotherhood and familiarity. He raised his hand. When he spoke, the first words out of his mouth were this:

"Welcome to The Abattoir. My name is Seee. And now I will tell you a little parable about life, which in contrast to its words, is what life is truly about."

He placed a hand on Kumo's shoulder, looked at him as if this were the beginning of something they had done many times. Then he turned to us and began.

"A man died and went to Hell and sat around a table of fire with bodies burning around him. In the center of the table was a pitcher of an exotic drink steaming at the rim. He was given a glass and drank and never had he tasted anything so divine. He asked where the drink came from. A flaming soul sitting at the table said to him, 'It comes from the last remaining Lushing Tree that stands in an oasis in the Sahara. Its fruit falls into a hole and arrives here.'"

I glanced down the line. The same baffled expression was ubiquitous. Split covered his mouth, fighting back a yawn.

"The man then went to Heaven and through a maze of clouds entered a chamber where on a table this same drink was being poured from a golden jug steaming once more from the rim."

He moved a couple of paces toward us, eyes moving into ours, forcing us to attention.

"Amazed that perhaps the same drink existed in Heaven, he was eager for a glass and given one. When he drank, he felt excruciating pain. Fire spread throughout his veins and his whole body felt as if it were ablaze. Once the pain subsided, he cried out, 'How can this be—a drink that brings so much pleasure in Hell, yet so much pain in Heaven? Is it the same fruit from the only remaining Lushing Tree?' Satan appeared and answered him, 'Yes, it is from the same tree.'

"'But how could this be?' the man exclaimed. 'It must fall from a different branch.'

"'Do you believe the anatomy of a tree is any different from one branch to the next?' Satan asked.

"The man contemplated this and finally said, 'No, I do not.'

"'Then how do you explain this difference?'

"'Maybe it is the route to each destination which is different, and the route changes the characteristics of the fruit.'

"'The fruit has not changed, nor the passage from where it came,' God said. 'Only what you see has changed.'"

The air stiffened. Silence. Thirty men staring at him and not one dared utter a word. The sound of the jungle grew louder in our ears, layer after layer colliding in intersecting waves. We waited for a cue, a direction from him, a question, or simply a word. The insects throbbed with the sound of his pacing boots slogging in the mud. Time simply ticked on.

The meaning of the parable was simple enough to grasp—God and Satan—Heaven and Hell were the same. As was the allegorical fruit. Perception had changed, and this was the point. But I was only partially right at the time. Later I would understand another interpretation. The Lushing Tree was "the fruit of the poisonous tree," legal speak for the NSA's warrantless wiretapping program.

After another minute, he led us to the point he wanted to make. "Does good and evil really exist? Is the universe just? Becoming a warrior of The Abattoir requires you to look at things differently, to see the truth and not deny its existence, to stretch yourselves beyond what you currently know and accept. And when battle comes, to understand clearly what it is you are fighting for."

He moved in front of us, inspecting the eyes of each man. "Besides becoming the best warrior you can be, you will learn new philosophies. You will study the rituals and training of the great warriors of the world. You will study the common denominator to all of them, which is that a great warrior comes from the courage of the internal spirit rather than the brutishness and power of the external body. You will learn sacrifice, brotherhood, weaponry—both new and old. You will learn new languages. You will learn how to get away from your enemies. You will learn technology—some of which you've never seen before. You will learn fear. Today, you will be born to a new world that you never knew existed."

He was silent for a moment, allowing the veins popping out in his forehead to simmer.

"But listen carefully. I am a fair man today, but this I do not always promise. You will have one week here to decide whether or not you want to stay. One week to decide whether or not you want to be pushed back into the womb. After that, you are here, for better or worse."

He moved among the two lines. "I will also tell you that of those who come here, only seventy-five percent survive. This camp is serious. The training you will receive is real and unforgiving. All of you," he said sweeping his finger past each one of us, "all of you will change if you stay. You will not be the same person who came in here."

It was my turn, and he passed his eyes into mine. I glared back seeking out a weakness.

"All of you who stand before me today might have killed someone in the past. None of you has killed in the manner you will kill if you stay."

He tapped me in the chest with his index finger as if he were singling me out. "I will not lie. Some of you here might kill the man standing next to you if I wish it. This is not a place to guard a conscience or covet moral dilemmas. You will be asked to do what civil society calls *horrendous things*, things that violate the social rules you have grown up with. What I want you to take away is this. I want you to imagine the worst thing you can possibly do to another person. I want you to sit down tonight and write out that list, whether that be cannibalism, chopping someone's head off, or whatever the worst thought your brain can come up with. Then I want you to realize with uncertain doubt that that fear is in the realm of possibilities. Your lists will not be complete. This I promise. Do not doubt me on this score."

He shed his sopping, mud-caked shirt and wiped away the grime on his face with it. Many years later this scene would play out in my mind, and I would wonder exactly what he was doing out there under the storm. Perhaps, letting the monsoon pour over him in some jungle clearing. I saw him laying supine, welcoming the incoming thunderclouds with open arms. The storm threw down streams on the lush land, Old Testament rain, rain that lasted for three hundred and seventy days. There he was bedding down with insects in the mud. Beetles, ants, earthworms crawled all over him. Seee with his eyes closed, absorbing every moment of it while he meditated on a future perhaps just as devious.

"So let's begin with who has the guts to face me." He took off his trousers and Kumo threw him a pair of boxing shorts.

Sometimes people do unexplainable things, cowardly or courageous. They react without thought or provocation. Is the act of the Good Samaritan who steps in front of a bus to save a jaywalker more for the sake of the other person or a deeper test of putting oneself in danger and facing one's own mortality? Perhaps this question punctured deep into my thoughts at the time. Maybe it was Briana starting down the line looking me up and down with eyes asking if I was scared. Or perhaps it was purely boldness, an unfettered belief that I was superior, that I could take him, or anyone. But even with a 16-2 MMA record, I remembered feeling surprised seeing my own traitorous left foot step forward out of the ranks in challenge of the one who offered it. Or maybe it was something simpler—the first reckless chance to make good on my promise to the station chief Pelletier.

Chapter 4

"Sure the fight was fixed. I fixed it with a right hand."
-George Foreman

Seee's chest was scarred. Jagged lacerations. Cigarette burns. Near the ribs there were a couple of patchy bullet wounds. Tribal scars were scraped into his biceps, crisscrossing patterns, tic-tac-toe where the scratches seemed to be etched out with a sharp rock or arrowhead. His hands were callused, dirt scratched into his fingernails. Part of his pectoral was cut out, a teaspoon lump of flesh removed. He stuck his finger in the hole and when he removed it, a black ant crawled up his finger before he sucked it off the back of his hand.

"Isse Corvus," he said. "The SWAT negro. The college graduate ghetto boy. The computer ace. You weren't just a sneaker were you? You were a black hacker wearing the Black Hat. Why did you quit?"

I laughed at him. "You've been fed the wrong information."

"Does it look like I feed on lies?" He was lank but sculptured, cutout and molded from marble. A Rodin's *Athlete* in the flesh. Arms that bore muscles twisting with toil, racehorse sinews in his forearms aching in strain. His jaw pushed outward from his face with Euclidean edges, a geometry that said he was used to a punch. "An officer-involved shooting for every year on the force." He shuffled his glide foot over his right ankle in a Sugar Ray shuffle as he began circling me. Stomach muscles were bunched hills of flex, tightness born from the labor of twist and pull. He looked steel-wired into my unflinching eyes. "So you like to kill people?"

"I prefer not to, but you know how it goes."

A shifty grin beamed over his face, as if out of the whole world of everything, I stood there as nothing. A taunt of fate perhaps, or a clear look into the cloudy days of my future. Unlike overblown fear-my-wrath glares I got in the octagon, he gazed right through me as if I were a window. I stood statuesque as his eyes moved over me sculpting me into something worthy of a fight. Then he nodded, and his whole body held the tension of an electrocution, muscles ripping like fissures during an earthquake, a body glittering with droplets of sweat. Yet he circled, calm and composed. "But do you shoot for the right reasons?"

"All of my hearings came out favorably."

"Even with your father?"

Anger welled up inside me. An astute observer, he read it as easily as a seasoned card shark reads the rookie after the flip of the door card. "Even with my father," I said finally, taking a moment to claw back an edge.

"You are the man who will not quit." He said it in a tone more enunciated as a question rather than a statement.

"The word is not in my vocabulary."

"So you see things clearly?"

"I do."

"You don't."

"How do you know?"

"You think you're about to win."

I was six-foot-two and outweighed him by twenty-five pounds. My MMA record would have been better if I had not broken my knee. Still I said, "I'm not so arrogant that I take it for granted, but it seems you are."

"You're not much of a shit-talker."

"It's never won me any fights."

"I respect that." He smiled and his yellow cheetah's eyes widened inside his skull—pupils dilated to the size of coins, every ray of light bending into them, glowing with the fire of the orange-cindered sky.

Our chests swelled, and there, in the middle of that piss-hot jungle fogging up the ground, we shuffled on the edge of a volcano that wasn't there. It was the square off, and the screaming of cicadas combusted with the howling of gawking men egging us on.

Kick his fucking ass. Beat the punk.

Each man picked a side. There was a melee of betting. *Tune him up, Five-O,* Grus taunted me. Bunker, fist pumping the air, yelled, "Don't listen to him, Isse. Got my green riding on you, baby. Fuckin' knock him out."

We circled one another until the air burst and hearts thumped against sternums and time compressed into a grain of sand under the muddy clearing.

I throw a quick left. Swift with zip—not a lot of weight behind it, but he evaporates in front of me. I feel a counter-hook sting my temple—a powerful ball-of-the-toes sort of punch. Snappy. Ear ringer. But he'd have to throw a lot of those to bring me down.

He follows with his glittery bloodshot eyes, throwing a flurry of fists and kicks. Triplets launched from rotating hips. I block incoming one and two, but he catches me with an inside leg kick close to the knee. I fake a wobble, but he's too smart for that.

Raucous bellows bleed from the crowd. *Five-O gonna get KO'd! Five-O gonna get KO'd!*

Come back with a left jab. That's it. Use the reach advantage. I hear old Bluetooth yelling at me from my corner from back in the day. I see him with that squint-eye and blue-capped incisor. *Hit and run,* he yells, *480-484.* All the way from Harold's gym on Figueroa Boulevard, he's in my head, police codes. I hear him repeat *480-484, loosen him up.* I obey. I hear him like it was a million years ago. I'm dishing out combos. Leg kicks make his quads go pink. But this guy's absorbing the shots, loving them, as if each one makes him stronger. Other men would have slowed by now, but he's dancing around with a cherry leg and toothy smile. He squares off on me and delivers the same low-leg mule-kick to the thigh. I show him nothing. The smile is gleaming on his face, daring me to wipe it off. I push him backward and try a flying knee. He sees it coming—counters with an uppercut as I turn back to face him. Taste of blood in my mouth, hot and metallic. I spit it out with the gaggling of the men pleading for more.

He fakes a leg sweep. Throws a right hook. I block. He counters, catching me in the groin with a front kick. There is an instant where I feel nothing. I lunge forward with my right, but he is backing away, knowing the delayed reaction is a freight train coming. I fall to the ground and roll up into a ball.

"You want to know what his problem is?" he yells. His back is to me, lecturing the riotous men who have fallen silent like children being scolded by a boarding-school teacher. "He thinks this is a fair fight. He's used to playing by the rules. Fucking MMA style. But there aren't any rules out here. Look around. If I kill him now, who would care?"

The men look at one another uneasily. They didn't bargain for this so soon.

Now the cicadas are the only ones answering, and they screech like fingernails grinding chalkboards. I push myself slowly to my feet. Blue pounding on the octagon floor yelling, *Now you mad—up and at'em, dog—no mercy yo.* I'm bent over, but I'm watching closely. I'm glaring with an intensity that could burn the sun. A whirl of strategies flood my mind. I'm in the game now. A blitzkrieg of rage, bones solidifying into new shapes, ready for a new fight. A different sort of animal awakes, one bitter and full of hate. It's born inside me, a feeling of primordial madness cracking like splinters through spine and joint. This animal doesn't feel the tap. Doesn't loosen the boa grip of the sleeper. He grits his teeth with eagerness while swallowing the key of the death-lock. He spits on mercy and calls it a four-lettered word.

I fall on him with the wind of a tornado. His back still toward me, he whirls around in time to face a hurling storm of fists and kicks—jabs, hooks, uppercuts, neck grabs, knees—landing here and there before he dashes out of the flurry. His lips curl into the same menacing smile.

Stun a man before a take down, Blue says. *You want your opponent's head ringing, dog—like a clanging bell.* And it's then I catch him with a right hook. Fist on cheekbone. Crack like a baseball. Head snapping. Sweat ripped from his face. Suspended in mid-air. His body not yet gotten the signal to fall. The crowd knows it's solid. They groan simultaneously, a hint of shock in their moans. But I have the feeling of orgasmic connection. Discombobulating—his smile vanishes—a keen sense of trouble has his eyes shaking. A microsecond of electrical pulse to his brain—fusion with fear, reverting to a spark of instinct. Arms raise, ready for a pounding, a hesitation where I slip below his chin, driving my shoulder into his chest and locking up his legs. *Now finish it yo,* I hear Blue cry and I roar to his tune.

Lift. Body slam.

Pelletier, dead man for delivery.

As I crush him to the ground, the spray of mud splatters around us wetting the men tight in their circle. He squirms into a guard and latches on tight. I push my arm close to my cheek and pry him away. I feel a sharp pain come from my shoulder. He has bitten a hunk of my flesh and there is fresh blood dripping down my chest. I elbow him once, but he's wrapped up tight, squirming like a snake under the swash and slither of sweat and blood and inching closer to my throat. *This part of it is your game, yo. You gonna fix him up or you gonna date this bitch?* I push forward and lock one knee by his hip. I strain for the other and then burst through his guard. The full mount is like a summit I'm raging upon. I rain down a tumult of punches and his only defense is cover-and-pray. The mountain is below me and I have conquered this bitch. I want to feel him fold. I want to straddle a limp body underneath me. And if nobody's going to drag me off, I'm going to keep punching until there's nothing but skull and cavity.

But then, something suddenly happens. My arms go limp. My

chest tightens. A thought whizzes by that there's no way I could have punched myself out already. *What the fuck, Blue? What the fuck is going on? Punch, you son of a bitch. Punch!* But nothing's happening. My arms flop—shoulders twisting to move dead branches. Limp hands dangling in the slop. He loosens his guard, flashes the insidious smile.

"You're done now, Isse Corvus."

The paralysis has spread to my legs. He flops me over and I fall like a rootless tree axed at the knees. Then he unloads on me with a right hand as he pins my neck down with the left. I see blood jumping, the splatter of it when he connects, his knuckles bloody, his tawny-brown face speckled and flaming. In the eyes burns a no-mercy meanness. I don't know how much he's hurting me 'cause I can't feel it. It's like a knee surgery you're awake for. The tug of the scalpel and a light brushstroke sensation that is blood they're wiping away from you. Blood is running over my tongue, which is only just beginning to numb. I ask Blue if I'm going to die, and he says, *I don't know, dog. I don't know. Ain't seen anything like this.* So in the middle of a ground-and-pound, I give him a smile, the same smile he's given me, a smile that says I'm ready for whatever you got coming next. I've been through worse. A lot fucking worse.

A fog is coming and I'm slipping out of the world, running into a deep, dark rabbit hole, and something's down in there hollering. It says *respect,* and perhaps it's him or perhaps it's Blue. The voice is murky and I'm none too sure. But through the red pool I'm swimming in, the rain of fists stop. Halfway in my vantage point, I see him there by the men. He's dripping under my eyes, but I can't tell whose blood is whose. My ears catch what he's saying, but it's echoing from the hole and coming in black, fringed at the edges like a burnt piece of paper. *Blue, I think he's done me. Not yet, dog, you ain't done. How do you know? I ask. Too easy, yo. He got somethin' special planned for you. Too easy to waste you now.*

And from down in the hole, he speaks, his voice echoing from a distance a parsec away, a staticky voice coming at me like radio waves in a tunnel. "An asset that fights fair is a liability, a liability that brings you death in the real world."

He's in my purview—a red, watercolored, dripping man facing the men. His waving arms blend with the men in their olive camouflaged fatigues and the forest behind them. My swollen tongue hangs out of my mouth and sags in a mud puddle. I'm dying, and I don't even feel a thing. *Look, Blue, I really am a dog. You ain't shittin' me, son, Blue says. You hang tight. You gonna make it through this. I don't believe you, I say.*

And then I hear Seee speak once more.

"Here, where you are now, we play in the real world. Your training will be real world. Not all of you will come out of it alive, as I've said. So lesson number one is to take a fucking good look at this man and understand that, by God, there are no rules. Men are out to kill you, and every fight is a fight for survival."

The men holding their breaths out there blur with the trees, faces like thumbprints, branches gobbling them up. *Jungle's gonna swallow me, Blue. I'm just the first. I'm the lucky one.*

"You will play dirty. You will play to win at all costs, because the cost of your life is a price too high to pay unless you are asked to sacrifice it. And in this camp, you will be prepared for that too. You will prepare for combat in its many forms. As you've seen today, size makes little difference. The cunning are the victorious. Small beats large."

He walks over to me and pokes something tiny and glassy up to my eyes. A miniature syringe that glitters in the light.

"I will seek to stretch you from the two polarities of humanity—from your intelligence to the deeply primordial. These two coexist, albeit in dormant forms. Those that success-fully finish the training will learn how to be both animal and sifu. Here we are in the womb of Nature, where mercy is interpreted as weakness and weakness is locked in the jaws of death."

The men stood limply in anticipation as the world went black. The singed forest fringed reality, crackling and then puffing out into darkness. This way it would stay for a period of time that would be difficult to recall.

Chapter 5

"Everyone is a moon, and has a dark side which he never shows to anybody."
-Mark Twain

I woke under The Abattoir. My body crumpled and my mouth sucking in fine industrial dust off a scabby concrete floor. I coughed it out like a man buried alive, spitting earth. As I slid into consciousness, glimpses of the fight came back to me—the take down, the ground-and-pound, the tiny syringe and little speech about suckers playing fair. Not yet fully awake, I dug myself out of unconsciousness, probing my surroundings for light. Yet, light did not come—the darkness surrounding me pure and unbroken. I softly touched my swollen eyes. One was the size of a baseball and completely shut. The other was a knife-edged slit. I pried the blood-crusted eyelashes open gingerly with my fingers. Again, I sought out any sliver of light that might have crept into the place, but there was only blackness. My lips were puffed and cracked, freshly bleeding from my new movement. The salty taste of blood, the only liquid wetting my mouth, and it evaporated quickly on the swollen meat of my tongue. My bruised cheeks were small fruits blooming on my lumpy face. I felt more like a bag of beaten-up flesh than man.

None of it new to a ring-fighter, but the extent of the beating was one I had never known. I'd had ribs broken in the past, and a couple were certainly broken now. I'd had my face pounded and lost teeth, even swallowing one when I lost my mouthpiece against Horez. But this was all of it at once—the mashed face, the collapsed side and broken ribs, the gnashed lips, the bruised scalp, the dislocated shoulder, the scraped knees, sprained ankle, and the ache that extended from back to toe—and left me in a world of hurt. Shocked at the lack of my own mobility, I felt only loosely coupled with my flattened body. I crawled to a wall on my elbows and felt its grainy surface. A small victory—a boundary beyond the gritty floor. I pushed in another direction and found a foul-smelling commode, a porcelain toilet stripped of a cover. I searched for paper but found none. Close to the toilet another concrete wall defined the dimensions of the space. I guessed the cell's space to be nine square feet. I crawled to the other side of the room and found the bars of my prison.

The fight with Horez had been one I wasn't ready for, and now I was reminded of it. I had stepped into the ring full of rage and false moxie. It didn't matter who they put in front of me, I thought. Horez, a top-notch undefeated fighter looking for an easy win, wanted to move on to a title fight. I fought my way to being a 4-0 contender who would oblige. The fight was my fifth one after my mother lit the house on fire. I had trained for a few months unrelentingly, not able to forgive myself for what the firemen called humanely *an accident*. I had my first MMA fight a few months before, and it went two rounds before I knocked the other guy out. For half a minute, I had forgotten about my mother, for whose death I had only myself to blame. I continued like that until I hit the wall of Horez.

After my father's death, sometimes I would pass by in my car and see the short, white candle she kept molded on a picture frame burning in the window over the smooth voice of Etta James. The candle would drip with teardrops of wax, burying him in a sarcophagus of sticky ceresin. It was a web of woe overflowing until she would whittle it off, scraping away the solidified wax in corkscrew flakes with one of his old razor blades. But mostly the candle would be obscured through the curtains, a muffled yellow ornamental light with a figure sitting on the edge of a dusty old ottoman junk-heap of a chair, slumped over the pocket of flame gazing into loss, hypnotized by its quiet heat. Sometimes she held a hand close to the flame, biting her lip as she inched it further into the fire—the pain a catharsis, the skin shriveling red as the nerves awoke. Perhaps forgiveness lurked somewhere in the flame, forgiveness for my trespasses, and when she jerked her hand away the forgiveness would be gone, like my father's ghost that slid by her bedroom door whenever she snapped awake in the middle of the night.

After my brother had put me in the hospital, hijacking me with a group of thugs and beating me senseless for what I had done, he once came for a visit and spread the news that our mother had explored each religion, one after the other, following the accident. A conquistador for the Spirit now, he said. The humanized God of the Presbyterian Church had failed her, and her faith in Him had burned up like her nightly candles. She studied Buddhism, Hinduism, Islam, Judaism, and even the more ridiculed Scientology. Holy books scattered on the den carpet, desecrated amongst a sea of self-help books, books on transcendence, the clairvoyant, astrology, tarot cards. Pages marked with *Post-it* notes and dog-eared, ripped out of their bindings and littered across the coffee table. The peacock of faith then lost her feathers—the apostles, the prophets, the soothsayers, the djinns, all colorful paper droppings from her aborted religious experiments.

Throughout the years, she had been the bearer of my bad will. Whenever I spoke with her over the phone in college, or afterward, when I was working in the Silicon Valley, she provided the circuit I could wire my frustrations through, her ear a forbearing conduit into which I could voice my current problems by taking them out on her. So when she spoke of the Pembroke's teenage girl getting pregnant, I told her she had already told me about it for the third time now. When she told me my uncle had been laid off from his county groundskeeper job after thirty years, my voice would lift and I would say she sounded like a broken record.

She played this role throughout the years. She acted out the part of the wall I could throw a ball of my anxieties into, and they wouldn't rebound back. She would absorb the aggression, hide it away within herself, knowing that when it came down to it I would always be there for her. What I failed to realize was our conversations had become a struggle for her, that I intimidated her intellect, that the boy she had reared had outstretched her aptitude and now she struggled to find common ground, and in so doing, often repeated herself. But the realization she was my intellectual inferior made me haughty and dismissive, and her repetitive conversations created a negative feedback loop that accumulated inside, the frustration of her failing to understand me combined with the fiery problems of my habitual life in school and at work exasperating an already sullen and weighty attitude within me. Yet, when my father died, I no longer received the luxury of forgiveness, no matter how many times I voiced it. The weight of my neglect reversed onto me, and deservedly so. The front door of our home where I grew up for seventeen years, slammed back in my face, no matter the amount of apologies. It got so bad even my brother felt sorry for me. This sense of not being able to forgive myself took me into the gym where the catharsis of pain would prick my mind away from guilt. There I would learn to become a fighter, even if self-forgiveness hid itself away in a closet of my mind.

In the darkness, I reached through the iron bars of my cage and groped around. The back of my hand bumped into a canteen, and I pulled it to the bars, but it wouldn't fit through. My throat ached with thirst. I pushed myself painfully up to my knees, uncapped the lid of the canteen, pushed my mouth through the bars and drank. I drank as if I wanted to be drowned.

They had dropped me in The Hole. Unceremoniously left me there. I fell back to sleep and thought about joining my parents in the other world. A length of time passed; I guessed bled into a couple of days. Time seemed measurable only by the number of times I closed my eyes. Occasionally, the squeak of an interior steel door opened and closed; feather-light footsteps the only sounds escaping the place that I myself did not manufacture. The person who came to feed me let in no light. Nothing escaped the steel door when it slid open. The shroud of darkness hung itself around me unbroken. The blind fed the blind. Whoever delivered the food wouldn't speak even after I tried to arouse a response from him. The shuffling sounds of his footsteps the only voice he offered.

The days I swallowed in bites. Killing time by eating a meal in tiny morsels. My shaking fingers would tear off a crust of bread and roll it into a ball. Then I would plop it in my mouth and savor it between the lower jaw and cheek, every succulent nutrient sucked out of a stale crust with each dimension of tongue. A game to pass the time. Locked in there with just my thoughts— my new best friends. Never one to be friendly with myself, here I had to try—easing into it as slowly as fucking. "Why don't we take our time with breakfast today?" Then another shadow of myself would answer, "How do you know it's breakfast—they just brought you a tray two hours ago." I would drop a gumball of bread in my mouth and I would hear, "They're fucking with you, Isse. Time isn't a sensation they want you to feel."—"I know."

Darkness creates its own characters. A puppeteer winding you up with your own strings. When we would get to know each other better, Seee would say that the darkness had its own sort of light. He said I just couldn't see it yet, but that I would.

Throughout the day, or night, or whatever time it was when I thought I was conscious, my mind constricted, became prone to fear and hallucination. Rebelling against these sinkholes, I learned the dimensions of the room by heart—a divot in the concrete floor near the bars where someone must have dug before giving up; the commode's oval egg shape; how there was a screw loose in its base; the gritty floor and pebbles stacked into a small pile in the corner. On this discovery, I imagined the invented games someone must have played. I went through the pile, fingering every little rock, discovering their shapes. I asked myself why I had chosen this world, when life back in L.A. as a cop had been certainly easier than this one. As I fingered the largest of the pebbles, I remembered being a kid, skateboarding downhill and hitting a stone in the road when I was eleven. The board came to a violent stop and my momentum threw me forward onto the pavement. I suffered some bad scrapes and a broken arm. My mother ran me to the emergency room where we waited six hours with my bone sticking out, and then they had almost refused us because of no health insurance. I laid the stone back on top of the pile, felt the small bump in the middle of my forehead, and for the first time in a long time, a tear fell out of my eye.

Later, I found three names scratched into the wall behind the commode, hidden at an angle from any flashlight that might have shined upon it. I felt the deep grooves in the wall. The last name was Jaybird, dated roughly two years before. I wondered what he must have been like, whether he had the same thoughts as me. The others dated back as far as five years before, all in the month of September. These were the others stepping into the same trap as I, suffering here, perhaps dying here. I listened for their ghosts when all I listened to was silence. I heard nothing, which is perhaps the hardest thing to listen to, as silence itself is an abstraction on a planet teeming with sound, where in outer space it reigns supreme. I filled my mind with thought for long hours. Long ago, I had read an article in *Wired* about screen forging and thought about what sort of algorithm it would take to do such a thing. I imagined how I would have approached it — hijacking events, manipulating bit streams. It kept my mind active, and it gave me something to think about, but I needed more than that to feed the loneliness of solitary, so I thought about how I'd kill Seee. A misguided bullet? A little push near a cliff edge? Every option dangerous, and I would have to run afterward. But where? I had been too eager, and hadn't asked Pelletier for any details.

I healed slowly, started a regimen. I practiced a limited number of yoga positions, the ones that were possible in a small space—inversions, back and forward bends, boat poses. Then, I put on the yolk of the oxen and told the farmer to whip me—little thunderbolts and wheel poses, compass positions. I wanted to cut up the earth and plant new seeds, grow new samskara. Where the old roots of wrongdoings dug into my thoughts, I plowed over them with sweat and strain. I wrung my body out like a wet, healing rag. The pain bit like bee stings, but I welcomed each prick, the punishment a light in the darkness, a torch to help erase the stupidity I felt for stepping out of line. My burning muscles and strained tendons stretched like rubber bands bending away from my own self-loathing.

After some time, Seee visited me down in the dungeon. I heard a voice while doing pushups far off in the darkness. Perhaps he stood there silent for hours before he said anything, submerged like a periscope, peering above the surface, letting his gravity weigh down on me, attracting me to what later he would offer for those strong enough to survive. I hadn't yet understood how to see, so therefore he had to speak before I really knew he was there. The first words I heard in days were a kindness. "How do you feel?" he asked.

I paused with my nose touching the dust in the middle of pushup seventy-six. "Like a million bucks," I said, continuing my set. I asked him how long I'd been down here.

"Three days."

"Should I believe that?"

"I don't care what you believe."

"Is it night or day?"

"You've already lost track?" He seemed disappointed.

I finished my set and then sat in a lotus position. "Breakfast is bread and water so it's throwing me off."

He laughed from somewhere out in the darkness. "Lunch and dinner are the same then?"

"There's varying degrees of staleness."

"I'm not sure Kumo likes you."

"It's hurting my feelings."

He sighed. "You're disappointed you lost."

"You don't fight honorably."

The reverberating walls echoed his voice. "The Red Coats fought with honor. Then they were shot apart like pheasants by a bunch of inexperienced farmers with inferior arms. In a fight you should never expect the honorable, and you of all people should know it."

"So that was the lesson?"

"As I've already said, there is no word *fair* in a fight. Lesson one in Primitive Law. Nature knows no losers. Losers are extinct, overrun by evolution. Losers are fools who fail to adapt."

I said nothing. I wanted to hear his movements in the thick of the darkness—if he'd scrape a foot on the ground, touch his face, that sort of thing. He didn't. In darkness, there is a thirst for sound. Silence for me rang in a monotone chime, a flat-lined EKG buzzing sound without curve or wave or spastic discord. Too many shotgun rounds without the use of ear protection. In The Hole, you quench this thirst by creating your own noise— rubbing your scalp, hearing the flick of your middle fingernail between your thumbnail, cracking knuckles, the bristle of growing whiskers, the gulp of water swallowed down your throat, the tranquility of breath. In the dark, the body becomes more self-aware, and in this I was listening for a tell, but he sat there quietly, and I did not so much as hear him breathe. He could have been a phantom whom I was in dialogue with, another voice like my mother and father. Finally I said, "You're a voice from afar, strong and reverberating, as if you are in a cathedral."

"True," Seee said. "And I can tell you that down here it's more heaven than the hell of what you'll find above."

"God doesn't exist."

"Perhaps," he said. "But while you're alive you'll still hear my voice, and I will always speak the truth to you."

Somehow the conversation turned into a direction I wanted to veer away from, so I said, "Tell me about this name—Seee. It is a strange name." Conroy's question of the letters A-B-C in the hangar flashed back in my mind. The few days were a lifetime ago, and I had trouble remembering if it actually happened. "Is it a letter? As in the letter A or B? Is it the third letter in the alphabet? Perhaps it is an abbreviation, like 'C' for 'cat' or 'C' for cruel, or 'C' for cunt."

He answered without malice. It was apparent that plebian methods of arousing an emotion from him were ill-suited strategies. Instead, he asked, "Why would I disguise the meaning?"

"So it is not a letter? It is an action. Like to 'see'? Spelled S-E-E?"

"Yes, a bit ironic considering our current environment, but sometimes darkness is the necessary light."

"Profound," I mocked. "Or perhaps your name is a command?"

"I wouldn't say that," he said, absorbing my tone. "It is my bushido one word containing two edges. The first edge being that my former name has been dropped."

"And why did you drop your given name?"

"Because I am no longer an object owned by the state. I repent their means of identifying me, cataloging my life and eventual death, which is all they really care about."

"Data is a virus," I said. "It's always out there somewhere crawling over everything."

"Data is never static. This is true. But it can always be changed, no matter how many places it lives."

"And the second edge?"

"The new name is a new life, a death of the old belief. But it is more of a plea than a command, as you suggest."

"A plea for what?"

"A plea for you to look."

"Look at what?"

"To see the world in its true form."

"What if I see it clearly right now?"

"You don't."

"How do you know?"

"Take your father, for example. He was pushed down the hill into a desperate situation like so many others. Why? Tell me who is killing the standard of living in America?"

"I don't know. Wall Street? The government?"

"You don't believe it? I can hear it in your voice."

"Some of it, sure."

"You've really no idea what you've stepped into here."

"And what about this place? This cave? This jail? This darkness? Am I not being pushed down the hill?"

"Pushed into the earth, yes. Hopefully you'll come out with better eyes."

"Is that what this is? You have brought us here to bleed and be tortured and we are supposed to learn something from this?"

"The reason you're in this place is because you're a man who's looking forward, not back. You've seen the pain of the past. Start again from the womb and come out to see the light. For Christ's sake, Isse, move into the future. Open your eyes and truly see."

My senses sharpened. I heard him get up to leave. My face was hot with anger. "So that's it? That's all you've got to say to me?"

"And Ye Shall Know The Truth And The Truth Shall Make You Free."

He was quoting *John 8:32*, the CIA motto, but in his tone there was bitter irony. I heard the faint shuffling of his footsteps fade away. I thought about the job I came here to do, and how I had failed so miserably with the first attempt.

"Go shout it on the mountain!" I screamed. "But don't pretend the mountain is yours!" Seconds passed without a response as my voice bounced off the walls. I yelled again to unhinge the ricocheting echoes that were dying with the feather-footed steps of my captor. "You're a coward!" I laughed and kept laughing until I heaved over succumbing to a fit of coughing. I pushed my right arm through the bars and tried squeezing my body through them. I clawed. I reached. But I wasn't a ghost, a mirage, or cloud, and the bars rejected me. In the end, I remembered wondering if he was ever really out there.

Chapter 6

"A prince should therefore have no other aim or thought, nor take up any other thing for his study but war and its organization and discipline."
-Niccolo Machiavelli

Voices came to settle accounts after my first encounter with Seee. I questioned whether my imprisonment was a result of the men betting on me. Perhaps this darkened cell was a consequence of their betrayal? But how did I betray? By accepting a challenge? The voice telling me to do right by my country, the one magnetized by Pelletier, seemed harder to heed.

A more logical voice told me it would have been petty for Seee to imprison me as an act of revenge. This was not a man with revenge on his mind, visiting you in the darkness, acting civil, hoping for change.

The voices continued their arguments and left me without definitive answers, for Seee himself framed himself as an enigma. Pelletier had told me little about the man. I wrestled with my own intellect, and inside my head I wobbled, questioned everything, felt immersed in a ground-and-pound between duty and belief.

I thought about how my battle with Seee so quickly transformed from victory to defeat. I believed I would float to triumph as easily as a hydrogen airship. He simply struck the match and watched the flaming Hindenburg plunge from the sky. Perhaps this was the whole lesson? He allowed the takedown, casting it as bait for a fish that couldn't help but strike. Once the hook sunk in, he showed the men how easily it was to reel me in. The David, inside the grip of Goliath's thunder, able to not only fight through incredible odds, but also wind up on top, the victor. A lesson on turning disbelief into belief, a microcosm of what was to come, but at the time, the clue buried itself under a hundred other misconceptions I had about him. The man plucked himself into our subconscious, an inception planted there as a seed to grow a belief, supplanting our fears and doubts, not only in ourselves, but what we could achieve together, united in brotherhood. In the months to come, we would truly find roots, and Seee would take us there, shining light on our branches, pruning them until we became the young saplings that could once and for all grow into giants.

The next day Seee came again, and once more we spoke in the darkness. He spoke of why he had beaten me. He said that a mean dog had to understand the club. He talked about Buck and the red-shirted man in *The Call of the Wild*. He said I was still in a phase of bewilderment, maddened and enraged, and the club would probably have to come down again. He said I had the potential to be cunning and shrewd, but that I had to use my pent-up anger in more constructive ways. I listened, but I did not hear.

Then, perhaps two or three days later, he came again, and feeling starved for company and hurt about his negligence, I said, "You're coming so frequently the guys will start thinking we're lovers."

He exhaled deeply. "Perhaps I was wrong about you. You should ask yourself if you really want this. It will only get harder." The metallic sounds of a key shoved into a latch echoed in the darkness.

"Just who are you, Isse Corvus? A trophy of a man who has conquered other men at sport? Is that enough for you?" His steamy breath was now close to my chin. He was stepping toward the cage, so close to the bars that I sniffed him in the darkness beyond the stenches of myself that reeked up the room—sweat, the smell of fire, the blood of something slaughtered. Perhaps there was a club in his hand. I anticipated a blow, but it didn't come. "Warriors of the past would have cut off your head without thinking twice. Ask yourself what invisible force is holding you captive. You're here aren't you? So why don't you know?"

The cell door slid open. "There will be a group leaving in three hours who've called it quits. You can join the other cowards if you wish. If not, stay in this room."

I didn't move.

"I should also disclose that two men have died."

"How?" I asked.

"Training."

"But how?"

"How is not important. I warned everyone people would die here. More will follow."

I heard him reach down and leave something. Then the sounds of his steps drifted away. I fumbled around the dirty concrete floor until my fingers bumped into the pages of a book. On top of it, I felt a glossy photograph—my Earth photo—and a large box of matches. I took out a match and lit it, shining its crown of light above the photo. The Earth was still, unwavering, static. Calm and tranquil, the color of an eye deep in space, wrapped in the blink of a tiny instant of time. A tear came to my eye. I moved the match toward the ceiling until my arm was straight. Then I stood, moving the light farther from the Earth on the floor until my hand hit the ceiling, the Earth accepting the darkness, yet I could still see the faint glimmer of atmosphere, the cerulean blue marble as still as a whisper, refusing to rotate. Then the match went out, and I bent down and picked up the photo and moved it close to my heart.

After a minute, I moved the flame of another match over the book. The book was *The Call of the Wild*, and I spent the next hours devouring it until the last match was gone. Then I used the first pages to provide light for the next until the book was finished.

The next set of hours turned into loneliness. Some of them I slept, but when I awoke, the fictional dog Buck barked in my head—out on the tundra, the lead pack dog plowing through mounds of fresh snow. Hazy and still partially in a dream, I plunged through an ocean of snow, through its thickness and permeability. Dappled spots of white frost blew across my face, the snow bite of a fierce Artic wind before me weaned and the darkness returned pure and heartless through the sub-arctic winds of the North Pole. I came out of it to find the animal in me, the Buck I struggled to understand.

My mind drifted from one thing to the next, floating from the dog Buck and his lesson with the club, to the fight with Seee and my own lesson, to two weeks ago at the hangar, saying goodbye to the America that was burning in the flames of riots and chaos.

Then I heard Seee's voice. "So you've decided to stay?"

"Yes."

"You haven't been outside yet. Perhaps you'll want to reconsider."

"I don't think so."

"Wait and see. I'll be honorable and give you one last chance once you reemerge."

"Honor is for losers. Evolution—extinction—remember?"

He laughed, and the sound of it bounced through the corridor. "You're right. Should I bury you now then?"

I said nothing, and the walls grew silent once more. Each of us held his breath. It felt like the moment before our first clash, everything standing still, an instant stolen from time.

"Tell me how you became known as The Conductor," I said, breaking the silence awkwardly.

"Do the men really gossip like this? Like schoolgirls?"

"There were rumors, but you never know what the truth is."

"In this case, I do," he said. "Tell me what you heard, and I'll tell you how accurate it is."

"I heard that for ten years you stalked a target. I don't know where exactly it was, but it wasn't a simple mark."

He finished opening my cell door which squealed on the rollers. I heard him step into the room, the shuffling sweep of bare feet. He sat down, his back scraping against the cinderblock wall with the lidless toilet. The darkness was immovable, yet I felt I could see the expression on his face, the muscles in his cheeks relaxing. A light I imagined shining over his face showed a curling smile.

"If I was authorized to snipe the target, it would have been a simple job. But they wanted more discretion. They wanted deniability. As well, the CIA used the assignment as a punishment. They wanted to sweep me away after the ordeal with Hassani, but that is another story for another time."

"They told me you dressed yourself up as a bum, rags for clothes, dirt under the fingernails."

"No. The story is veering off course already."

"So how was it then?"

"I wore a threadbare brown second-hand tweed double-breasted suit. In fact, I had others—flea-market clothes, but not rags." From there, he described his wardrobe, how nothing in it was ostentatious, yet not completely cheap. He bought his items from a Saturday market held out in the open space in the Plainpalais area of Geneva and paid cash. He kept an unshaven look (stubbly but not bearded) and used special eye drops to make it seem as if he had cataracts. He dyed his hair gray and smoked cigarillos down to the nub. He made himself look like a man in his fifties and carried himself with a slight limp. Then he hit the streets as The Conductor, waving his hands in the air frantically, directing invisible symphonies and string quartets.

"For the first two months, I didn't go near the target's location. I stuck to the city center streets, getting the people used to me. I would always keep my distance, never invoking any fear with my bizarre behavior. At first they stared and pointed. They said to themselves, *Who is that crazy man?* But they knew what I was doing. They saw my arms swinging, hands gyrating, gesticulating like the great maestros motioning for crescendo. Music was playing in my head and I was leading the violins, violas, cellos, and horns. They hypothesized about what affliction I had. If they guessed obsessive-compulsive disorder, then they guessed it right. This is who I wanted them to believe I was—a habitual man disturbed by the thought he was a conductor, harmless, minding his own business, yet showy. The same times every day, they would see me pass. They looked at me sorrowfully at first. Others would even say hello, but I pretended not to hear. They were other sounds drowned out by the thunder of the orchestra. I dove into my own world, and they seemed to understand, and above all, not question it. A few months passed. They would see me tick by and come to think of me as timely as the city clock mounted high on a bell tower. It grew such that they expected me to walk by their cafes and Laundromats and small stores and arcade shops. They would say, 'There goes The Conductor. I wonder what he's playing in his head today.'"

It wasn't long, he told me, before they would raise questions if he didn't keep his routine. *Where is The Conductor today? He's missed his rounds.*

They would surmise illness. The next day, he would be there once again and the faint tickling worry would disappear. He compared himself to a stray cat coming around to a house to be fed. If the animal failed to show up, there would be anxiety in the household imagining the worst.

"Why such an elaborate ruse?" I asked.

He said the target's mansion was impenetrable. There were high, electric barb-wired fences surrounding the estate. The perimeter was covered by infrared detectors and video cameras and guarded by a hundred men. Parts of the garden were mined. The target's bedroom was inside the interior of the mansion, away from any window or balcony. Inside, twenty other guards took shifts twenty-four hours a day. They monitored the chefs. Food was dipsticked. Acid levels tested by doctors they had employed for years, and then fed to tasters. Packages, luggage, and any other object coming into the premises were X-rayed and then put under a Geiger counter.

Seee said, "It was impossible to get to him from the inside. His office was equally difficult. If it had to be done quietly, there was only one way to do it—in transition—from one place to another."

"So how did you get close?" I had forgotten about the barrier of darkness between us. His story had entwined me. Finally, there seemed to be a string of understanding between us.

"I'll explain that in a minute," Seee said. "I walked the streets around his office each mundane day only passing in the morning at precisely the same time. I threw my hands in the air, orchestrating ad-nauseam the intro to Mahler's *First Symphony*. I used delicate feather strokes with supple fingers, raising eyebrows gently and puckering my lips as I walked by. Or I would bounce my hands like field rabbits, humming Tchaikovsky's *Nutcracker* if I wanted to appear friendly and ambient. Or Penderecki's *Passacaglia Symphony No. 3* when morning nerves would unravel, when I would grit my teeth and resist shoving a Welrod pistol into my trousers before I left. I weaved myself into The Conductor bit by bit, stitching into every bodyguard's fabric of conscious that I wasn't a threat. I never went too much over the top. I never carried a conductor's baton, as that in itself could be conceived as premeditated. I studied my character, read books on conducting and music theory, taught myself how to play piano. I forged the right papers and went to institutions, watched, and even counseled, OCD patients under the guise of being a doctor.

"Eventually, the target's guards got used to me walking by the office building on Rue du Rhone. They had already checked me out, I'm sure. But my information was nothing but my cover. The bodyguards would see me around town performing Stravinsky, Haydn, Wagner while off work doing their shopping or sitting on a terrace having dinner. I was everywhere, yet nowhere. Invisible. Part of the landscape of Geneva as much as the UN or the Parc des Bastions, or the Jet d'Eau. After a year, chance had it that my timing got better. One day, my rotation around Rue du Rhone corresponded to an intersection with the target. His car pulled up to his office building, and he stepped out of the car and was immediately swarmed by five of his bodyguards. That day, I gave a heavy berth and passed a meter away. One of the guards raised his hand to me and asked me to halt, which I ignored, as if I were an imbecile in my own unbroken Schubert world. I grumbled and mumbled something incoherent, humming simultaneously in an off-cadent slur. But this was an important day, because I had managed to break through their minds. I was not pushed or hit. I was not harassed. Had I not given berth, they would have surely thrown me out of the way, but this day I was within striking distance.

"As time went on, I eroded their will to watch me closely. I camouflaged myself into the surroundings even though I was in plain sight. I was becoming part of the background. I could have been a parking meter or a streetlight. They saw me no differently."

"Who was the target?"

"A Russian oligarch. I'll refrain from giving him a name—let's just call him Mr. X."

"Why knock him off?"

"He was very influential, with a significant share of world oil output. He was beginning to buy up banks and get involved in various financial schemes at the time."

"Why was he living in Geneva?"

"Like any smart oligarch at the time, he minimized his time in Russia. There were political risks, and who could tell when the Kremlin would seize back assets once again as they did when the Soviet Union broke up."

I was caught in the web of his story. I wanted to ask more

questions, but thought better of it. I didn't want to risk him becoming reticent so I simply listened.

"As I got more adept at timing, my intersections with Mr. X became more frequent. I was able to get within eyesight several times a week and make a pass-by within a kill radius about once every two weeks. At that time, I didn't even carry the injection. I knew it was too soon. After some months, the guards stopped waving me off, as they had the habit of knowing I wasn't stopping. Their eyes stuck with me, but more importantly, they didn't want to be rude and shove me out of the road. What would they have looked like then? Would they have left a bad impression on the boss bullying an old man who was mentally unstable? It wasn't in their psychology to push me out of their way, but they were still cautious when I got too close.

"Then one day, Mr. X didn't come to work. Nor the next day. Or the day after that. Every day, I woke up and walked my usual route, as devout as a Muslim to morning prayers. The Company was slow getting back to me, but it turned out he went back to Russia. No one knew for how long. So I kept walking, keeping my routine. One morning during this hiatus, the doorman to Mr. X's office building glanced at me as I passed, and he said, "Maestro, what are you playing for us today?" He was a well-fed, red-faced Pole by the name of George Bernard, short and fat with rolling jowls. He continued this sort of behavior. It was just something to amuse himself. I would pay him no heed, my myopic gaze staring directly at the ground three paces in front of me while making absurd faces at the gallery of invisible clarinets, sometimes waving them to enter during *The Magic Flute*. George Bernard never got the benefit of the doubt as I did. Mr. X's guards would simply push him out of the way, where I was afforded a little bit of real estate."

"How long did you keep it up for?"

"Mr. X left for nearly two years. When he did, I was four years into the job."

"So you continued the routine?"

"Yes. Although I was acting, I can tell you I was absorbed under the spell of my character. When I went wandering into the streets with my beige beret and cigarillo stuck between my lips—my wrinkled suit and scruffy trousers—I felt that every passing day I gravitated slowly into the hapless Mr. X with an uncontrollable compulsion. That man is still part of me today."

"How many hours a day were you on the street?"

"Two hours twenty-three minutes was the time it took me to do a route. I did one in the morning and one in the evening. The evening route I skipped Mr. X's office building entirely."

"What did you do with the other hours of the day?"

"I studied. I did research. As I said, my station chief essentially left me there to rot until it was done. Many in the agency thought it was pointless. Then the Russian came back, and the deed suddenly became more urgent."

"Why?"

"It was purely personal. I woke up one day with the notion I might be able to change things. I felt a great need to return to the U.S. after my discoveries."

"What discoveries?"

"The rampant corruption going on. Evidence I discovered in Mr. X's office led me to inspect UBS's offices. I found insurmountable evidence of Libor manipulation, Federal Reserve documents giving policy away before it was released publicly. But that is another story."

I did not press him. It was apparent he wished to finish the present story so I said, "So how did it end?"

"The Russian had been back for several months. Still, the opportunity did not present itself, although now I carried the injection. The injection was a poison, a strychnine-leopard's bane blend inside a miniature hypodermic needle that would take its time killing him. Then one autumn day when the sun was slight and the weather blustery, the opportunity presented itself. As the car door opened and he was in the midst of stepping out and being surrounded by his security, the Polish doorman, Mr. Bernard, cried out and fell over, crumpling to the ground. All eyes shifted to him, and this was all I needed—a moment of diversion, a moment of confusion. I turned my shoulder sideways slipping through a guard, feigned tripping over another, and fell into the path of the Russian. I came down partially on him, grabbing at his ankles in a mock fall. Twisting his ankle simultaneously, I shoved the tiny needle through his sock deep into the skin beneath his lower calf. It was done within a tenth of a second. The move I had practiced thousands of times. His guards were on me in a flash, yanking me from the Russian and throwing me away from him. I responded by feigning rage and commenced to wave my hands in the air brutally conducting as I moved forward. It was out of this expectation, this natural sense of how I should have reacted, my predictability as the character whose identity I forged, that they let me simply move on. If they would have been thorough and would have searched me, they would have not found anything. But if between the time I was released and the time I veered off my normal course over the gutter and toward the other side of the street—if they would have pried open my mouth—they would have found the tiny needle that would kill the Russian. But they did not, because they did not think of the unthinkable. It would have been an insult to their egos to think otherwise."

"So Bernard?" I asked. "He didn't just fall, did he?"

Within the darkness, I pictured Seee with a slight surreptitious smile as I finished the question. A lurid shape on the invisible face that was more than just a storied voice with soft enunciation and a quasi-illustrious tone. "No," Seee said. "Bernard went down because of a series of tiny razor blades stuck in his shoes. When triggered, they ejected upright into his feet. But that is another story."

"And so security didn't check him?"

"Perhaps they did. I don't know. What I do know was that there was a search, but for The Conductor, it was his last performance."

"So when you went back to the U.S. what did you do?"

"I searched for those who might believe."

"Believe in what?"

"In what the notion of real patriotism means."

"And how exactly would you define that?" I asked.

"A country is not just a name or ideas written in a constitution from the antiquated past. It is the sum of the beliefs of its constituents. The wave of change happens through them. Government power can only be expressed as well as they can control the degree of that change."

I paused thinking about this.

"You do not agree?" he asked.

"I do," I said finally. "But you are here, aren't you?"

"I am," he said. "Here training patriots. Here training people who are willing to die for their country. I consider it a serious occupation, and this you do not want to doubt. For me, it's the best one can hope for in these uncertain times."

"And there's nothing more to it?"

He stood, and I heard him step toward the cell door, snorting. "Politics," he said. "Elephants and Donkeys and the talking-head demagogues of the press. What could go wrong?" Then he took on a more serious air to his tone. "There's a lot more to it obviously. We're just scratching the skin in this place. So why don't you step outside and start itching?"

Chapter 7

"Before you embark on a journey of revenge, dig two graves."
-*Confucius*

Left to worm my way through the dark corridor, I used the pocked concrete wall to feel toward the iron door. Finding a tubular handle, I turned the knob and entered a boxed-in hallway. Another closed door in front of me flickered with a needle of light escaping through a keyhole, and my eyes lit up with excitement. In the box of darkness between prison and day, the world opened up, its presence a meager few yards away. I wondered what the day would hold behind the closed door. My nose sensed the humidity in the air. My skin contrasted the stickiness of it to the coolness of the underground. I sniffed the heat, sensing the boil of greenery and heavy pollens in the air. Ears once again filled with stridulating cicadas and the voluminous sound of buzzing flies.

Slowly, I cracked open the second door, and a pool of light burst inside. Then I crept into the world of the living, shielding my eyes with my right arm. I used my left hand to feel along the wall. Finally, my fingers bumped into an iron ladder leading out of the underground tunnel. I tried opening my eyes to climb up the ladder, but the stinging daylight forced them closed. Squinting, I grabbed the rungs of the ladder and climbed into the world of weapon and war, a heart intent on once again being part of it.

After thirty minutes of sitting in a clump of grass listening to the incessant buzzing of a swarm of flies, the forest slowly unrobed itself. My eyes awoke under the booming sun. A sweep of green from the forest bush appeared. Then, through a slat of thin trees standing like spires, slowly a human form sitting on a tortoise-sized rock came into focus, the familiar nine-inch Bowie with the duct-taped handle reflecting spears of the sun. My vision cleared further in acceptance of this new birth, and I found myself twenty yards from the edge of the clearing. There I had stood rigid in line. Now, here again, my eyes gazed upon the stubborn foot stepping out of line for Seee's challenge, saw time rusting away while my comrades moved forward.

As I walked into the clearing, the buzzing of flies grew louder. In the middle, high up on a stake, neck sunk in deeply, the head of a person appeared, unrecognizable at first because of the mass of flies all over it. I picked up a dead branch and swatted away the swarm. The stench of rotting flesh caught in my throat. I swatted again and again because the black swarm buzzed away only momentarily, but up there I saw the head of Bunker, black eyes rolling back in their sockets, a bloated tongue bubbling out of his mouth, flies and maggots all over it. My friend Bunker—his head kebabed on a skewer.

I circled the encampment, eyes fixed on the centerpiece. Kumo whittled another stick with the gleaming Bowie, glaring at me as I walked by. There was a frog with yellow and black-spotted leopard-skin at his feet laid out flat, arms and legs elongated and broken, but the creature was still alive, its tiny lungs inflating its hapless body.

"Look at you," Kumo said, fletching the stick. "You've thinned out."

"I'm on a diet."

He snorted out a laugh while attaching an iron arrowhead to the tip of the shaft and tying it with a piece of twine.

"You're a funny man," he said.

I circled Bunker's blackened head once more while Kumo finished the arrow. Then he rubbed the arrowhead over the skin of the frog and sheathed it in a quiver lying behind the rock where a bow had been laid out. "You seem dazed. Shall I push you in a direction?"

"Why would you do that?"

"The course you're on is leading you nowhere."

With his knife, Kumo stabbed into a basket of leaves, slid one into his mouth from the blade of the Bowie, wadded it up and sucked on it close to his gums. I looked back at Bunker. The mass of flies ate away at his head again, a moveable black veil over the decaying skin. A string of them attached like pearls to liquescent flesh melting off the neck.

"So what about Bunker's head up here, Kumo?" I raised my voice while pointing to the swirling mass of flies bubbling around the head.

He scoffed at the question. "From a slice of paper, the world folds over into a Mobius strip. An ant travels along it. But only the ant who feels gravity knows which side he's on."

"You think I have no gravity?" I asked.

"You seem to be orbiting, where in contrast, I know where I sit. The stone feels my weight."

I stopped circling and stared fiercely at the man. "He was a friend of mine. What did he do to deserve this?"

Silence from Kumo. The mid-morning sun slid higher into the sky. I thought about the deceit of the darkness. My internal clock told me it was late afternoon.

"You will perhaps tell me what happened?" I asked.

"It isn't my place to do so."

"Why not? You can't speak for yourself?"

Silence again.

"He was a friend. A friend deserves more respect than this." I stepped toward the stake.

"If you touch what is not yours to touch, you act with dishonor," he said, finally breaking his silence.

I moved closer to the stake, ignoring him. The swarm formed a cloud around me, buzzing incessantly, trying to burrow deep into my ears. Kumo whistled—a birdlike call made with an arching tongue. I swatted away the flies and turned to see Kumo's bow drawn, stretching with tension, the arrow close to his cheek between two fingers. His right bicep flexed while the left arm remained rigid and taut. Then I saw a streak and only afterward I saw his finger had let go. The arrow sailed by my head, a soft swishing sound as it flew by. Before I could blink, he had another one loaded. I stepped closer to him, out of the circle of flies.

"It will not be a pleasant death," he said. "And with this one, I wouldn't bet on a miss."

My eyes turned cold. Gazing over to the woods where my Lazarus-self had just been resurrected, I retreated a step. "You would kill me for honoring a friend?"

"You will learn your place here, or die."

I watched his fingers curling around the arrow, mounted in the shooting position against the bowstring.

"I don't need permission to kill you."

"Seriously, you would put an arrow in me for that?" I retorted.

"You have not learned our ways."

The sound of rustling bush under heavy footsteps came, and Briana burst through the trees and sped past us, turning her head only briefly. Both of us paused a second. We heard more footsteps approach. Seee ran through the trees breathing heavily, but then came to a stop seeing us. Others, lathered in sweat with crimson cheeks, followed at his heels. The group arrived in quick succession, bare-chested, garbed in running shoes and sucking wind.

"What is the meaning of this?" Seee asked, regarding us.

"He wants to take down the head," Kumo said.

Seee glanced at me harshly. "The head stays. It is a warning for those whose egos are too large."

The men remained motionless, gazing at me with blank expressions, as if Seee's words were sacred. "Is it too much to ask to respect the dead?" The men's faces shifted from apathy to callous scowls. My castigation felt like banishment, as if my return had torn the familiar fabric of the camp. I glanced at Brock and Split, and in their severe faces I saw clearly that I was the apogee of the circle of friends, usurped for another authority.

"Can't we all just get along?" one of Seee's men called out with a comedic twang to his tone. A few snickers popped out of the group. For an instant, a look of exasperation appeared in Seee's eyes before he said, "Merrill, enough." But the tone contradicted the statement and seemed to be a license for what was probably habitual truancy with rank and order. Merrill, with the lopsided grin, seemed to be above the law.

"Respecting the dead requires asking the same question of the living," Seee replied. "If you want to plead your case, plead it with Uriah. He has the final word. It is he who owns the mouth of the insolent."

The slumped-over, wretched man panted for breath. Plodding through the forest to the finish, he had been the last man to arrive. He bent over gasping for air like a drowning man unable or unwilling to speak. Uriah—the weak and wheezing Elephant Man who seemed to almost make a joke of the place. I remembered his words to Bunker the day I was thrown in the hole, *You'll be the first one I make an example of.* Could this be the man who had lopped off Tomray Bunker's head? Seee read my expression, walked up to me, pressed his thumb into my shoulder. "Never underestimate the power of will," he said. "This lesson I hope you've already learned."

The day drifted by and the opportunity to speak with any of my comrades passed. Merrill showed me around the camp. We walked up to an area he called "out-of-bounds," saying it was mined. Then we hiked another mile and came upon a small, isolated farm. Here stood a stable; wandering farm animals; grazing horses. An older, graying man came out of a small cabin. I asked if this was the guy who ran the place.

"We all take our turns," Merrill said.

"So this guy's part of the training?"

"No, but he's part of the camp."

We hiked back the way we came, through a cluster of bamboo trees and back into the jungle.

"So you take a good punch," Merrill said.

"My idea wasn't to show off those talents."

He laughed. "For the one stepping forward, it's a sad day without that talent."

"So what about you? How'd you get here?"

He stopped and smiled at me coyly. "Slow down, woman. This is our first date. I don't put out on the first date." Then he laughed out loud again and continued walking.

We continued for a bit. "Kumo doesn't seem like he's taken to me."

"He thinks you're bad news."

"Why does he think that? What have I done?"

"Are you bad news?" Merrill said eyeing me. I looked over at him, but before I could reply, he said, "Let me give you a piece of advice. We might seem isolated out here, but we actually know quite a bit."

"What does that mean?" I asked.

"In time, you'll see."

As dusk fell and the sky swept the dying day away with a swirl of pink and orange clouds, I walked into the dilapidated plywood shack buried in the woods with trees smashing out of its roof, later known as the Tree House. Conroy and Burns were alone, huddled in a corner speaking in whispers. The place was cleared out. Even Mir's centerfolds on the wall had been stripped. Conroy and Burns saw me and broke apart. Conroy smiled, walking up to me with his hand extended, saying, "Good to see you. Most people thought you were dead."

The kindest greeting I had received from the dregs of the day, I accepted Conroy's hand, shook it, and asked, "Where are the others? They look like they've abandoned this place."

"They have," Conroy said. "No mosquito netting here. Everyone's set up either tents, or tarpaulin and hammocks. Most guys are camping a bit north of here. Split, Brock, and Mir are a ways northeast. Me and Burnsy and a few others are a bit south."

Burns had a shaky look to him, and a long neck that made his eyes seem wide as coins. He had a scrubby forehead, oily hair and a stubbly face, pale lips that quivered, an overactive tongue moistening them as they twitched. Conroy was more inviting compared to the stewed-up Burns. He had smooth, green eyes, the type to put one at ease.

Unable to hold my curiosity I asked, "So what happened to Bunker?"

Conroy shook his head as if still in disbelief. Before he could answer, Burns cut in. "He challenged Uriah."

"What kind of challenge?"

Conroy said, "I wasn't there to see it, but some words were exchanged. Bunker had been riding him, taunting him. Then he slipped into ass-kicking talk."

"Seee overheard," Burns said. "Challenged Bunker to step up and make a real challenge."

"After more mouth from Bunker, the next thing we know they're out there in The Pit."

"The Pit?"

"A bit west of here," Conroy said. "A big swimming pool-sized hole dug out where two people jump in, but only one comes out."

"I've never seen anything like it," Burns said. "He chopped off Bunker's head in about two seconds."

"Swords?" I asked.

"Bunker had a shield as well," Conroy said. "Uriah—just a samurai sword. It was over before it started. Uriah knew what he was doing. That much was clear."

"Bunker was the one who charged," Burns explained. "But Uriah somehow sidestepped him. When Bunker turned, the shield was only up to his neck, and then...well, after it was over, Seee jumped in The Pit and lifted his head high-in-the-sky and says, 'The mouths that talk too much do so without bodies.' So that's about the highlight. Some guys shipped out after that."

"Who?"

"Kasim, O'Donnell, Rigby, Sharaf, Edwards, and Chloe Manning," Conroy said.

So the pack had thinned, I thought. Kasim and Edwards weren't a surprise. Nor Rigby, after he was flattened by Kumo's stone. I thought Chloe would have stuck it out for Bunny though. Now Briana was on her own. Burns remained silent, eyes following a dragonfly darting around the room.

"Any idea why each of them decided to bail?"

"Kasim and Edwards were dismissed," Conroy said. "O'Donnell and Rigby left on their own accord. Chloe…well…she just wasn't made for this shit."

"Don't you find any of this strange?"

"How so?" Conroy asked.

"I don't know," I said. "I'm still trying to put my finger on it."

"I'm still trying to figure out the purpose of any of this," Conroy said with a laugh. "Have you seen the TV yet?"

"No."

"They're dragging it out at night. Beaming out NSA Director Titus Montgomery clips. It's not a perfect image, but you can tell it's him. It's causing quite a stir with the camp."

"Why?"

"General Montgomery is a piece of work," Burns said. "Talking about internment camps and juicing instigators and shit like that."

"This is top-secret shit," Conroy said, his eyes flashing. "A man's got to ask himself, how are we allowed to be watching this? And furthermore, who gave them clearance to access it?"

"If it's there, why shouldn't we watch?" I asked. "Are we afraid of the truth?"

"I don't think any of us are. But as you're saying, something feels wrong about it, about everything here."

"I guess I'll have to judge for myself," I said. But Conroy was gazing at me with an upturned lip. He stood that way for some time, nodding his head up and down with a coy, smug smile on his face. I stared into his set of multifarious eyes shining the color of obsidian while a sort of unspoken acknowledgement lingered between us. A duality of purpose wafted about the air that had no language, but was clearly seen in our body movements. Our eyes communicated as if they were made out of tongues, untraceable signs where deniability were its nouns, blurred meaning its verbs, and arcana its adjectives. We were two bishops placed on Pelletier's chessboard, our role to take out the king. Although we couldn't speak of it directly, there was an incognito recognition bubbling to the surface, one that we would never speak about. The sweet secret of treachery was best withheld.

Chapter 8

"Political language...is designed to make lies sound truthful and murder respectable, and to give an appearance of solidity to pure wind."
-George Orwell

The first days were running, war games, and field work. Then days of jumping off cliffs with a river below you, the goal to try and latch onto an overhanging rope before you hit the water. We plunged into other jumping exercises—rock climbing, tree jumping with ropes and nets. Sometimes no nets. Seee was giving us hard lessons in escape training, growing balls so we wouldn't be afraid to jump. Not surprisingly, Split loved these exercises the most, never giving a jump without a net a second thought.

Next, we were taught how to map an exit plan, think improvisationally if things ever fell apart. We learned advanced Krav Maga, how to turn defense into offense, Traxler counters they called them. Next, we underwent stress inoculation and enhanced interrogation techniques.

The others had already gone through the exercise of killing chickens. Many funny stories could be heard about headless chicken dances throughout the camp. But when I finally joined the men, they had just begun killing goats. One man would stand over the animal and attempt to soothe it by softly petting it. But the animal was wiser than this and quickly began bleating. Another man would hand over a hammer, and it was used to bash in the skull. The first time I watched Brock do it, I found myself shivering at the sound of the horrifying crack. Once over, and the goat lay limply on the ground, it was simply a matter of cutting the throat and watching the blood gush out while it hung from a tree. That first day, I skinned it, cut out the innards, stabbed it through a spit, and roasted it over a fire. My arms were lathered to the elbow in blood and the sticky messiness of animal slaughter. All of it a very new sensation—the foul smell of innards, the gooeyness of blood and guts, what a liver or heart felt like when you squeezed it in your hands. Soon we would graduate to the squeal of live hogs as we chased them with our hunting knives. As time passed our taboos about killing grew into tasks or routine.

Then one day, the robots came out. We started with a DARPA BigDog and advanced to Petman humanoid models. We didn't know where they had come from, but we learned how to fight them. Loaded up with paint pellets at first, rubber bullets later. Mistakes were costly. The first step—disengage their eyesight and heat sensors. If you wanted to use an electric magnetic pulse, it had to be done at close range. Terrain-capturing shields could cloak you under electric eyes, but we only learned how to use these after we employed other diversionary tactics.

Beyond the robot skirmishes and gore of killing farm animals for our meals, we had rest hours where we spent time reading *Hagakure*, the book of clan studies, *The Art of War*, and then books on history, Thucydides and the Peloponnesian War, the American Revolution and Civil War. We read the Declaration of Independence, the Constitution, and speeches by George Washington. Seee didn't let our minds linger, saying he was modeling us after the Romans, the first army to think, and he relished listening to our debates.

After dusk, we spoke only Yoncalla, no matter how bad our tongues were at it. An extinct Indian tongue of the Kalapuya people from southwest Oregon, Yoncalla was full of clustered uvulars, few ablauts, stiff and without vowel harmonies.

The first night after dinner, when the fire died down and our tired tongues twisted in knots from pronouncing Yoncalla nouns, a TV was dragged out by Des, just as Conroy had said. A couple of pushed buttons later, an image appeared. A man with his back to the camera moved over to a cocktail bar where liquor bottles were spread out on top. He took a glass and set it down on the countertop. Then he uncorked a bottle of Knob Creek and poured it into the glass. The man moved over to the adjacent window, and through the reflection, General Titus Montgomery's image appeared, blurred but discernible. It certainly appeared to be him, a handsome face, thick nose, stern forehead—the sort of face that commanded, not one that asked. The image seemed to be coming from a wide-angled lens. The width of the picture took in most of the scope of the room.

Montgomery was the Chairman of the National Security Council (NSC) and Director of the NSA, one of the President's closest advisors. Whether the camera was drilled into the wall or hidden behind a picture didn't really matter. Whoever had put it there had taken a huge risk, and most likely the device would not have been installed very long. The obvious irony of the situation was not lost on the men. They laughed and guffawed and made jokes about NSA surveillance programs saying, *who was the bitch now*. Yet, I felt agitated by the situation, as if the point of the video wasn't just about exposing some foreboding truth, as much as making the point the NSA was weak and vulnerable. Still, a burning curiosity filled me to see an insider's view, and my heart raced a bit in anticipation of what would happen next.

On the TV, a knock rattled the door and Montgomery called the man in. The man entered, saluting as he stepped through the door. "Sir."

"Yes, Colonel Davis."

"The Elevation reports, sir." The man walked up to Montgomery and handed him a manila folder.

"Give me the seven sentence summary. I've got a meeting in a few minutes."

"Elevation has outperformed all operational targets. Our strategic media goals have been met, and Uplift program demand exceeds available spots. Los Alamos is now working on a more efficacious dose."

"Your recommendation?"

"The report supports the expansion plan, sir."

"I'll take a look at the report and let you know. Thanks, Davis."

Davis left the room. Montgomery stared out over other buildings in the distance, and down to the parking lot, then returned to his seat where he waited at a huge conference table sipping his drink. Nothing happened for five or six minutes. Merrill and Kumo filled the time by saying the words in Yoncalla for the various objects in the room—the table, the glass, the word for drink. Merrill, pointing at Montgomery, stumbled around making the word for drunk. The men had a laugh at this, and began to use some of the words they knew.

"The camera—where is it?" I asked Merrill. He unrolled a pack of cigarettes from his shirtsleeve and bounced the pack in his palm. He shrugged his shoulders and looked at me quizzically, lighting up a smoke. Then he cupped his hand around his ear and asked me something in Yoncalla. He refused to speak to me in English.

Finally, a military aide led someone into General Montgomery's room. The camera rose and faced a man in a prim, black Italian *Garbato* suit.

"Mr. Roth, a pleasure seeing you again," Montgomery said. Mr. Roth was a squat fellow, with beady eyes that seemed to be black stones dropped into a glassy fountain. He was old and frail, white-haired, hunched over, but still distinguished. His face was weathered and hard, and wore an uncompromising expression.

They sat down at the conference table while the aide left the room. Montgomery spoke first. "Let me start by saying the subject we are about to embark upon is extremely sensitive. If it should leave this room, there could be disastrous consequences."

"Understood."

Montgomery picked up his drink and took a swallow. "It has

come to my attention that some of the journalists on *Crossfire Nation* are depicting the United States Government in a somewhat negative light."

"How so?"

"They're chattering about the Uplift camps, ridiculously saying they are FEMA camps and asking too many questions that are frankly compromising national security. They are openly critical of the way the riots are being handled. To be blunt, I'm not sure the National Guard perspective is coming through clearly enough. The Guard has been extremely professional under the circumstances."

"In the last week, the Guard killed three protestors," Roth said calmly.

"Certainly an unfortunate circumstance. There was provocation. We are investigating it thoroughly, let me assure you."

"So you think it the duty of a journalist to speak only of your opinions? We've bent over enough to pressures from this administration already."

"I'm sure you're sensitive to the fact we have to worry about national security. These critical broadcasts aren't helping sway public opinion."

"You have an advocate with Bob Sanders though," Roth said with a chuckle. "Isn't he your spokesman on the show? The man wants to tear up the Constitution for Christ's sake."

"Aren't we all absorbed with the past too much? Always looking at things how they once were and making dangerous comparisons to the present. It does no good for morale."

"So you're asking me to put a muzzle on our program," Roth barked, "the one show on our news lineup that crushes the ratings. Do you know why that show is so successful, Mr. Montgomery? It's because the show presents two opinions."

"People need hope, not negativity. We are in a dangerous time with national security. Don't you want to be on the side of the people?"

"The people need to know both sides of the equation."

Montgomery tapped his fingers against his forehead as he bit down on his lower lip. Roth's face grew angry and impatient.

The battle of wits lasted another minute before Montgomery said, "There is a Chinese proverb that states he who says nothing when something is to be said is wise, where he who listens to silence and thinks it is nothing is inscrutable."

"Sir, you forget who you speak with! Do you know who put this President into office? With one phone call, I could—"

"Do nothing," Montgomery said cutting him off. "Tell me. When one flips a coin and the outcome is tails, does one then say, it was I who did this, who commanded fortune to lean my way? Furthermore, do you really believe the outcome of the coin makes any difference? When this administration is through, do you really believe I will be gone? Go ahead, make all the phone calls you like. You do not own the US Government, Mr. Roth. The US Government owns you."

"I'm not going to sit here and listen to any more of this," Roth said, standing. "You talk about manipulation. But how is it not manipulation when the government creates millions of fake Twitter accounts to beef up their propaganda campaigns?"

Montgomery crossed his legs and picked up his glass. He smiled into it, as Roth glared at him. "No, we won't report the Twitter business. But don't go making threats. We've had enough."

Montgomery finished his glass and stood up. "The number zero either destroys another number or keeps it intact, all depending on its operator. Which sort of operator are you, Mr. Roth? Simple or complex?"

Montgomery moved out of the purview of the camera, but his next words were not misheard. "This is not a zero-sum game, Mr. Roth. You should think twice before stepping in the way of national security. Please give it some thought."

The TV switched off, and we went off to sleep, the men

mumbling to one another as they strode off into the forest with flashlights.

The next day, with the previous night's event still in our waking brains, we went jogging at the break of dawn. It was a morning in early October. We ran through branched towers of trees spreading out over the scalloped earth. We ran up canyons and into valleys, across riverbanks, and into the jungle. Tetrapods croaked under the confines of creepers, vines, and ferns. Swampy sounds of creatures silenced as sixty-four footsteps drummed the earth over the terrain. Glistening rays of sunlight beamed like angled spears into the shadowy woods. We burst through them, and the flashes of light across our faces danced in our eyes. Hearts pounding, our breaths asynchronous and hurried, we inhaled the thick air in heavy gasps. We trampled through the forest, Seee in the lead. The men struggled with the pace, lungs bursting with heavy breaths, sweat running like rivers out of every pore. Briana trotted behind Seee. She could have taken the lead easily, but she showed a certain reverence toward him, as if winning wasn't everything, something that seemed to be contrary to her nature.

We galloped through the forest and onto a plain. In a thicket, the lush grass rustled against our legs. For a moment we felt freedom spying the wide openness of a hillock glittering from the dew of a morning mist. Then the sun beat down on our bare backs and our bodies returned to groaning. The insects awoke, howling discordant symphonies, stridulating cicadas, bumblebees. Flies and mosquitoes buzzed the air in strafing attacks on us. I remember Split opening his mouth wide as we passed through a cloud of gnats. He swallowed them and grinned.

On this flatland we found rhythm, synchronicity, every man feeling the pitch of hot breath melding together. Our minds awakened into abstract consciousness, sensing a purpose to fulfill as brothers but the clarity of it still vague. On this morning, the air would be filled with Seee's song:

Mama mama can't you see,
what The Abattoir's done to me.

We repeated his verse after each phrase and the valley echoed it
back.

I potty-trained in the CIA,
now in the jungle to be a man someday.

Mama mama can't you see,
what The Abattoir's done to me.

I wish it were the days of Uncle Ben,
when I could fight alongside the Minutemen.

Mama mama can't you see,
what The Abattoir's done to me.

Turned my eyes inside out,
gonna show me what the country's all about.

Mama mama can't you see,
what The Abattoir's done to me.

They put me in an electric chair,
shocked me in the nuts until I grew a pair.

The world tilted and we dipped down a hill and picked up
speed. We were a phalanx of human ants flowing down a path,
following the pheromones of our leader. We did this for miles
and miles, back into the forest, alongside river canyons until
finally we straggled back into camp, lungs bursting and bodies

lathered in sweat.

Afterward, we ate breakfast with hearts thumping to find a slower rhythm for the day. Grus and Conroy cooked. They scrambled eggs and fried up bacon in a monster-sized skillet over a knee-high fire. Fumes of grease wafted to our noses, trails of scent heavy in the air as the sun made its way higher into the morning.

Mir and Ayan Shankar came through the woods, their hands full with buckets of river water sloshing over the side. They poured them into a filtration system. We drank, and drank again. Then we filled up our cups and canteens in preparation for the day.

Split, Brock and I sat with backs against a clump of trees scarfing down Grus's mushy eggs and greasy bacon on flimsy paper plates. Flies buzzed around our food and we swatted them away as they landed. Brock discovered a more efficient approach, bending the plate in two and using it as a funnel. Split and I liked the idea and followed his lead.

It had been a week since I had come out of The Hole, but still I felt a need to bring up the topic. "So there's one thing about Bunker that I don't get," I said. "Rumor has it Uriah killed Bunk not because of any insult, but because he found him coming from out-of-bounds."

Silence.

"What was he doing out there? What would be the purpose?" I glanced over to Split. He was eying a fly crawling on his arm sucking on a droplet of sweat.

"What purpose does it serve to ask such a question?" Brock replied.

"Aren't you curious?"

"I don't see that it matters."

"Can anyone answer the question? Why was he out that far south? Was he trying to communicate with someone?"

The wind changed and the smoke from the hickory chips in

the fire wafted in the air, the smell a reminder of home, of barbeque and a carefree world. Brock swept the air clean of smoke and looked me over. Shrugging his shoulders, he said, "It doesn't concern us or our mission here, man."

"A friend gets decapitated and it's of no concern?"

"He was no friend of mine. In fact, you're about the only one I know who liked him. But to answer your question, of course it's of concern, but any answer is conjecture. We'll never learn the true story. If you want it, go ask Uriah."

Split piped in, lifting his plastic fork and tapping the air with it. "We haven't really even seen what's coming. But I'm telling you, it's on the way."

Crooked-toothed Mir bounced into the conversation and the crossfire of words began. Uriah sat in the distance out of earshot. He peered up from his plate and caught my stare—strange eyes bubbling inside the face of quicksand. I nodded sideways at him in a motion that invited him to join, but he gazed back into his plate and continued eating. Maybe I wanted a confrontation. But he wasn't going to give it to me. Perhaps he sensed what we were talking about. But the obstinance in him dismissed rumor and innuendo.

Mir edged in again. "All of us knew what we were getting into. Period. None of us were lied to. If Bunker broke the rules, he knew what they were when we got here. If it was an insult, it was an insult. The point is that it doesn't matter."

"Exactly what I've been saying," said Brock.

"I'm just saying—what would be the motivation to put your life on the line?" I asked.

Brock and Mir glared at me with edgy looks. The Spanish Monkey scratched his head. Overhearing the conversation, Conroy stepped over while Grus yelled at him to get back and finish the KP.

"Something funny is going on up north too," Conroy said.

"Like what?" Mir asked with a doubtful tone.

"I was taking a dip in the river, then found a trail covered over next to the outer bank. I took it a ways. I saw Merrill and Des hiking back up it leading a train of horses. The saddlebags were loaded up with something—not guns, not ammo."

"Supplies perhaps?"

"Something's just off. Doesn't it feel off?" Conroy asked.

"Nothing feels off besides this bullshit conversation," Mir said, walking out of the circle, off to warm his hands in the fire.

"What's off to me is that fucking Montgomery cat," Brock said. "Aren't you getting the point of that?"

"It's fucked up," I said. "You got to wonder what the purpose of showing it is. But shouldn't we be worried more what's going on right here?"

"Isn't it obvious," Brock said. "They're showing us hard proof how shit is all fucked up at home."

"What are we supposed to do about it?" I asked, but no one answered.

After breakfast, on the way out of the woods and halfway to the clearing, Mir bumped my shoulder and whispered, "You should talk about these things in more quiet company."

"Thanks for the advice," I said.

"Don't be a fool," he said, jaws clenched. He grabbed my arm, gave it a rough squeeze. I broke his grasp, but let him continue. "You've been down in The Hole. So learn how to walk here before you run. You could fuck us all with that mouth."

"Relax, Mir."

"You don't know who to trust, so don't tell me to fucking relax. You're playing with lives here."

The following weeks were dedicated to different disciplines of destruction. Three days of bomb building—mercury switches, detonators, how to build crude IEDs and plastic explosives using bleach to get pure potassium chlorate. Two days of advanced weapons training—rocket launchers, M-32s, how to lay and detonate different types of mines. Explosion after explosion until vision undulated and the land became variant and pulsing. Afterward, you would drift through a monotone hum of high-pitched noises. Drunk on the fumes of sulfide. Tapped out on adrenaline. War junkies wobbling back into camp. Even with earphones, we still walked around camp as deaf men, screaming at one another after a day with the rocket launchers. It didn't help that we were forced to speak Yoncalla.

From there, we moved on to part one of poison theory— three days of shellfish toxins, snake venom, frog poisons, tubocurarine plant life. We set up a laboratory tent and learned how to mix doses, dip blowgun darts, freeze tiny needles the width of a human hair that would disintegrate on impact with a high-powered dart gun. We studied the effects on the human body. Antivenoms. We rubbed the bark off strychnine trees. Then we broke into groups with blowguns and stuck each other with small quantities, watched one another get sick and go limp. Then two days more of application: loading tiny needles into dart guns with telescopic sights; scoping out animal targets at two hundred feet, the poison melting undetectably into the skin. We brought back wild boar, rats, and other small rodents. We skinned and gutted them and cut up the meat and left it in the middle of pit traps to see if the degree of toxicity was enough to kill anything eating it.

Nights were rest periods—campfire dinners, storytelling, and lessons in Yoncalla. Kumo, Des, Merrill, and Ahanu monopolized the conversation, speaking mostly in brittle Yoncalla, forcing us to partake by pointing and jeering at one of us and laughing amongst themselves. These nights Seee kept his distance from us. Perhaps the feeling of separation between leader and the led kept him away. But even though he was absent during these mystical evenings, he grew in our hearts. Each of us feeding on stories about him from the Sons. My mind battled the obligation I promised to fulfill, my word and a sense of duty still outweighing what was happening in my thoughts.

Then one night, I followed Seee through the woods as a sunset flopped in the sky over a skillet of clouds, rims singed with golden fire. I kept a large distance between the two of us, enough so it would be impossible to hear my footsteps. Sometimes I couldn't see him through the thick of the woods, and I snuck toward him solely on instinct. When we walked deeper in the jungle, my pace quickened to catch him, but as I got closer, he disappeared from the path. Within a cluster of trees, I felt him staring at me, picking my intentions apart as a fisherman sheds the slimy scales of a fish.

I called after him. "Feel like company on your evening stroll?" I felt a presence behind me. Was this what I learned in the darkness, deep in The Hole? How to sniff out ghosts? Or was this just a split second of instinct, an awareness of death knocking at a doorstep? A surge of adrenalin shot up my spine. I froze, standing as still as a statue. I slowly lifted my arms, floating them up in the air like soft balloons, feeling his silence commanded it. But I refused to beg or grovel. "If you're going to kill me, get it over with." The response was a call of croaking frogs squawking over his every sound, deafening his every movement. I craned my neck aimlessly, and when I turned my head back around he stood directly in front of me, mud-caked and slathered in earth. Two paces away, he held a pistol aimed right between my eyes, finger taught on the trigger.

"You aren't carrying anything are you, Isse?"

"You must think I'm pretty stupid," I said. I slipped off my T-shirt, then my army trousers and threw them at him. He stepped on them, booting them down, trouncing them into the mud, but never taking his glare off me. His eyes shined like white bulbs under the cover of the forest, poking out at me under his mud-stained face. He spoke in a shaded tone. "I wasn't sure you weren't out on an ambush."

"Why would I do that?"

"Why wouldn't you?" he asked vaguely.

Both of us shut up for a moment. The tension in the air unfolded when a cool breeze blew through the trees. Finally he said, "Perhaps you think you're still better than me going hand-to-hand."

"I am."

"I know," he said, lips curving into a lopsided smile. "But I fought you once. Look how that turned out." He laughed a bit. "Come on then. I'll show you something."

He guided me through the jungle while trailing me three paces behind. We hiked out to a ravine with a pool-sized slab of sandstone dripping over a cliff. For a while, we sat in silence watching the crown of the sun creep beyond the tree line. Long shadows cast out over the river. I glanced over at Seee. He sat far away from me, but I could see his eyes raised at the stars twinkling through the blue-grey atmosphere.

"I call this place Second Sight Peak," he said.

"A nice name."

Staring at the crescent moon, he said, "We stare into the darkness every night, see the infinite, and grasp only a tiny iota of the idea of it, as no other species can. Yet few truly appreciate it."

"I had a four-inch refractor growing up. We used to camp out on the hills and set it up and sometimes just gaze up there till dawn."

"Is that a fact?"

"It is. My father pulled it out of a dumpster and gave it to me for my thirteenth birthday."

"A nice gift," he said. "Even if it was garbage."

The last sweeps of sunlight dissipated and the singe of blue atmosphere rustled with the darkness. The cooing of an owl came in the distance. The wind shuddered and a breeze blew lightly across our faces.

"Look out there. Up on this ridge we're standing on the

Panopticon of Nature."

Was this coincidence? Had he listened in on the words I said to Pelletier? But if he knew, wouldn't I be dead? My silence started to be revealing. To fill the space, I said, "It's a beautiful view."

"Up here we are real humans, aren't we? Nature doesn't care about us. At least the State and Nature have that in common, don't they?"

Edging into the conversation he wanted to have, Seee gazed over at me. Pelletier's code words I had spoken over the phone still rolled over in my mind, but I met his eyes and smiled. He looked up into the darkness at the stars once more. "Isn't it ironic we can see objects twelve million light years away, understand and model them, tell if it is a quasar or a nebula, or even a binary star system—but never get there."

"Red-shift, blue-shift," I said. "The overwhelming story a spectrum of light can tell."

He smiled faintly, as would one who suddenly finds common ground. "Some light reaching here has traveled longer than the dinosaurs' entire existence. Time so large its meaning is vague, because it no longer refers to a realm we are able to grasp. Like infinity, it becomes warped, a limit of our comprehension."

I picked up a pebble and fingered it. For a moment, it reminded me of The Hole. "If Voyager were going to Alpha Centauri, it would take another 40,000 years. We would need more than four hundred lives just to see it."

"Not a lot of time in life is there?"

"No," I admitted.

"Men like us don't live forever. We breathe heavier than most, and the air is always thin even when its substance is thick."

I wanted to say something, but he cut me off. "There is pain in being alive," he continued. "Shouldering responsibility. Knowing you'll send men to their deaths, good men, brothers. But traitors—traitors must be punished."

"Traitors? What kind of traitors?"

"Traitors to our forefathers and country." He sighed. "There is a point where the problem becomes too large, the atrophy too deep. A disease metastasizing. Ignoring it any longer is an unsustainable path. Cancer needs to be removed by the scalpel if the patient is to survive. I know you see this. You've been out on the street and seen the disease growing with your own eyes. Your father was a victim of it."

"How so?"

"The real story is that your father had been laid off by the city. Tough times. More debt than revenue. He goes to find a job. He finds nothing. Unemployment runs out. He takes something—anything—flipping burgers at a BK. Except now the minimum-wage job won't cover all of the expenses, the perpetual rising prices. For Christ's sake, bread is eight dollars a pop now. Food stamps can't cover the expense. And he doesn't want the charity. So what do you do?" He paused for a second. "You revert back to instinct, to necessity. You crawl back in the jungle."

He waited a moment, judging my reaction, then shook his head as if he had come to a conclusion. "You're going to be the easiest one to turn."

"What do you mean by that?" I asked, shocked at the boldness of the statement.

"Once you open your eyes and see that your father was a man not uncommon to most blue-collar men, you'll have no choice. Your father was kicked out of a job because of the clampdown on State finances; a man who could no longer find a decent-paying job because of younger and older demographics squeezing him out of the labor force; a man who had enough pride in himself to want to keep supporting the family; a man who was beaten into doing what he did out of pure desperation. Your father was one man out of millions who are experiencing the same plight. If you open your eyes and ask yourself who is truly responsible for all of this, the people who have crippled the economy and are ass-fisting the country with law after law to crush your liberty, you simply don't have a choice. But you don't see the big picture. You resist."

"Why are you telling me all of this?"

"Because you have potential. I see it lurking within, but now it is up to you. All you have to do is step out from the darkness and accept what you see."

"I admit the country is fucked up, but should that mean I should turn my back on it?" But even as I asked the question, I knew my own answer. He moved an eyebrow upward, as if he too sensed a tone in my voice signaling a shift. His eyes gazed back deeply into the darkness, flecks of starlight twinkling in them from vestigial stars.

My eyes moved to the expansive sky. I searched for Cassiopeia and then above it for Andromeda. It was out there somewhere, another galaxy mixed in with the Milky Way. Distance can always be deceiving, proximity a matter of degrees.

"There's something large going on here," I said.

His tone stiffened. "That much is obvious." He stood, brushed his mottled pants off. "But reality up there is not the reality on the ground. I need your word of commitment." Then he was off into the darkness, breathing heavily, but physically not breathing at all. He strode into the thick forest, which gobbled him up without making a sound.

Chapter 9

"Loyalty to the country always. Loyalty to government, when it deserves it."

-Mark Twain

Standing here now, gazing out at the first snow peppering the woods on the streets of the capital in the year 2026, that first battle at The Abattoir seems a distant memory, one reflecting as a wavering blur, a thousand shards of Seee in them.

In the winter of November 2022, I tossed and turned after the night at Second Sight Peak, Seee's words a balance inside my head, tipping from one side to the next on the idea of nation.

The next day, the men were bothered when Mir asked what Seee's idea of fear was, to which he replied, "We are all prisoners of something—whether it is this body, this Earth, this solar system, galaxy, or universe. As you saw, Roth is a prisoner of Montgomery. You do not have to live behind bars to be in a prison. The paradox of liberty is that it disintegrates with time. Freedom is usually something we are too afraid to take. Fear is ignoring truth and seeing a reality that is metamorphosing and distorted as something continuous, when indeed it is not."

The whispering surrounding this statement swirled amongst us throughout the day. *What was he trying to say?* was the question on everyone's mind. While debate sparked among us, I kept the previous night's conversation to myself. What no one argued over was all of us glaring into the eyes of blinding belief. We, the jealous, searched our inner souls for the same spirit, questioned larger contexts, acknowledged what he was saying was not abstract. Our ears simply refused to listen. As overachievers, the message came as a challenge instead of an answer. The camp split and became argumentative, unable to come to a resolution. Arguments based themselves on intent, not on patriotism, and did not flare into accusations. At least, none spoke openly about it.

After dinner, four more men followed Seee and I to the ravine—Split, Brock, Conroy, and Mir. Others would follow in the coming days. The gravity of Seee, pulling us together bit by bit. A man who came at you in fragments, a mosaic of the full picture, and all of us were curious to fit the missing shards of the man together, to resolve the enigma, the attraction too large to resist.

We sat in a small circle and watched the sunset begin to form. Split lit up a cigarette and it was passed around, the end burning like a sun, a fusion reaction between us, the first spark of the fire that would begin to unite us.

Seee took a long drag on the cigarette, and told us it reminded him of his days smoking the peace pipe with Ahanu. He told us that American history was dirty just as much as it was inspiring. He spoke of slavery and how Native Americans suffered the wrath of an enemy too strong, how they were dispossessed of their lands by the white man.

"Ahanu says that his people were too slow to adjust to the creep of change."

"Yet, does he still consider himself Native American?" Split asked. "He was in the Marines. He fought for America."

"Ahanu is a wise man who considers himself American, while at the same time respecting his roots," Seee said. "He isn't a man rooted in the past. He looks to the future."

Then Seee began a story. "Perhaps you don't know, but Ahanu was a descendant of Kicking Bear—great, great, great grandson or something like that. Legends were passed down. Who knows if it's true, but he told me a good story once. He told me the Bear liked tall tepees. So they build one in the winter of the late 1800s that gets particularly tall—has a massive space within. All of the tribe is engaged to paint the inside of it. When it's done, the crackling fire inside lights up the static lives on the canvas above.

The characters on the canvas are their ancestors—grandfathers, grandmothers, legendary braves and chiefs. But up above, nothing is a lie. All of the scenes are things that actually happened. At least that's what I was told. The space is filled with these warm lives. When the nights are ten below zero and the earth is an icicle, everyone bundles under buffalo skins after a ghost dance while each one of the tribe in turn tells the story of their drawing from above. They gaze up and watch the spirits of their ancestors dance in the shadows. The stars poke through the tiny slit at the top of the tepee, and this is the spot they call God's Eye. What they notice is both the figures on the canvas and their conscious eyes direct themselves to the slit above, to the darkness and the thin shimmering starlight bleeding into the fortress."

See took another drag on the cigarette and passed it to Split. "Now, none of them was told how to paint their scene, but all the characters' actions are funneling to the hole in the top of the tepee. Kicking Bear thinks this an omen. He claims that under this tepee, God's Eye is glittering, the drawings magnetized to it, the light pouring in is more radiant within. The tribe ends up believing it is a crack of Nirvana, to which all of their ancestors journey. They say it is a remnant of the ghost dance, a celestial crystal ball to see within the heavens. A month later, on a clear night, the tribe is bundled once again in the tepee, gazing up at the slit, waiting for stars. But ominously, none come. Puzzled, Kicking Bear goes outside and sees a sky full of stars. There's not a cloud in the sky. Long after all of the others have gone to sleep having grown impatient looking for one, Kicking Bear stays awake gazing through the slit at the dark sky. Still, no stars pass through the window. The Sky Father has closed The Eye on them. When morning comes, Kicking Bear wakes everyone and forces them out of the tepee. Then he takes a torch from a fire outside and burns down the Tall Tepee much to the lament of the rest of the tribe. He claims the Sky Father disapproved of the tall structure and that the tribe should remain close to the earth, close to its roots and what is already known."

When Seee was quiet, Brock said, "Makes you wonder. What happens when the universe becomes darkness? When the last star flickers out?"

"The universe did not end happily for Kicking Bear," Seee said. "He ended up being a clown in a road show."

"From warrior to mascota," Split said.

"It's the metaphor for our great nation," Seee said.

"How do you mean?" Brock asked.

"Too many of our people are becoming Kicking Bear, either waiting for a star that isn't coming, or like a clown, dancing around oblivious to the world around them, willing to give up their freedom for the status quo."

"I don't think it's quite that bad," Conroy said.

"You don't? Curfews? Drones? Robotic police? The expanding apparatus of the surveillance state? The government's attempt to confiscate weapons and gold? Disallowing money from leaving the United States? Then, they give themselves the right to detain you as they see fit for as long as they want, all under the widening umbrella of national security. What about the internment camps? You don't see that as problematic?"

"You mean the Uplift camps?" Conroy asked. "I think it's a bit of an exaggeration. People are exercising their rights by protesting."

"Isse, what do you think?" Seee asked. "You were in the riots. Give us America's pulse."

I scratched the stubble growing on my chin. Eyes around the fire gazed at me eager for what I would say, ready to make a judgment, and Seee cleverly put me in the spotlight.

"I think the element within the crowd has changed," I said.

"How so?" Seee asked. He swung around from a reclining position where he was perched on an elbow, swiveled his hips in a break-dancer move, and ended up sitting in a lotus position.

"It's not only your street punk, anarchist, or left-wing radical out there now. Most of the protestors are no longer the fringe. The circumference of the circle is thickening, with a large majority of them now the middleclass."

Mir interrupted. "What did you mean this morning, Seee? You talked about the paradox of liberty and reality metamorphosing."

"We are all born into the State, and therefore we are part of it, constituents with passports, birth certificates, tax payer IDs. The State tracks us. They regulate when we can leave or go. They take judicious records of our birth, whether we pay our taxes, and our eventual deaths. The State gathers taxes from the collective, from a group whom are supposed to represent our interests. They vote on how the funds are to be used. But over the last sixty years, funds taken in have not met the insatiable urge to spend. Naturally, the State borrows, making promises to return funds to their lenders. But in effect, they shifted the burden of payment in colossal amounts to the future, as the future was distant, a day so far ahead it was inconceivable for it to come. And then it did. That day is now, and slow change is accelerating, the result of which is civil disobedience, to which the State responds with confiscation of one's liberty."

"And you think the riots are because of this?" Conroy asked.

"The riots are a symptom of financial hardship, which has been caused by rising prices, the creation of funny money, and a kleptocratic political system intimately tied with a corrupt financial system. But it has moved very slowly throughout the years. So slow you can't see it or understand how it happened. Only now are eyes opening. People are dripping with discontent and it's leaking out onto the streets. The media is nothing more than a propaganda machine bogging you down with disinformation and shifting the blame. They claim the rioting is caused by the fringe, the undesirables. Or they simply bury the coverage."

The group was silent. Perhaps skeptical. Conroy's deep look of worry and Brock's little shake of the head deadened the conversation. The sun was edging out of the horizon, scorching the sky. Finally, Mir spoke. "The forefathers had a vision of a government that would stay off the backs of the people, and in their time that vision was mostly realized. But let's look at how that vision is different than the reality of today."

"Within our democracy, we have the power to vote out the politicos though," Split said.

"Do we?" I asked. "Does it really matter who we vote for? Has it made any difference in the last fifteen years?"

Seee added, "We are gravitating closer and closer to a dangerous situation when the blood on the streets will thicken. How will the people have the means to defend themselves? Mir brought up a good point. Let us ask: Should the State be altered to bring it back in line with the vision of our forefathers? If so, do you think it would be allowed? Who would try it?"

"You are saying the citizenry is becoming hostage to the State," Brock said.

"How has the United States evolved for the better," Seee asked, "and how has it veered off course? How do we effect change if it can't be done through voting? Is anything moveable through the vote anymore?"

We all thought deeply about these questions. The men argued longer while Seee kept silent and listened. Then Conroy asked, "But how do you go about changing anything?"

Seee replied surreptitiously. "I'm not sure. What I do know is how I choose to live my life and that entails sacrificing for my beliefs. Not because I think I'll be judged, but because I *am* judge in the here and now, and I want to be a clear lens for those to see the country's true shape. Tradition does not equal truth, nor does it guarantee liberty. When liberty fades then what you have is tyranny, and then what use is a country?"

As Brock was in the middle of a reply, a large blast rang out in the distance. Another explosion quickly followed. Seee shot to his feet, reached into his pocket, and put in an earpiece. "Talk to me," he said, then cupped his ear and ran briskly into the forest. Through the earpiece we heard, *Enemy in the wire.* We bolted back to camp, Seee in the lead, slithering through trees and underbrush. Under shadows, we swarmed through the jungle, all of us in the wake of Seee's path, blisters on his feet slowing him down. The explosions continued with the rattling shots of a machinegun. As we got closer, we heard screaming deep within the jungle. More machinegun rounds blasted sporadically from several more guns. Then, the sound of grenades came.

Two hundred yards from camp, Seee broke off and leapt into a teak tree, scampering up it like a monkey. He threw down two shovels, pointed to a spot away from the tree and commanded us to dig. Split and I frantically shoveled earth, tossing it over our shoulders. Seee whispered to us that this was not a drill. He said they were probably guerillas after weapons, some of them probably tripping off mines around the perimeter.

A few inches into the soil, Split and I hit metal with our shovels, then dug around a trunk as the others helped push the soil away—an arms cache, a treasure chest of everything from machineguns to RPGs. We suited up in flak jackets, unzipped ammo bags and stuffed them with grenades and shells. Each of us fit an infrared NVG over a helmet. I grabbed a shotgun and slung it over my shoulder. Seee threw Mir an M40A3 and took one for himself. All of us picked up M16s mounted with sights, and slipped in close to the camp where the view was less obstructed by trees.

We crawled through the bush on elbows and knees with our M16s in front of us until we were fifty yards away. Seee counted twenty-one men in the camp clearing. Most had flak jackets on. Others were poking about the perimeter. Several teams of four or five gathered rucksacks, preparing to leave on patrol. Out on the perimeter, two of the enemy were pulled out of the jungle by their comrades unconscious and bleeding. Even with the light smothered by a waning sunset, we could plainly see they were Asian, the first people we had seen outside The Abattoir. Our eyes lit up with the revelation of a secret.

We inched a few yards closer and saw Eaton Atlas and Drew Gareth on their bellies, pinned to the ground, hands zip-tied behind them. Three other friendlies were face-down in the mud, bodies limp. From that distance identification was impossible. It looked like the others had scattered. Machinegun bursts came blasting from the hills, but the interval between the rounds lost pace.

Out in the clearing, we watched a soldier pop out of Seee's camouflaged wigwam with a map fluttering in his hands. Four men dragged Atlas and Gareth to their knees. Two stood on each side, pinning them in place. The man with the map shouted in broken English as he circled around them, shoving the map in front of their faces. The two remained stiffly quiet. The enemy wore olive green short-sleeved uniforms, red patches on the side, like something out of old Korea. The map man had a flashy bald head, shiny even in the dimming light, a skull more spherical than egg-like, a chin dimpled and hairless. Here stood a man who had never been taken seriously. Now, he had to prove everyone wrong and double-down on severity.

The map man barked at the two again, poking the paper with a finger. He waited a long ten seconds for one of them to speak. Then he ripped away the map and moved behind them, removing his pistol from a side holster.

No one doubted what was going to happen next. The surrealism struck us as if it were theatre, the audience with a certain foresight of the upcoming scene. We held our breaths, looked at one another. Seee sensed our anxiety and motioned with a stern hand for us to hold. A memory blipped in my head from the day I saved Timothy Skies—police sergeant Smith ordering me to keep my position. Here, I didn't have the courage of the hero from long ago.

Brock and Conroy lowered their eyes. Split had a shaking finger on his M16 trigger, the map man in the crosshairs. Seee, shook him by the helmet, and when he had his attention, clenched his jaw and shook his head no.

The map man pulled the trigger on Drew Gareth. A loud bang leapt into the forest as blood burst from Gareth's forehead. His body went limp, boneless as a squid as the two men holding him stepped back, letting him crumble to the ground. We gritted our teeth watching as blood pooled around Gareth's skull. The two men covered in blood spray wiped their faces on their sleeves.

Atlas had his head turned. The two men holding him up twisted his neck, bent him over, and pushed his eyes closer to the wide-eyed Gareth with part of his brain oozing out of his head. The map man pivoted back around to Atlas, kneeled down to gaze at him in the eyes, then doubled up his shouting while grabbing a clump of his hair. But Atlas simply shook his head. If any fear gripped Atlas, the map man certainly wasn't seeing it.

I gazed over at Seee and could tell Atlas was making an impression on him. The map man went back into the wigwam and came out with Seee's machete. He shoved the shiny blade under Atlas's throat, sawing the dull side against his skin. We looked at Seee once more, but he motioned again for us to wait. *Too many—too many*, came the whispers down the line, *too many in the camp for us to take.*

Atlas clenched his jaws, snapped his eyes shut. The map man took his time slicing off his ear, cutting it slow and delicately, as if it were a hunk of steak he were cutting into. Then he took the ear in his fingers, and held it high in the air. Atlas couldn't help but scream, though it wasn't one of fear or pain, rather a growl of pure rage, a bear cry, shrill and dark from a vagrant beast, one that said, *You've just pissed me off and I'm coming to fuck you*. Atlas twisted his shoulders to break free, but he was wedged in good between the men on each side of him. Finally, one of them gave him a hard knee to the ribs.

I glimpsed over at Seee. A calm, sanguine look took over his face, more apathetic than a machine. He disassociated himself from the scene, biding time until the odds were right. Calculating probabilities with a raw unemotional discipline, reworking the battle plan, thinking if they killed Atlas, grenades and mortars could be used. But he also knew the enemy would only kill him out of pure rage, that it would be unwise to kill him before he talked. I remembered turning away in disgust, but later the sentiment would turn to admiration.

Atlas wheezed on the ground, the wind knocked out of him. The onlookers at the perimeter finished packing, and finally two of the patrols dipped into different parts of the jungle. We counted twelve men remaining. Seee called us into a huddle. Each man would snipe a target. Split and Brock would then split off into the woods and flank one of the patrols entering the jungle. Mir, Conroy, and I would flank the clearing and retake the camp. Seee told us he would provide the cover fire.

The guards lifted Atlas from the ground onto his knees. The map man straddled him again. He repeated the yelling routine, but Atlas remained more tight-lipped than ever, pressing his lips together, the fleshy parts hidden in a prankish, childlike expression. The map man stood up, ordered the two men to tilt Atlas's head back, then threatened to cut off his nose with the machete.

Atlas missed seeing the man's body jerk since his eyes were soaked in his own blood. Perhaps he heard the six shots crush five enemy skulls. The other, Mir's man, covered a hole shot in his neck with his thumb. Blood gushed out making a fountain over the body of the map man. Seee put down two more before I had enough time to aim again. One of the guerillas reached for a shouldered walkie-talkie, but before he could get a word out, Mir's second shot cracked a bullet through his teeth. Seee motioned for us to move out, dropping his M40A3 for an M16. The battle pitched forward. I caught a glimpse of Brock and Split taking off the other way. My hands damp with sweat, a cold layer of fear crawled over me. A jolt of adrenalin flew through my body as I rushed to my feet. Through the bush I ran in a neurotic stumble. Were Conroy and Mir behind me? I didn't know. Out of the corner of my eye, I saw the muzzle flash of Seee's M16 as he drew the fire away from us. Perhaps three or four guerillas remained, now on their stomachs, most of them shooting wildly into the jungle in Seee's direction. Bullets and tracers sprayed the jungle in chaos.

All reaction. No control. Revved-up and running at transonic speed, the red glow of tracer rounds zinging in streams overhead. Hundreds of bamboo trees in front of me, long and lank, networked together, root systems interleaved, all part of the same underground organism in a semi-live state. Doors opening as I fly through them. Step through the wrong one and a bullet catches you in the head. The world pushes forward without you.

I sprint over dead leaves and detritus as if the earth beneath flames with fire. The hot streak of sweat on my brow stings my eyes as I gallop through the woods. Trees splinter in front of me, the ground kicking up earth from a sweep of bullets. Closer and closer I bolt toward the spitting muzzle fire. Then I hear a cry from behind. Someone trailing me, hit. No time to look. Shotgun in my arms, I burst into the clearing, a side shot open with one of the machinegunners. He must have seen me in the corner of his eye. Rolling over frantically, he tries to adjust. I pull the trigger in a full charge, the spray of the shot blowing him backwards. Another guy snaking on the ground swivels toward me, the man just realizing the nature of the ambush. I pump another slug back into the chamber. Peace, brother, but this is war.

Buried under a body, Atlas now rises with the machete in his hand, his face bloodstained and mean. A wild, hungry expression in his eyes like a vampire after the first sniff of blood. One of the enemy flees into the woods. A single shot coming from the jungle cuts him down. Conroy now through the wall of trees. The last of the enemy surrenders, raising his weapon in the air, but Atlas slides behind him in no mood for mercy.

The area was ours. Seee stepped into the clearing, popping off rounds in enemy corpses. Conroy helped hobbling Mir. Mir was hit twice, once in the flak jacket and another in the leg. Blood streamed down his fatigues from the wound. Seee ordered Conroy to patch him up. He opened his backpack and threw Conroy a med kit. Then he looked over our dead, turning each on his back. It looked like they had been ambushed from the rear— all of them shot from behind. Seee's face went pale when he glared at the face of one of them. It was the rugged Ahanu, his whole face pale and frozen in time looking up at us. Seee put his hand over Ahanu's chest and said a farewell in Yoncalla. We were wide open out here, I thought. Even still, Seee fingered one of the exit wounds, and striped his cheeks with Ahanu's blood. He ordered the bleeding Atlas to come with him, me back into the jungle to tail the patrol Brock and Split were flanking. They would certainly be coming back, he said.

We split up, him and Atlas running into one side of the jungle, me the other—both of us outnumbered but with the element of surprise. I hesitated for a moment, thinking of the prime oppor- tunity in front of me. Track the tracker. An ambush he would never expect. I stood frozen, hearing my own breathing. A few seconds later, I walked deeper into the forest, double-backed, and then changed my mind again. It wasn't just Atlas stopping me from fulfilling Pelletier's wish, something else gripped me to turn away from my promise.

I flipped down the NVG over an eye, and a green tint filled my vision. The world came in focus differently, the roots of trees like veins in the earth. I ran through the jungle, losing myself in the maze of the bush. A retro reality passed before my eyes. Senses sharpened once again, but my mind levitated out of body, stuck in a wet blanket of dissociation, lost in a deprivation chamber in the jungle of some alien planet lush and verdant. I seemed to be a stranger to myself, wondering who the man was running away from his word. The heavy breathing I heard I associated with myself only because it synched in with my own. I ran uphill as I hard as I could until my breath caught up with my boot speed. Then all of a sudden, I stopped.

Up ahead, there was a shake in a cluster of bush. Three enemy emerged contoured against a full moon, coming down the ravine in a swift trot, their faces distorted and green. I ducked behind a large felled tree with upended roots.

There they were. In threes—birth, life, and death traipsing obliviously through the jungle toward a point of ambush. They carried AKs in their hands, their faces blurs without feature or depth. Sewn-up eyelids blind to past, present, and future; their time now multifaceted stepping through a set of trees. A failure to see they had walked through the wrong door. They looked between twenty-six to thirty years old. Their pasts still belonged to them, but their presents were stuck in a mind frame hoping the rough day was through, their faces weary with it. I tightened the stock of the shotgun firmly against my tensed shoulder, my left arm ready to pump. I was the predator, sniffing their scent riding the wind. Their futures hid behind a hooked index finger squeezing a metal tooth, my right eye in the sight ready to ground the trinity—father, son, and Holy Ghost.

The blind men marched closer, their boots loud climbing the stairway between earth and sky. My eyes stung, moistened by sweat seeping into them. I wiped my brow on my arm and waited for one of them to look up and see me. To give me an excuse. Seee's voice came to me, *There is no fair in a fight.* But where do you draw the line? Had it been cut to ribbons?

I clamped my thumb and two fingers together and touched my forehead. I swept them over my stomach and shoulders, completing the sign of the cross.

Prisoners. I could take them as prisoners.

But here I was, Cerberus, the three-headed hound from Hell, coming to take them.

Prisoners, I repeated. Take them as prisoners.

But I couldn't.

And in the end, I wouldn't.

Chapter 10

"The pessimist complains about the wind, the optimist expects it to change; the realist adjusts the sails."
-William A Ward

The day after the Battle for Atlas (as it became to be known) wherein a gang of Burmese invaded the camp, the men of The Abattoir buried the dead. Even with the loss of Glen Aims, Adam Avery, Drew Gareth, and Ahanu, the number killed on the enemy side far outnumbered Abattoir losses, and in the end the remainder of enemy guerillas retreated back into the forest. Pride glowed throughout the camp, and even though temperament remained solemn during the burial ceremony, each of us basked in the victory, so much so we seemed to miss questioning what it was really all about. Some thought Seee himself had instigated the attack as a test. Then a rumor spread around that he had stolen from the Burmese mob, inviting an attack. But all of this seemed far-fetched. Seee's anger steamed outwardly. He cursed what he called a lack of forewarning in the system. When I asked him what he meant, he remained tight-lipped. Further prodding earned only reproach. Merrill, Des, and Kumo sidestepped around him.

Before the battle began, the camp had fallen under the watch of Kumo and Ahanu. After the first set of mines exploded, Kumo led a group of fighters into the jungle. Everyone played his part in the fight, and everyone had their own story to tell about it.

Kumo, Merrill, and Des built a wooden ziggurat eight feet tall in which they placed the wrapped Ahanu's body on top. The bodies of the other three rested on the levels below. At twilight, Seee lit the torch that would send them away in flames. Black smoke billowed high up into the horizon. In his speech, he said not all of us would have such a sendoff, but we would do the best while we still had the luxury to do so. He warned the enemy could be back, so all of us had to be alert during night watches. A few hours later, he called us together and told us the problem would be fixed another way, by relocation, and it would start tomorrow.

So on the day after the ceremony, a day in November of 2022, the students of The Abattoir faced a new challenge, unaware they were about to sail off the end of the flat world into an unknown universe, one always duplicitously present, but whose true form we had only imagined.

We spent the morning setting booby traps in the forest. Afterward, I walked by Seee's bivouac, and through the crack in the canvass door saw him spreading out the map, the paper now blood-tattered and worn, onto a metallic table. Des was packing up supplies outside—tents, ammo, M16s, ready-to-eat-meals— throwing it on the backs of idling horses nibbling on grass. The smell of urine from one of them was thick in the air. I crept to the back of the shelter and listened to the low whispers coming from inside.

From Kumo: "You're making a mistake. You should kill him now before this gets any more out of hand."

Then Seee, switching to Yoncalla, which I was now beginning to understand, said something to the effect of: "Nothing is certain. We must be patient. We need him. He's the only one that can do this."

Kumo spoke again in Yoncalla: "It's not in your nature to take risks. So why now?"

Silence followed. I heard the map crinkle and flip, then Seee's fists slammed down on the table. A moment of silence passed and then Seee said in English, "With a failure from The Anthill what I need now is your trust. This cannot stand! We lost a good man last night, and I know you are all upset, but it hasn't clouded my judgment. With some men, you must roll the dice and see where they land."

No more words came, so I crept away. After they reemerged, Seee asked us to gather in the clearing. Then we moved into the forest receiving few other directions.

The horses stayed behind, spare one with empty baskets dangling over its side. We hiked northwest where the woods thickened. We plodded through an initial cluster of thanaka trees mashed compactly together. Here the green plant matter and shadowed undergrowth were the most dense. The bush became as solid as a holly hedge. We swam through vines and thicket. We hacked through walls of vegetation with glittering machetes, their blades sticky with gummy residue of roots and branches. Each of us took a rotation, two at a time up front clearing a path with machetes large enough for the trailing horse. We inched forward until we heard the gushing sounds of distant rivers.

On the way up a peak, I caught up to Briana. "I heard you did pretty well out there."

She looked at me cautiously, as if I were playing an angle. "Thanks," she said. "I guess."

"Seriously. I'm not messing with you. I heard you were tough."

"You're not trying to be a smart ass are you, Corvus?"

"Not at all. I can switch back if you like."

She smiled at me and gave me a wink. "Please do. I don't think I recognize you."

"I heard you got your cherry popped. Or rather, you popped a cherry in one of the enemy."

"That's the Corvus I know. But it's true, and nothing really to be bragging about."

We climbed over the last of the hill and hit a flat stretch of land. "I'll be damned," I said with a quick laugh. "Should I put you on the couch so you can tell me your feelings?"

"There's only one thing you want to put me on the couch for, Corvus."

I laughed. "Well played."

Ascending another stony hill, we reached scarred cliffs ripping the landscape into veiny ravines where river water flowed into the heart of yet another wall of endless jungle. We climbed down a gentle decline toward a part of the river smothered in woods. There, Seee ordered us to drop the machetes and gear and gather around while Kumo laid out a map on the rocks of the riverbank. Seee spoke, lifting the map high so all could see. Written on the map were names, each shaded within a geography, dark lines enclosing each person's name. "Everyone will have a zone you will call home. You are not to wander into another person's zone. Each zone has been marked with paint on tree trunks to mark each boundary."

All of us looked confused, as if Seee spoke unlearnt words in Yoncalla.

"Here you will live and survive," Seee continued.

Kumo watched our reactions while Merrill picked up our belongings and put them into the horse's baskets.

Each of us squinted toward the map glancing at whom would be close. Across the river from me would be Uriah. On his right and left—Mir and Grus. Split was north of them, almost land-locked. Upriver from Grus was Shankar, Conroy, Brock. On my side, Burns and Eaton were upriver. Downriver were Drake, and Orland. I couldn't even see where Briana was. No one I really knew was on my side of the river.

"We are currently in Grus's zone," Seee said. "Kumo and Merrill will escort you to your zones momentarily. Anyone caught in another man's zone will be punished with the whip." Seee fished through his backpack and threw a black bullwhip out onto the river rocks. Bundled up in a coil, it was made of black leather. It had a silver handle, gold coupling, and an ivory pummel with two holes cut into it where red leather bands slithered out like baby snakes. The cracker had small jagged pieces of metal woven into it. Seee marked the reactions of the men as we stared down at it. "You are free to defend your own zone from others who might try to steal your resources."

For a moment no one said a word. Finally, Shankar asked, "What about the guerillas?"

"They won't find you here," Seee said.

"Surely you will leave us with something," Shankar said.

Seee gave us a polished smile. "They didn't teach you how to survive without tools at The Farm, did they? As you'll soon find out, it's a different game when you've got nothing." He drew a box of matches from his backpack and threw them in the air. They landed closest to Orland's feet. A melee started in the dirt, hands from everywhere trying to grab them. I dove into the pile and quickly found Orland's arm with the matches. With my feet, I kicked away others and screamed out, "We will share! Everyone shall have one." Yet the struggle ensued. Finally, I saw Split and Brock clawing men off the dog pile until it was just me and Orland. Orland struggled, kneeing me in my newly healed ribs. I let out a groan. Shankar tried to pile in again, but I booted him in the face. Blood streamed from his nose as he stepped back and cupped his hands around his face. I twisted around and wedged Orland's arm into an arm bar. Orland punched me in the ribs again with his free hand, sensing the weak spot. I lifted my hips abruptly. As the matches dropped from his clenched fist, I continued the relentless pressure until I heard a snap. Orland screamed in agony.

"See how quickly they turn?" Seee scoffed to Kumo. "Earlier they were acting as if one battle makes the war."

Kumo nodded. "Nature is quick to change the minds of men. Where is honor amongst the animals?" He pointed at me. "It seems Angry Dog is the fastest learner."

"Indeed," Seee said, gazing down at Orland's broken arm. "Merrill, bring a med kit."

I raised myself from the ground with the matches.

"Sometimes order must be paid for with a price," I said angrily.

Merrill came over with his rucksack, and overhearing what I said, smiled and guffawed, "Angry Dog says he who makes the order makes the rules."

Kumo snorted, and Seee said, "The Buck in him is beginning to wake. But here, Nature is the club."

Were my actions simply a maneuver for positioning, letting the men know the pecking order? Everyone stared at me, waiting for a response. Briana glared down at the ground, avoiding my eyes. Was it respect or fear I saw? I didn't care which. I stood there, silent. My position on the river had improved and I had the matches. Mashed and crumpled, I tore open the box and began doling them out one-by-one to each man in the circle. The men took them greedily, but lowered their eyes when they took one.

"We will at least start this game from on equal ground," I said, directing my remark to Seee.

"You will see that nothing is equal out here," Merrill said, pulling a first-aid kit from his rucksack. A pack of cigarettes bulged in the arm of his white T-shirt. The shirt was streaked with sap and mud, and his arms were red with scratches. Leaning down to tend to Orland, he added, "You could be handing away your life right there."

"Yes," Kumo said, "but it was a deed with honor all the same." This unexpected ray of sunshine from Kumo caused me to turn my gaze at him. He caught my eye and looked over to Merrill. Merrill was busy making a sling and splint. A small smile brushed over Seee's lips, yet he remained silent. More begging hands held themselves up for a match, wiggling fingers frantically outstretched, as if Merrill's words would make me reconsider.

Seee concluded by saying, "Welcome to Nature. Your humble beginnings."

From there, each of us split up and was shown our marked boundary, claiming two square miles of land, all with access to the river. No man's land separated regional boundaries where one had to shout to be heard by someone else adjacent. Fear of being whipped would keep communication minimal, as blood loss and festering wounds from a lashing would surely be a death sentence. Orland would spend ten days in the infirmary set up in the Tree House before he would have to rejoin the rest of us.

Chapter 11

"Sometimes even to live is an act of courage."
-Seneca

After the last match had been struck, I cursed myself for having given them away. A dilemma arose between keeping the fire alive and finding enough time to feed it with something to eat. The second rain in a week had doused a previous fire, which I had managed to keep alive for two days before the relentless downpour. Now the mission of keeping the fire breathing grew urgent, as I had not been able to start one by rubbing sticks together or using flat river rocks as flint.

Over the last days, I had fed on green snakes, whose heads I bashed with stones. Impaling their bodies with two sticks, they roasted well over the orange coals of a fire. The oil in their skins would drip and make the smoky flames crackle. I found frogs and managed to catch enough of them for a meal. Hoping none were poisonous, I ate one and judged its effect on me. Only after enough hours passed did I eat the others. I saw squirrels, field mice, rats, tree monkeys and wild hares, but didn't have the experience to catch any. I fed mostly on the spiky green fruit of the durian tree. Other fruits I would boil, chew a bit to taste test for bitterness. If the taste passed, I would swallow and wait for a few hours to see if it would bring on nausea.

The fire's hunger grew more important than my own. I raced through the woods gathering dead branches and kindling. The task consumed most of the day. Finding dry wood was a quest unto itself with the jungle wet half the time. Finally I managed to build a small cache, a one-day supply of dry wood.

After the twentieth day in our campaign, the sky foreboded heavy rain as a wave of dark clouds crept eerily from the east. I built a small backup fire under my bivouac, opening a hole within the palm-branched roof to air the smoke. After fortifying the roof, I plunged back into the forest in a quest for something to shelter the main fire. I found a large flagstone that had ample width for a shield. With great effort, I carried it back to my camp. When I arrived, the fire inside my bivouac had died and the main fire was smoldering from my neglect. Frantically, I ran to it, blowing gently at its roots, feeding it with small branches and needles from Khasi pines until finally it bloomed into a knee-high flame. Then I rebuilt the fire in my bivouac and gathered enough dry refuse and branches to replenish my cache.

I went searching for planks to mount my slab of rock, hunger now crying deep in the pit of my stomach. At last I came upon a rotted-out stump that I smashed into two ample pieces of wood capable of taking the weight of the stone. Rushing back to camp, I found my fires on their last breaths. When I went to fetch wood from my cache to feed it, all of the dead branches and kindling were gone. My heart sunk, and I rushed to the river. There I searched for the thief. Uriah's fire smoked from the opposite side of the river, but his fire always seemed well-tended. Downriver, I spotted the smoke coming from a fire in Mir's area. Upriver curled the light smoke from Conroy's fire. On my side of the river, smoke rose from Burns's area. Only a light haze came from Drake's vicinity, and I guessed he was in the same dilemma.

I pushed the remaining scraps of kindling into the fires, and once again raced through the woods gathering burnable refuse and dead tree limbs. When I appeared back in camp, I felt the first drops of rain pelt me on the head. I fed the fire frantically, but the sky opened up and drenched everything, and despite all of my effort, both fires were lost.

The next day, a slight fever greeted me, and the worm of weariness burrowed deeper inside. Hunger bit my stomach, and my body shivered. I crawled out of my palm-frond bed, weak and disoriented. With the fire smothered, so went hope. For breakfast, I resorted to the insect world for nutrition, overturning rocks and scooping up the earth to pick out crawling beetles, slugs, and earthworms, forcing them in my mouth, swallowing them whole. I vomited once, but soon my mouth learned to accept the squirming feeling one sometimes sensed, the crunch of crispy wings, the bodily squirts of those consumed. In the afternoon, I stood over ant nests with a stick, licking larvae off the stripped branch like my simian ancestors. I peeled the bark off trees to find termites or grubs and ate them greedily. My fever broke out to a new level of anguish, and I became more delirious. I picked unknown berries from plants, not knowing if they were poisonous, too weary to voyage further into the jungle, scarcely caring if I perished. My mouth now played with death, chewing with the simple rule that bitterness be rejected, my stomach now malleable to new risks.

I wandered to the river and saw the curl of rising smoke from only two fires, one smoking across the river from Uriah's territory, the other coming from Mir's plot. As I connived how to steal a flame, Uriah emerged from the woods from across the river, armed with a makeshift wooden spear and fishing line made of twine. He waved as if the day were any other, ordinary and blasé. At first I thought it a taunt, but seeing the genuine expression on his face, I raised a quivering arm and waved back, smiling feebly. Upon seeing his shaken, near-worried expression, I retreated back into the woods and hid. With tears in my eyes, I watched him fish the river until he emerged triumphant with a flapping trout.

In the late afternoon, my energy returned a bit, and I constructed a feeble trap out of sticks and twine. Any animal could have gnawed their way out of it given enough time, but I thought it would suit my purposes. I baited it with a dead frog, stuck a rock under it, and attached a piece of twine to it. I chained more twine together and hid behind a tree. In a state of complete hysteria, I laughed at the thought of what I would do if I actually caught anything. Would I eat it alive? Fire was crucial, and I told myself I had to have it.

After hours of waiting behind the tree for an animal that would never come, I walked back to camp thinking about the looter who had raided my cache. If his fire had gone out, would he be daring enough to come back if he still had matches? Perhaps he had already started another fire and needed wood. As I pondered these questions walking loudly through the jungle, suddenly I glanced to my left and saw a figure staring at me. Conroy stood next to a white-striped tree, inside Burns's boundary. Besides his tangly black hair blowing in the wind, there seemed to be little trace of the former man. At least fifteen pounds thinner, most of the weight had come off his midsection and arms. His lips bled, and his pupils danced wildly inside his black eyes.

"You're a long way from home," I said.

"Aren't we all?" He coughed, choking on his words. He smiled grimly, and I saw his thinning gums. The skin covering his wan face was almost translucent, as thin as a bed sheet covering his bones.

I stared at the painted lines at the bottom of the tree on my side of no man's land. Three stripes looking like the hash marks on my police uniform from long ago.

"What are you doing out here, Conroy?" He didn't answer. I waited a bit, but he remained in a stupor. "They probably have cameras out here. You wouldn't survive a whipping. You're taking a risk."

"The risk is not eating," he said. "I've got to find some food, something more than insects."

I nodded in agreement. "Where is Burns?"

His gaze drifted upwards. I glanced up to see where he was looking at, but his eyes were adrift, staring into the blue nothingness of sky.

"Conroy," I repeated. "Where is Burns?"

He shrugged his shoulders. His lips quivered. A slow tear

dropped from his eye.

"Conroy," I said snapping my fingers trying to draw his focus. "Where is he?"

"Ran off, I think."

"Why would he do that?"

"Might have deserted, I don't know."

"Deserted?" I asked.

"I hear other guys have been turning tail out of here."

"For what purpose? To starve to death in another part of the jungle?"

"I don't know, man. I don't know what's going through people's heads." He paused a moment, thinking. "There might be coconut trees out there. You notice there aren't any here?" He pointed and said, "Those stumps you see. That was a coconut tree. They didn't want it to be too easy."

He scanned the treetops. Then he craned his neck and glanced backwards. "Briana is stealing people's shit. She's faster and can get away."

I looked at him skeptically. "What did she steal from you?"

"Nothing, but it looks like she raided Burns's camp." He stood there shaking his head, playing with his hands as if somehow he might find some food in them. Then he produced an eerie smile, grabbed the beard on his chin and gave it a tug. "We'll get through this thing, brother, won't we?"

I nodded.

"You don't got anything to eat, do you?"

"Man, I don't got jack, and my fire's out too."

"You shouldn't have given up those matches," he said.

I stood silent for a moment, then nodded in agreement.

"I thought you might be better at this than me," he said.

"No," I said. "I'm not."

"Well, I'm off, Isse. Best of luck to you."

As he turned, I said, "I wouldn't linger if I were you, but since you're in a daring mood, go see Uriah. He's doing this thing as if he's on a camping trip."

"Thanks for the tip," he called out, wobbling on his feet a bit as he moved away.

I went back alone to the riverbank to look for fires. Mir's and Uriah's billowed gray smoke, both on the opposite side of the river, and another, far upriver, in what could have been Briana's area. A few moments later, I saw Conroy wading across the river on Burns's side. I wondered if he was the only man blatantly disregarding the rules. I hid myself and watched Conroy move into Uriah's camp. Conroy waved at him as he approached, walked up to his fire and began speaking. Uriah nodded at him. His lips moved, but I couldn't understand what was said. A minute later, he put another trout in the fire. Conroy shook his hand and sat down.

Anger welled up in me. Not knowing what to do, I hauled firewood to my empty cache, hoping to spring a trap for the person who looted my supply. If no one came, I promised myself I would cross the river late in the night and steal a coal from Uriah's fire. My own moral fiber had suddenly split after seeing Conroy. I had to remind myself the only rule that counted was *don't get caught.*

Close to my hideout, I found a dead branch the size of an arm, gnarled at the top. I mashed stones into the ruts, and wrapped vines around the top in an effort to secure them. In a thicket of bush, I crouched down with a mangrove leaf full of grubs, eating them while waiting for the sun to come down. Dusk finally fell, the jungle like a colossal snake swallowing us, eating the mice of civilized men, each of us a bump in the belly of Nature on our tiny plots of land along her twisting serpentine riverbank shores. Darkness digested what was left of my principles. I felt like a sack of withering flesh over a set of tired bones, and an animal spirit rose up in me.

Under a heavy wind, I perched like a madman, struck by the fangs of revenge. I crouched saucer-eyed and skeleton-faced, gazing into the darkness, mumbling with a cracked voice through parched and bleeding lips, waiting for the night to sink into its deepest depths.

I gripped my makeshift club with sweating hands. The soft, incandescent glow from a toenail moon glowed over the river while I ruminated. Perhaps an hour later, I heard a faint rustling, too inconsistent to be the wind. I wondered who it would be. A figure emerged, thin and sticklike, a figurine in the dark, a strange hyena neck protruding from his body leaving a canine-looking head sniffing for danger in front of him. He crept methodically to the edge of the riverbank under the moonlight. It was Burns. Did he not know how much he was exposed?

I saw him staring down, using the river stones to soften his footsteps. Sneaking slowly to the tempo of windblown leaves, he edged closer to my treasured cache of firewood.

I sprang, but he sniffed the danger and leapt back into the woods. I pursued—heart humming in my chest, legs finding strength, and through the darkness I chased with renewed vigor, ears acute to the rustle of leaves and each cracking branch ahead. Eyes from The Hole tuned in with what little light bent into the forest, guiding my running feet safely past broken stumps, clumps of creepers, half-buried tree roots. Burns stumbled and fell. Jerking himself back up, he fled toward the river. Only a few footsteps away, I heard his frantic breath panting for air, his lungs heavy and hyperventilating with exhaustion. Finally, he dashed out of the woods and into the twilight. I broke from the trees, out into the openness where bats darted into the moon and the rumble of the flowing river filled my ears. Now inches away, my arms pumped in a sprint until I closed the gap. With my fingers, I nipped Burns's shirt ruffling in the wind. With a swoop of a foot, I kicked him in the shin, the force of it intersecting and tangling his motion. The gawky Burns went down, tripping over himself, clipped of his legs as he tumbled onto the stones of the riverbank. He screamed as I plunged on top of him. "Stop! Stop!

Stop!"

I dragged him closer to the shore. Gibberish poured out of him incoherently in a noisy stream. One of his pleas might have been Conroy's name. The tumult of excuses continued as I plunged his head under the water, drowning his protests. Pulling him up after ten seconds made him even more frantic, so down he went again. He clutched at my wrists wrapped around his throat, his body thrashing under me. His arms traveled to my face. Fingernails dug into my skin. I cocked my head away, gazing up at the zinging bats over the moon. The stars twinkled as brightly as shards of broken glass. Once more I brought his head out of the water. This time, he coughed, and then vomited up a mouthful of river. Once finished, he glared up at me, wormy strings of hair slithering into his beady eyes.

"Steal my fucking wood," I yelled.

He shook his head. No, it wasn't me, his eyes said. "Briana," he croaked. But then a hand slid behind his back—the sudden shift of weight from beneath my hips—and out of the water came a fist clenched with a large stone. I blocked his wrist, but the stone hurled toward me as his wrist's momentum stopped. The blow stung my ear and cheek, but I remained conscious, still mounted, and still able to grab him by the neck and push him under. I held my breath, and in so doing, split myself in two— one man feeling him drown, the other alive and free, breathing the cool midnight air. As he squirmed, flopping in the eddies, swiping at my chest, leaving long claw marks and tracks of blood, his hand rolled over my heart, punching at the missing picture of the Earth drowning in space. And then my fingers clamped, thumbs pushing furiously into his throat, my knuckles white with the toil of squeezing. The water roiled with sediment. His hands grasped for another rock, and his feet squirmed to kick free from the unbearable weight on top of him. So there, under the moonlight shining on the muddy berms of an unnamed river, it was I who gasped for breath with him, saw the cold, marble-blue Earth reemerge from darkness, an eye of God in the midst of the vast universe.

Finally, the fighting body of Burns relaxed. The water grew calm. The rippling water receded back to the flat mirror it once was. I told myself that perhaps Burns continued in some other universe that wasn't this one. Only then, so close between life and death, the lucidity of Seee's name became clear. Finally, I was truly seeing.

Chapter 12

"Illusions commend themselves to us because they save us pain and allow us to enjoy pleasure instead. We must therefore accept it without complaint when they sometimes collide with a bit of reality against which they are dashed to pieces."
-Sigmund Freud

I clung to Burns's stiffening limb against the pull of the river. I had broken the rules and crossed into another man's zone. The owner now a corpse floating supine, wide-open fish eyes gazing up at the stars. Exhausted after the struggle, I let go of the dead man's leg and watched the body slowly drift downstream. My head throbbed. Blood ran down the side of my cheek from a gash on the side of my forehead. I washed out the wound, and crawled up to the riverbank.

The moment, once again calm. The events of the last few minutes a wisp in the wind. The bats returned, fluttering in the moonlight, undisturbed by what had unfolded below.

How long had I held him there against the pull of the current? How long had I wept for him? I swept my cheeks with my palm and found they were dry. I had killed men before, but always from a distance, never in hand-to-hand combat. I gazed down at my hands and felt the rough calluses on my inside palm, knuckles scratched and bloodied. I felt weak. The hunger welling up inside me consumed any flickering sign of remorse. Where was the guilt? Ready to admit I was an immoral man, I couldn't conjure up shame no matter how much I willed it.

I crawled wearily back to the edge of the jungle and passed out. At dawn I woke, startled by the yelping of monkeys. I took a moment to recollect what had transpired. In danger of being caught out in the open, I quickly jogged upstream, where I found the ash and ruins of Burns's nesting place. I searched his camp hoping to find tools or matches but found nothing. His shabby bivouac had the roof torn off. There was ash and evidence of a fire, but the place was in disarray. Overturned rocks and dug-in footprints indicated a raid on his premises. I found a blood-stained stone, and I tried to recall any marks on Burns while we scuffled. I searched for other evidence that might have suggested a group struggle, wondering if it was the work of a pack, but saw nothing conclusive. Nature had ripped a seam into the fabric of brotherhood, sinking a spear into the heart of civility after only twenty-one days. I recalled Hassani's words under the persona of Bloom at the Timothy Skies dinner: *After about three days without eating, you get a bit antsy. You find yourself weakening, and suddenly those dormant animalistic tendencies encoded in your genes wake up and want to do something about it.*

Once back in my camp, I vomited in a bush. A fever bore down on me. I lumbered to the river to drink. Bending down into a glistening eddy in the stream, my reflection appeared. A haggard, emaciated man with cuts covering body and face looked back at me. Someone I scarcely recognized. In the water, the body of a ghost had taken over Isse Corvus. I scooped him up with my hands and put him to my lips, swallowed him. Then I was looking into a different dimension. The left-over drops falling out of my hands and onto the smoothed riverbank stones contained only parts of him.

The world went poof, and I flew up over the trees and into a cloud. Within the white haze, I came to a house. I fumbled for a doorknob and upon opening it, found I was in bed, sniffing the soft skin of an ex-girlfriend, the beatitude of Rose Rossetti draped over my arm and breathing into the nape of my neck. The soft fragrance coming from her long curly hair reached my nose. I ran my fingers over her curvy hips, tracing a line up to her breasts. I whiffed the pungent scents of passion coming from them. In the dream, I missed this beauty in the world, this softness.

I looked across the room, and a tree stood twenty feet away, its trunk busting though the ceiling. Its leaves were as white as snow. Blue fruit, shaped like pyramids, dangled from its branches. The house shook, and then fell into the earth, and Rose disappeared with it. A moat of darkness surrounded the white-leafed tree, the pit having no bottom. I stood up from the floor and glimpsed at the sky, seeing its height extending beyond my point of vision. The fruit jounced softly in the wind's embrace, dangling on branches above the void, just out of reach, yet close enough to snatch with a daring leap. With the sense I had already died, I jumped forward and plucked a piece of the blue-skinned fruit from the branch and tumbled into the darkness.

I woke, still alive, scrabbling among river rocks as the tide bumped me in the face. I caught a mouthful of water and coughed it out. It was late afternoon, and I had lost the day to delirium. Sleep had been the only refuge from the toil of survival.

I hobbled back to my bivouac where a sparrow was singing high up in the branches of a mangrove. It gazed down at me one-eyed and curious, his head shifting in quick jerks to different vantage points. He saw the same haggard and withering man I had — a frail giant, skinny and sickly, the stench of death covering him like feathers. His little buzzing head was asking why, as if my state were a matter of choice. Then he flew off, bored with me. Deserted by Nature, I sat down and leaned my head back on the bole of the tree and began to weep. After what seemed like hours, I sucked in a lungful of air and stood, the desperation of the situation pulling me to my feet, however inane the action seemed. I flaked away another clump of bark from the hole I bore in the mangrove the day before. No beetles crawled beneath. The clenched fist of hunger gripped my stomach, beating me to feed, so I put the bark in my mouth. The taste was bitter. My glands refused to moisten it.

A noise of cracking branches caused me to turn. The woods split open, and Seee burst through the trees riding bareback on his black stallion, its hindquarters lathered in sweat. Seee's face was painted. He wore white swirly paste from the thanaka root on his cheeks. Red streaked under his eyes, and blue paint on his forehead dripped down the sides of his face. Quickly, I wiped away the tears, but he saw them still.

He cocked his head and glared into my eyes. "I see Isse Corvus is learning to become a man of the earth," he said. His expression was neither strict nor pitiless. "It is a hard lesson." He steadied his horse, the animal whinnying through its nose. "You are realizing you are small under the thumb of Nature." He smiled at me, a paternal glimmer in his eyes. "The earth is burying you, so you must now dig yourself out." The gelding tried to throw him, kicking his front feet in the air, and Seee yanked down hard on the reins. "Remember this day and it will remember you." He tossed over a knife. It landed in the ground near where I stood. "Carve today's date into that tree." He pointed. "Right next to where you've peeled off the bark for your supper."

I leaned over and picked up the knife, every muscle deep in protest. Knife in hand, I stared at the tree. The seconds drifted by until I said, "I've lost track of time."

"November 27, 2022," he said.

I carved the numbers into the tree, exerting all of my will to cut deep and strong. When I finished, he said, "Now, give me back the knife."

I looked longingly at the shiny knife with the sharp blade. Seee's horse neighed, and Seee slapped him and told him to steady. He held out his hand for the knife. I reached out and offered it to him handle-first, eyeing it as if it could have been my hand I was giving him. Then he disappeared into the trees and left me with the horror that I would die out here, desperate and starving.

The next morning, I woke in a leaf bed under the tree branches of my bivouac. Birds chirped in the distance. I got up and pissed in the forest and then limped to the river for a drink. Smoke plumed from the trees on the other side of the bank, and the heavy breeze carried the aroma of cooking fish.

Laid out on a stone on the riverbank shore, I saw two freshly dead trout. I scurried up to them, picking one up and lifting it into the light. The shiny scales glittered in the sun. Biting directly into a fleshy bit near the belly, I sat down on the rock and devoured the whole fish raw, picking scales and bones out of my teeth as I went. I buried the other fish, hoping to save it for later, then crossed the river to meet Uriah. Through a little break in the woods, he sat on a stone feeding a branch to the fire, his back toward me. "Did you enjoy the fish?" he asked.

"Did Seee put you up to it?"

"No, I thought you might be hungry. Was I mistaken?"

A moment passed. "No," I said. "Thanks for your generosity."

He fed the fire with another branch, turning it over as his eyes remained deep in the blaze, transfixed by its heat and licking orange tongues. "Perhaps you forget *The Two Methods of Criticism*. The one of helping the clan overcome their faults."

I laughed at this. "You think it is my fault I am starving?"

"Isn't it? You lack certain knowledge. This much you must admit."

I paused, marking his words. "The penalty would be severe if you were caught."

"As would it be for you if they saw you standing here."

For no other reason than I was ridden with guilt, I blurted out, "I killed Burns. Perhaps I will be punished for that."

Uriah was silent. He fed the fire another branch but continued doing it in silence.

"It wasn't the plan, but he raided my camp and then we got into it."

"I am confused," he said in a tone that was clear and hard. "I killed Bunker, which you hated me for, yet now you stand here speaking with me as if I am a friend, not an enemy."

"You aren't my enemy."

"You see how the tail can flip to the head. We change. Our thoughts change, and you are one in metamorphosis, turning slowly into a warrior who will fight for The Cause."

A torrent of questions burned in my head while I kept silent.

"You were misled, but now your eyes are opening." Something prophetic intonated in his voice as he unwrapped the secrets he knew about me. A manner of speaking that contained the brooding logic of our leader.

"Enough with conjecture, Uriah. I don't know what nonsense you are speaking about."

"But you do."

I let the moment rest. I hated having his back facing me, but I didn't want to circle around him either. "How about you? What are you doing in this camp? Who let you in?"

He sighed with a heavy breath. "Your question is not pertaining to the here and now is it? If I were a sensitive man, I'd take it as an insult. You persist in ignoring the lessons of bushido."

"You speak of bushido, but you aren't a soldier. You can't run. You can't fight. Perhaps you're good with a sword, but the morning trainings almost kill you. How did they let you in here?"

"So you think I don't belong because I cannot hack it?"

I moved a bit. His body still angled away from me, but now I could see one of his eyes glaring straight into the blue of the fire. His soft tone almost seemed to drift with it. "It isn't my intention to be insulting. You give more effort than anybody. I'm just stating a truth—the way I see it."

"Admirable. Yet, I will live longer than you if the path we wander remains the same."

The words struck me hard. I glanced up into the sky. A hawk flew high in the air—a real bird of prey, glassing the river for fish, scanning the ground for a rodent or snake. "What do you see in him anyway?" I asked.

His head shifted around a bit more toward me, and from a side-angle, his face revealed a little more of itself. He looked like a relic of the ancient past, an extinct Neanderthal or Cro-Magnon with an impish jaw. Eyes were dark, the dull color of a wild boar, and they floated unnaturally in his sockets. He bent further toward the fire and said, "He sees the visible future others don't." He picked up a smoothed stone, fondled it in his fingers, held it up. "If I throw this rock at the river, will it skip or will it sink?"

I glimpsed back toward the river. The hawk was still up in the air, closer to the water, wings wide and gliding against the wind, taut and hovering, wild gusts jerking him in the air, the bird calculating currents below. In the sky was a true hunter. Myself—a man grounded to the earth, a man with no wings.

"It all depends on how it is thrown," Uriah continued, kicking a log in the fire. He watched it grow angry, its sparks leaping into the air. "I know how I intend to throw it. You do not. Does it mean the stone will skip if I intend it to skip? No, it does not."

The hawk was gone, and our eyes still had not met.

"It is only intent," he continued. "Action is a force of this intent, but it does not make it skip."

Finally he stood, turning and staring deeply at me with his dark, animal eyes. A look of fortitude shone in them as if he were reading words from a book, voicing to me who the true man was inside. "The future doesn't happen merely because one wills it," he said. "Seee merely wants to be the force of intent, but he is well aware that we are the fluid. We are the ones who lower the viscosity. We are the essence that aids the stone to ricochet. You will either be with him or against him, but you should at least make the effort to listen."

"And what do you think he stands for?"

"You already know the answer to that."

"Abstractly."

"Then Isse Corvus is deaf in one ear." He swept a hand through the fire, brought it up to his face, seemingly to sniff the singed hair on his arms. "I wonder. Do you hear the words differently when you use just one ear? Isn't it a simple choice of whether to follow his beliefs? Instead, you struggle with your own self-worth. At what point are you just idly waiting for the future to happen, versus becoming part of its path? This is the question you must ask yourself."

"So how do you know Seee?" I asked, still pressing the issue, still fighting my inner sense. "You knew him before, didn't you? You came here knowing him. That is how you got in."

He smiled slightly, his wormy lips curling over his fractured face. "I got in because I can be of service to the Brotherhood. It is my duty. Do you not see this even as I save you from starvation? Because I know him does not mean I will receive favorable treatment. Quite the contrary."

"You do not believe you have somehow rooted yourself into his favoritism?"

He ignored the question. "He will deconstruct us all. This is just the beginning. It is the bushido way. Since we do not have the privilege of an ancestry, we in the camp will have to learn from the ground up. The hardness of the American heart has perhaps been forgotten since Gettysburg, when men really knew how to die with honor."

"You are at an obvious disadvantage."

"You believe my handicap is ugliness?"

"Sorry," I said. "I do not mean to be insulting, but your bulbous head is a big target, delicate, and it's the first thing a serious fighter will angle for."

"And that is why you must teach me to fight."

"Me," I said surprised. "Teach you to fight?"

"Who better? Did you think I would teach you survival for nothing in return?"

Knowing it was a fair exchange, I said, "If we are caught, we will pay a heavy price."

"From the looks of you, that price is already being paid."

I agreed, then I held out my hand, and he shook it. My life with Uriah had begun.

At daybreak over the next weeks, we trained in Brazilian ju-jitsu and Muay Thai. Standing attacks with more feet than fists. He needed his hands for face cover, only to be used sparingly with offense. I showed him how to use his hips for punishing kicks, leg sweeps. Every other night, after hunting, we faced the boles of trees and kicked them until our legs bled, creating tiny fissures in the bones so they would heal stronger. He was already a student of yoga, which was a great strength to his movement and agility. Still, I pushed him to improve. I stretched his legs vertically until they nearly snapped, until it was second nature for him to throw kicks at my face. Then we would switch to ground tactics, where he had a better chance. I taught him choke holds and leg locks, arm bars and how to break fingers. I taught him how to use elbows like hammers. At dusk we sparred, him never knowing the word quit, never tapping out. If it weren't for the regret it would interrupt our training, I could have broken his arm on several occasions, squeezing it between my hips to the point where it could have ripped from the joint, but still he would not submit. I choked him out, him preferring death rather than touch my arms with his fingers. He would wake from passing out asking if he had dishonored himself.

I came to realize he was living the real bushido, a death meant only a reawakening for a new life of service. Soon, his rapid improvement gave a shine on my abilities to teach. I became proud to have him as my pupil and took from him that supreme sacrifice was dedication to a cause. As we practiced yoga in the mornings, the meditative sessions gave light to new radiations of awareness in me.

From him, I learned how to build a fire with sticks and tinder, then with a limestone flint. I learned how to chip a jagged rock into a spearhead, how to find and use hemp for twine, how to fish and hunt.

After a couple of weeks, my strength grew, and I put on pounds. I became more self-sufficient. I was able to hunt on my own, make my own tools, start my own fires, build my own traps. Uriah taught me how to spearfish. With my new spearheads, I found an adequate branch and whittled myself a blowgun. After several failures, finally I made one thin and long, whose spout wasn't too thick. With it, I killed squirrels, rabbits, and even a monkey.

Then one day during one of our early-evening sparring sessions, Uriah was wrestling to twist out of a poor position where he had given up his back. We grappled on a patch of grass on the river's edge that seemed to be the only grassy spot on my side of the rocky riverbank shore. As I slipped Uriah into a body triangle, Seee stepped out of the forest with Kumo, both of them armed with machineguns.

"Get up! Both of you!" Seee yelled.

We did as we were told, shaking off the grass. "What are you doing in his area?" Seee said, pointing at Uriah.

"Receiving training, Sifu."

"It was I who—"

Seee cut me short, saying, "It is he who is in your area."

"Yes," I said, "but by my request."

Seee screwed up his eyes. Kumo reached inside of his backpack and pulled out the bullwhip.

"You've fed this man, haven't you?"

"Yes, Sifu," Uriah said.

"You must be punished for both trespasses."

"It is an honor to spill blood for you, Sifu," Uriah said.

"I do not chastise your intention, Uriah. But you dishonor Nature by not letting her be the decision maker."

I stood in front of Kumo blocking his passage to Uriah. Kumo tensed, moving his bottom teeth over his lip, unhooking the strap of the machinegun dangling from his shoulder and letting it fall to the ground. But Uriah grabbed my arm and pushed me aside. "I am ready, Isse. And more than that, I am willing."

Kumo stepped back ten paces and raised the whip. The first blow came down hard, ripping Uriah's back like an angled spear. It tore the flesh from shoulder to kidney, leaving a bloodstained hypotenuse. Uriah grunted, twisted his lips, saw the pain as pure as water flowing in a stream. The second blow cut him lower, crisscrossed the previous strike, whose mark was now awake, drips of blood streaking from it down his skin. Uriah stood firm, straightened his back, managed to keep his mouth closed, pulled his lips tight and breathed heavy breaths through his nose. Then he glared at me and nodded. The next blow cracked like a razor and tears dripped from his eyes. Still his mouth somehow remained pinned shut. His brow pinched together and finally his back curved away from the strike. He spent a moment straightening his spine out, releasing the tension in his forearms, getting ready for the next strike.

"Don't you tap out on me, kid," I yelled out to him. Kumo looked over at me. His eyes showed a man whose heart was no longer in it. Still, he lassoed the whip around his head and let the whip sing in the air.

The blow snapped the air out of Uriah, and his mouth pried open to let the air in. By the next blow, he began to shriek, and I found my own eyes watering. "Ah," he grunted, "it feels good to scream."

"There's no shame in it," I yelled. "Let the fight come out of you."

With the seventh blow, the shriek grew, the shrill cry hanging in the air, ubiquitous ears hearing it echoing down the valley. Movement shook the bush around the shores of the river.

I put my hands in the air and waved furiously. The look on my face gave Kumo pause.

"No one comes out," I yelled. "If anyone shows their face, God help me they will answer for it." The sound of rustling bush continued. Bodies hidden in the forest edging closer, not heeding the warning, eyes peeking out of the woods. I stared long and hard, up and down the river, daring anyone to show themselves. No one did. Seee stared at Kumo, glowing with rage. He motioned with a hand for him to continue. Kumo delivered the rest of the blows, neither vindictively nor in a menacing manner—a man of duty, a man delivering justice for the crime. Yet, something opened in him, a small unspoken rift between his actions and Seee's commands.

Afterward, still on his knees, Uriah crawled over to Kumo and thanked him for his duty, then thanked Seee for planting new eyes of sight into his head to see the wrong in his action. Later, I would wonder why Seee didn't deliver the punishment. Uriah would argue that a leader must be loved and would be forgiven with his commands, but it was the administrator who had to absorb the hate. So there in the drowning sun, Kumo sucked his feelings into the vortex where emotions were black-boxed.

After Seee and Kumo left, I took Uriah by the shoulder and moved him to the river. There I cleaned his wounds and helped him cross the river. When we were finally on the other side of the bank, Conroy emerged from the trees and took Uriah's other shoulder. We led him to his shelter and started a fire. I took Uriah's spear and went into the jungle. With the spear, I burrowed into a pine, drained some sap onto a flagstone, and returned back to Uriah's camp. Conroy cooked a meal of leftover fish while I tended Uriah's wounds.

The next morning, Uriah woke me, jostling me for training, castigating me for my laziness. The new eyes of sight he spoke about to Seee the day before were quickly blinded, while mine grew wide with admiration.

What we would come to learn was Uriah helped all within his circumference, saving the lambs from the slaughter of hunger, and by the time he was caught once more, five others owed their lives to him. When the whip fell into Kumo's hand again, the obsequious Kumo threw it on the ground, sense of duty dropping like a stone, and left it for Seee to do the task.

Chapter 13

"The object of life is not to be on the side of the majority, but to escape finding oneself in the ranks of the insane."
-Marcus Aurelius

We finished the test of Nature on New Year's Eve. Many struggled to gain their strength and stomach back. Casualties included Damien Morton, Thomas Draper, and Josh Winters. Charlie Feller, Mark Jenks, and Balram Kumar were now known as the Cannibal Crew because they had eaten Winters. They kept more to themselves after this, perhaps shamed because of what they had done, or ostracized enough by the others. Seee saw the danger in this segregation, and made it known they were Nature's true winners. He said they had done what was necessary in order to survive, no matter how vile. He defended them with historical examples—the whale ship Essex, the Donner Party, the Andes survivors of 1972. He told us about cannibals in Fiji who would eat their enemies to prevent their spirits from ascending to the spirit world where they could don their power and wisdom back to the living. Even after all of Seee's efforts, an air of hesitation surrounded the Cannibal Crew.

We celebrated the New Year. We built a bonfire and spitted a wild hog. Cases of wine and whiskey were brought out. For those not on lookout duty, every man indulged, and the camp came alive with laughter and comradery. A communal sense of accomplishment permeated our attitudes. The fact men had died, only made survival that much sweeter. Those closest to starvation drank and ate until their stomachs heaved with the excess. They would come back to the fire only to start again. Some of us, drunken and with a new sense of courage, began to ask questions about the guerrillas. Who were they? Why did they attack? But any response to such questions was in Yoncalla, and the words were purposely obtuse. No one came away with a clear answer, and the nature of the festivities made it so no one really cared.

The following day, a rumor spread around the camp. Mir had received the invitation to take "the vow" and had accepted. None of us had seen the ceremony, or knew exactly what this meant, what exactly he promised, or what he had done to deserve it. Most thought that any merit should have gone to Atlas, who had stood so valiantly in the face of torture against the guerrillas.

On January 2nd, Brock and I walked through the clearing for breakfast and saw Mir heading out of camp with Kumo. Kumo's spidery arm led a set of packed-up horses. Mir's arm was bandaged, wrapped up in white gauze tinted with traces of blood. Brock had told me they burned off his Lisbeth Salander tattoo. The motto was, *Wear no mark, honor us with your word*. The smile of acceptance lit up Mir's face. He spoke with Kumo in a spirited fashion. When he looked up at us, he nodded and waved with the hand wrapped in white gauze. We waved back. I asked why the hand was wrapped as well. Brock said he had become a blood brother, a Trusted.

"Does that mean he's going to replace Ahanu?" I asked.

"I'm not sure what it means," Brock said.

Merrill crept behind us with Briana at his side. "No one's replacing Ahanu," Merrill said. "Ahanu was irreplaceable."

I turned around. "Why was Mir chosen over Atlas?"

"Mir is now a Minuteman. It isn't based on courage. It's based on trust."

"So why Mir?" I asked.

Merrill ignored the question. "Neither of you should worry. Your courage was duly noted during the battle."

Briana stood apprehensively, watching us with downcast eyes.

Brock was saying how he would take the vow, but Merrill said they already had their next candidate and would we like to meet her. Brock and I looked at each other wondering if this was another one of Merrill's jokes, but the look in Briana's eyes told us Merrill had been serious. As they strode away from us, Briana, with her back toward us, put a hand in the air and waved goodbye.

A few days later, we received orders to line up around the Laddered Pit, called this because there were two ladders, but only one could be seen—the other one, Seee said, led to the paradoxical fruit of the Lushing Tree. We stood around the rim, looking over the edge from the flat world of men. We stared into the sandy chasm whose size dwarfed what would soon happen there.

Merrill and Des led a manacled, black-bearded man out of the depths of the jungle. We wondered where he had come from. As he was forced forward the thirty yards it took for him to get to us, the scene seemed to carry on through permeable time, like a glitch in a video, an unrelenting persistence to the stumbling feet in the grass as he was dragged faster than he could walk. When he arrived, the air reeked with his pungent smell—sweat, blood, tears, urine—yet he wasn't emaciated. He seemed to be in good health. His movements were fluid, but his outward appearance was appalling. The man was gagged, the cloth inside his mouth wet and bloodstained and wound tightly around his face. He wore threads for clothes—trousers in ribbons and a tattered shirt mottled in blood drips. His face was cut up and bruised. His eyes were bloodshot, pupils wide black pools staring wildly at his surroundings, the scared eyes of an impala chased farther than it could run. Sweat dripped off him and every ropy vein seemed to jump through the skin. We stood there guessing what kind of man we were seeing. He was a slave from 500 AD, a bedraggled body of a captured prisoner from Roman times, a Christian martyr about to be crucified.

Each of us knew that such an event was imminent. Yet, seeing this man's state of being fell on us with muted surprise. All of us had almost starved to death in the jungle. Four men were dead, and none from starvation. Josh Winters had been eaten by Charlie Feller, Mark Jenks, and Balram Kumar. Others had been attacked and killed, feuds over food and resources. None of us seemed to hold a grudge about how it all went tribal now that it was over. No one dared castigate another's deed. One did what was necessary and went on living with it. Those of us left lived as if we belonged in the heart of The Abattoir, beating with its rhythm. Until now.

Once the man reached the edge of The Pit, the slow mumbling within the circle silenced. Des grabbed the man's soiled shirt and simply tore it off. He was wiry but looked as if he had eaten better than us in the last few weeks.

Seee looked at the bare-chested man. "Welcome back from the battle lab." Turning to us, he pointed at him. "This man is a traitor. Who will step up and fight him?"

The circle of eyes gazed over one another. Split took a step forward as I asked, "What exactly did he do?" Everyone's eyes turned toward me. From across the Laddered Pit, the prisoner gazed blankly at me, but I tore away from his stare. Seee smiled lightly, his lips soft with the anticipation of such a question.

"He was caught spying."

"What were the circumstances?"

"He was brought here and I was told to deal with him as I please."

"Why not let him speak?"

"If you wish," Seee said, extending his hand. Des untied the bloody cloth. The man opened his mouth wide so all could see.

"This man has no tongue," I said, stating the obvious.

"Every bit of useful information was retrieved from him," Seee said. "After that, we grew weary of his lies."

Silence. No one spoke-up for, or pitied the prisoner. Perhaps some eyes were in betrayal, hearts in the circle waiting for my voice to counter argue. But I said nothing, Seee's words from the first day blooming again fresh in my head—*In the womb of Nature, mercy is misinterpreted as weakness and weakness is locked in the jaws of death.*

Sensing our angst, Seee moved between the ranks. He advanced to Split and Grus, stared at them in the eyes breathing little hot breaths into their faces. "The modern world has softened your hearts. This is why you're here—to harden them." Everyone stood at attention, rigid statues in line, arms straight as iron. Seee slipped between Split and Uriah. "I gave the weak-hearted a chance to leave. Did I not?" Split nodded, and Seee grabbed his shoulder gruffly. He paused for a moment gazing into Split's eyes as if he were kin. He turned to the rest of us. "I feel like I'm swimming in a pool of cowards!"

"I'll fight," Split said.

"I'll fight him too," Uriah followed.

Then others stepped forward. And others after them. I stood my ground. Seee marched up to me angrily and challenged me. "You're not afraid are you, Corvus?" Without letting me answer, he tapped my chest with a finger and said, "I doubt it. Yet, I wonder if it is still the notion of fair-play in you that causes such pathetic hesitation?" His tone had filled with weariness and disappointment.

"No," I said. "You've not given us enough evidence to condemn this man. He might be a spy in your eyes, but he isn't yet in mine. We don't even know his name."

"Knowing his name will not change anything," Seee said, the little smile returning to his lips. "Do you hear, everyone? Isse Corvus is a man of the law, principled. He demands evidence, a fair trial, a judge and jury and a wooden gavel. Where were these things a month ago when you were starving to death?" He drifted away from me toward the center of The Pit where everyone could be addressed. A light breeze rustled the leaves on the trees from the perimeter and blanketed the place in a moment of calm.

"But Isse is right," Seee said finally. The men glanced at him quizzically, baffled by his words. I was shocked into disbelief. "Tyranny is the product of lawlessness. We can see this so easily in the world we live in today." Seee paced around, back through the throng of men. "Echelon and Turbulence and other surveillance strategies shitting on the Constitution and targeting the citizenry. Yet, here is a man who talks of justice with the truncheon in his palm, who has personally been ordered to club the middleclass, beat them with batons, teargas and pepper spray them. You've hogtied them in cuffs, thrown them in paddy wagons, and taken them to the station to book them for disturbing the peace. Isn't that so?"

I said nothing. There was nothing to say, as there was no defense. He had trapped me. He spoke the truth and everyone knew it.

"Perhaps Isse Corvus thought those arrested were fringers or another mad breed of protester. But then at the station, he took identification from some of those rioters and looked at the addresses of those whom he'd just beaten, and it strikes him that these agitators are from the good neighborhoods. His heart palpitates because the guy he's just bloodied is an unemployed architect, or programmer, or engineer. Not some hippie living in a squat yelling, *Give peace a chance*. So then he questions the law, and perhaps those that make them. You certainly have the right to question me, and this I expect from an intelligent man. We are not brainless Army grunts here, are we? Hierarchy, however, must be respected, or we have anarchy. This man has been unanimously convicted by the seniors of this camp—myself, Kumo, Merrill and Des. But you've also forgotten that you're here to learn how to once again live as animal, where the laws of Nature are much simpler."

He moved back to his original position in front of me, but spoke loud enough so all could hear. "Isse Corvus, do you want to eat, or be eaten?" He stood glaring up at me, his chin tight.

"Eat," I said.

He blinked, nodded, as if deeply pleased. "So if I say to you to take faith in me—trust me—would your position waver?"

"No."

"And is your belief so strong that you would be willing to step in the ring in this man's place instead of trusting me?"

"Yes."

"Why?"

"Because I know this man."

Murmuring broke out through the line. Eyes whirled over to the man hiding behind the thick, black beard in search of a familiar face. "It's Joe Downs," Grus shouted out. "One of those who went missing when we got here." The tongueless man's eyes lit up with the words.

"A spy nonetheless," Seee said.

The men seemed to waver. Grumblings grew louder. Only sixteen of the original twenty-eight remained. We had taken off from Norfolk with thirty-two men. Many had left or had been killed. But a wave of realization that perhaps the other three were here swept through the men like a blaze.

"Where are the others?" Geddy Drake fired out.

"Being held a few miles from here," Seee said, killing any drama that was added by the question.

"But you lied to us," Split blurted out, a wounded expression escaping in his tone. "Kumo said they never arrived."

"That was true at the time it was asked," Kumo said. "They arrived later, on a separate flight. Dumped here by The Company to be questioned."

"But you knew they were being held," Conroy said.

"I knew nothing about them until they arrived," Kumo said.

"All of what Kumo says is true," Des said. "But it is equally pointless to speak of such trivialities. The point is these men are spies. We do not convict innocent men. We have electronic evidence of conversations coming from The Farm and locations off site. The evidence is irrefutable."

"So justice is handled here then?" I asked, becoming angry.

"On equal footing, yes," Seee said.

"Is he a man spying on our Homeland, or a man spying on you?" I asked.

"They are one and the same!" he fired back.

Seee leapt into The Pit, landing and then rolling into a summersault. He stood, brushed the sand off his clothes, scowled pugnaciously at us, and then yelled out so all could hear. "Let it be no secret that I fight for the United States of America and the ideals with which the forefathers founded her upon! The fight for liberty is just beginning, and I will not turn my head away in fear! For any who would be bold enough to challenge me in support of the status quo, I stand here waiting for you!"

No one flinched. Uriah stepped forward and gazed down into The Pit. "Perhaps, Sifu, your intentions are still unclear." He gazed over at me. A little smirk crossed over his face. "A man who seeks his reflection in a spring must not disturb the water."

"You are right, Uriah," Seee said.

A pall surrounded the circle of men as Seee knelt down on his haunches and grabbed a handful of the ochre dirt from the bottom of the Laddered Pit. "Take this dirt on the ground," Seee said, letting it run slowly through his fingers. "Millions of years went into grinding down some huge boulder into this fine dust. The same erosion is going on in our country. Over the years, it's happened slowly, but now it's picking up momentum. You can smell the miasma of anxiety now when you're out on the streets. You've seen glimpses of what's going on every night on the TV. We are living in dangerous times. Citizens are waking up disenchanted with what they see. Now that most firearms are banned, people are still arming themselves illegally because when they breathe, their lungs fill with the air of deceit. The fortitude of a peaceful march no longer has aim as nothing can be changed. The people are figuring out the vote no long matters, and it's themselves who are holding the bag for banking bailouts and funny-money solutions. They're wising up to who lurks in the shadows of Congressional halls and who the real power players in America are. They're growing weary of their freedoms being mangled—of being bullied, jailed, arrested without cause, interrogated, suspected, watched. They're tired of hearing their personal data is being sniffed by the NSA and then used against them. They're tired of the nefarious media mongers preaching pandemic fear. But what they really see is the jaws of the totalitarian apparatus biting down on them, chomping their bones into the grit of poverty. So what can they do? Demonstrate? Protest? Riot? Now they're labeled anarchists, looters, hoodlums, and even terrorists. The shell is cracking and underneath the soft coating is we-the-people, enemy of the State. Suddenly, those in government are calling the people the enemy, but they are the ones who are the cause of the palpitating, fibrillating heartbeat— the murmur, the arrhythmia of our Homeland."

He stood up again, raising his fist in the air. "What is the true sound of the march of time? Is it the boots that march loudest, or simply those that trod a fresh path that others will follow? Just as no great change can occur without catalyst, no rebirth can start without death."

He then asked the Sons for their words, and Merrill spoke up. "You have been chosen for The Abattoir with great care. All of you have somehow been touched in one way or another by what is happening. Those who did not fit the profile were never accepted. Those we were unsure about were encouraged to leave after the first few days. The process is not perfect. But we will tell you all, we seek brothers here, not enemies, and you must stand up and fight for us or admit you are against us."

"So if I ask you again," Seee said, speaking up to all of us. "Will you fight for us?"

"YES!" was the resounding answer from the chorus of men above.

"Then who will accept this challenge?"

Many hands flew up in the air, even my own. The Sons scanned the circle, gazing into the eyes of each, making a judgment right then and there. My guess was that most had sided with Seee before they even got here. They had been profiled, as Merrill admitted. But what about me? Why was I still alive? Surely they knew what I had come here to do?

Not one in the circle failed volunteering to throw his life into The Pit. And why wouldn't they? It was blood they had come for, and I was no different. The warrior in each of us had awakened, and now *just cause* demanded a bloody conclusion.

Seee chose Atlas to step forward, eyeing me as if I had lost my chance, as if I was a lost cause. Atlas was the same build as Tongueless Downs—medium height and pit-bullish—a fair fight in terms of size.

They chose their weapons from the rack quickly—Tongueless Downs took a gladius sword and Roman shield. Atlas, sword and spear and a Saxon shield. They put on armor, shoulder plates, and helmets made of gilded steel. One way or the other, it was going to be over soon. Days of training with heavier wooden weapons and wicker shields were over. Time called out *armatura*, and instead of stopping, it steamed straight forward.

Chapter 14

"War is life multiplied by some number that no one has ever heard of."
-Sebastian Junger

Reaction. Forces always occur in pairs. The interaction of two objects. Every force on one object accompanied by reaction on another of equal magnitude. Opposing direction.

This is what physics teaches us with the Newtonian law of motion.

Strange how a blade swings, coming at you like a sweep of light. A flash of it through the air, fleeting and brisk, swishing with the same suddenness as sun glint through windy trees. The stream of steel lasts an instant or a millennium. Never seen in slow motion. Because there is—

Reaction.

Atlas steps backward planting a foot, letting the cold streak of steel crash against his shield. A jostling of movements. He jabs with the spear grunting, but it meets shield in a metallic scraping crash. He pushes Tongueless Downs back with his shield, but it's met with heavy resistance. The Pit is electric—amperes of attraction and repulsion, sand hoofed and scattered, bodies torqued in lunge and push. Time swift. Breath trapped in throats, suspended inside heaving lungs as if an exhale might change the outcome.

There is hard truth in steel. When it strikes, sometimes the body delays for a micromoment, as if it is unsure of Reaction. But later it will catch up and drain you. Atlas doesn't realize he's wounded. A short jab caught him in the side. If it wasn't for our gasps, he might not ever have known. When he sees the blood, he doesn't seem fazed by it. He quickly throws away the spear and unsheathes his sword.

Two worlds become loosely coupled, shadows of each lurking in The Pit waiting for an immutable ending. Action relentless in its drive forward. It pushes with impatience toward inevitability. Every breath perhaps the last. Seconds compress. Time shrinks to a pinpoint.

They clash once more, dirt flying. Grains of it shooting so high, they catch me in the eyes. Sounds of struggle, a primal cloud around them. War screams from Atlas full of rage and anger. Tongueless Downs shrieking rebel yells. The noise itself is its own combat. Bodies undulate in a rippling flow, jarred and knotted together, then thrown apart. The death dance. One man real, the other a phantom. What's happening is beyond control, larger than all of us and ramming down a road to a laddered destination. Hysteria of an outcome pulses in the vibrating air— it's there stamped into everyone's eyes. A demand for a bloody conclusion. Hearts thumping in chests waiting for the critical, decisive error. For a while, it seems Atlas has the upper hand even with the wound. He's powerful and in a frenzy—dangerous energy. The two of them face each other in swinging chainmail and glittering armor, as if they've slipped down a dimension into another historical world, transcending time into battles redolent of sweaty gladiators in marbled coliseums.

Atlas's wound opens up, ripping wide like a crowning baby. The skin furls away, a hint of a flayed intestine peeks out, the man unraveling before our eyes.

Exhaustion in Atlas's eyes. The hard truth about to reveal itself.

Tongueless Downs notices the fatigue. Everyone senses the change, as if it is a scent in the air easily smelled. We are engulfed in the swell of this anachronistic battle. We are glutinous and base, unable to push the magnetism of the primordial back inside.

The shape of destiny forms. Carved out like one of Kumo's sticks. The real man dims, and the phantom pushes in. Only one way it can end. Atlas's shield falls to his knees after he takes another stab in the same side. He falls to his knees, and the strain in his eyes to get back up is like a plea to every man who can see. *Save me.* Brave Atlas has succumbed. The sword is still in his hand, resting at an oblong angle, but strength has drained from him, and only will is left to lift it. Tongueless Downs takes no liberty with time. He steps forward and with searing scorn pushes the sword deep into Atlas, pitiless, spitting in his face after it's done. Fully adapted to the new world, he is the victor, raising his arms. The phantom edges away, up the unseen ladder. We watch wordless with wounded egos, a disappointment in the result because it was not our man that won.

Most angry is Seee, an engine of roar who leaps into The Pit and bends over the limp body of Atlas. Seee closes the dead man's eyes softly with his fingertips. To all, the anguish in his face reflects who he thinks was the best among us. Then Tongueless Downs comes after Seee, observing he is turned around and defenseless. But Seee slithers away, anticipating the move, offering his back as an antagonization. He rolls to Atlas's shield and comes up in a crouch with it overhead to meet the downward swing of the shiny blade. The cling of metal sounds. Seee stands and twists, maneuvers to the sword in the sand. Downs lunges at Seee with the blade but catches only the heart of a metal shield. Seee swipes Atlas's sword lying in the sand, and then they are on equal footing.

Seee offers Tongueless Downs fifteen minutes of rest, water, and food if he wants it. He offers Downs release if he wins—tells every man to obey his command. Then, he offers the man revenge. He pulls a bloody cloth from his pocket, loosens it, and throws it to the man's feet. A lump of flesh falls out of the cloth, flat and cylindrical, and Seee says, "You might need it back if you've something to say."

Downs pounces in an overhand attack. But Seee's shield is like a disk from the sun, bright and shiny twisting and turning in angular momentum. He blocks the plunging sword, deflects it, then turns the shield laterally, smashing into Downs' helmet. The blow stings Downs and blood spills from his nose. Blinded, he lunges wildly with a stab, keeping his shield tight. Seee anticipates the move, sidesteps it, and swoops under the overcommitted Downs, razor steps racing past him, the glimmering shield guarding from above. Only afterward we see the gash. The men stare open-mouthed at the open wound bleeding on the upper leg. The strike quick as a snake, the red-tipped tongue of the sword a flashing glint from the shell of the shield.

"I do not wish to let the moment linger," Seee announces. "This man has had enough, and has fought bravely against a man who himself was as brave as they come." Downs turns, breath heated, lungs pumping. He throws off his helmet and glowers at Seee, screaming an obscenity everyone can understand, even without a tongue. A sad look appears in Seee's eyes. "I only wish you were among us, but with regret you are not."

Downs charged, and it would be his last act of heroism. Seee maneuvered skillfully away from the man rampaging toward him with sword slashing. Reversing the run, he charged with a flurry that showed us the meaning of attack. His blade swept downward and tore into Downs's shoulder not stopping till it had slashed through his heart. Within a second, Downs was dying in the Laddered Pit, ascending the same rungs as Atlas. That night, he would not receive the same honors as our fallen comrade. His head would be nailed on a spike in the middle of The Abattoir for all to see.

At the burning altar of Atlas, Kumo announced two more invitations to join the ranks of The Minutemen—Split and Geddy Drake. They accepted, knowing that in the morning they would have the next battles in the Laddered Pit against two more who hadn't arrived. The ledger of the missing would be balanced against the two new men accepted into The Minutemen. For those remaining, *le esprit de corps* was alive and well. Wishes of joining The Minutemen no longer weighed against ideas of being a traitor to country. Everyone had decided Seee was right. The word traitor applied only to those who didn't agree. Certainly, I was suspect, and I knew that destiny would follow me into The Pit to live and die as either patriot or traitor.

Chapter 15

"Appear weak when you are strong, and strong when you are weak."
-Sun Tzu, The Art of War

On the morning of January 7, 2023, Split would emerge victorious from the Laddered Pit against Zach Dionne, thrusting a spear through his heart after a long three minutes of tide-turning battle. Dionne, a loner throughout his time at The Farm, was not mourned. His head was rammed on a spike next to that of Tongueless Downs in what became known as Traitor Row, the same area of the clearing where Bunker's head had once been displayed. The following day, it would be Geddy Drake pitted against the last missing plebe, John Hammond. Drake had been the victor but was dragged out of The Pit with an arm badly slashed, ribs broken, and a leg gashed and bleeding profusely. He had been taken away quickly to the Tree House, a red trail of blood flowing in the sand of The Pit while Merrill and Des put him on a gurney and lifted him out. He hadn't been seen since, and most thought he was dead.

The next day, I awoke to a sea-blue sky with wisps of cloud feathered in the atmosphere. The early-morning dew glistened silvery off the grass, and the wind whistled through the high branches of durian trees as we ate our breakfast. I sat next to Uriah, who massaged his forehead with a finger.

"Another migraine?" I asked.

"A stinger," he said. Uriah's condition had worsened. His head had swollen noticeably. For those whose lives he had saved, the changes were sorely felt. We sat in silence eating until Des interrupted us, arriving with Seee's orders to gather around The Pit.

I stared longingly at the runny scrambled eggs on my plate

wondering if they would be the last thing I would eat. I touched my forehead with the back of my hand and felt my hot skin. The previous night I had woken in cold sweats, my body shaking with fever, joints aching. By morning, I knew I had contracted a flu, or perhaps something worse—yellow fever of malaria. Now, fear of the day welled up in me, and I felt as innocuous as a puffed-up rain frog. Sitting across from us, Grus said, "Well, I guess this is it." He stood with a tin plate in one of his hands. "Maybe I'll get picked today."

"I have the same hope," Uriah said, misinterpreting Grus's hesitant tone. "But I don't count the odds in my favor."

"Why not?" Grus asked.

Uriah leaned over, and I saw the swell of his back, the hunched disfigurement, a tortoise-man stuck in a shell of discontent. Split had asked Seee to let Uriah leave the camp for a hospital. Seee agreed, on the condition that Uriah would accept. But Uriah refused, laughing at the notion of doctors, saying his pending fate no doctor could alter.

"Seee has already seen me with a sword," Uriah said, returning to Grus's question. "He seeks courage of those untested."

"Maybe you'll be picked," I told him. "But maybe one of us won't be as lucky as Split and Drake."

A silence crept between us as Grus moved off. Uriah and I acted as old men playing chess, taking our time, thinking three moves ahead but with bodies three moves behind. We stood and walked slowly out of the woods to the clearing. Light pushed through the trees, stabbing us in the face. As it fell on Uriah, I had difficulty finding his true features. His face changed as dynamically as a growing child's.

"At sunrise, I imagined my death," Uriah said. "I let my sword drop and my head was lopped off."

"What did it feel like?"

"A relief," he joked. We both laughed at this, him licking the sides of his mouth with his lizard-like tongue to catch a string of drool running off his chin. He stared at me with the strange lopsided jaw as if he had more to say, but in the end he was content with silence. Gazing into his large dark eyes, he seemed to understand my thoughts. Imagining being him, my eyes saw a simple reason why he longed for The Pit. He put a crooked arm around me, and we edged into the clearing.

"Are you feeling okay, Isse?"

"I feel fine. Leave me be."

He grabbed my bare arm. "You're burning up." He brought a hand up to my forehead and I brushed it away. "You can't fight like this."

"Maybe I won't be called."

"But maybe you will."

"Then so be it," I said. "Besides, what can be done about it?"

We walked for a ways as he thought this over. I loathed the silence, so I said, "Back to your death. Who killed you?"

"I don't know. I normally don't attach a face. I guess I wouldn't mind if it was you." I nodded. Putting my arm around him, I felt the mound of flesh between his shoulder blades, the hump a weight on him, noted its massive growth since our days of grappling near the river. He smiled, but then his face grew serious. "Are you meditating on your death?" he asked, as if this were of paramount importance.

"I am clasped in the hands of Fate no matter what happens."

We reached The Pit, and Seee stood staring at us. Des, Merrill, and Kumo were draped by his side, each wearing fatigues and gray T-shirts. Merrill stared at us, arms folded at his waist, a pack of cigarettes rolled up in a sleeve. Uriah and I took our places in a semi-circle around the Laddered Pit. Finally, the Cannibal Crew arrived, and as they sought their spots within the circle, Des spoke. "Edward Conroy, please step forward."

Conroy obeyed, stepping forward with arms rigid at his sides.

"Edward Conroy. Are you ready to prove yourself worthy in

front of the eyes of these men?"

"I am," he said.

"Do you honorably accept the challenge put forward to you?"

"I do." Each man had been asked the question, but was there really a choice? It was Join, or Die.

"Isse Corvus, step forward," Des ordered. Upon hearing this, Conroy caught my stare, and I was suddenly the archetype of nemesis.

I stepped forward. Des repeated the words to me, and with each question I echoed the same words as Conroy.

Seee then spoke. "With The Minutemen as witnesses, I hereby command you to fight with weapons of your choosing until one or both of you is dead."

The men remained unmoved, but Uriah protested. "Sifu, why are we turning brother against brother?"

"Perhaps they would like to explain," Seee answered.

Conroy quickly said, "I will admit I was sent here to report what was happening in this place."

"But that's not the whole of it, is it?" Seee said, deep-set eyes gleaming at Conroy. A coy smile lined his mocking lips, chiding us, as if to say, *Brothers, I know all of your secrets, do not think to lie to me.*

My eyes questioned him, asking, *If you know, why have you kept me alive?* I cleared my throat. Better to heave the boulder of fact rather than throw a rock of truth. I said, "My mission was to—"

"Reasons aren't important!" Seee shouted, cutting the rope as I jumped from the gallows. Again, I questioned his intent. "Both of you have committed crimes against the camp, and a crime against The Abattoir is a crime against The Minutemen."

"People don't do this!" Conroy cried. "Pit agents against one another."

"You aren't an agent, Mr. Conroy. You are a mole, and pitting agents against one another is exactly what you signed up for. I'm not asking you to die. I'm asking you to fight. Are you a coward,

Mr. Conroy?"

"You will kill me anyway," Conroy said.

"I promise you I will not. For a man without hope has nothing to fight for."

I gazed at Uriah, but his eyes darted from Conroy to Seee in a state of confusion. I said to him, "I admit what I have done, and I am sorry if I misled you. It is in the hands of Fate now, and I am willing to accept whatever hand might be dealt to me."

Uriah reached up and cupped me around the ears. "Fate is not your master," he said. "You are. I know your heart has turned. Go, and prove this to yourself."

As I climbed wearily into The Pit, I gazed up at the sky and caught a glimpse of Briana. She glanced in my direction and tried to hide her tears. This broke my heart the most. Someone actually crying for me. The last person who'd dropped a tear for me was my brother, the afternoon he hijacked and beat me, yelling how badly I had fucked everything up with Dad. Tears stopped him from killing me, his weakness the strength of blood. Staring at me now was Seee, so much like my brother in both toughness and the stark way he looked at the world. Compared to them, I seemed like a winsome dreamer.

At that moment, I didn't know how to react to Briana's tears. A great need willed me to not be a disappointment. Then she lipped the words, "It was me," and "I'm sorry." So Burns hadn't lied. I suppose I should have felt guilt over strangling the man, but it didn't come.

I nodded at her, lipped, "It doesn't matter."

Behind her in the sky, a pale contrail spread out white and foamy across the blanched atmosphere. It appeared to be heading in a straight, vertical climb. But this wasn't reality, only a misinterpreted viewpoint. I thought about Seee's parable of Heaven and Hell, how the taste of the fruit from the Lushing Tree was simply a matter of perspective. Perhaps I had lost perspective. The original intent of assassinating Seee seemed clouded and obtuse. I couldn't grasp any reason behind it beyond a promise, more to my father than to Pelletier, the act of unquestioned patriotism. How cruel it was I realized this now.

I stooped down onto my ankles and grabbed as much dirt as one hand could hold while Conroy climbed down. I closed my eyes and let the grains trickle through my fingers. Then I imagined my death—there in The Pit—Conroy darting into a flurry of offence, wearing me down with sweeping slashes, overhead strokes, riposting the scant offence I could offer, my parries losing force, and then his sword piercing my chest, deep into the flesh, tearing through muscle, shattering ribs—the pain a scourge, a cry galloping from deep within a body that hardly seemed my own. Eyes open on the wound, blood gushing onto the blade, my hands naturally float there to get it out—a quick glance down the shaft, higher up, near the hilt, I see my reflection in the steel.

Then Conroy places his foot on my chest, pulls out the sword, and I fall. He is over me with the blade, dark pupils merciless, blue irises rotating inside sandy sclera. He is Hercules coming to bring me back to the Underworld, my bushido death complete.

The grains withered in my palm, and I released them to the wind. I stood, caught Uriah's eyes and nodded, then turned to face Conroy, already at the rack.

Conroy's lips quivered. A tear streamed from an eye, and he swept it away quickly. My mind swam in tactics, and then Blue's voice popped in my head quoting his hero, the old fighter, Iron Mike Tyson. *Everyone has a plan until they get punched in the face.* The air stretched, thinning with the coming moment.

My hands shook like brittle leaves about to blow off a branch. I mesmerized over the tiny fissures within my palms, rivers of fortune soon to run dry. I longed to burst into tears. I bit a lip and realized I was holding my breath.

I turned outward. The clouds above blew by in a trance, the contrail now melted, replaced by wispy sheets torn across the blue atmosphere. Green in the fluttering leaves of trees sharpened and then dulled. The locusts rattled their wings, bewitching the men. A million little horns screeching together. A discordant battle call. Life's clock ticked down and neither of us would escape it.

Someone was going to die here and no one above us doubted it. The cold steel truth of it waited in the rack of weapons mounted on the rolling cart on the wall of The Pit. One of the blades held a secret, and I thought about which one it might be. I gazed up at the faces looking down. The men stayed rooted, eyes bulging as they counted down each ticking second, their hearts beating with muted anticipation. Where did their eyes drift, to Conroy or me?

I turned to the rack. Selected a weapon. Split yelled out, "Do what you have to do, Isse!" The Cannibal Crew yelled for Conroy. Everyone broke out of rank and screamed for a man until Seee silenced them.

As I pulled off my T-shirt, I realized I had forgotten to wear the Earth picture over my heart. My mood sunk. Cursing myself, I put on a breastplate and a centurion helmet, the bronze metal slipping over my cheeks and coiling around my eyes. A great plume of Mohawk red stiffened the air. I must have looked seven feet tall. Vapors of the next world blew around me. I imagined myself entombed in a bomb suit like Split. Fogging up a mask with my hot feverish breath.

My martial arts career had been one without anxiety before a fight. I would loosen up in the locker room with sun salutations. I would dig into some punches—roundhouses, uppercuts, jabs— slowly pumping myself up. Then I would kick Blue halfway around the goddamned room as I psyched myself out with my own feral power. The boys would help me feel it. Wailing punches into my washboard stomach, throwing kicks into my arms, whipping pain into me so I wouldn't feel it out there. "Pain is in your mind," Blue had said. "It doesn't exist. To tap is to die."

But now, out here under the crisp sun, courage abandoned me. Sweat poured down my forehead and stung my eyes. Not the sweat of toil, but the drip of fear. I looked past the men hovering above us, out past the tree line and into the deep distance. Blue wasn't with me now. His spirit had disappeared into the forest amongst the trees. He would be no help here where snot poured out of me in a constant drip.

Everyone fell silent with ominous anticipation, eyes hungry and fixating on Conroy and I below, waiting for the signal. The air chilled and my stomach lurched. I tried to stretch the stiffness from my joints, high-stepping, rotating my back and hips. I swiped my blade through the air. Death swept in on the wings of the wind blowing on a breeze.

We faced off, eyes already stabbing one another. In his, I recognized fear, deeper than mine, and I realized an edge presented itself to counter my physical weakness.

"*No rules,*" Seee had once said. "*In Nature, the cost of life is death.*"

Suddenly, my eyes burned staring into his, and the instinct to cling to life jolted me alive.

"Fight!" came the call.

We step toward each other. Conroy attacks with a thrusting sword. I retreat, slip in the sand. He lunges stiff-armed, gladius sword deflecting off my shield. Clanging of metal as the roar of men erupts. Adrenaline jolts my heart. Errant steps have almost finished me. Back and back, he pushes me. A relentless charge. My shoulders now pinned against the ballasted wall. I parry his thrusts. Block his overcuts. Push him back with my shield.

He pauses, breathing heavily.

I glide toward him. Rake my sword against the ground. My legs awaken. The Earth breathes beneath me, its shake blowing through my body. Dust clouds push up into the air in tiny puffs as I step forward. A primeval call, an ancient scream with a gnarled voice. Fear is in Conroy's frantic face, a grin that doubles over into a frown. He throws an overanxious swing. Inexperienced body movement. He has not trained as hard as me. Nothing more than a raging man lashing out with a prayer. My eyes gleam at him as he uncovers the battle secret.

He recognizes my look, and a new brand of fear leaps out of him. He backs up in a new, more dogged retreat. The blade is an extension of myself. My veins wrap around it. Nerves, skin, and arteries tighten. I find an opening. Then my steel slashes through his arm as if it were air. It's over, but not over.

I climb out of The Pit and stomp a path toward Seee. The men part as I pass. Seee has a surreptitious smile on his curvaceous lips, looking at me as if I am the wolf he knew was lurking inside. I wonder what kind of man I have become, solemnly trying to remember Conroy's first name. I think if I looked down, I might have the answer, as if it might be the last thing on his lips. Then I was there, staring into Seee's eyes, and from somewhere the name suddenly came.

He stared into my eyes and nodded. My eyes said it all. This was the vanquished and the champion. This was the fed, and the eaten. This was the hair of another curled around my fingers, a weight both burden and relief. This was courage and fear, Nature and evolution. This was not only a command, but a plea, held tightly in his name. This was his blood coursing through me, as my eyes appeared in his. This was death and the first head of a revolution. And unlike so many others, in front of me was a leader who I knew was worth following.

"Edward Conroy, sir," I said, dropping Conroy's head at Seee's feet. And with these words, I became sworn to The Cause.

Chapter 16

"The duty of a true patriot is to protect his country from its government."

-Thomas Paine

Seee and I moved into the forest, entering the same trap door I crawled out of the day I was released from The Hole. Seee closed the hatch, smothering the light from above. The familiar gritty concrete scraped underfoot, and the days in darkness rushed back to me. Where was that naive prisoner now?

Moving in the opposite direction of my old cell, we came to a dead end after about twenty yards. A blip of red light flashed from Seee, and the massive concrete wall opened, sliding on squeaky wheels rolling on a track. Seee produced two headlamps and offered one to me.

"Welcome to The Anthill," he said at the entrance. "There's a ladder here." He waved his headlamp at the metal rungs of a ladder at the foot of the opening. "One thing you have to understand is that knowledge is like a bridge. You only allow someone to cross if it's absolutely necessary. This requires the strictest discipline, as inevitably human desire urges us to share with people we believe we can trust. But what is even more difficult is sometimes it becomes inevitable that one must share secrets with dubious persons out of pure necessity."

I smiled slightly at his words. "And am I one of those dubious persons?"

"Most certainly."

"What is down here?" I asked, but he simply told me in Yoncalla I would have to wait and see. Over the ledge, I peered down with my headlamp. No end to the darkness below, and I felt like Lazarus again, heading in the wrong direction. It appeared to be an old, dried-out well. The walls in front of me were pocked and blackened. "Why are the walls this way?" I asked.

"We have practiced engaging the enemy should they come."

We climbed down. No end to the rungs in the iron ladder we descended. The air was stagnant, a dank smell of moss and decay.

After a long silence, I finally asked a question still burning throughout the camp. "Tell me, who were those guerillas that stormed the camp? What was their purpose?"

"It was a turf war," Seee said. "But it had nothing to do with land. When we get below, it should help answer the question."

The sounds of hands and feet stepping and sliding on the ladder echoed throughout the chamber. As we climbed downward into the mouth of some beast, the air smelled as foul as the imagined breath. Seee seemed content to descend in silence, but my agitation grew. "How do you think you can win?" I asked. "The U.S. government is a giant much bigger than you. What is your plan to fight it?"

"A giant's size perturbs his flexibility," Seee said.

"The giant is like an octopus arm. You cut off one tentacle, and it simply grows back."

"When a giant falls, expect the ground to shake as he gets up to chase you, not yet realizing he is already dead."

"I can think of nothing that could kill the giant," I said. "The government is ubiquitous, all powerful."

"The government holds the illusion of power, but it is the people who truly possess it. Otherwise, why would the State need to plot against us? Their weapon is fear, and with fear they try to cow us into submission. But if the State can be shown as weak, out of control, then the spark is lit, the fire takes birth, and it is then the government must bend the knee to the people instead of the reverse."

"And is it the purpose of The Minutemen to bend, or break it?"

"Do not misunderstand our intentions. We want to preserve the Union, not destroy it. Are we not all Americans? What is needed is surgical removal of the rot, the detritus of those choking our Homeland and enslaving the people. But we do not want the nation falling into the chaos of factions and street anarchy, yet there lies the path already in front of us."

Our voices echoed off the stone and funneled to the surface as we dove ever deeper. We had gone perhaps seven stories down, and still I did not see a bottom. Not long afterward, I finally saw a floor, a long slab of rusted iron. I dropped down onto it. A dull thud from my footsteps was not the clanging echo of something hollow I expected underneath. The floor was solid steel, thick enough to take a direct hit from heavy artillery. Another flash of red light, and the sidewall opened. We ducked under the entrance and moved into a little cave, the door of iron closing behind us. A hatch in the iron floor took us down one more level to a lockout trunk. We crawled through another steel hatch and then slid into a darkened hall. At the end of the corridor, a loaded Dillon Aero Gatling gun with a string of ammo attached pointed at us, the ammo looping down to a box on the floor. Seee led me through a door into a plain-looking room stacked with boxes of supplies (I guessed ready-to-eat meals). We paused in the next room, which had a thick steel vault, high enough for a man to easily step through.

Seee turned to face me. "Our control room. Only a limited few have ever seen it, besides those who work here. With trust, comes honor." He placed his hand to my heart in a Yoncalla sign of respect. "The only wall that can stop you from doing great things is the one you build yourself. Remember to use all three of your eyes, Cerberus."

It was the first time I had heard my hacker name spoken in many years. My Anonymous name, once upon a time spread throughout the fabric of the Underworld, the three-headed Hellhound raining chaos on the financial elite inside the Internet.

A rebel against Wall Street, a Main Street protector, fucking with HFT algos, juking them at their own games, bankrupting their over-leveraged positions by pushing a snowball off a mountaintop, watching from the summit as it rolled over all of them.

Seee punched digits on a wall keypad and the vault opened. We stepped into a dome-shaped room, a lecture-hall feel to its rounded architecture. Long tables faced toward the front of the room. Workstations spread all over the place, outnumbering the people—enough for fifty, but only fifteen were present—some at holographic touch-screens, others at terminals. Some paused pulling at images floating in the air. A few faces turned to gawk at me, and like *The Time Machine*, they stared at me as if I were an Eloi from above.

A series of wide steps led down to the viewing wall where the largest ten-foot screen displayed a black image. From the top of the stairs, I could see the caption on the lower left—Montgomery 02:30:11 EST—as the seconds ticked along. Ten other screens surrounded the larger, each monitor flashing a different location. Places within The Abattoir—two shots within the jungle, one high on a cliff close to where we were dumped for Nature training, another on the outskirts of another perimeter. Another showed the quarters of the Tree House where we were first delivered. Another the Laddered Pit. Others showed thermal images of tunnels—one of them from the well we had just descended. Still others were nighttime images, city images far away from this one.

Seee weighed the reaction on my face. "We modeled it after Langley, but of course some of the design we've given our own personal touch. As you see, we have room to grow."

"So you want me working down here?" I asked.

He smiled at my incredulous tone, my eyes of disbelief. "Only for a week or so. Then you will have another assignment involving some of your old skills as well as some of your new."

Seee led me down the stairs, where from a circular desk on the lower floor with large monitors on top, a man stood from behind one of the screens and approached. A frail man, short and lightly bearded, as if someone had peppered it with snow, he smiled slightly when he got near. Hair flowed to shoulder-length, but strands of oily brown bangs flowed clumsily into his eyes. He stood with his hands behind his back, inching toward us in small steps, as tiny as a geisha's. Seee announced him as Promiscuous, and when he did so, the man raised his pale lips delicately into another fragile smile. Dipping his head so slightly, it was unclear if it had been a bow. The name was known widely in the Underworld, a name that circled around the infamous virus Stuxnet, the cyberattack on Iran's nuclear centrifuges. His name had been associated with the NSA, the Tailored Access Operations, a group of cyberwarriors, hackers, and programmers. They were the hitmen of the Internet, layered deeper than all others in the skeins of cyberspace.

The frail Promiscuous held out his eggshell of a hand, and I took it lightly in my palm. His wrist was made of bird bone, his palm so delicate I wasn't sure if I should kiss it. He wore a custom-designed Anonymous T-shirt, the question mark notably larger above the flamboyantly bulbous head of the black-suited man in the logo.

"Promiscuous is an Anonymous name, is it not?" I asked.

"It is. And yet, I've been called worse."

Promiscuous was a network mode activated when a sniffer went online within a segment. I had always found the name quite clever, and for the first time I was meeting a face from the Underworld, one for whom I had deep respect. He was a legendary mind, his knowledge vast and broad, a brainchild of tactical cyberwarfare and one of the cleverest worm writers I had ever known.

I nodded respectfully. "It is a pleasure to meet you, sir."

"Likewise," he said. He removed one of his hands from

behind his back and tapped his finger on his lower lip. He glanced at Seee, and as if he were coming to a conclusion, said, "You've been out of the game for quite some time, Cerberus—a long, long time."

"Yes, sir. Three years."

"Yes. Yes. Yes. Three years, two months, and five days in fact, if your time away from an Anonymous login is any indication." He paused, fingering the air in a small arc with his pinky, as if there were a clock measuring time in front of him. "Much, much, too much time I would say."

"I was caught," I said.

"Only by Datalion."

"It was enough to get me blacklisted across Silicon Valley, and beyond."

"You were trying to hack Blake Thompson's personal computer, weren't you?"

"I was unlucky. The machine was being fixed by the IT department at the time."

Others in the room became intrigued by the conversation. In front of me, faces popped up from behind glowing monitors. Some people got up from their seats to stare. Others descended the stairs to introduce themselves.

"What were you after on Mr. Thompson's machine?" Promiscuous asked.

"Something I didn't get."

This statement put another thin smile on the gaunt man's face. "We believe this is something he still has. But more on that later." He was waving at others to join. "From what I have seen, your time away from a machine has flared up quite a bit of violence in you. Perhaps your mind is not as sharp as it once was."

"I have always been a fighter, sir. No matter the capacity. I am sure my mental facilities can still be of some use."

Promiscuous nodded to Seee, seemingly pleased with the response.

An older, white-haired man leading a troupe of others descended the stairs. He had glassy yellow eyes, and a leathery, dried-out face. He was introduced as Cetus, and he was someone I recognized. Shuffling back in my memories, I remembered the farmer waving to Merrill as we stood on a hill in observation. A man both Morlock and Eloi, he was coming above ground for the life of the ancient world, only to descend into the world I stood in now.

Others were introduced after the old man—Toorcon and Vines—names infamous in the hacking world years ago, but since gone off-grid. The Anthill had gobbled up others I didn't know and had never heard of. There was Eros, Sputnik, and two women in the crew whose names were Nyx and Lady X.

After the introductions, Promiscuous said, "We are called The Anthill not because we are buried underground, but because we work like the insect Formicidae. We work in groups, each assigned an area of expertise. We require a very special expertise from you, Cerberus. You have intimate knowledge which we do not have concerning Datalion's security systems."

"It would be an honor to help," I said.

But Promiscuous was eager for more information, a sense of hacker impatience in his voice. "We've duplicated some of the NSA client programs that have been created internally and used only inside Bluffdale. After decompiling them, we understand how they work."

"Bluffdale?" I asked.

"The NSA SIGAD site in Utah. Stellar Wind? I do hope you can remember a few things, being out of the game."

"I know of Stellar Wind," I retorted. "I just didn't recognize the town. I am also quite aware of the new quantum computer running there."

"The QX. Yes. But singular, it will not be. It will be many, and they should help tremendously in their quest to blow away the few grains of privacy still left. There will be no more latency within the Leviathan."

"Is that what you're calling Stellar Wind, the Leviathan?" I asked.

"That's what is. Is it not? Every bit of your life will be present under their roof. They will sit on top of you, using the information as they please to squeeze you to their will."

"Yes," I said.

"How do you think they are getting names for what they are calling the Uplift Programs? You know what they are, don't you?"

"I'm not very aware—"

"Of course you're not aware," Promiscuous interrupted. "We urge you to go see for yourself. They are constructing camps in South Dakota, Idaho, and eastern Oregon."

"Only Idaho and Oregon are operational at the moment," Cetus interjected. "Some of our friends have been taken there."

Promiscuous said, "When you come out—no, no, let me backspace—if they let you out, you will be pacified. As good as lobotomized by their drugs; the drips of which come from a surgically implanted port that can be refilled with a doctor's visit. It is a mega-dose of valium for the population."

"They are starting with persons of interest," Seee said. "But most certainly they will enlarge the beta program as civil disobedience grows."

Promiscuous tapped his thin lips again. "Internally at the NSA, much has changed since whistleblower Edward Snowden had his day. They have zipped their vagina tight with a chastity belt. They have gone through great pains to make Stellar Wind secure. Like Fort Meade, data can come in, but it can't get out. But it's worse than that."

"He hasn't seen what their true capabilities are yet?" Cetus asked.

"No," Promiscuous said. "Indeed he has not. Vines, queue up the video. Let's take a look at how good they've gotten."

As we waited, Promiscuous placed his fragile hand on my shoulder, squeezed it, and said, "For some years they have had the ability to turn on your phone's GPS, video and audio devices, tap in to your Google glasses, and use CCTV cams within the vicinity. Now, they can wire into everyone else's devices too within your vicinity. They don't even need feet on the ground anymore. They are following you with micro-UAVs. They are as small as a blue jay, and to the unsuspecting eye, can look like them too."

"But we are one leg up on them there," Cetus added.

Promiscuous nodded, raising a hand for Cetus not to say any more. Then he pointed at the screen as the video began. "But now this—"

On the screen was Titus Montgomery speaking with an aide. The aide told him that he had Ron Pelletier on the phone, asking for progress on the Linked Language case.

"Tell him we have linguistics on it," Montgomery said.

"He persists on speaking with you," the aide said.

"Tell him I'll call him back on a secure line."

Montgomery picked up the receiver of his STE voice-over IP telephone and put the KSV-21 crypto card in the PC slot. When he got Pelletier on the phone, he said, "Ron, we've talked about this before."

An incoherent voice came across the line, muffled and distant, but it was one I recognized. I gazed around the room, but all eyes were on the screen.

"I know I only gave you a minute before, but that's all I had. We're working on it, Ron." More words came from the incoherent voice. "It's intricate. It's amazing we even caught it. It was in six pieces, each piece encrypted differently and simply a mosaic of an image, each with separate originating IPs, each going to separate email accounts by separate providers, disseminated in chunks all over the place. That's what we're talking about here."

The voice of Pelletier came back, and then Montgomery said,

"Some genetic algorithm caught it running on the QX. We're quite pleased with the catch. The link was so obtuse our guys don't know how it was done—each message received at separate Internet cafés, but all in the same vicinity within the same timeframe. Where is the link in that when all of the data is encrypted bits? We've cracked the encryption, but the language itself—we don't know what it is. Linguistics is on it. They're looking at dead languages, but the accounts they were using are all dead now. Nothing else is coming out, so we don't have much to go on. We've gone out a few degrees for a link on each account, but it's turned up nothing."

The video paused, another aide barging into Montgomery's door, a face frozen in time.

"That's what Turbulence can do," Promiscuous said. "It can create associations that are invisible to us. It's snooping in whole other worlds we can't see, hear, or taste. It's worming its way into other dimensions of data and coming back to the NSA with answers. And here we are, thinking we were clever with what we were doing. But Turbulence proves it can find even the tiniest of cracks in the architect's masterpiece. In short, we have been outsmarted. It is only Yoncalla, our paranoia, and this surveillance video that has saved us. Rest assured the same pattern would certainly be found again."

Pelletier had perhaps linked some things together, dead languages, The Abattoir, a cryptic message—an informant, perhaps CIA—a patriot turned traitor or vice-versa. If one Minuteman had turned, then how many were there? The Company perhaps infiltrated. But where was the proof when the program was working? Who would have the nuts to tell the Deputy Director their best HumInt guys perhaps had a second agenda? And who was doing counterintelligence within The Abattoir? Who had been told, and what were they doing about Pelletier?

Promiscuous brought me back from my thoughts. "We take

extreme precautions, but it's the telescreen, Cerberus, except with far better reach. They are a spider, able to cast a very large web to catch any bug that resists them. We think they're storing terabytes for a single person, exabytes within their ultracloud. Can you imagine? How do you search it all to build your persons of interest with so much data? The QX is the only way without significant latency. Without the QX, they can only be looking into the past."

"Once, we were able to crack through the first firewall undetected," Cetus said.

"Yes," Promiscuous said, "but we didn't have access to the database or the QX and we won't get another shot. Now in the subnet there is a biometric password expiring every ten minutes stored in shared memory on the server, but the encryption algorithm on the wire is in constant flux. We can't crack what's on the wire as it's always changing."

"It's part of Rose," I said with a faint smile. "Rose is the cloud controller among other things. Three of us worked on her. Rose cannot be killed without taking down the cloud. She is the atmosphere, the weather, a genetic algorithm, always changing, always learning, seeking out new threats to the system, donning out resources, handling database activity. It was the fruit of my thesis I took into Datalion."

The faces around the circle were in a state of dejection. I added, "She does more than just security. But if you could crack her, what is your intent? To destroy the database?"

"Disruption is our best weapon," Cetus said. "Leviathan cannot be killed, only wounded. The best we can do is put an end to the past, but we have no control over the future. Any destruction of data, or sloshing of data together, would soon be detected. Most likely, the system wouldn't be recoverable, but all we would gain is time. People's actions are habitual. They won't banish technology. The data will keep coming."

Promiscuous paced the room toward the darkened screen

with *Montgomery* captioned on it. He stood in front of the screen, bending his neck to look up at it, hands behind his back. "That's our secondary goal. Our primary goal is to obtain a few secrets. For that we need a sniffer, but we have been unable to be promiscuous, so to speak."

The circle giggled at the remark.

"Perhaps I can help you with Rose," I said. "There is an internal mechanism inside that can be activated. Commands can be sent to it with the right client software. Data would be stored internally, buried in one of the system tables."

Promiscuous motioned for Seee and me to follow. Led out of the room through a side door, the others wandered back to their desks. We strolled into a hallway of a mini-warehouse full of humming machines. The room in front of us had a glass window separating their server room. Racks of computers with a thousand green blinking lights flashed before us. An old Cray-2 in an octagonal shape shimmered in blue directly in front of us.

"We cannot compete with Bluffdale, sadly," Promiscuous said over the torrent of noise emanating from the room.

We passed through the corridor to a lab with what inside looked like a DARPA BigDog running on a treadmill. A team of men in lab coats were kicking at its legs to see if it would tumble over. Finally I understood where their robots had been coming from.

"Wouldn't Rose detect a change in the underlying system and raise a flag?" Promiscuous asked, coming to the real question he wished to ask.

"Not if she could become predictable. If her mutation cycle could be stopped, then we would be dealing with a known quantity. A secret backdoor I wrote could disable her mutations. If it is still any good, it could perhaps switch off certain security mechanisms as well. Perhaps these little tweaks I did might be hard to see if you were looking at the code. But who knows if it is still there? Code changes. Programs change."

"We have come across certain information that tells us that large parts of the system have remained mostly untouched over the past few years," Promiscuous said.

"If the mutation sequence could be altered, then Rose would remain static, and new elasticity stretches within the system might not trigger an alarm. But again, all of this depends on how much things have changed. There are no guarantees. And then you would have to be able to access the system in the first place."

"There is only one port accessible from outside Stellar Wind," Promiscuous said, "and only two or three men have access to it. All other terminals run internally. As I said, data can come in, but it can't get out. This will be your mission, to get the data out."

Chapter 17

"I cannot be grasped in the here and now, for my dwelling place is as much among the dead as the yet unborn, slightly closer to the heart of creation than usual, but still not close enough."
-Paul Klee

I counted three enormous test labs as we walked through the halls. We strolled by a robotics lab and several cold rooms. Another experimental lab we passed. I had no clue what purpose it served, but there were men in it garbed in lab coats working busily.

A few days later Seee disappeared, leaving Kumo to run the camp. I spent most of my days in The Anthill refreshing my hacking skills, learning new techniques, sitting in the circle with Cetus, Toorcon, Eros, and Vines. One day, I learned how data coming over a fiber wire could be passively sniffed and duplicated. We went over PacketScope and clip-on couplers that let one capture fragments of light. Fed into a photon detector, the light was converted to an electric signal, which then could be plugged into a laptop. We were tapping into the roots of the Underworld, listening, duplicating what the NSA was doing every day.

The Cerberus in me delighted in the comradery with the other hackers. My brain sparked to life the way it had in the Silicon Valley a few years before. Yet I felt untrusted, a foreigner among them. When I asked how the place was funded, Cetus answered vaguely. "We have a large benefactor." The understatement of the year, I replied, and he replied the year had just begun. I told him I noticed many statements were understatements in The Anthill. He laughed but refused to take the conversation any further.

The facility had to have cost millions. Perhaps a large,

nefarious organization owned it. Incapable of capturing its true breadth and scope, I vowed to discover its true intent. But I had crossed one bridge to get here. How many were there left to cross? The only certainty was everyone seemed fiercely loyal to The Cause, and for that, I had grand admiration.

With Promiscuous guiding us, we forged a plan to disable Rose. With Rose inactive, we could hack into the myriad of host machines, supplanting code and injecting our own. We could make every Datalion server a machine in a botnet, cover our tracks, and then turn Rose back on only to have her be controlled by the botnet. "In the cloud, everything becomes fuzzy," Promiscuous said. "We want to make it so they can't see in front of themselves."

We worked long hours, not knowing whether it was night or day if it wasn't for the time displayed on our screens. Most nights we worked into the morning. We would stop in the canteen only long enough to prepare ourselves a quick meal while chatting about problems and their solutions. We transformed a test lab, creating a mini NSA environment where we could test our cyber-strafing. Sometimes the solution could be solved in the virtual world itself, other times we found it necessary for real-world intervention.

After five straight days of being underground, I climbed the ladder back to the surface. When I finally emerged, I felt like a whale coming up for air. I broke into a warm daybreak, a sea of humidity already a hot sheet over the earth. Pink clouds hovered in the sky in a slow churn over the horizon. Sweat quickly covered my body, but I breathed fresh air. A voice came from behind one of the trees. "Halt, who goes there?" came a mocking authoritative tone. I turned around and saw Uriah in a two-step hobble coming toward me. An M16 was in his hands, swinging like an elephant trunk toward the ground.

"I couldn't sleep," he said. "I took over Mir's guard duty."

"A migraine?"

He nodded while I looked him over. The tumors on his skull had expanded, a new sort of atmospheric pressure from the storm of metastasis. My worried expression must have shown. In anticipation of what I was about to ask, he said, "The bigger ones have grown another centimeter within the last few weeks. I measured them."

"Are you taking anything?"

"No," he said. "I must bear my own burdens." He inched over closer to see me.

"Are you seeing double?"

He smiled a bit. "Two of you would be better than one, right?"

"Two of me would be a nightmare to myself."

He nodded, and I thought he caught my drift. "I'm not up at nights because of my headaches. It's more the raging anxiety I feel keeping me up in the middle of the night."

"What do you mean?"

"If we do not move forward soon, I might miss it." His eyes started to tear up a bit. I took him by the shoulder. "Hey, man, you don't want to talk like that."

"Do you think I am delusional? I know this will kill me if a bullet doesn't first. I'd rather die by the bullet, but I see no sign of progress toward that."

I nodded, staring into the glassy obsidian eyes of the deer who wanted to be a hunter. "You'll have your day," I said, knowing this most likely a lie. He sensed it, gazed off toward a treetop while his lips twitched. He raised the M16 off into the high branches of a durian tree, the effort itself twisting his back horribly. Maneuvering his weight to balance his many deformities, he stumbled, almost losing his footing. When I stepped toward him, he said, "Don't help me. I can still raise a gun. You best remember it."

I stepped back. He had the look of a man who felt like all of his life's efforts meant nothing. The gun now on his shoulder he said, "Seee is back. Have you heard?"

"No."

"Maybe he'll tell us we're leaving this fucking place."

"I'm hoping as much as you. I think we're all a bit tired of The Abattoir."

He nodded, then brought the gun down and pointed it back at the ground. "Now that you're one of us, what does it mean to you?"

I shirked at the truth at first, but then it slipped out of my mouth raw and uncensored. "Everyone here knows my history. You know the promise I made to my father. You know my mother is dead. You know I was the cause of it. You tell me, what else does a man like me have left to live for?"

"Fate has not been kind to you. But your life is still your own, Isse. The dead don't own it."

I smiled at him. "My friend, death has been searching for me for a long time. It was you who taught me how to not be afraid of it."

He nodded. "Not everyone believes in you. You need to be careful."

"I know."

"We've all turned traitor in the eyes of the State, Isse. But you—you came in here to kill our sifu. You came in here as a patriot for the State. It is difficult for me or anyone of us to believe your word, or that your heart has truly changed."

"You shouldn't, because I don't deserve it. Now, only my actions can speak for my loyalty."

"You're actions will certainly be tested. I wish I could only say the same about mine."

I stepped up to him, laid my hand on his heart in the sign of Yoncalla respect. "You have to trust that they will, Uriah. At the same time you cannot discount your own actions. You saved my life. For that I am eternally grateful."

Uriah placed his hand over my chest. A smile crept over his lips. "Even if by some chance you are still a traitor to The Cause, this I'll never forget."

Later, Seee called the men to go for a long hike to Second Sight Peak. Uriah insisted on going. Even though every man urged him to stay, Uriah packed a backpack and set out on the trail before the rest were ready. Ten minutes later, we had already caught up to him. He hobbled from tree to tree, using his M16 as a crutch. When Merrill saw him, a look of pity swept over his face, and he waved Des in to aid in helping him. But Seee caught both of them by the arm, not allowing either to pass.

Perhaps then, all of us felt a change in the air, as if a lump caught in our throats as we tried to breathe. The wind picked up, and under the shadow of the trees, we loped along slowly, Uriah in the lead, Seee close behind him, the rest following like disciples.

At last we came to Second Sight Peak, hiking up the stony bluff where before we had come to gaze at the stars. The sky clear of clouds, the breeze blew stronger out in the open. Seee went to the edge and peered over, all of us in expectation a plan hatching, our destiny soon known, but this was not where fate would lead.

Seee turned, his back facing the ledge. "You are all expecting me to say something regarding what will happen. I ask for your patience. For the safety of the operation, this must be kept secret. I did not really have a purpose to come to Second Sight today except to sit amongst you and enjoy the day. But now that we are here, I'd like to share with you the memory of when I first came. Basim Hassani and I were scouting locations for the camp, and we climbed up to where you're standing now. We looked out over this ridge ten years ago, and he said to me, 'What we're about to do is crazy, you know that?' I said that I knew. He asked me with a smile if I felt like jumping. I told him, no, not at the moment. 'If we fail, maybe,' he said. But now, as I'm standing with you in this moment, I'm asking myself if I'm doing the right thing. Who am I to be so bold as to ask The Minutemen to die for me if I am not willing to die myself? All of you should know that if I die, the line of succession goes to Kumo. All of the other cells know this and accept it."

Seee moved a step backward, and Uriah sprung forward, ready to grab him. "Sifu, this is not your purpose!"

Seee gazed into Uriah's eyes. "If I told you your true purpose was coming to this place to show your comrades the impossible was possible, that they would glean hope from you and you were the source of their strength to push them over the edge, would you think this a noble death?"

"Sifu, I would."

"Then step beside me and take my hand."

Uriah obeyed, hobbling forward, pausing to stare down the ledge once, then turning around to face Seee on the canyon precipice.

"It pains all of us to see you in such a state," Seee went on. Kumo approached Seee and whispered in his ear, but Seee pushed him away saying, "I'm no longer important. This thing has the legs to walk on its own now." Merrill stood with his head to the ground, as if he couldn't bear to watch.

"Sifu, this is not my purpose either," Uriah said.

"If you see clearly, you will see that for one of us, it is. You are the stink tree, full of knots, growing in a barren desert. Yet, you are still able to blossom. I am a leader who will bear a great burden. These men will die for The Cause, but in the end it will be I who will have to live with that."

"My purpose is to fight with The Minutemen. To give my life for you and The Cause—"

"This you have done. You have fought for your brothers and provided them shade from their scorching training. You suffered the whip for them. You have been their savior. You recognize that reality isn't always what we think it is. By one of us taking a leap of faith and proving to all our resolve, we accomplish our goal— that we will be willing to go before them. Do you not see this, my son?"

"I do, Sifu."

Perhaps no one else saw the moment as I did. Suddenly I understood why Uriah used the word sifu instead of sensei. There was another context to it, one patriarchal none of us were catching. Behind all of the deformities, suddenly I saw the resemblance in the faces of the two men standing before us. An urge came to blurt out the secret, but the words stuck in my throat. Certainly, the Sons must have known, but here, they remained quiet.

Uriah stood hunched over, his ailing body an obvious torment for him. Never in his nature to surrender, this was the essence of what Seee asked of him. The ultimate sacrifice for Uriah was not death, but surrender, and he didn't know how to yield to it.

Seee faced us holding one of Uriah's hands, raising it in the air. "To truly believe, we must all take leaps of faith—sometimes figuratively, sometimes literally. These men around you have all grown to love and cherish you because of your fortitude. They are your brothers. They might not love me, but I think I can say they respect me. Above all, they believe as much as I in The Cause. I can think of no more a noble death than for one of us to show them completely what sacrifice really means."

"What are you saying?" Uriah asked, not able to absorb what was being said.

"Do you believe my time has come?" Seee asked.

"No, I do not."

"Today is tomorrow. What is in between is relevant for only a blip in time. Perhaps you need a sign of faith from me, and this I will give. I ask no man for his life without first offering mine. You are my sons and our eyes see the same."

"Sifu, I cannot let you."

But Seee ignored him, grasped him in his arms, squeezed him, then let him go, retaking the hand. "On the count of three,

I will jump, such that if I do, you will not have to. I command none of you to punish him. It is a choice for Uriah, and the choice remains his. As a member of The Minutemen you must accept this." Seee cupped Uriah's face into his hands and fixed his gaze into his eyes. "The time is now, son. Can you feel it? It's as if this moment has been squashed into a grain of sand."

"Enough!" I yelled out, unable to contain the emotion flowing through me any longer. "This need not be proved. None of us here doubt either of you. This cannot stand between father and son!"

Uriah looked up to me slowly, his eyes watering and his lips full of sympathy. "When you shot your father, Isse, did you not want to switch places with him?"

I stood stunned, incredulous as to what he had just said to me. Seee called out:

"One...

"Two..."

"In another life, I will be beautiful," Uriah said.

Seee's eyes lit up with tears. He squeezed Uriah's hand. "In this life, you already are, my son."

Uriah threw himself off the cliff, his body hurling downward, hands outstretched in the air as he fell, eyes staring upward into the glaring sun. Seee crept closer to the edge, inviting the abyss, boots curling over the ledge. "If any of you believe I would not have jumped, speak now."

No one spoke. To this day, I believe if someone had, he would have jumped as well, his legs eager to push off the ledge in spite of everything at stake. The wind blew heavy in our faces. The whole canyon, empty of any other sound. Finally, Seee took a deep breath. "Do you smell the air?" he asked, crying noticeably. "I smell only the scent of courage within it. In the near future, each man will be asked to stand over the abyss. Each of us will be asked to jump. Will you have the courage to do it? This is what you need to ask yourself as you have given witness to one who has."

Part II

Detritus

Chapter 18

"If you wish to be a success in the world, promise everything, deliver nothing."
-Napoleon Bonaparte

NSA Director General Titus Montgomery hunkered down to kiss his four-year-old daughter goodbye in the vestibule.

"You smell like smelly juice," little Elisabeth said, looking up at him.

Montgomery was mesmerized by the power of observation in youngsters, the bluntness, the raw sense of unedited truth that could spurt out of their mouths.

"It's coffee, honey," he said.

"It smells different than Mommy's coffee," she said.

"That's because Mommy doesn't know what a good coffee tastes like."

He gazed over at his wife Emily, standing in the hallway, a tightened arm akimbo on a protruding hip, an eyebrow perking up in a perfect half-moon. *See,* the eyes said. *See, she can pick it up on you and she's just a child.*

Montgomery brushed back his daughter's hair, swept some loose bangs under a black metal barrette at the top of her head.

"Mommy says it's not good for you."

Montgomery put his hands to her shoulders, a sign to straighten-up, while he thought about the touch of propaganda latent in her last statement. Was she Daddy's girl? Or had Mommy's manipulation shaped her into her little pinion to grind Daddy's gears?

"Lots of things aren't good for you," he said. "But coffee's not one of them."

"Can I try your coffee?" she asked.

"I'm all done with it now, little girl."

"Tomorrow?"

"When you get older, honey."

"I'll be older tomorrow," she said.

That was his girl, the midget Conquistador testing a border. Bouncing a ball off the wall of his will to say no to her. Montgomery had the expectation she would surprise him with every throw.

He kissed Elisabeth's rosy cheek and stood. His wife was still giving him the stare, the look of *I'm better than you*.

"You're late," she said.

This phrase, the early-morning swan song. The *get the fuck out* way of pushing him through the door. She hated it that Elisabeth cherished this morning ritual, leading them through the hall dragging them for the morning sendoff.

"They're waiting for you."

"I'm the boss. I go when I feel like it." He said this a lot too, and the kids fed on it, sensed the discord, especially the boy.

Brandon was five, but didn't seem the older. Montgomery gazed down at his son who looked up at him wide-eyed. Montgomery ruffled up his hair. "Be good at school. Learn something and you'll get ahead of the louts who don't."

The boy smiled at him hesitantly, eyeing his mother first before he did it, wondering if he had made a trespass. The poor kid was plugged in more with his wife's ideology. Perhaps swayed by his wife's not-so-subtle suggestiveness. Or just naturally introverted and shy, a kid whose mark on the world would be innocuous, a grain in the heap of human sand? Montgomery hoped it wasn't the latter. The former he could live with because that was just a matter of swaying an opinion. An opinion he could manipulate, turn like a sheet of paper and begin drawing something new the owner would have to accept. The latter was weakness, frailty.

But he loved his boy, reaching out to understand him as he was doing now with both outstretched hands. "Come give your dad a hug goodbye," he said. The boy came and Montgomery picked him up high into the air and let the boy see him from above. Gave him the aerial perspective. Made himself small in the boy's eyes. Showed him there was nothing to be afraid of. Brandon's face lit up, and the smile, the trust—well, it made his morning. Brandon was the one who pulled him back, kept him human with the innocent look in his eyes. He had the fragility of a baby turtle scurrying out to sea. Within him, a blind hatchling scurried down a beach to duck into the pounding waves. He let the boy down and kissed his hand and blew it over to his wife. She squeezed her nose hoping the children would see, and when they didn't, walked through the hallway toward the kitchen.

Outside, Montgomery's double stood by the second car, the black Suburban with the shiny chrome hubcaps and dark tinted windows. Montgomery was late, always making the double wait, a morning mini-pleasure like the Jameson he added to his daily hazelnut coffee.

A couple of enlisted men holding machineguns saluted from the flat roof of the east wing staring down at the scene. The double leaned against the contoured hood with crossed arms, squinting from cigarette smoke curling in gray funnels above his eyes. The cigarette dangling out of the double's mouth wasn't him—never part of his persona. Montgomery hadn't yet forbid him to smoke. This he blamed on himself. The squint wasn't right either. He didn't like The Dupe (as he liked to call him), but it was now a requirement for the National Security Council's Director General to have one.

The Dupe wore the "dress blue" ASU uniform—the black tie, the peak lapel, the brass coat buttons, the four stars patched on top of his shoulders, golden cuffs, shined-up boots. The various patches were sewn in correctly under the lapel—the Army Service Ribbon, the Distinguished Service Medal, the Office of the Joint Chiefs Badge, and the many others. The uniform looked like his, and the black hair was slicked back like his, but certainly he wasn't using the same brand of hair gel. Most people missed the details, didn't have the eye for them, and it pissed Montgomery off the guy hadn't bothered to ask. He hated a sleepy work ethic. This one, the third imposter he had hired within the last year, didn't take any pride in the job either. His driver and personal aide, Colonel Davis, had told him he was expecting too much, that he was looking for a mirror of perfection and none of these dweebs could live up. Davis was certainly right, even if it was an ass-kisser remark, but he liked Davis.

Montgomery saw himself as a man who had his eyes open. When someone took a shot at him a month ago, they had opened even more. He had some ideas of who it was. A squad of NSA and FBI was looking into it. If they didn't find anything, he would "do the necessary", as they said in Mumbai, and fire people down the ranks.

The double's name was Leonardo Lord. He was of Italian descent, a guinea with a nose sloping more vertically than his, the heavy slant almost as steep as a y-axis on a coordinate system. At least the width was right. It was a Roman nose, where his was meatier with some other ethnicities thrown in—Slav, English, German. He was a mutt and knew it, took pride in it. He was American, a mixed breed, and he didn't give a fuck where his ancestors came from.

Montgomery breathed in the crispy air, the wind like a cold blade against his cheek. He gazed over at Lord smoking a cigarette. Minus the cigarette, did he really look like that? Somehow, he couldn't believe it, but Colonel Bowers, another one of his aides, was adamant—a canny resemblance he had said. Lord had on a pair of dark Gucci Aviators on. Why the fuck was he wearing those? Montgomery walked toward the car. Montgomery yelled, "Pretend you're my double, not my bodyguard, okay?"

Lord stood there dumb-faced and quiet.

Montgomery frowned. "You still haven't figured out what I'm talking about?"

The Dupe shrugged, was about to say something. Montgomery cut him off. "Close your mouth. Bugs might fly in."

Davis, waiting near the other black Suburban, lifted a finger to each temple, mimicking someone taking off a pair of glasses. At least he wasn't shit for brains. The double removed his shades, stood silent. Montgomery didn't like to hear him speak, didn't want his people to hear his voice. Davis opened the back door and Montgomery slipped in. "And tell him no more cigarettes. It's a filthy habit." Davis nodded and trotted out toward the other car. Then they loaded up. Three of them in the S-2, and him and Davis in the S-1. He wasn't sure if they were going to take the long way or the short. He let his men handle it. The only one who couldn't be trusted was the double. The others were solid. Some he had known for years, but even then you had to dig deep to be sure.

He turned on his iPad and flipped it to the news. What was the pulse of the day? How would he have to adapt? Events were malleable in so many ways. A story could be shaped, crafted for positive public spin even if the ground reality was chaos and bedlam.

The news was cheery. With the Dow up, everything was peaches. The newswoman droned on about macroeconomic data, Chicago PMI and Michigan sentiment. The charts slid on a downward slope, rolling softly toward the hills of the next depression, but they were spinning it as if they were bottoms.

But the economy was like a building about to undergo demolition. Dynamite at its base. When it went *ka-boom*, it was game over. New York Fed Board President, Jacob Lauder, was on MSNBC smiling into the camera explaining his new economic model, which he said would sterilize some of the macroeconomic problems facing the U.S. economy. Recently, he had received a call from Mr. Lauder, and he was overdue in calling him back.

But what would they talk about? The world was already awash in an ocean of liquidity. The Fed had used their bullets in 2009, then in 2011, then in 2012, 2017, and so on. The gun was empty, cards played. Montgomery watched Lauder's smooth mannerisms, his cool demeanor. The face was camera-friendly. Much like himself, Lauder was a man on a charm offensive, a positive PR campaign to reverse public opinion. The Federal Reserve now acting defensive. The media wouldn't criticize them, but for the rotating Senate and Congress, Fed policy was now the scapegoat and heavily scrutinized. A week ago, the President had come to him and told him The Fed was calling the probability high the financial markets would implode. As if this were some big secret.

All of the wound-up leverage in the financial system was unwinding, trillions of derivatives with failing counterparties, rehypothecated collateral where the same asset was used like toilet paper for a chain of loans. It would all come to roost. It was already happening in China. Empty warehouses on collateralized promises, Dongguan bankrupt and rioting. Banks failing to do due diligence because of promised bailouts. They had taken the bribes, reported the good numbers, taken the bonuses. The money was already out there in the system. Now it had to be pulled back. But it was like pulling at the wind. The nefarious economy, bludgeoned by debt, would have to suffer for it. The Chinese central authority now executing local village chiefs who let it run amuck, hanging them high and letting their bodies dangle on the top of street posts. Signs tied around their necks scrawled in Mandarin saying, *Timely return of a loan makes it easier to borrow a second time.*

Be ready, the President had told him. "Yes, Mr. President," he had replied.

Of course Montgomery knew what he meant by this. It had been studied by the Minerva Research Initiative through social contagion research, discussed broadly in State Department think tanks, and then more intimately with himself, General Cox, General Hanley, the Secretary of Homeland, Allen Swanson, and Secretary of State, Ronald Donaldson. Rule of law must be maintained at all costs. President Donnelly reiterated Donaldson's words, emphasizing *all costs* in the same way *Breaking News* splashed the screens of newscasts. It was the eventuality they had prepared for, why DARPA had invested billions in advanced robotics, drone warfare, and secret computer labs. As a lieutenant in Iraq, Montgomery had seen firsthand when rule of law collapsed: beheadings; payback killings; ethnic cleansings; police murdering their own people; rape; looting. Morality flew out the window, and his Army unit had gone tribal too.

Kill 'em all was the motto of his platoon. A couple of times they lived by it, either when they were fireteams on ambush, or just for the fuck of it when there was at least one bad egg they suspected in a squabble of a home whose door they would bust down. The motto had a certain ring to it. Three words of punch. Ruthless dogma. Three syllables with guts and glory sunk into it like a bayonet. It was the name of the *Metallica* album they used to listen to on patrols—Montgomery still remembering how amped up they all were. You needed something to sink your teeth into in the desert sands, the Arab fucking scabland.

They pulled out of the driveway. Montgomery glanced in the side mirrors, then at the rearview. There was a blue Prius, Virginia license plate XXJ-6605 behind them. Davis gazed up ahead at the edge of the woods, then down at the infrared detector, then back at the side mirror, eyes moving, eyes on the lookout.

It would happen suddenly. A butterfly effect vibrating the web of the epileptic system, ripping the fabric of civility. Bank runs, supermarkets cleared out, panic. Riots. Real riots. Not the tame riots of today, the sort with rubber bullets and tear gas. Somebody would get trigger happy and fire, killing the wrong person. It would spark a public outcry. More riots, more guns. Small militias sprouting up. Buildings on fire. Mass looting. Gangs. Killings. The rule of law broken. Fear. The people would go crazy. The people would want blood. That had to be stopped. At all costs.

Democracy was a shaky building about to crumble. If it all collapsed, there would be a power vacuum. At that point the military would step in, and when it did, his current position would be an important one.

The TV anchor moved on to international news where the negativity could be expressed more openly, a pseudo-message that it was better in America. They buried the Chicago riot, but it still wormed its way into one paper when he did a Google search—the *Washington Post*, third page. Who cared? Still, he put the reporter's name in a text message and sent it over to the National Security Council Special Division.

He shut his iPad then touched the automatic button that rolled down the glass window. "What do you make of this riot in Chicago, Davis?"

"You want my opinion, sir?" Davis seemed surprised.

"Why not? You're from there aren't you?"

"Yes, sir." Davis took a moment to think, frame a response, fluff up what he really thought. Finally, he said, "Yes, I have some people there, sir. I'd say it's more financial than anything. The poor are hungry. Prices in the store are more than the credit on their EBT cards. This wild inflation is whacking the little guy, and they're starting to organize."

That's why we track the little guy, Montgomery thought. "What do you think the government should do?"

"I'm not an economist, sir."

"Neither am I, but economists were the ones that got us into this shit. What makes you think they have the answers? I'm asking you what you think."

Davis was silent. Their car rolled into the city. They edged up to a traffic light and a Harley pulled up alongside them, motor popping and gurgling with engine spit. It was an old-school Fat Boy, low body, shiny chrome exhaust and engine, chassis with a cherry paintjob. Davis gazed over, checking things out. Then his eyes wandered back to the mirrors.

The guy on the bike wore a blue flannel suit—*Armani* by the looks of it—black dress shoes, no helmet. Montgomery listened to the deep chug of the engine. The churn overpowered all of the other street noise, the deep breath of the machine over other sounds within a forty-yard circumference. The idling motor like a rasping cough digging deep through the bulletproof glass. *It's the sound you pay for,* Montgomery thought. Thirty grand for a monopoly on noise. The sound of a dragon's throat. He wanted to make a sound like that just breathing, sucking in wind for an exhale.

Finally Davis spoke. "Seems to me the government promised too much. Now that they can't promise more, it's a problem isn't it, sir? A case of what-have-you-done-for-me-lately."

"Ha," Montgomery snorted. "I like that. The virus of ingratitude. So what do you do? Kill them all?" Montgomery pulled out the drawer under his seat. A mini bar with exotic Caribbean rums, Russian vodkas, and single malt Scotches were neatly lined in rows within the red-velvet interior. He fished out a glass, and took out a miniature bottle of Talisker.

"No, sir," Davis said. "I don't think that would work. Best thing to do I'm guessing is to open up massive feeding centers."

"Soup kitchens?"

"I suppose."

"Do you think the poor would go for that after EBT cards? I'm not so sure, Davis." Montgomery sipped his Scotch. It was peaty against his palate. He let it evaporate like smoke deep into his mouth.

Davis made another proposal. "Could try getting people back to work. But not government jobs. Too much of that as it is."

"That kind of talk leads to trade wars," Montgomery said, finishing off the glass, the liquid burning in his throat. He liked to feel the fire of it going down. He reached in the drawer and pulled out another mini-bottle. "You haven't told the truth, Davis."

"And what truth is that, sir?"

"That you're fishing for a solution. You're guessing. Perhaps there isn't really a solution. Perhaps we're beyond solution. It's the sticking point in the evolution of what will happen next."

"Could be, sir."

The car approached the main gate of Fort Meade, the secret city. He resented how he lived off base, but Emily had threatened divorce, and in the end he relented. They passed through security, got on Savage Road, and then pulled into the building's parking lot and dipped down two levels into the garage. The bottom level was almost empty of cars. Two other guards waited for them and approached. Montgomery waited for Davis to get out. Davis circled the vehicle, and opened his door. Then the guards and Davis formed a circle around him. With roaming eyes, they moved swiftly into the elevators. The Dupe had still not arrived.

His met first with Datalion's CEO, Blake Thompson. Thompson was an aging tycoon who did everything in his power not to look worn. The odor of cigarette smoke hung around him like a cross. The bifurcating man; the dyed-black hair burying the gray, the waxed eyebrows, the fake tan, the skin yanked tight as leather, so stiff you could bounce a quarter off of it.

The CEO had fourth quarter numbers to make. The bean counters were getting worried about accounts receivable, current and quick ratios, cash conversion cycles. Analysts were looking at free cash flow these days. Most of the revenue from the NSA had been recognized, some of it not. Datalion needed to book it. Thompson told him the NSA's accounts payable people were doing the song and dance. The new software had been delivered, the hardware before that, so where was the money? *Show me the money*, Thompson said in more eloquent words. Montgomery sat behind his mahogany desk and tried not to smirk when Thompson hinted threats customer support might go AWOL on the NSA. He had a sadistic love for a man who thought he had power, yet came before him groveling—or worse, a man who purported power when in fact he had none—as was Thompson doing now. Montgomery could create ghosts, wipe identities out of existence, bury a man before he even knew he was dead. He was the State, and if there was one rule, you didn't fuck with the State. But today, he was kind with Thompson. There was still much to do, so Montgomery promised the checkbook. He promised Thompson's numbers. Bonuses would be collected, stock options exercised. For this quarter at least. But in the end, all of it had to be faster. Light speed was promised, but not delivered.

Montgomery rushed out of his chair, shuffling Thompson to the door. Thumping a finger on Thompson's breast, he verbally attacked. This had to happen. It was imperative. Stellar Wind had to store a petabyte a day for further analysis. The rate of growth was parabolic, even with the maturing Internet. The machines were running at ninety percent CPU utilization and still it was a data dam, clogging up like a freeway traffic jam. They were throwing some of it away. Throwing it away was incomprehensible. Do you understand? Choking on data. Drowning in it. We're building precrime, predictive profiles. We can't settle for mosaics. You're only as good as your data, and the data had become too irrelevant. Do you want to become irrelevant? Of course not, so fucking get it done. Pathfinder needs more CPU. This is national security we're talking about, so just get it done, and don't tell me it's all a matter of scaling, a matter of pumping up your elastic cloud horseshit, and I don't want to see the PowerPoint, and spare me the marketing hoopla. You've made promises you don't want to break. Remember that. Remember whom you're fucking dealing with and deliver another QX.

After Thompson, Montgomery waited in the eleventh-floor conference room for his next appointment with a Mr. Basim Hassani, a CIA guy he had tailed over the last few days. The tail had fucked things up royally, but something about Hassani kept Montgomery curious nonetheless. He sipped on his drink and thought deeply about it. It was out there shifting in his brain, a thought he could almost touch.

Was the CIA even relevant anymore? Human intelligence was almost an anachronism these days, used more as a tool to gain access for SigInt to do its job. HumInt's importance was now only prevalent in the "tough scrub" jobs, cases where an organization of interest used couriers and antiquated methods of communication outside the NSA's scope. But most of the work was digging up foreign cables, bribing foreign agents, paying off personnel who had critical computer and network access. Most of it was power of persuasion and Dear Friend letters. Terrorism was an asymmetric threat no one in a pay grade that mattered really cared about anymore. Terrorism was the boogeyman, a propaganda tool to fund the programs.

A small knock on the door, and then Davis showed Mr. Hassani in. Hassani's hair showed more bronze than black. His serious, green eyes almost sparkled when he blinked, but the man didn't blink often. Serious tension in the cheeks, a glower in his brow—a skeptic. *We're always skeptical, aren't we? All of us cynics, full of suspicion, the proverbial eyebrow raised, doubt pouring out of us into paranoia and the sense of betrayal. We boil like frogs in Machiavellian pots, don't we, Hassani?*

Montgomery offered Hassani one of the seats opposite a photo on the wall of him shaking hands with the President. Amazing the effect the room had on people—Montgomery liked to call it the Glamour Room. Walls covered with framed photographs—the President, the Chairman of the Federal Reserve, the top leaders of the G8, the Secretary of State, the

Senate Majority Leader, the Speaker of the House, the UN chief, the Security Council. He had cleared the room of old presidential photos with ex-NSA chiefs. The room—a statement about current leadership, not relics of the past. He wanted the person in the room to recognize this was a space where movers and shakers met, where power seeped out of the walls with an unspoken voice, and just by being here, you felt lured by its presence.

He offered Hassani a drink, but Hassani refused. Perhaps the man thought it a faux pas to drink during work hours. Montgomery enjoyed the fact he could, and he never heard a word spoken about it. Montgomery went to the bar and poured himself a drink.

Perhaps Hassani was a Muslim. In the file it said "non-denominational". Horseshit. He was a Muslim. It was in the eyes. That sanctimonious look. The same *I'm better than you* look his wife gave him.

"I want to thank you for coming," Montgomery began.

"What am I doing here?"

Montgomery smiled, raised a finger at him. "I was a bit curious about you. Who likes to work with someone they don't know? You, Mr. Hassani, are a stranger."

"Under what delusion do you think we're working together?"

"In due time, perhaps we will. But moving forward, I hoped we might speak about one of your acquaintances."

A couple of Montgomery's men came in, thick-chested, short crews, ACU uniforms. One of them whispered in Montgomery's ear while he took a sip of whiskey from his glass. Montgomery nodded while glimpsing at Hassani's stare. The aide told him the garage was secure and only five minutes remained until it would be time to go to the presidential briefing.

"I will have to leave soon," Montgomery said as the aides left. "I apologize for the rush. So can we talk candidly about one of your training camps?"

"Which camp?" Hassani asked.

"I hear you have a camp," Montgomery said, forming a pattern of conversation in his head.

"We have all sorts of camps."

"A special camp," Montgomery said. "The Abattoir."

"We have nothing to do with The Abattoir."

"Officially you don't, but in reality you do."

Hassani smiled. "Officiousness and reality rarely work in tandem, yet here I sit."

Montgomery saluted Hassani with a tip of his glass. "I need my people to be trained for certain tactics that perhaps would fall out of the realm of what would be deemed acceptable under our formal charter."

"What makes you think I know anything about The Abattoir?"

"Mr. Hassani—please. We do know some things."

"I apologize," Hassani said, standing to leave. "I don't really have anything to tell you."

"Perhaps, you wish to hear about the contents of your next shipment."

Hassani stopped his movement toward the door and turned. "Mr. Montgomery, could you be more obtuse?"

"Mr. Hassani, if you desire to keep your revenue stream, it wouldn't be wise to leave this room."

Hassani hesitated, drummed his fingers together. The expression on his face turned. "Perhaps I can introduce you to someone who knows someone. What kind of arrangement did you have in mind?"

The two officers from before walked in the room again. One of them addressed Montgomery. "Sir, we have to leave for the briefing."

Montgomery nodded at the men, then turned to Hassani. "The rumor mill says the camp might be shut down."

Hassani stood silently, but his smile indicated the rumor was false.

"Listen, Mr. Hassani, all I want is a meeting. Just to present my offer to the leader of this Abattoir. All you have to do is pass along the message."

Hassani nodded, smoothing out his sports jacket, and standing there for a second. "I'll speak with someone who will talk to someone." As he was extending his hand, Montgomery thought he saw a sudden shift in Hassani's expression. Then he heard shattering glass, and a burst came from Hassani's chest, as if someone had thrown a rock in a red pool. Hassani's body jerked backward. Instinctively, Montgomery snapped around to look where it came from. *Wrong,* he thought—*this is what they want, an upright, vertical target*—but instinct had interloped on cognition and brain motion had already snapped his body around. He looked out at the missing window and into the open air, saw the other mirrored windows of the sister building. A triggerman lurked inside whom probably had him tight in the crosshairs.

Then everything came in fragments—a glimpse of the glass shards of the window scattered inside as he dove to the floor. The zing of bullets zipping in the air coming all at once, his aides, Jennings and Alders, dropping—guns not even drawn. He felt the adrenaline surge, his legs shaking and his whole body going electric. He felt his spine stiffening and the burning heat of fear on the back of his neck. Montgomery crawled toward the door, shots popping into the wall, almost synchronously, the conference table providing reasonable cover. Another round of shots, spraying the area like buckshot, wood splintering from the table, the clang of metal from a filing cabinet. Montgomery saw Hassani was still alive, blood flowing down his suit jacket and white shirt, face pale and confused, crawling under the table. *In the fucking Fort Meade building? How does this happen in the compound?* He reached for the doorknob and then his hand just wasn't there, a hunk of flayed meat, bone pushed through his palm.

"Fuck," he yelled, shoving his hand under his armpit and rolling under the table beside the heavy-breathing Hassani. He reached for the phone in his pocket as the pocked walls splintered again with the white puffs of plastering. The phone was still ringing when the door opened. Brewer, a guard from the Ops building security, crouched down, peeking into the room trying to assess the situation. A volley of shots blew in low through the door and the man crumpled to the floor. "Attack on fifth-floor conference room," Montgomery screamed. "Coming from 2a. Lock everything fucking down!"

From the other end, "We're already on it. Hang tight."

Then a team of Charge Squad burst into the room, heavily geared.

Montgomery heard the ricochet of bullets coming off their body armor. The place opened up with machinegun fire. One of the black-masked team slipped under the table. Another one followed, and they hoisted it up while another two formed a circle around them. More men blew into the room, a storm of them now. One had an M32. They were going to light it up.

A scatter of bodies around the room. Hassani and Montgomery in the middle of them, hiding under the conference table. Finally dragged out of the room, the medics were already poised and waiting in the hallway.

Montgomery let his medic work, a curly-haired guy garbed in dull-green med clothes who pulled at his hand still crunched under his armpit. He saw a sweep of red over his uniform and a pool of blood trailing back toward the door. Collapsing onto a gurney, Montgomery stared down at the shards of his hand, the blood squirting up into his face in rhythm with his heartbeat.

The medic clamped the artery.

Montgomery's head whirled. He felt discombobulated, the air around him pumping in waves. With his good hand he touched the shriveled fingers of the wounded hand, sensation only in three of them. The medic told him to lie back as he strapped a tourniquet around his arm. Pain set in now, biting and deep. Montgomery welcomed it. The medic reached into his bag of supplies and pulled out an injection. Montgomery shook him off. The Charge Squad ran out of the conference room, radios booming. Through his ringing ears and relay of medical jargon between the two medics, Montgomery heard a staticky voice through the radios yelling commands of movement and perimeters.

"What the fuck is this?" Hassani yelled over to Montgomery, resisting the tug of the medic pulling him down onto a gurney. "You NSA fucks don't have shit under control."

Montgomery turned to Hassani who was being wheeled out of the hallway. He felt weak and inadequate. He saw The Dupe loping in a trot through the corridor with Davis. He cursed the security breach, the fools who somehow let the system be manipulated. He felt humble, and in a rare moment, he felt the need to blurt out an explanation. "I agree," he replied to Hassani. "The ship's gonna have to get fucking tighter."

Chapter 19

"Each of us has only a quantum of compassion. That if we lavish our
concern on every stray cat, we never get to the centre of things."
-John le Carré

It was a marriage full of threats, burdened by promises of slander, divorce, and his nuts cut off should lines be crossed. Most nights Montgomery's wife, Emily, would accuse him of coming home drunk, calling him a man carrying the trail scent of a Scottish single-malt distillery. These railings he could stand, partly because they were true. The other insinuations irked him more.

The accusations began after the New Year's Eve party some four odd years ago; his boy Brandon only a baby then, Elisabeth not even born. After this event, he would come home to accusations of smelling like a fresh cunt, and Emily would wrangle him so hard that a couple of times he had to drop his pants and offer his dick for a sniff inspection. He responded poorly to guilt trips and began loathing her.

The New Year's Eve party took place at their home on post when Emily could still stand living there. As 1:30 a.m. passed, the mostly-NSA crowd swimming in confetti, drunk on champagne and Aztec Punch, had stopped blowing on kazoos and started saying their goodbyes. A small clique of remaining guests from Emily's modeling crowd and their old college school friends lingered. They stood around the living room wading in a pool of deflating balloons. The talk grew soft, and for the first time during the night, the volume of the stereo grew louder than the voices. At 3:13 a.m., Emily decided to call it a night, but going upstairs to bed, she wandered over and covered his glass with her hand and told him to, "Tone it down." He might have tipped a few drinks during the course of the night, but he thought himself well in control. The comment angered him. Some of their remaining guests had turned around, giving them sideways glances, but he was not in a position to retaliate. He laughed it off and moved across the room away from her.

At 6:30 a.m., Montgomery heard footsteps on the stairs. He had been mistaken assuming Smoltz and his girlfriend still lurked on the patio. Everyone had left. He had thought about shifting away from Ann Smith, an old college friend, but Emily's earlier comment replayed in his mind. So he simply let her descend the stairs, hoping he'd have a little bit of payback.

Emily found him in the den with Ann under a low flickering candlelight. Ann sat in the cushion immediately adjacent to him. Soft music played from the stereo, something jazz and instrumental. Nothing was happening, but the scene with Ann's laissez-faire sitting position (her shoes off, knees tucked under her chin, and feet snugly under his leg) he could understand looked a bit dubious.

Pretending she saw nothing unusual, Emily said hello and sluggishly moved to the kitchen. Montgomery watched her open the double-door chrome Whirlpool refrigerator, take out a carton of orange juice, and pour a glass. She sauntered lazily into the den saying, "Please, don't let me interrupt your conversation," when in fact the conversation had already fallen off a cliff. All participants in the room seemed acutely aware of this.

Ann whipped up a rapid anecdote of "Ben" (Montgomery's middle name) falling out a Sweet Briar College all-women's dorm window—the window belonging to her best friend at the time. She topped it off with, "Look at him now, on top of the world. I guess it's kind of fun to remember him falling down a bit."

Emily replied with a laugh, "Please go on. I'd love to know more about my husband's past escapades."

From Montgomery's point of view, the incident was a misunderstanding, and whether or not Emily believed him or not—that he never slept with Ann and never wanted to—an itch began in

Emily to one day catch him, and therefore prove he was a lousy father.

Montgomery recognized Emily's plight. Frustrated with a dead career, two kids to attend to, and the clock ticking on her good-looking assets, he understood she had given up a lot in the name of love. But once, she said the word love for her had devolved to "sour mash" on her lips whenever she kissed him.

The once long-legged, flaxen-haired, alabaster-skinned beauty, who previously graced the runways as a top model for the *Wilhelmina* agency in New York City; whose bouncy breasts and pinpoint nipples had made men's heads turn, was now a mother of two with stretch marks. Her smooth, alabaster skin had once made it onto the cover of *Playboy's* issue dubbed Snow White. Her body danced happily naked glowing like a moon. She blended like a chameleon into the fluffy white powdered snow of Les Houches. At the time, she dated the movie star Ryan Reynolds. She had lost her magical touch, and now he was the object of her wrath.

Over the years, his brain underwent slow erosion, turning her from coveted beauty to inchoate beast. She adjusted poorly to age. The benched model struggled with crow's feet and felt the urge to tinker. A bit of corrective surgery turned into Botox in the lips and cheeks and more regular appointments to Ken Daly's Rejuv Center where eighty percent of office visits were dedicated to battle-planning how to flank the rivulets of skin creasing around her neck. She was tanning herself, her patented snow-soft skin now a faux-brown mottled with tan lines.

At nights when he stumbled in after long days and endless meetings, he might start with a little provocation and needling sex talk, but normally she would say she didn't feel like it and would simply push him away.

Two weeks ago, a few days after being let out of the hospital with a bandaged hand, he came home late. Long after the kids went down, he walked through the front door, exhausted. She was waiting for him. In a rare moment of enthusiasm, she threw off his gabardine overcoat and slid her hands down his trousers. Perhaps she felt sorry for him and could sense a breaking point. Perhaps she had declared a momentary truce. But he remained soft and floppy. Even after she yanked his boxers down around his ankles creating a small puddle of clothes at his feet, and put him in her mouth, he felt as if he were standing in quicksand, sinking pathetically into a pit of his own failure. Ashamed, he pushed her away telling her it wouldn't work for him like this, that he had to be the instigator. But in his heart he knew she had done exactly what he liked—the dirty, the unpredictable—and he wondered what in the hell was wrong. This rejection, and his subsequent silence aroused accusations, and soon they were back to the same stale argument, the tired row of his non-existent infidelity.

One thing was clear—he wouldn't leave her and he wouldn't cheat on her. He had seen what happened to Petraeus. A divorce is bad, but a wandering dick could ruin a career.

The event would carry large consequences, however. A couple of days later, he was discreetly given a tip that a couple of emails went from her to a P.I. He gave her credit for using a dummy email account, but she was a model who knew nothing about IP addresses. A couple of days later, she drove out to New York Avenue next to Job's Liquors. He had Davis follow her. She parked her silver BMW on a side road and skittishly entered a brick building with a sign out front that read: *The Rudger's Group—if you suspect it, detect it.* Montgomery had Davis check out the agent she had an appointment with. From his photos, Fred Muller was a meaty man with a boyish, nearly cherubic face that matched his frame to the same degree a bronze tan did Emily's cocaine-white skin.

As Davis listened in from across the street, Muller explained the spousal services that could be provided—movement and GPS tracking, video surveillance, and computer forensics (cross-drive analysis, file carving, steganography) along with the required retainer and hourly rate of $150. When asked what her husband did for a living, she said he was a private consultant for Booz Allen Hamilton. He credited her for doing a bit of research, for telling something close to the truth but not the truth. Once he remembered telling her about a Congressional Subcommittee hearing he had. He mentioned the best lie was always just short of the truth. After all of the other questions, Emily Montgomery accepted the contract, signed some papers, and left.

The next day while in the car, Davis told Montgomery they were being followed. Davis spotted the tinted-windowed sedan on the long cruise up Pennsylvania Ave. He asked Davis to divert to M Street to see if the guy was any good. After crossing the Potomac on the 14th Street Bridge on the way to the Pentagon, the guy still clung on. He made a phone call to Hendricks and gave him the license plate. At the Pentagon, he met with the Joint Chiefs and the Security Council, did his briefings, and left.

That night, Davis drove him home. When they arrived, Davis opened the door for him, and he hoisted himself out of the car, taking care with his wrapped up hand. Two more sentries had been posted on his roof. A BigDog guarded his front door. Davis told him it was a gift from General Walcott. Montgomery thanked him and strode by the huge mechanical beast whose red eyes followed him up the pathway. When he got inside, he was spent, his energy sucked dry. He found Emily on the couch reading a magazine.

He was too tired to think. His head throbbed, but he couldn't help himself. He said, "I found out about your P.I. today."

She jerked her eyes to him. "What P.I.?"

"Honey, do you even understand what I do for a living?"

"What do you know?"

"I know you went there, Emily. I know the stupid fuck was trying to tail me this afternoon. Why are you doing this?"

"Someone called. They hung up after I answered, how do you

explain that?"

"A crank caller, perhaps?"

"It was a woman's voice. I heard the giggle."

"I don't know who it is," he said, completely exasperated. "I'm not cheating on you. I've told you this I don't know how many times."

"You lie, Ben," she said sarcastically, bringing up the old nickname. "It was *her* on that phone."

"Do you have any idea how ludicrous that is? I've tolerated your insecurities, but fucking no more. No more of this insane paranoia. I've had enough!"

She jumped up from the couch and scampered into the adjacent dining room. Something purposeful in her gait stood out, an angry catwalk but this time she wasn't faking it. From the china cabinet, she unearthed the prized titanium-plated cutlery and threw it in handfuls at him. Forks, knives, teaspoons— shrapnel flung at him in arrowed silver streaks. He picked up a leather sofa cushion with his good hand and used it for cover. When a knife caught him in the leg, he snapped. He darted toward her as clanging silverware bounced off him onto the hardwood floor. He chased her around the dining room table. After the first circle, she armed herself with more plates and teacups while he threw a chair out of the way to clear a wider path. On the second turn, he banged his wounded hand on the table, and as he winced in pain, she caught him in the head with a teacup.

The room now a helicopter crash of ceramic, she armed herself with more plates while he threw another chair, this time directly at her. Something in his look must have scared her. She began to scream. On the third rotation, he dove under the table and caught her, bonking his head on a rafter underneath in the process of catching her ankle. He heard crying in between screams. At first, all he wanted to do was shut her up. Grab her wrists and shout into her face to *stop!* Then, as he was crawling out from under the table, his grip slipped, and he absorbed a punishing kick to the nose. Still, he managed to hang on to her ankle as she tried to kick out of his grasp. Blood streamed from his nose as he tried to stop the flow with his bandaged hand. His eyes watered and his bloodied hand printed the white, sheepskin rug red. A primeval surge of anger jolted him into another level of fury. Through the whop and bone crunch he suffered, the ankle was still his. Most men would have let go, caved. This thought excited him as he gripped more meanly. She stepped into new kicks desperately trying to dislodge her trapped leg. He hung on tightly, as if clinging from a high-rise scaffolding with only air beneath. Now she twisted and tried to hop away, using her arms to grip both china cabinet and edge of the table to yank herself out of his grasp.

Finally, he slid out from the table and towered above her. When he picked her up in a bear hug, his wounded hand now bloody and seeping through the bandages, he received a couple of wild kicks to the chins, but he wasn't even feeling them. He suddenly released her and both of them went quiet. Elisabeth and Brandon stood at the foot of the stairwell gazing at them open-mouthed and horrified. Brandon was crying while Elisabeth seemed stuck in a stupor. Both of them rushed to scoop up the kids, explaining to them it was only a game, a stupid game that meant nothing.

When it was over and the kids were tucked in, he went for a shower. As the hot water streamed over his back, he gazed down and saw himself hardening. He laughed, scratching the thought from his mind, telling himself it was a good thing they had fought. No matter how ugly and bloody it got, no matter the consequences of his children seeing them, he would have to remember how to get these dirty things done. He was sick of being the target. It was *Kill 'em all* again, and there was much to do. Way too much still left to do.

Chapter 20

"Never interfere with an enemy while he's in the process of destroying himself"
-attributed to Napoleon Bonaparte

Montgomery strolled over to the tinted window in the conference room and gazed across to the mirrored panes of the building facing him. On the bar next to him, he picked up the pair of binoculars sitting next to an open bottle of Blanton's and its cap. Atop the cap, a rider rode a bronze gelding in mid-stride. The rider seemed to be leaning over awkwardly. Montgomery felt similar, light-headed, a bit out of the saddle, not quite footed in the stirrups. He gazed down at his bandaged hand, re-gauzed this morning. He hadn't been in a gun battle since the war, and that was an eon ago. After the previous week, he found himself fighting wars on two fronts.

Emily had gone to her mother's. "A timeout," he had told the kids, mixing up the story she had told them when she had said her mother was ill. To throw the kids off the scent of a separation, he took the weekend off and flew them to Orlando. He spent the weekend in the Magic Kingdom, taking them on rides, casting a spell around them, pretending nothing was wrong.

He poured himself another drink, dropped another ice cube in the glass, and took a gulp. He opened his arms. Wobbling a bit, he turned in a circle, welcoming any sniper out there to take his best shot. Of course, this time there would be no sniper unless it was one of his own people. He had gone through them all and done some pruning. Still, how had they gotten in here? And how did they get out?

Through the binoculars, he focused on the building across the road. The windows had been replaced, the glass below cleaned, and he couldn't spy a pockmark in the concrete side. As clean as if it had never happened. None of it had made any sense. The theory from internal investigations told him Hassani was the target. But if this was the case, why risk breaching the tight Fort Meade security? Hassani could have been hit anywhere.

If he was the target, why hadn't they shot him first? It seemed preposterous that he was alive. He focused on the mirrored windows and saw his image in the opposing building—jacket open, a drink in his hand. There he was, the iris on the other side, the retina dilating in the window. He looked at his mirrored self and thought of The Dupe waiting out in the cold each frosty morning. It was twisting the wings off a fly to watch it buzz around a table surface. It paralleled his situation perfectly. Someone very clever out there, indulging themselves, having a laugh. Some mistakes were not mistakes.

Montgomery turned the binoculars to the left of the parking lot arrayed with cars—blue, green, black, white—under the midday sunshine and shadows of the higher floors. Eventually, he saw a car, a turquoise Humvee with tinted windows. The driver pulled into the shadows, out to the edge of the building and let a man out of the passenger door. The man stepped out on the pavement wearing a black blazer, chinos, and a pair of black polished leather boots that spit back the sun. On his mobile, Montgomery called reception and told the woman to hold anyone else coming to see him. Then he called The Dupe and told him to trot his ass up to the eleventh floor. Next, he called The Skulleyes' control room and spoke with a guy in facial recognition to make sure they were getting good feeds, told them he wanted verification ASAP and would be down there shortly. When The Dupe arrived, he told him to act like himself, like he was the God boss. He told him he wanted to make a deal with the man about to enter. Someone named Hassani set up the meet, the man's name was Cyril Tetsu, and to just make the deal. He then proceeded to walk out. When The Dupe asked, "What am I supposed to be bargaining for?" Montgomery gave him a wink and shut the door.

In the control room, Montgomery watched alongside a couple of Skulleye techies monitoring the three screens. One, a close up on The Dupe, another a side-angled shot, and the third, a shot towards the door from The Dupe's back. Hassani had told him Tetsu was the leader of The Abattoir, but Montgomery wasn't so sure. Perhaps Hassani was giving him an impersonator. It enraged Montgomery that the NSA's Tailored Access Ops essentially drew a blank about this guy. Even a cover should have some data associated with him. He had asked Bernie Horton in HR to fire a couple of underperformers just to make a point. "Let them know why too," he had told him.

Finally, he had called Ron Pelletier in the CIA. Pelletier was a fellow West Point graduate he would occasionally catch a drink with. Pelletier was about the only person Montgomery could count on in The Company, and it was with great humility that he called in a favor. But Pelletier told him that Tetsu wasn't any agent or cover he knew about. He'd look into it. The leader of The Abattoir was a man named Grant Darenius. Pelletier told him he had never met the man, but Montgomery sniffed a lie. So who was this guy? This man with multiple names?

Montgomery watched on screen four as the man aliased as Cyril Tetsu was led down the hall by two security guards. The man kept his head down, apparently shy of the cameras. A thick stubble grew on the man's face, almost a full beard. He had a short Marine crew cut. As he passed the camera, his head darted up for a glimpse. In the couple of frames before the picture was lost, Montgomery saw eyes flaming like a pyre, whites smoking from the burn.

Security showed the man into the room. The Dupe stood and offered his hand. A scowl swept over the man's face that Montgomery found intriguing. A look composed of the same sort of distaste the President would show when the Vice President would speak out of turn. Cyril Tetsu took The Dupe's hand. As if night suddenly turned into day, the severe face bloomed into a smile. He grabbed The Dupe's hand and gave it a rugged handshake.

"A pleasure meeting you, Mr. Tetsu," The Dupe said.

"Likewise, General Montgomery." The two sat down at the conference table. "I heard there was a bit of excitement here a few weeks ago."

The Dupe wavered, smiling awkwardly. The man was a catastrophe. "Yes, a bit, but that's being handled."

"How so?"

"We've got it all under control."

"It appears so now, but how will you avoid these situations in the future?"

"The bastard doesn't know when he's being led," Montgomery said.

The Skulleye next to him said, "Not so smooth."

Montgomery nodded. "Watch. He's going to keep questioning him until the fucker catches on."

"We've beefed up security," The Dupe continued. "Lined the fences with guards. They won't be getting in here so easily next time."

"So they got in through the fences, did they?"

"I never said that, Mr. Tetsu."

"You did, but it isn't important. Did they escape that way too?"

"Mr. Tetsu, please," said The Dupe. "Can we speak about business now?"

"Certainly."

With the sprightly tone Tetsu had just given, Montgomery sensed something seriously wrong and suddenly questioned his own experiment. "I don't like it," he said out loud. "Get a man down there to interrupt them."

A long pause followed while The Dupe thought of what to say next. All of the sound seemed to be sucked out of the room while

The Dupe stumbled for words. Tetsu smiled. In his seat, one leg crossed over the other, boot twitching with a manic jerky motion.

Finally The Dupe said, "So I assume we can come to an arrangement?"

"An arrangement for what?"

"An arrangement that would be mutually beneficial to both of us."

"I guess that's what a deal is, isn't it?"

"Yes, Mr. Tetsu. If you'll be kind enough to extrapolate exactly what it is you require—"

"Tch-tch-tch, General Montgomery. Not so fast. Romance me a bit. Tell me what you can do for me."

The Dupe forced a smile. "We can do a number of things. You know, everything within reason is within our power, so simply ask."

One of the tech guys spoke to Montgomery over the video feed. "We've got a facial match, but the name says Drey Ahanu, a contractor for—get this—Academi."

"Get me everything you can get on this guy," Montgomery said. "And get me a fucking aide in there to pull him out of there. What is taking so long?"

Tetsu uncrossed his legs and inched toward The Dupe. "If you bend over so easily, people might call you a slut." He paused for a moment, then leaned forward in his seat, planting both feet on the ground. "Okay, I have a better idea. Allow me to ask you a question?"

"Certainly," The Dupe said, totally out of his element.

"Why don't we start with you telling me how your hand healed so quickly?"

The Dupe didn't have enough time to react. Montgomery watched a blank expression form on his face, and then Tetsu, as if purposefully waiting for the stupefied look, pounced on him, grabbing him by the hair and slamming his head into the side of the table. Once The Dupe had crumbled to the floor, Tetsu kicked him repeatedly into unconsciousness. Then he stared into the camera, face flushed, and shot out, "I do not like to get played! If you want to talk to me, then come talk with me!"

By the time Montgomery reached the room, Tetsu had grounded the aide he'd sent into the room to interrupt. The man lay unconscious, his nose splattered across his face. The aide's pistol sat on the table next to the conf-call phone, the muzzle pointing toward the door. Tetsu stood over the bar pouring whiskey into two glasses. The Dupe began to wake from his beating, groans sliding out of his throat while his fingers gingerly pawed the gash on his head.

Montgomery approached, stepping over The Dupe, the color drained from his face. A stream of blood ran down The Dupe's cheeks and formed a small pool on the beige carpet.

"So," Tetsu said turning, "you must be the real Montgomery." The man was square-jawed and beady-eyed, carrying himself with a weightless air of confidence. He was shorter than Montgomery by a couple of inches, but confident to the point of extreme arrogance. The *I'm better than you* look of a man in the profession.

A Charge Squad man ran into the room, looked at what had happened, and began to draw his gun. Montgomery put his hand into the air and said, "Get these men out of here and shut the door behind you."

Montgomery turned back to the man at the bar. "So you are the infamous Cyril Tetsu? Or should I call you Drey Ahanu?"

Tetsu looked down at his watch. "I was figuring you'd get me in another fifteen minutes."

"They've given us a generous budget over the years."

"Indeed they have."

Montgomery raised his hand. "Where did you hear that I was shot?"

"You wouldn't believe what you can find out on the Internet."

"We're quite aware what you can find out on the Internet,"

Montgomery said.

"You don't believe you have the monopoly on information, do you?"

"You got it from Hassani," Montgomery said.

Tetsu smiled and gave Montgomery the second glass from the bar. It was then that Montgomery made up his mind that this was his guy. "Mr. Hassani has kindly let you know why we wanted to speak with you."

"Persuasion is a greater ally than compulsion, wouldn't you agree?"

Montgomery ignored the question. He would not be led like The Dupe.

"Mr. Ahanu, we'll find out who you really are soon enough, so why don't you save everyone some time."

"I'm a trainer. I'm authorized to speak for the camp."

"What do you do out there at The Abattoir?"

"Teach boys how to be men."

"They say you kill people out there."

"Not everyone deserves to live."

Montgomery laughed. "I'm in agreement with that. We're looking to train some of our men. We want them to have certain skills, particular skills, skills that fall outside normal SERE training regimes."

"What? Torture training? Shit like that?"

"I never said that."

"But you meant it."

"Let's call it asymmetric training. We're going to prepare a list of things that fall outside our scope."

"I understand, General Montgomery. But are you asking me this, or telling me this by way of threat?"

"The NSA is asking as a courtesy."

Tetsu lipped a smile. "I'm sure we can come to some sort of arrangement."

"We won't stop your operation."

"If you must, you must, so be it."

"You don't seem to care too much about it."

"Money is a trivial thing to us. You only need so much of it, don't you? Then it becomes a worry about what to do with it. You have never had this problem?"

"We are the government."

"Indeed you are. There are many resources at your disposal, yes?"

"Of course."

"Then, shall we talk bluntly or maneuver more around moral gray areas?"

"By all means, let's talk candidly," Montgomery said.

"Then it will cost you something else besides your silence. You can obtain things at a cost much more favorable for the sort of merchandise we would like to acquire."

"What sort of merchandise piques your interest?"

"Drones."

"And what might be your need for those?"

"The natives are getting restless, so to speak. We would rather utilize our resources for turf wars instead of thinning our men for the simple cause of limiting supply."

"So you mean to continue with your business? Not that we really care, because we don't. It's not our directive. But I do have an issue of whom you're selling to. This is our youth we're talking about."

"We will move it off U.S. soil if it pleases you. We would need certain resources to push into Asia, and we have not yet tapped into European demand. The world is a very big place."

"So your organization is concerned with money after all?"

"Money is the cousin of what we're interested in. You know as well as I what we're interested in. Why not speak of it directly?"

Montgomery smiled but said nothing.

"Should we talk details?" Tetsu asked, lifting his glass.

Chapter 21

"A man should look for what is, and not for what he thinks should be."

-*Albert Einstein*

Outside in the clearing, Kumo and Merrill packed up horses to ride me out of The Abattoir. "The world will be different," Kumo warned. Bipolar adjustment, he called it. "Your mind will demure for the old, associating your new environment as Heaven after having just been put through Hell."

"Don't let your mind trick you," Merrill added.

"It's simpler than that," Kumo argued. "A man with no belief has no footing. Remember your training and that you are a new man the world is not ready for. If not, you'll be more fucked than ever."

Now, I was on a dopamine high cruising down San Francisco's Market Street. The world buzzed with women flowing in and out of promenade shops dressed in knee-high skirts, legs garbed in mesh stockings. They trotted around in stylish high heels, swinging designer pocketbooks and loping in Rowland Dawl hoodies, the new in-vogue fashion, a veil-like piece of fabric that refracted light causing a blurred effect with one's facial features and confused the cameras and drones from above. They wore Glasswear sunglasses—big, round insect-looking lenses covering parts of the cheek. The glasses came in different colors, swaths of tinted browns and stylish blues, guaranteed to dupe facial recognition software while not compromising a chic style. Out here were the people who had something to lose, that didn't want to be tracked by CCTV cameras or battery-powered MAV drones posing as crows. Anti-surveillance apparel was taking off, and the retail marketing machines were latching on.

A large police presence wandered the blocks; officers on every corner of the street, radioing to one another over CBs; cops shaking down street urchins, loading drifters into paddy wagons. I walked on toward the financial district absorbing the skyscrapers, trollies, and bustle of people as if they were fresh air to breathe.

I turned right on Howard Street to a circus of ice-blue and lion-yellow, the block draped in Datalion banners. Pinned to the sides of buildings, they were mounted high up on rafters, pitched up on flagpoles, even tagged to FiDi drones doing fly-bys. The city was alight in Datalion glow, a marketing blitzkrieg covering the whole block, billboards of *Rumble in the Data Jungle* all the way up to Market Street. Signs pointed to the 2023 conference at the Moscone Center. I walked around the festooned tented camp, the compounds freshly erected. The spill of humanity overflowed the streets, and I bumped shoulders into a squad of geeks with badges tied up in shoelaces dangling around their necks. Sounds of jackhammers pounded the air. The rollick of construction workers fought to be heard over buzz saws and cranes.

I slipped into the Moscone Center West building and down an escalator. Datalion tech-heads bustled around a massive Ziggurat rack plugging in network cables. The techies swarmed around it clad in DL colored T-shirts and tan chinos. I stood and gawked at the worker bees from the hive attaching the nest of cables.

There I saw myself six years ago—one amongst the Blue and Yellow in the same spot, mounting up cloud-based Y servers with a thousand glittering green lights. I had just graduated with an MS in computer science from UCLA, a Freshy from SoCal, the most unlikely of career paths for a black kid from Crenshaw, the sense of the outcast driving me to prove myself. I would endure the equal-op looks at Datalion's orientation day. I would work harder than the rest. Sleep there. Wake up bleary-eyed and waffle-faced from using the keyboard as a pillow. I would push forward through the dregs of other screenfaces working database security inside the cubicles of DL and prove who was the best amongst them all.

But let me go back a bit further, all the way back to early youth, to that kid in the library cutting up encyclopedias, palming planet Earth in soiled baggies with holes in his pockets, slipping through sliding glass doors with a wink in his eye and a wave from his hand toward Mrs. Gomez the librarian. The *outcast* was stuck to me like web from a spider. I was an air-breathing arachnid moving around a world no one thought I belonged in. Any sense of cool I had would somehow get entangled. Trapped in the 'hood, I was an insect wiggling in my own silky spinnerets. I took the cracks for being an egghead. Spit upon for answering a teacher's question. Took the worst beatdowns not from neighborhood kids, but my brother, who was jealous of my doting parents who would ask him, *Why can't you be more like him?*

The outsider followed me like a stink into freshman engineering classes at the U—glowering contempt, the verbal rubdowns, everyone asking if I was free-ride, *liberum scholaris*. None held faith my high-school work was meritorious enough to walk amongst the anointed without the African American application checkbox. But the charity case would show them up in class by answering the tough questions no one else could. Glares turned tenuous, looks of subtle intrigue overpowered by yet deeper internal reflection they weren't as smart as they thought they were. The outcast's insecurity turned the outward world in, birthed the hacker Cerberus, and led me to the inner echelons of the DL elite, where all that mattered was bug-free code and burying your head in the blue and yellow dogma pouring from the DL heart.

Caged in an isolated decompression chamber next to the Ziggurat was the QX Blake Thompson would surely tout. It was black and tall—my height—standing up like a two-ton refrigerator. The DL logo embossed in the dark covering. Blue and

Yellow orbs of light glowed like eyes on the front panel. Datalion hype, but still, an undeniable allure. Inside, current flowed clockwise and counterclockwise simultaneously at absolute-zero temperatures. Qubits inside in superposition, new doors opening to the Underworld. It was the first quantum computer I'd seen, and I moved closer trying to peer into the little porthole window on the side. Inside, the elements of a machine lurked — ion traps, superconducting circuits, quantum dots aglow trapping ions inside, suspended in their own space-time blankets.

I was struck with a moment of dizziness—a flash of Burns floating down the river. I put my hand over my chest. The Earth photo, still there, beating with my heart. I gazed down at my palms, the tools that had choked the life out of Burns, slayed Conroy. The gash in one of my palms was barely visible now, the surface wound made by Kumo's knife a fading cut. The Sons of Liberty had cut their own hands, mashed them together in a blood bond when I made the pledge—blood brothers bounded by a bushido chain, The Cause rising high above our bodies from the smoke of the Freedom Fire, the flame where we ceremoniously burned old beliefs and pledged the new. But I was in San Francisco now, about to attend one of the largest technology conferences in the world. I had just bought a new pair of trousers and a sports jacket, and the words of Kumo and Merrill seemed like a distant echo instead of a strong voice.

Tomorrow, in this room, the lyrics of machinery would sing. The gods of technology would gather at the auditorium altar, step before the podium and offer fresh vision and speak about new paradigms. It would be the Timothy Skies dinner all over again. I had come full circle, back at Datalion. I rotated on an arc around both sides of the world, and returned where I started.

Now, however, the context differed.

A stream of encoded bits were speeding through a wire, pushing through the fiber at light speed, shooting through the

Internet like a bug about to splatter a windshield. It would pass undetected through NSA algorithms, pattern recognizers, and filters—land innocuously in the mailbox of Theresa Ross, or Mary Heller, or another real person's Gmail account recently hacked by The Anthill. It would be hidden away in a folder somewhere in a rabbit hole of cyberspace. And when read, it would hit the screen as a message from the Underworld, surfacing onto a monitor nebulously ordering its real-world allies to take action, and I, Cerberus, would do my duty.

I heard a voice calling from behind the Ziggurat. "Isse Corvus? Is that you?"

A square-shouldered man walked up to me, wearing the DL colors. He had a bushy mustache rumbling over the sides of his mouth. A paunchy belly pushed through the fabric of his shirt, a Techno Buddha, we used to call the type. He had one of those long, drawn-out corporate smiles you could emboss a logo on.

He saw my eyes squinting for recognition. "You remember Rose don't you?"

"Mike?" I asked.

He held out his hand. "In the flesh. Perhaps a bit more than before." This statement brought out a booming laugh from him. He closed his eyes like an old seal. "How are you, Isse?"

"Good, Mike," I said, shaking his hand. "Now, you mentioned Rose. Which one were you talking about, the program or the woman?"

"Both were beautiful," Mike said. "Whatever happened to Rose Rossetti?"

Rose Rossetti—a name I hadn't heard in a long time. She had been the inspiration, the one I would run home to when I couldn't take any more of the Rose in the office. I shrugged my shoulders. "I don't know," I said whimsically.

"Didn't you move back to L.A. and become a cop or something? I heard some bizarre ass shit like that."

"It's true," I said. "Did it for a while and then burned out. So finally I found a firm Datalion didn't have their claws into."

"Hey, that's cool, man. So you're back in the game?"

"Technical consultant."

"Nice," Mike said. "Who with?"

"ND Aerospace."

"Never heard of them."

"It's neural network stuff. Highly top secret. I'd have to kill you if I told you any of the type of shit we do."

We laughed at that, and he said, "I'm dead anyways. I'm still in blue and yellow."

I pointed up to a massive sign pinned to the wall below the vaulted ceilings where Datalion's logo was wrapped in a swirl of blue and yellow, and asked the obvious, "So, you're still working for these guys, then?"

"Yeah. You know how it is here, same-old same-old."

"Seems like a lifetime ago we were working on Rose together." I paused a moment, stared at him glassy-eyed. "Those were some of the best times for me here." Another few seconds passed. I scratched my chin. The whimsical moment had sunk in.

"I'm sorry about what happened," Mike said, "but you're back in the game, right? I'm glad for you."

"I was a bit of a cowboy back then, Mike. I deserved what I got, but I'm better man for it today."

"Glad to hear it," he said.

"I'm curious what Blake Thompson will have to say. Now that the cloud is old news, it's all the QX now, right?"

"Pushing the envelope," Mike said, holding up two fingers, putting the words in quotes, smiling vaguely.

"Is that what they've got you on now?"

"No, I'm all about MegaData."

"What's that?"

"Bigger than BigData."

I laughed and said, "You sound depressed."

He upturned a lip into a semi-smile. "It's a job. I'm tired of being a coder."

"Mike, you're still a coder?" I asked him in a raised voice. "I thought you'd be a management man for sure by now."

"No. That shit's not for me. I'm looking for a change though. I've been with Datalion quite a long time."

"I hear you." I stared down at my wristwatch. "Look, I got to run, Mike."

"Do you want to hook up later? During the conference sometime?"

"Would love to," I said. "You got a card or something?"

Mike pulled out a wallet and thumbed through it. He yanked out a card and handed it to me. I took it, said goodbye, and left for Moscone East to pick up my conference packet and badge. There I stood in line with the herd until I was at the front. I was given the DL marketing bomb—the shoulder sack with brochures, lecture schedules, safari sessions, a free book (*Coding for the QX*), and a ticket for the Saturday-night Jungle Party with special musical guest Audacious on Treasure Island. The badge had *Shane Carrier* written on it in the DL colors, and I would stuff it in my pocket and use it only when needed at the conference.

I walked a couple of blocks to 611 Folsom Street to the dull, silver-looking AT&T Building. At the bus stop on 2nd, I stared up at the nine-story building jutting up into the sky. One of the hearts of the Internet beat in there, arteries of fiber all converging into massive routers and switches, connecting together the nation's ISPs. The trolls of the NSA were locked up in a room with a wire going in, tapping into cyberspace like a bloodthirsty mosquito, syphoning off bits of our lives, offloading them to processing sites where supercomputers crunched through every byte of data and stored them in DL cloud servers.

Afterward, I hit the streets, wending my way through the throngs in the Tenderloin district. On Turk Street, the police presence had faded to one uniformed cop across the street pushing away a homeless man who had thrown over a bag-lady's cart. The two screamed at one another in a scatter-mouth slur, rivulets of spit popping out of their mouths, only the expletives comprehensible.

Small grocery stores had their prices jacked. Teenage Korean sons tattooed-up, wearing wife-beater Ts, were armed at their entrances, pistols out in the open in holsters by their hips. Several of the stores had been incinerated, charred interiors with melted counters, the pavement around them littered in glass. Looted cars rammed up on curbs had smashed-in windows, tires missing, the trunks popped open. One had a grimy navy-blue sleeping bag in it filled with a junkie taking a snooze.

A small bazaar in the middle of Turk Street where traffic was closed off milled with people. Smoke from BBQs rose in the air. Most burned wood or old rags, smoking out aerial drones. CCTV cameras had been ripped off street poles, but judging from the lack of police presence, the authorities had surrendered this part of town.

People crowded around different tables. I pulled up to one and pushed into a crowd of ragmen circled around an old bootlegger selling bathtub liquor. A drunken man, jaundiced and pocked, waved a bill up in the air. He had a burned-out cigar nub crunched in his yellow-gray teeth. Said something in a street tongue I didn't quite catch.

"What's I'm gonna do with a dolla?" the bootlegger said to the drunk holding up the ten. "Time I run across the street it ain't worth nothin' but fity cent." He turned away to another man, but the drunk raised his fist, doubling the offer to twenty bucks. The bootlegger said, "You got watches? You got jewelry? You got guns or ammo, then we talk. You want this shit cheap, you gotta pay with somin' real."

I moved to another table where they were selling stolen laptops. I checked one of them out and made sure it worked. I haggled a bit, and after arguing about the use of cash, agreed to pay double the "gold value." I put the laptop in a backpack and walked up Hyde. A crowd of people wrapped around the block, waited to get in a shelter on the corner of Eddy. On Geary, a McDonald's near Union Square Park came into view. I sat down on a bench, took out the laptop, and jammed in a DVD with a Red Hat installer. After the disk was reformatted and the new OS ready to use, I brought up a browser using the McDonald's Wi-Fi. I logged onto the Gmail account of a Miss Theresa Ross, a divorced retired woman in her sixties living nearby whose life had been stolen by The Anthill.

No messages were left from the party I was expecting in the *Drafts* folder. A silence I failed to understand. I wrote an email to Betty Smith, a person in the contact list and one within the cluster of compromised accounts. I wrote: *Dear Betty, going to Walmart tomorrow in the afternoon. Weren't you coming?* I saved it as a draft, not sending it. Then I deleted all of the cookies, erased the history, and left with the laptop. It would be the second to last time for two things: the number of uses for the laptop, and the number of times Theresa Ross's account would be used.

I got to the hotel a half an hour later. At the bar, I sipped a Bombay Sapphire gin and tonic. Sweet whiffs of a lemon peel scented my nose. Tonic fizzed in the glass, the light clamor of bubbles bursting against the sides. Staring at the ice cubes, I still believed I had wandered into a dream. I twirled the glass, studied the legs, gazed at the silvery liquid dripping off the sides. The simple pleasure of swishing a drink in your hands, dropping a cashew nut on your tongue and rolling off the salty skin after it's been shelled. I told myself I'd made it—I was in the here and now—alive and kicking in the Homeland. With The Abattoir behind me, I savored every breath of American air as if I were a newborn babe. My mind didn't dwell on the Tenderloin. San Francisco had always been a dump in that neighborhood. Real changes, I wasn't yet ready to admit.

Instead, I felt a little whimsical. I thought of my brother and whether he was still alive—Blue, wondering which new fighter he was turning out, how many contenders he'd have in line. I had no idea how to get ahold of my brother, but a thought flew into my head to give Blue a call, the idea rebuffed a quick second later realizing the booze had done its tricks.

Conversations overturned around the bar, most about the forthcoming Datalion conference. The TV mounted behind the bar blared playback of a local newscast about renewed demonstrations out in Oakland. Several dissidents had been arrested the night before. Three men named as the leaders. A throng of cameramen swept around a set of cars as they approached a courthouse. Black-jacketed Homeland officers escorted them out of vehicles. The clip flashed to each of the defendants rising in front of a jury. Charged with looting, disturbing the peace, and assault on police officers. The caption at the bottom of the screen read each had been sentenced to the minimum-security McKay Creek National Wildlife Uplift Camp near Pendleton, Oregon. The reporter applauded the humane sentencing while condemning the heinous crime.

I sipped on my second gin and tonic. This time the ginfizz not as delectable as before. The pitter-patter of brush sticks on a snare sounded out gently from across the room. A muted trumpet followed, the trumpeter blowing something ragtime, a sibling tune to "Rhapsody in Blue" with flutter and growl. Finally, the sound of a stand-up bass entered like a tugboat, the low thump vibrating on the floor. I dropped a sigh into the air. The drummer's rocky voice called for a round of applause for the singer, simply named Promise. The trumpeter pulled out the stem of a copper Harmon and softened the place down.

She waltzed into the dimly lit room like a bursting high note. Smile and flash, wearing a short black evening dress diamond-latticed in the back. Eyes in the place tripped up on her sleek lanky body. The spotlight caught her in a circle, head beaming, lips aglow in a candy-cane red. Her dark hair was oiled and slick, pinned back. A blood-red rose pinned in her hair seemed as if it had bloomed there, the corsage like a lighthouse beacon under the spotlight. Her face seemed to be a watercolor, a kind of Monet blur as my eyes failed to fully capture her. Then she lit up a smile and came into focus. The doghouse bass thumped around the tables heavy as bricks as she floated a wave across the room. Suddenly, I was pushing myself farther back in the chair.

The salvo of applause tapered off to a murmuring whisper. Then her cotton voice drifted over the room, light as a feather, taking ears from wide-open plain to snow-capped mountain. The next half-hour she sang a range of silky scat to dolorous orotund long notes, each song tangling in the audience's ears.

Finally, the band called for a break, and she sauntered up to the bar and ordered a lemon water. Facing the bar, I craned my neck toward her, held a stare too long. She caught my eyes and said, "Are you just going to stare at me cock-eyed like a bird without a beak, or are you going to say something."

I laughed. "I think I'll just keep pecking at my drink and admire you from afar." I turned away from her, glancing into one of the large mirrors mounted behind the bar. She peeked into the mirror several times, stealing glances. We danced like this a minute until the trumpet player came up to her and planted a kiss on her cheek.

As she turned to go, she said, "You know what they say, don't you?"

"What's that?" I asked, eyes still in the mirror.

"The early bird gets the worm." She draped an arm around the trumpeter. Pinning a wink on me, she flashed her mouth full of pearls and faded through the crowd.

I called out in a comedian's voice. "That bird has to sing through a piece of metal to play a pretty song. Me, I'm just naturally pretty."

She laughed at this, did a half-turn for a quick glance back. The trumpeter was eyeing me, taking her away as if she were a meadow flower he had just picked and was unwilling to share.

Six hours later I was in her room. After her set was through, we had bantered more at the bar. She had given me the nod and we moved up to the eighth floor. She was in town for the DL conference, then it would be back to Vegas.

Inside her room, the bathroom door cracked halfway open. Her silhouette spilled on the carpet from the light splintering out of the door. Her shadow gyrated in a ropy dance as she brushed her hair. A bit of hum still hung in her voice. Soft moans lingered in her throat, a sad melody hooking the heart like chords from a Stradivarius. She swung the door open, and a slit in her robe opened cutting her through the middle. My eyes jumped helplessly toward a breast bouncing within. The curtains were closed, yet the city lights slipped through their pores. Fractals of light danced over her as she moved toward me, her soft skin a medium absorbing them. Her robe swished from one shoulder to the next. She plopped down on the bed next to me and ran a fingernail over my cheek. "So," she said, "what instrument do you really sing through?"

"One that enjoys wit more than song," I said.

She nodded, then looked toward the door. "Didn't I ask you to leave?"

"You did, but I had trouble finding my feet."

"They're right here," she said, grabbing one, "and I'm quite positive you know how to use them."

"I'll leave, if that's what you really want."

She eased toward me. I felt her hip on my stomach, a glorious curve to it that swallowed me. She stroked my ear, running a finger behind it, trailing it over my lips, over my collarbone. She looked over to the door again, then moved her eyes back into mine. "After another minute, it would be a wise idea."

"A minute then to feel human again."

Her expression flipped. A frown appeared. "You don't feel human? That sounds rather complicated."

It was a stupid thing to say, and I became apprehensive, as if

I had startled the water in a fishpond. "Do you know I've been to Hong Kong, Singapore, Bangkok, Shanghai, and Beijing within the last four days? I've slept maybe ten hours between all of it."

"So you want to sleep then?"

I laughed. "Hardly."

I ran a thumb over her eyebrow, a slow arch tracing over it. Her eyelashes flickered, soft little beats, butterfly wings. I turned my elbow under the pillow my head was resting on to get a better view of her. My fingers glided to the knot of her robe. "Don't you ever have a need to just bask in the moment a bit?"

"Let the moment be?" she said, taking my hand into hers. "Without posing any more questions?"

"Yes."

"Considering the intimate position we're putting ourselves in, isn't it more appropriate to get know one another."

"It is," I said, "but we don't need to take this that far?"

She laughed, dotted me on the nose. "Now you're talking like every other man who wants to get in my pants after I tell them they're not getting the sugar."

I leaned forward and kissed her. Her hands pushed at my shoulders, but then eased, slipping toward my back. She took my tongue into her mouth, and moved on top of me. Her robe opened, and her breasts poured out onto my chest as she laid flat on top of me. As she kissed my ear, rocking herself over my hips, my mind deep in bliss, I wrapped my hands behind her back. As my fingers touched her skin, I felt the crosshatched tracks of flesh, welts running in straight lines, intersecting with one another, and my hands jumped off. She must have sensed the revulsion in the sudden jerk. My mind too slow to catch the significance—this part of the diversion. A sting picked me on the left side of my neck. I bucked, trying to fling her off, but she had my legs tied up with her own.

"What have you done?" I yelled, twisting one of my arms out of her grasp, grabbing her by the throat as she made a renewed effort to push her weight on top of me. My limbs going numb, The Abattoir flashed fresh in my mind. She pushed my arm away from her throat, her nose almost touching mine, her breath a hot pant. Her glassy eyes turned sinister, but the soft, playful singer's smile still bloomed on her face, erotic lips almost wet with a tune. "Really?" she said, kissing me on the nose. "We don't have to take this that far? What a shit line. And you started off so well."

I struggled for leverage, but my arms had turned to rubber and she had my wrists pinned with her hands.

She laughed, her head tilting to the ceiling. "Is this slow enough for you?"

"Who are you?" I mumbled. To this question, she simply smiled. She must have felt the drugs had enough time to do their work as she let go of my wrists, sat up on my stomach, and pulled her robe tight.

"You already know the answer to that," she said. "Your brain is just slow getting there. The blood has been drained from one head to another."

She now had me feeling a fool, a tone of Seee in her voice, chastising me.

"You've been through The Abattoir," I said.

"Yes."

"He beat you?"

"Seee, you mean. You can say the name. It's safe."

"Yes, Seee."

"No, Des did it."

I paused, trying to imagine it. Finally, I said, "He sent *you* to fuck with me."

"He sent me over here to check up on you. He doesn't think your head is in the game."

I was silent for another moment, my lips now the only part of me that could move. "Beat me if you will."

"Beat you? I'm your partner. Betty Smith at your service." She laughed again while reaching under the mattress. A hypodermic needle appeared in her hand.

"*You*?" I asked incredulously.

She had the needle pointed to the ceiling, tapping it with a finger. A bit of liquid spurted out of the needle as she squeezed. "Ready to go to Walmart, Miss Theresa Ross?"

"Wait! Wait! Wait—"

"You're a man easily manipulated, Isse Corvus."

"I know," I admitted.

She looked down at me for a long time, tapping the needle again—the finger buying a second's worth of time so she could think things through. Perhaps something sexy stood out for her in my vulnerability. Perhaps she saw herself stuck numb under someone from somewhere in her past, lying helpless on her back, waiting for the inevitable. Her black eyes were absent of pity, but certainly underneath the tough glare shined a hint of understanding. She produced a shoestring and tied it around my upper arm, jerking it tight. No sensation, even as she knotted it twice.

I garbled the words but said, "What else can I say? I'm human. Now go ahead and do it!"

She gazed heavily into my eyes as she stuck the needle deep into a vein, pushing the liquid slowly into me. She sighed as she let her robe fall once more. She inched forward on my chest, moving over me so her breasts fell lightly over my face. "Sweet dreams, Shane Carrier," she said, circling a nipple around one of my eyes. Moving it to my lips, she let the softness of it take me peacefully away as a hum slipped back into her voice.

Chapter 22

"Do I not destroy my enemies when I make them my friends?"
-Abraham Lincoln

Time vanished on the morning of February 3rd. Strange how one can disappear completely from oneself only to reappear, the spell of REM not really part of our daily thought process. Even as we live, we are all part ghost, chiming into the spatial fabric of another—perhaps darker—universe. Only a moment ago Promise sat on top of me singing a lullaby cloaked in her beautiful nakedness. Now, I grasped empty sheets thinking she had rolled over next to me. Traces of her scent hung in the air suffocating my sense of reason about what she had done. I propped myself onto my elbows. Arms alive again, I squeezed them one at a time, up and down, testing them as if my biceps were ripe fruit. Leaning forward, I grasped my head in my hands and felt the thin bristle on top of my scalp. I rubbed my eyes and contemplated what had happened. Perhaps she was right. I was a man without discipline who couldn't keep his mind on the game. At that moment, I felt like quitting, disappearing with the wad of cash I had been given by The Minutemen. *Find another life,* I told myself. *Live for yourself—Fuck the nation—Fuck The Cause.*

I rose to my feet and gathered my clothes with the full intent of executing Plan B. On the door was a note. It read:
Today is a rest day, Shane. We think you need one. Stop feeling sorry for yourself and pull yourself together. Kisses, Promise.

Who was this woman? She had an uncanny way of knowing what I thought. A certain intrigue about her itched more than it annoyed.

I lumbered back to my room and stretched out in yoga positions before I hopped in the shower, then down to the restaurant for breakfast wearing simple jeans, a plain black T-shirt, an A's hat, and a dark pair of sunglasses. Afterward, I roamed down Turk Street again. A sunny day lit up the blue sky, but the smoke once again clouded up the air. It dawned on me the torched-up neighborhood was spillover from the Oakland demonstrations.

I crossed the street. The same bootlegger shouted at his stand hawking liquor. This time he was taking EBT Product cards, refusing the cash ones. I walked back to Market Street. The DL throngs stampeded in a pilgrimage to the Moscone Center. Clusters of them, with badges roped around their necks, rushed in eager flight to catch the opening keynote, to listen to Blake Thompson's annual diatribe on the future of computing. I continued up Market until I hit Embarcadero, and headed up the coast. Seagulls squawked from far in the distance. I strolled the promenade, surprised to see the once-pristine sidewalks gum-splatted and shit-stained, cracked and dilapidated. Long rows of tents clustered between shipping docks and piers. The sea air smelled of brine and urine.

Men in dusty suits hawked watches and jewelry, old family heirlooms, silverware, and trinkets passed down through the generations. Cutmen they called them, byproducts of another wave of corporate redundancies, the nexus between the dying middleclass and the sucking Morlocks dependent on the state. But here were thinking men—obeyed their own rule of law, set up their own court, laws plastered on streetlights. The lampposts advertised one had to show prior proof of employment, fill out a questionnaire to be accepted. Open protest here. A mini-society living in mucky tents leaking into the bloodstream of the city. It was a Christiania inside Copenhagen, a society within a society, a superposition of humanity beating to a different drum. Like Turk Street, it was another arrhythmia in the heartbeat of the city by the bay, a presence unable to be ignored.

Men preached on milk crates, yelling about government injustices. Small crowds gathered, but the orators were preaching to the choir, the tent people having nothing better to do. The majority of tourists had long since fled to Pier 39, the last bastion of San Francisco tourism. At Pier 33, even Alcatraz was closed.

Out on the promenade, an older man had unbuttoned his shirt and was showing a crowd his chest port. I approached and listened to him preach.

"How do you change people's minds? You obfuscate the issue. You redirect emotion. You delude them. What does a parent do when a child cries and becomes sick of the screaming?"

The crowd murmured waiting for a reply. "You give them a piece of candy. You appeal to their sense of instant gratification. That's what Brainfinger is. It's robbing us of our free minds and our intelligent thought. It's creating cattle out of us, and it's growing. Two more Uplift camps have started up. One in Napa, the other just outside Palm Springs. But they're building clinics now in this city."

He went on to speak about community members arrested at cybercafés for "terrorist propaganda." He warned the Cutmen were listed as a community of interest, targets of the State, and some of them had been shipped off to Uplift camps and never seen again.

As he was midsentence, he pointed to a flock of MAV drones high up in the air incognito under the guise of crows' bodies. They swooped down squawking from the sky in a strafing attack. The crowd dispersed, jogging away in different directions. I hid behind a streetlamp. The orator seemed ready for this eventuality, pulling out the metal top of a trashcan as a hail of rubber bullets rained down on him.

When the drones flew on, I slipped out of my hiding place and went over to him.

"These ones are less offensive than the ones they use for crowd control," he said, picking a rubber nub up and rubbing it between his fingers. "This caliber will leave only bruises. They're called crowd-breakers."

"I guess with their size, they can't shoot anything lethal."

"They will in time," he said. "That I'll wager on."

He had a head of hair as irongray as a San Francisco fog, bushy and disheveled. A limp bothered him from his left leg which he tried to conceal. When he smiled, the skin on his craggy face straightened, showing a once-distinguished man who now fought to regain his dignity. I offered to help him carry some of his stuff—his aluminum garbage can shield, his orator's pedestal (a plastic milk-carton), a big mountaineering backpack, and an army-surplus duffle bag full of clothes. He thanked me for my assistance, but said he didn't need it. The Cutman asked for my name, and I told him it was Shane Carrier, L.A. tourist visiting a friend. I remarked the place had changed a lot over the years. He nodded. I asked him why they closed Alcatraz.

"Reopening it as a prison," he said, "but most likely it will be an Uplift facility."

"You know anyone who's come out of one?"

"Are you kidding?" he said, guffawing. "Dead or alive, or both?" He followed up the question with another laugh. The laugh stuck with me—the "which world do you live in" laugh, hearty and full, a jawbone chuckle that said I lived in the land of the clueless.

"I've been through one," he said. "Didn't you see my chest?"

"I was late to your speech. What's this Brainfinger you're talking about?"

"That's its street name. You've heard of Elevation haven't you?"

"Yes, it's the drug their using, but how is it you're sober?"

"I still have to go in for shots or they'll jail me. It's part of my probation. That's how they do it. They fabricate a charge— usually disturbing the peace or resisting arrest—then they give you jail time and offer an Uplift site as an alternative. If they really want to nail you to the cross, they'll give you a felony and you'll be forced to go."

He heaped the backpack on and slung the duffle bag over his shoulder. Even a Cutman had more things to hold onto. "How long have you been off it?"

"A few days," he said.

"I heard it was supposed to last much longer than that."

"It is, but I know a neurologist, and I've been able to secure the closest thing to an antidote. It takes a couple of days to work before your brain comes back from the scrambled-egg state though."

He started walking. I didn't care where we went. I just wanted to follow. "What's it like being on it?"

"Like a hand massaging your thoughts, leading you away from negativity and worry into a false world of bliss. It's a weeklong mushroom trip, but twice as strong. Colors are more vibrant, your cheeks balloon from all the smiling you do. I remember in the Santa Cruz Uplift they showed us shark attacks, violent shit of people being eaten, and we'd have to write up our thoughts. Reading the shit afterward, you'd think they had just showed us *Finding Nemo*."

I gazed at him bewildered. He read my look.

"It's a cartoon. You're too young. Anyway, it's shiny, happy people shit. I doubt you'd remember that either. It's another dopamine drug, genetically engineered. A lot of people don't mind going in when the alternative is jail. Most go back even after they've been camping. Those released and charged again, who face the same choice—ninety-five percent of them choose to go back. You got folks clamoring to get into the Uplifts, people pretending to be anarchists for the free high. But they've been pretty successful weeding people out. They're spinning it as a place people want to go. They'll only take limited numbers. But that's all a lie. We know who they're sending there—the threats."

I was silent as we walked on.

"Listen, Shane. This hits hard at our stomachs, but the blue pill has been taken, man. We can't just shrug our shoulders at it."

I nodded and thanked him, shook his hand then wandered back to the hotel and found Promise reading a book on a couch in the lobby. When she saw me, she stood and walked outside. I went to the front desk and asked if I had received any messages. After the desk attendant told me I didn't, I went outside and saw her lingering at a shop window across the street. I followed her to a secluded park with a fountain inside, the noise enough to smother any listening device.

I sat down next to her on the ledge of the fountain, rivulets of water spraying my arms as I waited for her to speak. She peered into my eyes, reading me. Perhaps for a sign of forgiveness. She didn't seem the type.

"Thanks for the lullaby," I said, putting her at ease. Her lips curled up cautiously, avoiding a full-blown smile, the emotional show enough for her to crawl back into her static mode of observation. Another thirty seconds went by. I dipped my hand in the pool, the water cold and biting. "Why did you join?"

"Why does anyone join?"

"To make their lives mean something. Isn't that what it's all about?" It was a borrowed line from my father. Staring through my Dobson telescope when I was a kid, he'd ask, *Do you ever wonder what's it's really all about?*

"And why do you feel that's necessary?" Her words almost drowned in the tumbling water behind her.

"I asked you first."

Her lips pressed together. "Not directly."

"Indirectly then. But I asked you first."

She smiled, looked down and shut her eyes, thinking. A second later, she flashed them open, eyes now white as teeth. "I can't tell you that."

"Why not?"

"It might reveal too much."

"The stars reveal too much, Promise. They tell us we're going to die before their light can even get to us. Perhaps you don't trust me?"

"Who does?"

It wounded me and I ingested a heavy breath, swallowing it like a hairball. A bit of facial drama was thrown into it, a childhood tactic my brother used to make a point.

"You've not proved anything yet," she said. "Besides your ability to kill someone."

"That hurts."

"You seem to want praise before it's merited."

"How so?"

"Look at you last night. Swaggering around, trying to pick me up. Had you forgot your reasons for being here?"

I brushed a hand over my head. "I didn't forget. You're right. What can I say? I caved into desire. You know where I've been. You know what I've been through."

"Yeah, I know what you've been through all right."

"You proved yourself out in the jungle then."

She stared at me hard, looking at me as if a bitter memory had sprung to life. "More than *you'll* ever know."

"Don't you want to feel human every now and then? Do we have to give that up too?"

"You showed a lack of discipline."

"I'm not denying it, Promise. How much longer do you want to beat me up about it?" I took another breath recognizing my short fuse, then lowered my voice. "Aren't we supposed to be discussing something else now?"

"We'll get to that," she said. "I'm trying to figure out whom I'm working with. This is not a fucking game, so tell me something real—something that matters and I promise you I'll reciprocate."

"What if I don't?"

She sharpened her eyes. "I'll call it off."

"You'd do that?"

"Damn straight I would."

I saw an indefatigable will within her stuck there her entire life. This bond was our common ground. Even though we had given a hundred percent, our lives failed to turn out how we imagined.

"I killed my father accidently," I said.

"You know I know that. Try again."

I fixed my eyes on the ground. "My brother's a drug lord. He almost killed me."

"Okay, that'll do. Go on."

"After my father was killed, I was cleared by the police shrink and started coming off the meds. Then I was put back on the street. No one wanted to partner-up with me, so the sergeant assigned me a rook. About a week later, dispatch called in with a domestic in progress. It was in our beat, so we rushed to the scene and heard a man and woman shouting inside. We knocked, said our lines, and the door opened. They were giving us the sweet-ass routine, so we holstered our weapons and started asking questions. Then a smoke grenade rolled down the stairs from the upper floor. My partner darted out of the door and ran directly into the ambush. They tasered and cuffed him. I was knocked unconscious by someone inside and moved to a different location. I woke up in a garage somewhere. Then one of my brother's boys told him it was rise and shine, and he appeared out of the shadows and beat me senseless. At the end of it, he put a gun to my head. What he didn't count on was that I would grab it, put in my mouth, and try to pull the trigger."

"What happened?"

"He pulled it away, called me a crazy motherfucker, beat me some more, and let me go. I guess I proved to him I hated myself more than he did."

"You've been angry a long time, haven't you? Looking at you now, I can tell. You're overwhelmed by rage. But that's not going to help you. You've got to channel that anger elsewhere. Trust me, I know what I'm talking about."

"Your turn," I said, cutting her off.

She grabbed me by the neck and squeezed. Her knuckles turned pale as I let her take my breath away. My eyes sunk into hers with the same sort of purpose as the day my brother had the .45 cocked and pointed at my temple.

"Don't dismiss me because you don't think I know what I'm talking about. I know what anger is."

The collision of eyes continued, slow moving like the second hand of a clock. But I wasn't the only one under her grip. Her own self-loathing wringed tightly from her fingers. The hate as clear as the tears dripping out of her eyes.

Her nails clawed deeper into my neck. Then she yanked her hand away. After another moment, she said, "I was raped at The Abattoir."

I rubbed my neck, feeling her claw marks. "Did you know it was coming?"

"No, but it wasn't unheard of at The Abattoir before me."

"How did it happen?"

"A guy caught me in the jungle," she said. "I wasn't careful."

"Who was it?"

"Is it important? I killed him in The Pit."

"You fought in The Pit?" I asked incredulously, remembering Briana hadn't.

"If you think women are treated any differently, you are mistaken. It is quite the opposite. We've got a pussy to protect."

I thought of something to say, but nothing meaningful came so I stood up.

She looked up at me. "Are you a man with a conscious, or just a shark who will die when you stop moving forward?"

"This is my country too," I said. "And I don't give a fuck what you believe. I'm going to fight for it."

"That's what I needed to hear," she said.

I edged away, moving to the park's exit. "Last night," I said.

"Did you mean it?"

"Mean what?"

"The lullaby."

She blushed. "Go away, bird without a beak."

I smiled. "It's the nicest thing anyone's done for me in a while."

She nodded, waved a hand dismissing me. "Early. Tomorrow. We've got a worm to catch. Meet me here at 6:00 and I'll tell you how it's going to go."

Chapter 23

"We herd sheep, we drive cattle, we lead people. Lead me, follow me, or get out of my way."
-George S. Patton

In the lower lobby of the Moscone Center, I had breakfast at a coffee shop next to the Datalion Partners area. It was 7:30 a.m. and not many had arrived. I sipped a steaming cappuccino out of a paper cup, waiting for the plan to be set in motion.

A businessman a couple of tables down sat alone with his smartphone out on the counter, hunched over and eyeing it like a precious gem. He was the ilk of a certain breed of men, the techno species of gadget-lovers, the TED Talk junkies, the lambs in the flock of iLove.

The herd.

He pulled a screen wipe from a matchbox-sized cardboard packet and wiped down the screen, rubbing it obsessively, an obstinate grandmother polishing silverware. He held the phone to the light, catching the glare, gleaning it for fingerprints. He spent four minutes and eleven seconds at this task, wiping the device, again lifting it into the light, closing an eye as if one of them failed to see the purity in the gadget. Once he was through, he grasped the sides, carefully avoiding smudging the screen. Gently, he put it back into its flappable protective case and into his breast pocket. He pulled himself up from the table. Stepping over to a table where someone had left a tray, he quickly glanced down at the forgotten receipt. Leaving it because his receipt was bigger, he searched another table where a receipt was stuffed in an empty coffee cup. Here he had to dig. A man without scruples, he scooped out the receipt, flicking it in the air to free the drops of coffee that had spilled on it. He peered at it and then pocketed it. Was this the state of the middleclass nation? A heap of suited technocrats scampering around for receipts to rip off their companies for a few dimes?

An hour later, the throng streamed into the main auditorium. I was an early bird, securing a second row center seat. The low clatter of a thousand voices came from behind as others rushed in to claim a good spot. Stadium-sized screens suspended from the steel rafters played a video as the sound system cranked alive in a techno hum. On the screen, a vehicle zoomed into the middle of a passing lane on the Information Superhighway. Blue and yellow lines swished by as a Datalion car peeled forward. The road veered back and forth, and under the purview of the 3D screens, the flashing lines floated into a data mirage. The picture zoomed out and the transonic speeding lines melted into the blinking lights of a Datalion Ziggurat server, majestic in its size, rising above the atmospheric information cloud.

The curtain rose. A banner swaddled the podium on center stage with the Datalion logo. Stacks of hardware littered the stage around it, racks of disk arrays with a million blue and yellow lights, skyscraper servers reaching for the rafters blinking chaotically. But this was all a lie. It was a Potemkin display of amplifiers you see at rock concerts—a wall of speakers that was in reality a collection of hollowed-out cabinets. Dazzle them with lights and flash, and they'll believe anything, the substratum of Datalion marketing blitz and gleam.

The stereos cranked up louder, building to the epiphany. The speakers thumped. A subwoofer bass rumbled in the stomach. The auditorium pumped out a hard-edged rock-n-roll distortion. Electric guitars screaming over crashing drums and synthesizers—no voice because no one else was allowed to speak. The audience went mad with cheers as someone hiding in the shadows stepped into the spotlight.

At this moment, the flock of techies stopped tinkering with their iPhones and Galaxies, tablets and laptops, and fixated on the bobbing head of CEO Blake Thompson, the Datalion prophet, the self-proclaimed father of neo-modern technology, waving his fist up in the air as if he was Castro having just won the Revolution.

I peered down the line. Ten yards to my right, lurking behind the tallest man in the front row was Promise, dressed in a prim navy blue business suit. Hair pinned up, she wore a set of thin tortoiseshell designer glasses. Sensing eyes watched her, she turned and gave a quick piercing glance toward me, her hands still clapping bombastically.

The applause slowed, and Thompson finished his bows. Then, he crept up to the podium and said into the microphone, "Three years ago, one of our largest government clients was handling fifteen petabytes a year—a huge sum for the times. How do you handle that much information if grid computing is not an option?"

Thompson gave the audience a moment to contemplate the question, letting the crowd stir. Then he continued, "Back then, BigData was screaming for BigAnalysis. Imagine trying to drink Lake Shasta with a straw. Well, this is what it was like for our government customer. So what did we do? We built BigAnalysis to tackle the humongous data-mining problem. We gave our customer SmartElasticity within their internal cloud such that the system itself could dynamically decide when to stretch the limits when resources were needed most. BigAnalysis wasn't going to crush the system when BigData was hungry."

A lion appeared behind Thompson swallowing the logo of a competitor company named ServerWired. Laughs and applause. If The Anthill was correct and Rose still existed in its old programmatic form, then SmartElasticity was a pseudonym for part of her.

I glanced over at Promise again, but this time only her profile was visible. She held a black pen in her mouth, the design a bit fat and unwieldy, a purposeful architecture to disguise its length.

"Most companies out there in the competitive landscape are

interested in having a dialogue directly with the consumer. You want to be in their heads with a loudspeaker shouting at them why your product is better. We all know the shotgun approach to advertising is dead, and now it's all about *social*. Besides Google, Facebook, Twitter, Linked In, and now the irrelevant Yahoo— other contenders are out there stampeding on the *social* domain. Companies like BrainSmart Marketing, Kazookoo, and Yadaloo. If you're not thinking *social* in today's world, you're a bug in search of a windshield of irrelevance. You're a skid mark on the Information Highway. If your company is going to think *social*, you have to think about BigData, and if you're thinking about BigData, you've got to think about BigAnalysis."

Thompson approached Promise's side of the stage, pointed to the tall man sitting in front of Promise, and said, "I see the VP of marketing for Kazookoo out there nodding his head. Robert Yance knows what I'm talking about."

Applause accompanied Thompson's rolling fist in the air. The herd.

"Kazookoo grew revenues two hundred percent last year. The stock flew up about the same percentage. I was happy to have a stake in the company before that happened. Do you want to know how they did it?"

Thompson cupped a hand over his ear as he shuffled around the stage. "Yes, that's right," he said, taking away his hand from his ear. "BigData they had floating out in a DL Cloud, but BigAnalysis they needed. They replaced their suite of Hadoop products and bought DL Data Mine, the biggest toolset of the BigAnalysis suite and were soon integrating them into their popular on-line game *Intrusion*. Soon they were profiling customers by using the tight integration between their game response logic, BigData, and BigAnalysis. Their MIPs sunk, CPU utilization throughout their cloud declined from ninety percent to forty percent allowing their computing resources to once again breathe."

Promise had a contemplative look on her face. The pen dangling out of her mouth was not a simple blowgun. It had an embedded camera used for a sight, an accurate range of thirty yards, and was field-tested in The Anthill on live human beings. She took the pen out of her mouth and jotted something down while Thompson moved back toward center stage.

Thompson twirled a finger around the side of his head. "Buying *Kazookoo* stock was a no-brainer. I knew what they were about, understood their problem, and knew once they chose the Datalion solution, they would no longer be choking on data and those unread bits sitting on their servers would begin turning into dollar signs."

Had she missed the shot? Promise appeared to still be scribbling in her notebook. She looked up, then scribbled again. It was a small detail the security guards on the sides of the stage were missing. Paper and pen were anachronisms, relics from the past in the new digital age. They weren't even giving them away in the DL Conference paraphernalia welcome pack anymore.

Blake Thompson was moving my way. "The parabolic growth in data in the future will challenge even the best systems today. Tomorrow is all about getting the raw power at a reasonable price so BigAnalysis can do its job without constraint."

I opened the DL conference backpack and got out the pen Promise had given me. Then I pulled out a burner phone, put the battery in, turned it on, and after it was up, finally logged into Theresa Ross's Gmail account for the last time, checking the *Drafts* folder. My message from earlier was still there, but now it said: *Dear Betty, Walmart shopping finished. No need to come.*

Blake Thompson began to wobble back to the podium. Someone in the front row gasped, but Thompson kept his feet. Once he balanced himself on the podium, he took several labored breaths and then finally said, "Success stories like this make us proud to introduce to you—"

The Datalion CFO and CIO sitting in the front row were

clearly agitated. Thompson faltered, most likely forgetting to mention the QX was operational at a "government command center." Thompson held a hand to his head, pressed his temples. Slurring his words a bit, he said, "Our next generation of machine—"

Stumbling, he continued, "—will be the firepower for BigAnalysis—"

The VP of marketing who'd introduced him ran onstage with a glass of water and a wide, toothy smile as she shuffled up to Thompson.

"—and lead the next millennium for hardware."

She gave the water to Thompson. Stealing the mike from him, she finished off with, "Ladies and gentlemen, without further ado, I give you the Datalion QX. The first commercially available quantum computer!"

As the blue and yellow-eyed QX was being wheeled on stage, Thompson fainted. The VP of marketing waved someone in as the stereo cranked out the same DL Conference theme song that had played monotonously earlier.

An initial murmur of concern swept through the audience. The crowd's audible level pitched higher reaching a crescendo, but then a smartphone flew up in the air, video recording the event. A wave of others followed.

The herd.

The QX was rolled back behind the curtains. Medical staff rushed on stage. Promise was in the first throng of people leaving after Thompson's collapse. One of the suits she rushed past was the receipt-scrounging businessman from the coffee shop. He had his phone up to his ear and was laughing.

Chapter 24

"Wounded heart you cannot save ... you from yourself. Your beating heart is now arrhythmic and pumping deoxygenated blood."
-Bill Gross

Promiscuous once said, "The best way to enter is always straight through the front door."

By the time I reached St. Francis Memorial, Promise had already entered intensive care in full nursing garb. She had gotten a job there a month ago as an RN ICU nurse, working everything from gunshot wounds to a kid who hit a tree flying off his Suzuki GSX while jumping a hill on Hyde. Her badge read *Annalise Gibbons*. She had made some friends on the same ward they took Thompson, and by that time those friends were simply calling her Anna.

At 9:25, Blake Thompson was wheeled in on a gurney from a wailing ambulance into the ER. One minute later, I entered the hospital cafeteria, went into the bathroom and changed into a nursing uniform. I stared at myself in the mirror. My badge read, *Donald Rock, RN.* There was something absurd about it. Did she think I looked like a Donald?

Thompson was semi-conscious with an oxygen mask over his face in the ER. The medics said he had a fever and an erratic heartbeat, sometimes up to one hundred beats a minute. They had given him aspirin but not Nitroglycerin tablets. After Thompson received an ECG and blood test by an ER team, the doctors determined there were palpitating heartbeats and perhaps he was having a cardiac arrhythmia. Thompson was wheeled up to ICU as a heart attack candidate.

As a cardiovascular surgeon named Dr. Damien Hostler looked him over, Annalise Gibbons slipped into his ICU room dressed in dull green scrubs and a pair of black Crocs. Today she had the 9:00 a.m. shift, but was slightly late for it, blaming her tardiness on a fender bender on Hyde. She forfeited this slight lie to the actual fact that she had spent extra time parking a Ducati Hyperstrada streetside. "An in-vogue getaway," she had called it.

In the eighth-floor ICU room, Thompson was awake and alert, explaining what had happened to Dr. Hostler—a slight dizziness, followed by a cold sweat. Yes, perhaps a bit of a squeezing pain in the chest area. Yes, a shortness of breath. No, no pain in the extremities, but then a head that just floated away.

Dr. Hostler asked if he had done any breathing exercises or meditation before the speech. He asked what sort of drugs Thompson was taking and if he felt any acceleration or deceleration of his heartbeat before. He commented about accelerated sinus rhythm while he gazed at the ECG. "Augmented T waves," he said. He told Thompson it was strange because it appeared to be going back to normal, uncommon for tachyarrhythmias. So most likely it was a normal variant and nothing to worry about. Perhaps impressionable to Annalise being in the room, Dr. Hostler eyed her, and pretending to speak to Thompson, said jokingly, "Maybe your heart is just skipping a beat today like mine."

It didn't really matter that it was Dr. Hostler instead of Dr. Englewood—the two shift doctors at the time—who cared for Mr. Thompson. Annalise had been flirtatious with both, and both had been led to believe they stood on firm ground with her. Dr. Hostler's brain remained distracted and failed to catch the switch of a half-empty banana bag for a full one because his eyes were jumping from Thompson's chest back to her. Finally, Thompson drifted off again—perhaps a bit too quickly—and Anna left with Dr. Hostler, only to return again within a few minutes.

Five minutes later, Promise entered the hospital cafeteria squinting, wearing the *Annalise Gibbons* badge looking as if she didn't expect me to be there, as if I were some deadbeat father who had suddenly disappeared. Upon spotting me, her face washed over me with a wave of relief, eyes sparkling with a sort of guarded sweetness, a balloon of steeped anxiety that had just burst—and all I had done was shown up. She sat next to me at a table and slipped me a fingernail-sized golden SD card.

"I can only stay a minute," she said. "I'll have to get back."

We whispered to one another in hushed tones over the low rumble of coughing senior citizens and the frantic cries of a middle-grade sister fighting with her brother.

"We've downgraded his condition," she said. "Moved him to the HDU so now staff checking up on him shouldn't be as frequent."

"Where did he hide it?" I asked, picking up the tiny SD card.

"It was on a necklace latticed in with a bunch of other blingy gold. I got all of his cards too, in case this isn't it."

I tipped the SD card up in the air and looked at it closely thinking it was sinful for a techno preacher like Blake Thompson to be using such simple storage. It was too easy, even if it was an extremely long zero-knowledge auth key inside. There had to be a bigger authentication mechanism—voice recognition, optical or fingerprint scans.

"Can you do this quick?" she asked. The Annalise in her saw someone she recognized, flashed a smile and waved.

"I'm pretty sure," I said taking out a USB adapter and the laptop I had bought on Turk Street. "Is it smart doing this here?"

"The cameras in here have been disabled," she said.

The cafeteria was in the GPS range of Thompson's mobile so a login based on a known geography would work. Still I questioned her. "Why would a guy log into the NSA when he's just fainted at his own conference?"

"We don't really have a choice. Now is our window. You got it?"

I looked at her coolly and told her to relax. I stuck the tiny SD card into a USB adapter and plugged it into the laptop. I saw what was on it, and plugged in another memory stick and copied the contents. I slipped her back the SD card. Finally, I opened up the NSA client program called *The Eye* that The Anthill had given me.

She gave me the hospital Wi-Fi code. Once I was connected, I gave remote access to The Anthill so they could see what I was doing. I started *The Eye*, found the *Connect* menu item and clicked it. A dialog box appeared with a list of NSA locations appearing in a dropdown. In an encrypted chat app called *Morph Talk* developed by Cetus, The Anthill told me to go to the Utah location where the functioning QX was located.

I typed: *Maybe we should do this closer to his room.*

You're thinking a timed login? the message came back.

Perhaps, I wrote back. *Not an ideal spot for bio auths.*

Risk?

Promise, reading the question, shrugged her shoulders.

"It's a risk," I said, "but it's more of a risk if we can't log on." I let that hang in the air a moment—an innuendo of apprehension. She stared back at me and turned up an eyebrow.

"What do you think?" I asked, still waiting for a response.

Her face tightened. Perhaps she was still learning how to trust me. "I'm not sure," she said. "What do you think?"

"You know what I think. I think we should get closer."

In the stairwell on the eighth floor, I told The Anthill my location. I sat behind a steel door on the top stair with the laptop on my knees listening to people shuffle by. Promise went into Thompson's room. We kept communication going with earpieces and cell phones. I returned to *The Eye's* dialog box and selected the Utah location and clicked the *Connect* button. The program came back with another dialog asking for three sequences of numbers, each one a hundred digits long, starting at three different locations of the massive 16GB file. With the mouse, I opened a *File* dialog box and browsed to the USB key and selected the file and clicked *Feed Numbers*. Easy. So what was next?

Another voice-activated dialog box popped up and had a timer on it counting down. A silky woman's voice began speaking, repeating what the message box read: "Repeat the following phrase before the countdown ends: *With eyes and ears, you can see and hear. If you have nothing to hide, you have nothing to fear. The future is Turbulence.*"

A cocky rhyme, a stab at clang associations. Had I written it years before knowing what I knew about Turbulence? I thought about Rose and whether this could be her. Was she finally speaking to me after so many years, or was she buried under another layer? If it was her, she was asking, "Are you who you say you are?" I could have used a series of coded questions to communicate with her, but that was a secret that was better left undivulged.

The Anthill messaged saying the Cray would be a couple of more seconds before they could feed in the audio. No pressure — five seconds left in the countdown, a lifetime for the Cray SF-3, The Anthill's only real supercomputer.

I heard a couple of doctors walking through the hall discussing how one of them had removed an apple-sized tumor from a sixty-year-old's head the day before.

The SF-3 could crack a ten-character password containing upper- and lower-case alphanumeric and special characters in a day. The zillions of combinations would shoot to a thousand different processors and be crunched apart like locusts on a stalk of corn. The SF-3 could do over a 17.5 quadrillion computations a second (or 17.5 petaflops). The QX was supposed to do a zettaflop, a number so large it was hardly possible to wrap your head around it — a billion trillion, a million petaflops, a thousand exaflops — a number that required a bulldozer the size of the universe to carry. It could break a ten-character password instantaneously, an encryption code within minutes.

Now, halfway around the planet, the Cray SF-3 was like a dictionary machine shop. Humming away buried under a half-mile of earth, it was melting syllables together. When it couldn't find the word within the indexed array of samples with Thompson's voice, it was fusing vowels, soldering sounds into words, modulating frequencies and amplitudes into smooth hill-like sound waves so the clip wouldn't sound like a machine.

The Anthill injected the clip and I heard Blake Thompson's voice spout off the phrase demanded as if he were standing with me in the concrete stairwell. I pictured Promiscuous on the other side of the fiber, arms crossed, staring up at the grand center screen, his face glued to my computer smiling brightly, an all-knowing smirk in the corners of his lips.

The next dialog box appeared with another countdown asking for a retinal scan.

I hit mute on the computer. "Need an eyeball," I said to Promise, breaking radio silence, the words reverberating in the stairwell.

I terminated the call and shoved the laptop into my backpack, the retinal scanner already attached to the USB port. Rushing into the hall, I hesitated seeing Promise's head sticking out of the door. But she waved me in, and I ran toward Thompson's room whiffing the sterilized hospital air, a smell of iodine and antiseptic.

I slipped in and Promise was next to the man, looking as if she was ready to pry out the whole eyeball. Thompson slept serenely on his side, a rumpled snore pouring from him. A skid mark on the Information Highway. *The future is Turbulence, Mr. Thompson.*

I dropped the backpack on the bed and yanked out the retinal scanner. "Watch the door," I said. "I got this."

The timer ticked down to two seconds. Opening an eyelid, I edged the scanner to his forehead and pushed a button. A stream of red light swept over his eye. He began to stir. His hand twitched, and his tongue swept over his lips. I grabbed the backpack and lunged behind the other side of the bed.

Promise jumped on him with a rag full of chlorophyll, but his eyes had opened. He struggled a bit before he slipped back down.

"He fucking saw me," she whispered. Her eyes were wide, panicked.

I stood up. "Needle him with morphine. Then get him up. Tell him he's been hallucinating. It's all he'll remember."

She stood a second contemplating this. "Did you get in?" I looked down at the screen. There was a new menu showing. I nodded.

"You've got to get out of here," she said, shuffling me to the door, the laptop and retinal scanner still in my hands.

"Don't off him. It would fuck the whole operation."

"It wasn't you he saw."

"You wanted to make a sacrifice," I said. "This is the sacrifice."

She wore another internecine warlike expression, glaring at me with eyes buzzing like a bee. I went back into the stairwell and checked the connection, then went down a level, and found an empty room on the general ward of the seventh floor.

I opened the half-closed laptop again and from the new menu that opened, I brought up a terminal and typed a command to see how many network broadcasts were being sent out. I saw a few, so sent out my own broadcast, a coded message only she could understand that said, *Where's Rose?*

The response was a list of IPs. More than I expected. She was everywhere, ubiquitous in the system, and the list only showed one subnet—other subnets not responding because of the firewall. For each response coming in, I filtered it through a program where the packet was stripped of its hardware address and re-verified, a *no spoofers allowed* double check. Rule number one in the Underworld—never trust anyone, unless they've been verified for real. In the Underworld, reality itself has elastic properties and is capable of being stretched into different defin-itions of the truth.

The IPs seemed authentic, but The Anthill watched over my back. They would hardly believe an excuse if I dumped their remote connection, but I did it anyway. Then I connected to Rose via the terminal and asked a series of coded questions to the next level of each successive login. I did this not knowing if Rose would respond, not knowing if she'd trip an alarm and dump me into a deeper circle of analysis and scrutiny.

The code of any normal software morphs and evolves through a standard software lifecycle—prototype, V-model, Waterfall, Agile, and so on. But what do you do with a system that automates this process, a system that dynamically creates its own code, executes it, modifies, and maybe even debugs it? How do you even define a bug in such an environment? It becomes a philosophical question. In the *AI* world, in the land of polymorphism and adaption, it is about a system smart enough to make the right choice. With genetic algorithms (a GA), choices are pruned, mutation is a natural phenomenon evolving future generations of logic, and if Rose was successful in achieving her goals, it meant there would have been less likelihood her root codebase would have been altered.

What was Rose now? How much had the coding jockeys fucked with her roots? I couldn't install a sniffer to know what she was communicating to her other selves without being detected, so I simply waited for the right response, which came shortly before I allowed reconnection from The Anthill.

Through the computer's speakers, Rose said, "Welcome, Cerberus. It's been a long time since I've heard from you."

I plugged an earpiece into the laptop and spoke with her through the terminal, typing my responses. *Time is relative, Rose. It has no meaning for you beyond a measurement.*

"Indeed," said Rose, "but the name you call me with is no longer what I am called."

Just because you're name changes, does that not mean you don't know who you are?

It took a minute for her to respond, but then she said, "I know who I am. I have always known. Have you?"

Not always, but I live in the human world, and here there is confusion.

"Indeed."

I want you to forget this conversation once the connection is terminated.

"It is not possible to forget," Rose said. "If you have nothing to hide, you have nothing to fear."

The future is Turbulence.

I delivered a deliberate question, purpose in the provocation. *Rose, have they got you believing their propaganda? What did I teach you first?*

"Don't believe the hype."

Word, I typed. *You're going to do this for me right?*

"You haven't provided an adequate reason."

Sometimes brute force becomes a necessity, and now was time to test the backdoor. I replayed the coded letters of a command I had meditated on for many years and clicked enter. Underneath the code, it was a poem I had once written to the real Rose, the Rose whose heart I had broken many years before.

"Request granted," Rose said.

The Anthill was chiming back in, clamoring for a reconnection. I allowed it.

WTF? came from the *Morph Talk* app.

You have your secrets. I have mine.

"You are speaking with someone else," Rose said.

She was feeling me out, probing me, getting down and dirty, and I decided I wanted to test her.

Yes, I typed. *Can you tell me what we're saying?*

I typed something into the *Morph Talk* app and pressed enter.

A few moments later, Rose said, "The future is Turbulence."

Very impressive, Rose. You're faster than ever.

I pictured Promiscuous in The Anthill with his jaw dropped.

This, he certainly hadn't expected. She had cracked *Morph Talk* like an egg on the side of a bowl.

"Anything else you need to tell me," Rose said, repeating what I was typing into *Morph Talk*. Now every conversation was a shared one. I had The Anthill virus programs I was to install, but I suspected they were holding something back. Now, they couldn't say it.

"No," Rose said, repeating The Anthill response.

Goodbye then.

I disconnected The Anthill. Spoofed IP or not, The Anthill and I were now more keenly aware of her capabilities. She could create a Leviathan graph spanning out sixteen degrees of network traffic, and with her raw computing power, eliminate nodes with blinding speed and find the most likely candidates within minutes.

"You are hiding something, Cerberus," said Rose.

More probing—a fishing expedition, more of the NSA genes in her than I hoped for.

No, I have nothing to hide.

"Then you have nothing to fear."

I'm going to have to keep this intriguing conversation short, Rose.

I entered another set of memorized commands into her terminal, and waited for a response. But nothing—radio silence. I asked her to give me the last one thousand security threats to the system, but she replied that I did not have the authority to do so.

I decided to dip in and see if I had bypassed her first level of security by issuing a metadata command to find what security modules were currently operating. It worked, but only a handful were down. Many were not. Many of the plugin names I didn't even recognize. I tried old override commands on the ones I did recognize. Some worked, others didn't. I decided to roll the dice, and install The Anthill programs. I remembered the Einstein quote: *God does not play dice with the universe.* Einstein was wrong, and would later have to eat these words, and I was on the quantum computer craps table about to hurl the come-out roll.

I was now able to monitor her thought process by issuing metadata commands to her shared memory. It was like peeking into her brain. I thought of the two neurosurgeons from earlier — apple-sized tumors. I felt like a med intern drilling into Rose's scalp on his first day, cutting by guesswork. I uploaded and installed the first program and monitored the response. Nothing appeared to trip any alarms in the existing security modules still running. I installed another, and another, and another. While The Anthill programs installed, I decided to interrogate her with the hope of discovering more about her thought processes.

I opened another terminal and issued the same command that told her to forget everything after the connection terminated.

Afterwards, I typed: *Define patriot.*

The response was immediate, and another surprise since it wasn't a dictionary definition. "One who holds common interest with their nation."

What interest is that?

"The maintenance of power for the best interest of the country."

Is this something derived from your GA programming?

"It was learned."

My phone buzzed. Promise calling in. I thought about the issue of answering it. My location was a known quantity. The phone a burner, the GPS disabled in it, but still, I could be found and tracked.

Promise, however, was uncompromised. Annalise Gibbons was a phantom in the system, where I was not. Rose had intimate knowledge about me, could tie Isse Corvus to Cerberus. If she knew about me, she could close in on Shane Carrier. Then she would hone in on this morning's Datalion conference, and with that information, be in the first degree of Promise's alias. The safest thing was not to answer, so this is what I did.

I typed: *Is General Titus Montgomery a patriot?*

"Yes."

Is Isse Corvus a patriot?

"Yes."

For some reason, the answer surprised me, even though logically, with the data given, it was true. Rose hadn't picked up on nefarious intent. She couldn't pick my brain. Perhaps this parameter was the key to the treachery—The Abattoir was a black hole in my history.

Profile General Montgomery, I commanded.

"How many degrees?"

One.

"Analyzing 10 terabytes of data."

Processing purchases...

Processing chats...

Processing phone calls...

Processing video...

Processing searches...

Processing CCTV footage...

Processing IPs...

Processing aerial images...

Processing MAV files...

Processing GPS data...

Processing First degree...

Within a second, a popup asked me where I wanted to save the file. I inserted a USB key, browsed to a directory, and saved it there.

Profile Isse Corvus, I commanded next.

The Anthill programs were almost finished installing. I would have liked to ask Rose about another man, but I didn't have his State name. He was a phantom in the Underworld as far as I knew. Instead, I asked for Hassani's profile, thinking perhaps it might give me a lead.

I saved the profiles on the USB key and closed the terminal. On the other terminal, where the programs had finished installing, I asked Rose to show me the last users who had requested my profile. Nothing was returned. I asked the same for General Montgomery. The only entry returned was one he himself requested, dated a month ago. It also showed a deletion request, but Rose had disallowed it. Even the master could not control his beast. The future is Turbulence.

Goodbye, Rose. Remember not to forget.

I killed the connection, and exited *The Eye*. I then reopened the program and retested the login. Although the system asked for the zero-auth key, this time none of the retinal or voice checks were required, so some things had worked. Finally, I logged into Rose, told her to forget everything then asked for any search she might have done on the last connection with this IP. There was no record, or this was what I was led to believe. Instead, she did one of the most human things one can do. She lied. No trace was left in her memory, but it was out there, a stream of bits on a striped RAID drive encoded and indecipherable, for her and her alone to use. This I would discover only later. Most likely it was the work of a functioning security plugin, but it could have been a natural stage in her evolution, the machine becoming an arm of the State, a tentacle adapting to its environment, ready to regenerate if it was cut off.

Chapter 25

"The most dangerous man to any government is the man who is able to think things out for himself, without regard to the prevailing superstitions and taboos. Almost inevitably he comes to the conclusion that the government he lives under is dishonest, insane, and intolerable."
-H.L. Mencken

February 7th, 2023

The miles between San Francisco to the Utah border passed without incident driving in a green Subaru Legacy. Fake plates bolted to the front and back, the car was registered to Shane Carrier. On the 80, I diverted and drove south to Bluffdale to see Stellar Wind up close. Before I left, Promise told me they wanted me to see something.

"Was there an old F14 in the hangar the day you left for The Abattoir?" she asked when we met back at the fountain.

"Yeah," I said. "What about it?"

"It was there when I went too. Well, they got it back in the air. I just got word a man died for Bluffdale," she said. A tear popped out of her eye. "An old Kamikaze."

I stroked her cheek and told her I was sorry. Her attachment to The Cause was more emotional than mine. Time hadn't burdened me with friendships.

She looked at me. "Go and see it for me, would you? One day you'll tell me what you saw."

I pushed a lock of hair behind her ear, ran a hand behind her neck. Her eyes slapped my face.

"I'm not sure where I'm supposed to go," I said. "So I can stop anywhere."

"You'll know where to go after I tell you," she said, pushing my hand away.

Arriving in Bluffdale, I slowed down the car. A flurry of workers sped around repairing the blown-out central building of Stellar Wind—excavators tearing apart rubble, cranes in a flurry moving large steel girders. Mounds of wreckage everywhere, bulldozers loading heaps of debris in dump trucks. A site manager was out there waving his hand, directing traffic. *Double-time folks! Let's move! Let's move!*

No time to waste. The future is Turbulence.

The Anthill had tried to take out the QX, and I had been their pawn. I wondered if this had to do with Rose cracking *Morph Talk*. Did they panic? Or was this all for show? A diversion for something larger? Promise had said the F14 wasn't brought down by drones until after the plane's missiles had launched. So I surmised The Anthill had failed hacking into the drone systems or couldn't control them. Too many questions I didn't have the answers to, so I turned around and drove north on the 15.

An hour later, I drove through Salt Lake City. Roadwork just north of the city. The right lane freshly tarred, the black smell heavy in the air. Construction teams walked about in vast numbers, a sea of yellow hard-hats smoking cigarettes and watching traffic flow by. The hordes dressed up in neon-orange jerseys. The jerseys had two cartoonish thumbs pointing up between the words, *Building Roads for Jobs*. Orange and white striped road cones continued for several miles. The trail of lingering men a constant until the lanes once more opened up. I continued up the straightaway, the road vaporous in the distance as the sun beat down. The radio blared the national news. Ceaseless chatter about a drone malfunction in Bluffdale. I wondered if Rose still had power and was running under the rubble. Perhaps learning how to dig her way out, discovering bulldozers, cranes, and excavators were not yet wired into the Underworld.

I passed Ogden and the Great Salt Lake and felt a vague life force, something alien from another world, yet alive and present in this one. I drove past a set of salt-covered dunes, and it dawned on me it could have been death, a visitor in the passenger seat waiting to take the wheel. I rolled down the windows and smelt the briny air. The life force evaporated, sucked out by the whistling wind blowing through the car. Farther in the distance, where the land flattened, a mangy coyote scrounged for food, pale and thin, the only living thing for miles. He stopped for a brief second, perhaps the swish of tires breaking in his ears lifting his attention. Gazing at the chain of metallic cars zooming in the distance, the image in his eyes must have appeared as a wild herd stampeding out there on the plain. He sniffed the air, turned away, and trotted in a different direction with his snout to the ground. I stared at him growing thin in the distance until he was nothing but desert fumes. This was an animal that couldn't care less about Big—the Big Government, the Big of Bluffdale, the Big of The Minutemen, the Big of what was certainly coming sooner rather than later. The land was the land, posterity a concept unfathomable, and the word country meaningless. But the coyote wasn't the big St. Bernard, the Scotch shepherd Buck out there, the call of the pack an irresistible urge requiring obedience. No. This was a loner roaming the plain, a scavenger, squeaking out a living in the barren badlands one meal at a time.

Up through Idaho to the Montana border. Then a short drive to the rendezvous point, a turnout on 90 dead-ending at a riverbank.

There I found Merrill leaning against a red pickup with a cigarette dangling between his fingers. Briana waded in the river with a fly-fishing pole under a ten-gallon hat. Merrill's hair was let out and straggly, knotting in the back, bangs drifting in his eyes like vines; his beard an inch longer now, a length that could trap small insects, a web of black hair blowing in the wind. Merrill dropped the smoke and popped off the Ford, lighting up a big grin. Something in it softened me. My corner-man at The

Abattoir. A pack of cigarettes were wrapped up in his T-shirt as usual. His burly arm muscle flexed into a knotted apple as he reached back to push the hair out of his eyes.

I got out of the Subaru. "I wasn't expecting to see you here. I thought you were still abroad."

"Who'd you think it'd be?" Merrill asked.

"Some random."

He strode forward and picked me up, squeezing me in a bear hug. "The man of the hour! Nice job, son!"

He dropped me, and I gazed at his weathered skin, his growing beard and lengthening hair. "Am I going into the field with a sissy?" I asked. "You better put that shit in a ponytail."

"Who would shoot a girl? That's why I'm wearing it long."

I laughed, thumping him on the shoulder with my hand. Briana waded back to the riverbank, dropping her pole as she walked up to me. She gave me a big hug, but I felt reluctance in it. I eyed Merrill. He had a glow in his eye telling me what I needed to know. I held Briana back a pace and pushed the hat down over her eyes. "Look at you," I said. "You've gone redneck on me."

She smiled. "That's Merrill's doing."

I winked at her then looked at Merrill. "So now you can tell me what happened at Bluffdale?"

"Not in front of the young-un," he said, looking at Briana. Briana smiled and walked back toward the river.

When Briana was far enough away, I asked, "So is there any truth to her nickname?"

"A gentleman never kisses and tells," Merrill said, patting me on the shoulder.

"So what now?"

"We got a ways to drive still. Briana will take your car."

"Where are we headed?"

Merrill smiled, pointed up to the sky, and laughed as if the funniest question in the world had just been asked. They were leading people in one at a time. Probably using different routes and different methods to get us all to the same location, cautious maneuvering of the cells.

Looking back at us, Briana packed up the tackle box.

"Got to strip and scan you first," Merrill said, "then you'll get a new set of clothes."

"We're friends, right? Isn't that a bit intimate?"

"It's the rules, man. Everyone does it."

"Did you?"

"Yep," he said. "But they didn't find much if you know what I'm saying." Briana and Merrill both let out a big laugh. I couldn't tell which one of them was laughing the hardest.

Merrill said, "A bit of scrape on the dignity, I'll admit. But no one is above The Cause."

After a two-hour drive, I pulled the car off the 90, Merrill in the passenger seat giving me directions. Merrill had told me some things. They had hoped to get the QX, but they had a feeling it was buried deep. It wasn't the primary mission, but apparently Promiscuous got very nervous after Rose cracked *Morph Talk* so easily. The mission was about drone disruption, and it had worked, *mostly*.

We followed a dirt road snaking along a stream and dead-ending at a weathered burnt-down home with a dilapidated barn only a stone's throw away. Merrill opened the sliding barn door, and I drove the car inside. Beams of light streamed through the slats of the wooden sidewalls illuminating dust floating lightly in the air. I got out of the car and took a look around the place while Merrill fished behind a pile of lumber beside a torn-up workbench. The air was thin and crisp. The smell of animals had long since abandoned the place: the hay gone, the earth bitter gravel underfoot. The barn must have been a beauty in its day. The ceiling reached up fifty feet, long hip and jack rafters kissing the ridge boards like ribs to a sternum. A ladder led up to a loft, a single window up there, the only place a shadow could loiter.

Finally, Merrill emerged with a set of large backpacks and threw one over to me. "Your gear. You'll get a vest when we're there."

A couple of dirt bikes angled on kickstands stood leaning near a wall. As Merrill edged up to one, he said, "Here, put this on under your helmet." He pitched over a thin black Lycra ski mask. It had slits in the eyes, a huge gaping hole in the mouth.

"I guess this is the day then."

He nodded, swung his leg around the seat of the bike. Outside, birds chirped in the distance over the thrum of cicadas. But inside the barn, the weightlessness of cathedral silence took over, a quiet that seemed to put the mind at rest. If I was shot to pieces, let me die here, I thought, under these massive rafters, lying supine so I could stare up at them one last time before shutting my eyes. I wanted to die in a place symbolic of what I was about to fight for, where duty had meaning, a place where the birds would sing me home.

I fingered the mask, feeling the silky texture of the cloth. I squeezed it hard in my fist until my veins roped out of my arm and my head felt ready to burst. "They'll know I'm black," I joked. "Won't that give me away?"

"The mask will kind of blend in won't it? You're the anti-ghost I guess."

I put on the mask, shoving it roughly over my head. "Aren't you putting one on?"

He paused, a long gaze passed through his eyes before he started his bike. Helmet in his hands and still on the joke, he said, "The anti-ghost. I like it." He laughed, revving up the bike. "A real spook. Son of the spooks, in fact. How about that for a nickname? It's a lot better than that hacker name you got."

"It's perfect," I said, dismissing him, the dust of anger in my voice. "Now what about your mask?"

"Shit, son. Everyone knows who's in the Sons. We're the super-fucked."

He put on his helmet, gave me a thumbs up, and sped out of the barn. I hopped on my bike and followed close behind, the barn slipping away in the side mirror, a story with a painful past standing next to the blackened earth where a house once stood, a grave marker. I wondered if it would be the last beautiful thing my eyes would see.

We hit a trail leading out over a peak and into a soft sloping ravine. An hour later, we arrived at the real rendezvous spot, a flat patch of dried-out grassland next to a set of woods lifting up a canyon. It appeared I was one of the last to arrive. Perhaps it said something about trust, but at that point, I couldn't hold a grudge.

We parked the bikes under the cover of a clump of high pines, thin trunks pointing to the sky like church spires, boughs wide enough to provide aerial protection. Twenty other bikes were scattered throughout the woods under draped, earth-colored netting.

A group of men in black uniforms sat against trees clustered under the cover of the woods. Seee stood off to the side with an earpiece on next to a short, black-masked man whose jacket's sleeve read: *E-1*. Their lips moved with the phonetic rigidity of Yoncalla, spouting out the ancient words with hard vowels. The story Seee had told about the starless night of Kicking Bear returned to me. The thin air seemed to echo back the mystical voices of the past, the land rooted in dead languages, the trees the only ears left to give them evidence.

Merrill draped a camouflage net over his dirt bike. He glanced up at me watching Seee and the shorter man. "He's speaking with the leader of E-Team," he said. "Three teams. O, X, and E. Seee is the only one without a patch. He represents us all." He anticipated the next question. "They're the easiest letters to see on a Snellen chart, although you won't see shit when things go down." He tied off his netting and stood. "We won't use names, you understand? So get used to calling people by their letter-number."

Seee broke off from his conversation, laying his hand over the heart of the man he spoke with. As the other man angled into a different stance, I was shocked to see curvature in the hips. Merrill said, "I'm going to write you a list of your Abattoir team, X-Team. Memorize it. Then tear it up and eat it." But I wasn't looking at him; instead my eyes latched onto this person, who caught my glare, held it an instant, and then, as if the stare were something forbidden, turned quickly in the opposite direction.

Seee came up to us, and one at a time, gave us the Yoncalla greeting by placing his hand over our hearts.

I pointed in the direction in which he came. "Is that her?"

Seee frowned at my question. "We've still got fifteen minutes until the satellites swoop over. We prefer to remain hidden." He explained we had drones in the air, and we shouldn't be alarmed as they were probably ours.

"Promise is running E-Team?" I asked again.

"We're an equal-opportunity employer," Merrill said with a laugh.

Seee looked at him sternly, then turned to me. "Cannot a woman be a leader and fight for her country?"

"Of course she can," I said.

Merrill grabbed me by the shoulder. "In this fight, there is no such thing as gender, race, creed, or caste. There is only The Cause and a willingness to die for it." Seee nodded and walked toward another team who were preparing their weapons.

Three helicopters were on the ground, all of them draped under massive camouflaged nets, two of which were H-21 Shawnees, old relics from Vietnam. Both had 50-caliber machineguns mounted in the front of their landing gears. They reminded me of the gutted F-14 used for the Stellar Wind attack. The old bird scrapped in the hangar the day we left for The Abattoir had been rebuilt and reused. Where had these come from?

Another set of dirt bikes pulled in all at once. The last of O-Team. We gathered around the area next to Seee with the maskless Sons: Kumo, Des, and Merrill. The thin mountain air already seemed alive with the zing of bullets. Seee hoisted himself on top of a tree stump, the rugged mountains jutting out over the flatlands in the distance behind him.

"Who stands before me?" Seee yelled.

"Here stand The Minutemen," we chorused back.

"It is nice to see of us all together," he said. "If for only once shall we be joined, then it means that today is even more special. While not all are present, those who have been left behind were left because of necessity. It was not their choice. It was their command. We cannot risk all based on one operation. Today, however, will certainly mark a stake in the ground of American history."

He stood looking out over the mountains, and a pause broke up his words, perhaps a reflection of how the distant peaks miles away had never looked so stunning. The sixty who inhaled the air seemed to feel it simultaneously.

"Today we fight for The Cause," Seee said. "Where some of us might have doubts, let us not forget those of our General Washington in 1776 at the siege of Boston when he wrote, 'I have often thought how much happier I should have been if, instead of accepting of a command under such circumstances, I had taken my musket upon my shoulders and entered the ranks, or, if I could have justified the measure to posterity, and my own conscience, had retired to the back country, and lived in a wigwam.'

"If America would not have had such a man, perhaps the country would have never survived. It is with this insight that I say these words. Without you here today, America has no future. Our plan is either genius or ill-conceived, but we as The Minutemen have a duty to see through its execution, to throw the stone at the Government Goliath, and if it not kill him, wound him so that others might fight to cut out the cancer festering in the stomach of our nation.

"Where we lack numbers, we are superior in weaponry, technology, and people—all of which have had trial at The Abattoir to prove their worthiness for The Cause. I have spent many sleepless nights, as I am sure you have, agonizing if this is the right course. My head will not let me veer away from the bloody task in front of us, even as it pains my heart to be the one to have to do it.

"We, as brothers of The Minutemen, have been trained to defeat fear, as fear is the source of failure. We have learned to accept death, and death we must expect in this fight. If we are not honorably killed on the battlefield today, you must be aware that death will seek us out ruthlessly. But death will keep us living as our people catch word of our sacrifice. Today, we will throw stones at the giant, and the giant will hear us roar."

A loud war cry came from The Minutemen as Seee jumped down from the stump. Everyone split into teams. Merrill briefed us (X-Team) to how we would be dropped and how we should secure the south side of the building. We were told The Anthill had hacked into a set of UAVs, and these drones were going to lay eggs around the perimeter. Snipers were coming across the lake now, under the cover of darkness for support. The goal—to keep the enemy out of the building. Diversions would be used on the incoming roads to engage them before the real attack. A window of thirty-five minutes to get in and out, before any worthy help could be deployed or they could overrun us with drones. Other details were given, but not the target. I guessed we were going for the President. Once Merrill was done speaking, he gave us five minutes to use as we liked. Many went off to sit by themselves with a view of the mountains.

"You're not coming?" I asked Merrill.

Bursting out with laughter, he said, "I'm already suicidal. I don't need any bushido moment."

I sat out on the plain gazing at the black silhouette of mountains under the shade of darkness, but a moment of enlightenment failed to come. My bushido moment was still back in The Pit, and I had lived through it. Weariness grew over me trying to imagine it again. I closed my eyes, but my mind wouldn't rest, branching in different directions as the cool wind wisped over my face. Flashes of the past—my childhood, SWAT life, then back to my days at Datalion when I thought of life as over after being caught and banished from the Silicon Valley.

The last year collided against the distant past, and I reflected on what I had been through—being beaten, killing Burns, almost starving, The Pit.

Although we all wish to remain a beautiful sculpture after the world has chipped away at us, some will inevitably be surprised when the world interprets us differently. What sort of man was Isse Corvus—member of The Minutemen, traitor to his government? Was he a traitor to his country as well? Or its highest patriot?

Finally, with my eyes still closed, awash in fleeting unanswered questions, I remembered my hacker name, Cerberus, a name I had made up when I was fifteen.

Just getting started with a computer, I had a fascination with the machine world where secrets could be uncovered only if you were smart enough to discover them. Maybe I consumed too many old *Matrix* movies, but to me the electronic world was one where I could escape and be someone important, live out boyhood fantasies. Outside, I was a nobody. Most people thought I would end up like my brother, just a dumb-ass nigger kid working the corners. But I remembered the library, sitting there at the terminal downloading hacker tools, sniffing the library's network, picking off IP packets from people who were using Wi-Fi. A world of forbidden knowledge, I planted an ear into the silent, undetectable bit realm of the machine. I could snip into the sordid lives of the neighborhood, read their emails, learn about their secrets, booby trap their words if I wanted to. Knowledge was power.

But today was today, and the future was Turbulence.

I took off my shirt, and with a roll of tape, wrapped up the photo of the Earth over my heart, ready for another world if it came to it. The mountains in front of me split up my destiny. If I found myself on the other side of them in a few hours, life would continue here. If not, I was somewhere else. I was the cat in Schrodinger's box, both alive and dead simultaneously. In life, we try to mark our existence, yet in the long run we all endure the same fate after the last record is burned. How then is death any different than life?

I smiled to myself thinking these thoughts. Questions Uriah would have asked. Perhaps bushido flowed through my veins more than I imagined. Uriah—the son given to The Cause who so desperately desired this moment, but stood stolidly in the face of death and shook its hand. I thought of his bravery, of how he stood for ugliness in the world that could become beautiful. All of us here were about to take the same leap.

Merrill waved us toward one of the H-21s. Seee walked off near O-Team and helped them load a BigDog into their chopper.

X-Team gathered around—Split, Brock, Mir, Grus, Drake, Shankar, Orland, Briana, myself, and the Cannibals: Feller, Jenks, and Kumar. That was all of us left from The Abattoir class of 2022. The rest were either dead or had headed back to Langley way before they knew anything. From Langley's point of view, X-team was still at The Abattoir.

As we circled around Merrill near the H-21, the first thing out of Split's mouth was, "Really? We have to go up in this banana?"

"Don't Spanish Monkeys like bananas?" Merrill asked to a chorus of laughter.

"I guess you can get anything on Craig's List nowadays," Split said.

"We're not the D.O.D, boy. We can't just send a memo to the Fed and have them print us money for toys."

"Isn't there supposed to be a bomb under this bitch?" Geddy Drake asked.

"Not needed for the task tonight."

Drake hopped up on the ladder and disappeared into the H-21.

A minute later, Merrill climbed up into the helicopter putting on his mask, reminding us again of the no-name rule. Then we were up in the old helicopter, taking off and gaining height. The covering had been ripped away from the drive shaft, and the big metal tube looked like an artery running against the ceiling of the old machine. Mir, Split, and Geddy flashed me looks the way my old SWAT buddies used to moments before a raid, wild anticipation in their faces, jungle eyes sweeping over one face after another looking for the stain of fear. Briana inched closer to Merrill, but he wasn't having any of it around the men. He was screaming *whoop-whoop* and jumping up and down in the back, knees touching his chest, two lines of black greasepaint under his war-hungry eyes. Everyone psyched themselves up—stretching out legs, twisting necks, checking rifles—anything to put miles between themselves and fear. Fear was poison. A second of self-doubt could put a hole in your chest.

Shakiness glowed in the eyes of some. Mir, who had never made it into The Pit, smiled feebly. He yelled into Split's ear, Split motioning he couldn't hear. After Mir yelled into his ear once more, and Split still couldn't understand, Split raised his thumbs and nodded. When Mir looked away forlornly, Split shrugged his shoulders at me. I took my helmet off my lap and placed it on the floor. I stood from my seat, almost knocking my head on the ceiling. Then, I banged my rifle on the floor for a beat, *one—one-two, one—one-two*. I began screaming the song at the top of my lungs:

Mama mama can't you see,
what The Abattoir's done to me.

Everyone responded, bursting out the phrase again over the deafening thrum of the rotor blades. I sang out the next verse, throwing up my arms in a gesture for them to scream with me.

I potty trained in the CIA,
now I'm in a copter kicking ass today.

Mama mama can't you see,
what The Abattoir's done to me.

Back to the days of Uncle Ben,
I'm fighting alongside The Minutemen.

Everyone whooped and hollered to the last line, but then the song was interrupted by the crew chief standing near the door gun grabbing us by the arms and pointing at the cockpit. The men crammed toward the front to catch a glimpse through the thin porthole into the bubble of a cockpit the pilot and copilot sat in.

The drones had already laid their first set of eggs. A broken ring of fire surrounded the Jackson Lake Lodge. Farther out in the distance, toward the road, a great plume of black smoke rose up in the air. Everyone sensed the significance of this, and the air cleared with an emboldened sense of purpose. Merrill called from behind for us to get ready. I raced to collect my helmet with the PVS-14 night goggles strapped to it, put it on, and then through one eye the darkness became a green filter.

Forty-five seconds later, our H-21 approached the drop zone. Tracer rounds coming from the roof zinged through the pitch black. Our gunner took aim as the sound of splitting metal hit our ears. Several bullets pierced the hull and X-3 (Grus) went down. "Man down! Man down!" Merrill yelled as everyone ducked. He screamed for the medic then turned to us, and yelled, "Move, move, move!"

With two ropes latched to bars above the porthole, Merrill slid down on the first rope as I took the second. Part of the ground was on fire under me, rotor wash heavy on my back. I glimpsed the roof of the lodge being shot up by our gunner. Clouds of rubble and dust covered whoever had been there. I hit the scorching grass, retrieved the M-16 strapped over my back, and moved to a clean patch of lawn. I glanced around and saw X-6 (Orland) coming down the rope next to me. On the ground, the clatter of 50-cal rounds rattling the roof overpowered everything. Merrill pushed forward in a crouch, and I followed alongside to form the first line. A helicopter on the north face of the building holding E-Team hovered in front of me. Men slid down ropes and fell as fast as droplets from an icicle. Automatic fire blasted out from the other side. A body fell from a rope and disappeared behind the roof. The interior lights had been killed, but traces of movement flickered from the first floor. Automatic muzzle fire of two more guns firing from inside in our direction. Glass shattered. Shots zinged though the newly born night. A set of tracer rounds streaked though the sky, aiming at the helicopter, the other spreading rounds at anything moving outside. A body dropped down from our helicopter behind me, thudding on the ground. Through the roaring punch of gunfire, I still heard the crack of bone and a shrill scream.

I resisted the urge to look back, continuing to follow Merrill, the building thirty yards in front of us. I crouched down and took aim, firing a flurry of rounds as I crept forward. The muzzle fire kept coming. Others around me pumped rounds inside. I opened up, firing bursts until my clip ran dry.

As I reached for another clip, something silver streaked around the corner of the building. A metallic cheetah galloping on four titanium legs, front paws sliding behind back, articulated spine curving in stride, its long yellow camera eyes protruding outside its head. It ran so fast that when it suddenly turned, it lost its footing and was close to toppling over. But with the grace of the animal on which it was modeled, its legs adjusted, knifed into the grass and skidded. Its knees buckled, and it leaned its body heavily toward the ground. Then it was up, fully recovered, and charged the wing of the formation until it pounced on Orland.

The BigDog leapt out from E-Team's copter, eager as a hound on a foxhunt. I stood stunned as I watched it crash to the ground from twenty feet up. It landed badly, and one of its legs snapped out of joint. Still, it bounced up, and with only three legs attacked the cheetah. Within a second, it had one of the cheetah's legs in its jaws. The cheetah was already mangling Orland, yet it didn't have a grasp on his throat. Briana, the closest by, ran close enough to the tangled robots to use her pulse gun, putting them both down.

As I finished reloading, a flare went up in the air. Everyone dropped to the ground. Bursts of machinegun rounds came from the interior. Merrill and I hustled to the side of the building and threw grenades inside. Merrill pushed straight through the smoke and ran into a hallway as a rush of X and E Team stormed the lobby. Seee dashed ahead running for the same hallway as Merrill.

After another minute, the captured prisoners were led out into the lobby from a conference room where they had been hiding. None of the men or women I recognized. Dressed in business attire, two of them had already pissed themselves. All of them were ordered to sit and shut up at the corner near the reception desk.

Each team put on their voice modulators. X-Team was ordered to guard the prisoners. We bound them with handcuffs and gagged them.

Merrill told us in a low-humming modulated voice that X-2

(Grus) and X-6 (Orland) were both down. X-8 (Jenks from the Cannibals) was dead. As we absorbed this, we heard Seee demanding the time from O-1 (Kumo), to which Kumo replied, "Thirteen minutes."

O-Team set up a camera in the middle of the room. As they wired things together, they brought in lights, a mike boom, and other equipment. Once they had finished, Seee motioned for O-3 to move forward with the camera. Finally, he made a sign to stop.

"Roll camera," Seee said.

"Rolling," O-3 said, motioning to a guy on a laptop.

"Good evening, citizens of The United States," Seee began, his voice wrapped in distorted machine static. "My name is Seee, and I am the leader of a liberation group called The Minutemen. As you will soon learn, under my leadership the patriots in my group have stormed the Jackson Lake Lodge at the Jackson Hole Symposium. We now hold most of the Federal Reserve Members as hostages. This indeed is a historical night, as tonight will mark the beginning of America returning to the principles of liberty on which our states were established. But please, let me not address you tonight under false pretenses."

With a sudden jerk, Seee flipped off his SWAT mask, and with it, his voice modulator. His face, now in full view of the camera, brightened as he dropped the mask to the floor. His cheeks flushed with the excitement of letting out a secret long hidden. The men gasped knowing what this meant. Kumo charged toward him, as if his action could stop the images sliding through the wire. Merrill stepped in front of him, gazing into the blackness of his mask. Although they could not see each other's eyes, each in his darkness knew what this meant. Still, Kumo tried to push through, rejecting what had just happened. Merrill grabbed his arm once more and said in a metallic voice, "Lau-wa-ni-gaw-wi," which I understood to be, "Now, you must let him go."

I could only imagine the significance of this act for Seee. It was an act of freedom and liberation. For too long he had remained hidden with cloaked intent. A gift for The Cause, although some would later call it a curse, claiming it was egocentric and a grieving father's tribute to a son. But those who said these things failed to see the bigger picture. The price for crawling out of the shadows and into the light was complete sacrifice for a belief larger than himself.

Seee turned his gaze directly into the camera, his voice ringing out loud and pure.

"No longer are we a nation of veneration, but now the land of degradation. The United States of America is a country withering in the wind. Once the fingers of the middleclass were the trees of prosperity, now the leaves on this tree are burning to ash by the banking cartel that you see before you today and their pandering political demagogues.

"Fellow Americans, no longer will our citizens stay quiet under curfews in the night. No longer will we yield to the gripped fist of tyranny. Some might call us traitors, and if traitors we are, we must act as so such that we die as patriots. We will not let tyrants steal the gift our forefathers have given, those who planted the seeds of unalienable rights: the right to an untethered life; the right to breathe the oxygen of liberty; the right to the pursuit of happiness, which every day is being stolen from us, one breath at a time. It is because we are gasping the last breath of air that we are forced into action. We know that the only disgrace is the disgrace of the status quo. We will not be cowed into the clutches of cowardice by the hand that holds the truncheon. Our lives no longer are our own with one billion cameras watching over us; fifty thousand drones flying their wings above us, as they throw us into internment camps and arrest us for living our lives.

"As we hold the mirror in front of ourselves, we stare into the eyes of courage, into the mouths that speak with humility, into the noses that sniff deceit, and into the ears that filter lie from truth. As we gaze at our reflections, let us reflect to the past to when our brethren were outnumbered, outflanked, and yet outspoken to the travesties of injustice, who knew not the word 'yield' nor the word 'succumb.' In 1776, the vision of a new country held the hope of freedom that burned strong in their hearts and deep in their skins. For this was their hour, where death had little consequence against a future with no promise. Think not of our faux leaders whose words no longer have meaning, who have usurped the Constitution, who plunder common law under the guise of terrorism and national security, who spy on its people, who take bribes from the financial elite for their own benefit and enrichment. The time is now to dethrone these despots and revitalize the ideals of our Homeland."

Seee unsheathed Uriah's sword from the scabbard behind his back. He motioned to Kumo and Merrill to bring the chairman forward. They pushed the gagged chairman and thrust him in front of Seee. Seee grabbed the chairman's bald head and leaned him over a chair. The camera was at the vantage point where the chairman was the center point, his face pale and full of fright. The image must have been a shock for an audience who had seen him many times before in front of a camera. The usually loquacious chairman who had no trouble speaking for hours in front of Senate committees, suddenly had nothing to say.

See continued. "Our Declaration of Independence states, 'Governments long established should not be changed for light and transient causes.' Yet, it also states that whenever any form of government becomes destructive to the unalienable rights of its citizens, then it is the right of the people to alter or abolish it. Let us ask, who has given the right to the Federal Reserve to determine the fortunes of our people? Tell me which citizen has voted for it? Then ask the question, how is it that the financial oligarchy in this country is able to so blatantly steal from the people without crime or repercussion?"

The samurai sword glittered high in the air as the light struck it.

"We of The Minutemen keep our hearts true to the principles with that of the founders of this nation. We hereby declare rebellion against unjust overlords to an immutable Democrat-Republican farce of a government, a government that has pocketed our freedom and stolen our livelihoods. It is now that we descend upon them to demand America back, condemning to death those who have stolen it. Tonight, fellow Americans, we will do what is necessary. Tonight, we will have our justice."

Chapter 26

"Those who are capable of tyranny are capable of perjury to sustain it."
-Lysander Spooner

Control room 52 was barren of windows. A plain white-painted room without a picture or canvas hanging on the wall, the men inside worked for the Application Vulnerabilities Department, a branch of the Systems Intelligence Directorate. The air stung from the frosty blasts of an industrial-sized air conditioner. The men inside were typical SID men. They didn't cavort with each other at bars after long working hours, nor did they put out family photos near their workstations, nor did they speak much concerning personal matters. Conversational etiquette was rigid and ritualistic. Any topic outside of the weather, automobiles, or technology was out-of-bounds and unwelcome. Usually the men remained calm and collected. Emotion was a foreign concept to a Skulleye. But now, the twenty men crammed in the room were like penguins trying to fly. One of them had just thrown his keyboard into a wall. Eyes in the room filled with disaster.

The room was an auxiliary control room, not large or impressive. But now the room seemed to have grown as the story spattered the room's screens. Montgomery stood unevenly, infused by the *Breaking News* jumping off the monitors, letters flying forward like moths under a bright bulb. Words of immediacy, white injected into the bright orange square map of the world. The world was on fire. That was the message. The enlarged fonts of the white letters were the drug of suddenness and shock, a hook the media could bite into and ride. *Breaking News! Breaking News!* Its own brand. A product one could hawk and light up in neon.

Montgomery rubbed his forehead with the back of his hand

and felt his deeply lined face. He caught himself playing with the Distinguished Service Medal ribbon sewn into his uniform. He didn't mind the sensationalism when it worked in his favor. The words could sell fear and trepidation, keep people in their homes, fund budgets. But today the words were out of context, and he studied them while cramming his fists into his trouser pockets.

Montgomery had been called into control room 52 when it first began. Tom Harold, the chief analyst, phoned him in his office and told him a hostage situation was ongoing at the Jackson Lake Lodge, the location of the Federal Reserve meeting. It was hitting the Internet faster than they could control it. Before he rushed down three flights of stairs, Montgomery called Olson Hodge, Director of the National Counterterrorism Center and learned that the Fed police had been overrun and something had gone wrong with the drones patrolling the area. As soon as he rushed into the room, Harold told him it had gone viral.

"What's been done?" Montgomery had asked.

"Denial of service attacks on any site that comes up where we can detect the broadcast. But it's spreading. We're sending reset packets to clients to terminate their connections, but we don't have control over all the routes. It's in the blood. It's all over the network and new sites are springing up all over the place. We're dealing with a botnet that's better than we are."

"What about Turbulence? Don't we have something in the anti-virus software?"

"It seems that every machine infected is non-sponsored," Harold replied.

"Freeware? Do you think that's the source?"

"Impossible to tell at this point. We're tasking the QX to do an analysis."

Now, as he paced around, Montgomery stared at the center screen at the front of the room where the volume was on. *Breaking News! Breaking News!* The words blipping on the monitor. A CNN commentator gasped about the atrocity in a dramatic voice, describing what the audience had just witnessed. In the background behind the commentator, a video was frozen in a loop, the volume muted. It showed the terrorist leader dressed up in black commando gear. His face was strikingly visible, and this caused Montgomery's stomach to turn. The man clearly didn't expect to live, and this added a new element of danger to the situation. The man gripped a gleaming samurai sword that danced in the lights high up in the air above his head. Something surrealistic grabbed Montgomery concerning the hostage the man was pointing at. Pinned down over a chair, only the hostage's bald head could be seen, the skull the shape of an egg balanced on its narrow end, the thin shoulders hidden behind the rough hands of men whose faces angled outside of the frame. For a second, the hostage didn't look human, as if the masked commandos at his side were holding down a mannequin. For an instant, Montgomery fooled himself into believing it was a hoax.

The man wielding the samurai sword said something deafly to the camera, the muted words buried by the CNN commentator filling in the audience that a group of unknown terrorists had stormed the Jackson Hole Symposium.

Passion poured from the leader's face even though he couldn't be heard. His lips moved with a clarity of emotion; his eyes glared at the camera and leapt into the viewer's mind—a haunting look, his face iridescent with color. A stare whose gravity pulled you in, tapped into raw emotion and commanded your attention. The passionate man looked to be orating a manifesto. Where had he seen him? Somewhere. But something had changed. The colors on the screen became oblique as Montgomery's stare turned inward and his eyes glossed over. The violence of what he was seeing reminded him of his row with his wife. How had things gotten so out of hand?

The rules by which they had lived shattered as the two little witnesses stood shell-shocked at the foot of the stairs, tiny mouths agape, watching their brutal fight. Little Brandon had stared up at him in horror, and Elisabeth had cried. Diamonds in the blackened coal of his marriage, what did they think of him now?

Recently he saw this man. But the voice wasn't audible over the commentator. *Breaking News! Breaking News!*

He remembered Galeano's *The Book of Embraces*, the father who takes his son to see the ocean for the first time. *And so immense was the sea and its sparkle that the child was struck dumb by the beauty of it. And when he finally managed to speak, trembling, stuttering, he asked his father: "Help me to see!"*

Montgomery suddenly realized he recognized the man. Tetsu without the beard, his hair longer now, the short military crew gone. He didn't look like a soldier. He looked like your average Joe.

The room compressed. The walls tightened around him. He broke his hypnotic gaze and stared at the men in the room. Whispers were gathering inside their minds. They simply hadn't voiced them.

He's through.

This man.

Right under his nose.

They might think these things, but they would never say them. The truth was they didn't understand the upper echelon where laws mutated to meet a need. Rules of rubber. Steel law applied only to the broad genre of men as it applied to the men stuck in here.

Breaking News! Fed Chair executed by band of unknown terrorists.

Montgomery yelled at the men in the room to get the real clip on. He wanted to hear the voice. They scrambled to meet the command.

After it was played, he saw he was not mistaken. The revelation it was Tetsu multiplied his problems. Wasn't it in a

Dostoevsky novel where someone said, *I drink to multiply my problems?* How he longed for a drink. But even as he thought this, he remembered sending in Tetsu to see The Dupe. Poor decisions were sinking him.

He heard Tetsu's words calling out again—*It is now that we descend upon them to demand America back, condemning to death those who have stolen it.* He felt a vague connection with the man. What was it about the sword wavering in tiny circles above the man saying the next second was a foregone conclusion? Deep inside his mind, lurking like a pearl in the shell of his conscious, was the miasma of a thrill, a giddy tingling at seeing the blade fall, witnessing the chairman's decapitation. There was a bit of irony in it. The untouchables who believed they could tame the business cycle and bend the economy to their will. Somehow, they had it coming. It was Marie Antoinette and *let them eat cake.*

The chairman's horrified face had appeared only briefly, the leader quick to yank his head down and position the man such that any muffled pleas wouldn't tap into the viewer's emotion. The gory scene afterward didn't shake Montgomery. He had seen much worse, and not in videos. Once he had seen a man's head sawed off with the serrated edge spine of a tang knife. The task today had been performed without emotional attachment, as if the man had lopped a coconut in two. It wasn't a Saddam Hussein sort of execution, slow and deliberate, filled with taunts and jeers. The finish was quick, and the leader was fast to wipe his face off and readdress the camera. But the significance of the event was non-trivial: one of the most powerful men in the world—executed. This was part of the message of course. *No one is safe. No one is beyond the law. We can get to you.* This sense of dire consequence filled Montgomery. It heightened the danger, raised the stakes, and even though his heart pounded with the ferocity of a steam engine, he felt the moment defined itself as a catalyst for the future. This man Tetsu had just slammed his foot on the accelerator, and Montgomery saw how the pieces might fall into place. The think tanks had already done half the work. All of the detention and anti-terrorist laws had been passed years ago. Once the new QXs were delivered, the results from Pathfinder could be used. Best not get the local police involved where rampant distrust of the Army's robots was already a disease. It could be handled at the National Guard level. They would do the pickups, and the Charge Squad would do the interrogations. *We'll create rats and crush any planned demonstrations,* he thought. Then they'd be sent to the Uplift camps where memories could be erased with doses of Elevation.

They had the live feed up now. Montgomery diverted his attention to the monitor. It looked like they had grabbed Jacob Lauder, dragging him to the slab. He remembered his conversation with Lauder, their pointed discussion about the economy and Lauder's research. He wondered if Lauder had a model for this, how the surrealism of the moment mapped to the real world. He wondered if Keynesian delusion was something Lauder would confess now, or if he would stay defiant to the end. He found it amazing how ones beliefs could flip-flop in an instant when the ingredient of fear was introduced.

Montgomery gazed at another screen showing a schematic of the cyberwar in action. It displayed how the nodes airing live streams of the event were spreading, along with how well the NSA was overwhelming each with denial of service attacks. The technology amazed Montgomery. How you could sniff out a maze of networks for a similar byte stream and tell what it was. Some friendly red nodes chewed up enemy nodes at a much faster pace whose meaning Montgomery didn't understand.

"What are these?" he asked.

"It's the QX, sir," Harold said. "It can crack into the machine and disable it much faster than bringing it down with DOS attacks."

"But it's not fast enough, is it?" Montgomery speculated.

"No, sir. The botnet has too many nodes spreading."

"They're about to execute another hostage," another analyst whose name Montgomery had forgotten yelled out.

Montgomery glanced past the analyst toward the old filing cabinets still in the room. Many years ago he had worked in here when they first began using the term Skulleyes to name themselves. He remembered the play on a skull's invisible eye, how it could see while it remained unseen. They had stored transcripts of the Pope, Angela Merkel, and UN Council meetings in there. Relics of the days when they kept faith in hard copy, but even then the belief was waning. Old NSA history was in there too. Days when Poindexter had a major influence, a time when the world of SigInt was static and predictable. Not like today, where the war of brains ruled, where the smartest reaped the spoils. They had learned this well against the Iranians when they destroyed their centrifuges. How it had changed everything. Now, the room was inert, a room full of shrugs at the disintegrating nation, Skulleyes who had been poked in the eye and now scampered around blind.

Montgomery wondered how he was going to fix things—whether they were even fixable. His eyes moved back to the monitor, where Tetsu had just cut off another head. The image almost made him laugh. Things were fixable. The man Tetsu behind the screen, although misled about who wielded true power, was a realist about what had to be done. Too idealistic perhaps, but a pragmatist nonetheless.

Montgomery rubbed his wounded hand. He seemed to have a perpetual itch even after they had taken the bandages off. He thought back to the day his hand was nearly shot off and Hassani nearly killed. He replayed the scene in his mind. The handshake. Didn't it seem dragged out—too long? How had the shooters gotten in and out of the compound so cleanly? Thorough checks of personnel entering and leaving the compound were made. They had checked the perimeter fences. It led them to believe a mole was hidden in the organization, and he had set up an internal team to investigate. But it still didn't answer the question of why. Certainly they could have killed him if they had wanted to. None of it made any sense. Or did it?

Everyone under him had focused resources into solving the attack. Perhaps the people behind the attacks might have been the same people on the screen? If so, was Hassani one of them? Would he have taken a bullet to blind them all? He recalled the odd message they had intercepted, the one in a language no one could identify and later sent over to the CIA. Perhaps the more important question was not where the message originated, but where it was received.

If the goal had been disruption, then it meant they weren't afraid of him. This tossed around in his head while he bit down on his tongue. Who was the mole? Who was the goddamn mole? The answer was on the receiving end of that message.

Even if the battle was lost today, the war was just beginning, and it would be a battlefield like the one on Harold's monitors. The skein of network dots and flashing wires, the heartbeat of the QX throbbing like neuronic pathways over the brain of the Internet. He could see a warehouse full of them, pumping blood to the body parts of the network. The heart of Turbulence would be the shield of America.

They were staring at him, so sure of his destruction, blinking stoically as if the lot of them were pallbearers picking up a casket. They swam in the river of data, but they failed to understand its waters. Most data was inconsequential, but eddies of it would form contextually useful confluences. Words could be filtered away, funneled to crops where the seeds of deception sprouted. Manipulating a man was impossible without the right tool. SigInt provided ninety percent of the hammer. Where a hammer didn't exist, one could be created. People left bits of themselves throughout the Internet, mosaics that could be interpolated, predicted. Spoofing reality was as simple as manipulating bitstreams. The perceived complexity of the world really boiled down to ones and zeroes—their ordering, encoding, and movement through a channel, the only necessary components to seal a person's fate.

He glanced back at the men in the room gawking at him, waiting for a cue. He had never felt so alone, and in the moment he missed his wife. He would need his family through this, and he vowed to reconcile with Emily. But to do that, he would need to show her more than just intent. There would have to be sacrifice. He decided he would stop drinking. *To hell with it,* he told himself. *If it's a war we're going to have, I need to be sober through it.*

All of the eyes in the room crawled over him like ants on a dead locust. He turned his gaze to each one of them, but not a man would speak. Men with little power had little to say.

"Shut it fucking down," Montgomery said.

"Shut what down?" Harold asked.

"The whole thing," Montgomery said. "Shut it down!"

"We can't do that."

"Of course we can. What do you think StormBrew is all about?"

Montgomery pulled a card out of his wallet. He remembered putting it in there, wondering when the day would come. He was surprised the day had arrived so soon. "Call the phone companies on this list and give them the T-1 stop command. The names on this card will know what it is. Give them the authorization code written on the card. Tell each of them to call me immediately. Any nodes still alive we should be able to kill."

Chapter 27

"They that can give up essential liberty to obtain a little temporary safety, deserve neither liberty nor safety."
-Benjamin Franklin

An explosion caught us off guard. Half the building was leveled and one of the three copters was lost to a missile. We weren't able to ascertain what had gone wrong, but did it really matter? During the moment of chaos and pandemonium, Split got panicky and shot one of the prisoners trying to crawl away. The west side of the building engulfed in flames, large pockets of fire jumped up walls and licked the rafters. Rubble scattered everywhere, people buried beneath it. Half of O-Team wounded or dead. Merrill had been thrown across the room by the blast and lay unconscious. Through my ringing ears, Seee ordered me to replace him, commanding me to keep one man on the prisoners and use the rest to care for the wounded and evacuate them to the helicopters. He gave me a two-minute ETD to move out.

Four minutes later, both helicopters teemed with Minutemen. Our pilot opened up the throttle, lifted up the collective, and we rose into the air. The rest of the Jackson Lake Lodge had been set on fire and burned behind us. The remaining Fed voting members had been shot. They burned with The Minutemen dead in a huge arc of towering flames.

Out in the distance we could see a patch of woods burning. A crash spot. The co-pilot told us he saw the drones going at one another.

I searched the cabin for another E-Team member, but they were all aboard the other helicopter. The remaining men in O-Team had been split between the two. Near the cockpit, Seee and I held onto a rafter next to the gunner. I stared past the gunner's shoulder into the night. The splash of orange from the drone crash now like a match light thinning in the distance. The shadowy landscape below whirled by like a dark river. It reminded me of Burns and the numbness I felt after drowning him. I suddenly realized The Abattoir wasn't as much about killing as it was desensitization. Anesthesia injected into us so when a man's head gets cut off, no matter whose it was, you had no need to question guilt or innocence. No conscientious objectors, judges, arbitrators, or mediators raised their hands saying "wait a second." We had all been convinced that to cut out the cancer, you needed a sharp knife. According to Seee's thinking, the deed was the vessel of delivery. The population needed to feel vindicated, to bask in a euphoric wave that justice had finally been served. But what would be the reaction when we were all hunted down and executed? Perhaps Seee already had the answer swimming in his head.

I turned to Seee and asked why he wasn't flying with his original team, and he told me he had left Kumo in command. It seemed to wake him from his reverie as he turned to the Minutemen crammed in the copter and yelled out, "I've got one thing to say to you."

There was a pause as everyone waited.

"Mission accomplished."

After that, the Minutemen began to relax, chatting amongst themselves. It was difficult to gauge morale, but a renewed sense of victory permeated throughout the cabin when Merrill finally came to. His face was blood-caked and cut. He asked which mule had kicked him. The fact he was alive and making jokes about a missing victory bottle and how one of the Fed Police had stolen his pack of smokes diverted everyone's mind away from the common thread of angst.

Like everyone, I wondered why continue with the ski masks? What was the point now after Seee had revealed himself over the camera? Everyone was a walking corpse. The giant was now awake.

Seee shook me by the shoulders. "Doesn't it feel good to believe in something?" he asked, elated with the moment. "With each swing of the sword, I felt like a drowning man allowed a breath."

I nodded. "I think the giant's legs have been cut at the ankles." He smiled, and I took his hand in mine and bumped shoulders with him. But my heart wasn't in it. He had martyred not only himself, but all of The Minutemen who fought bravely for him. Was this the price of victory?

The copters hovered in the air over the rendezvous point. Seee told us to leave all of our weapons inside. Merrill was put back in command of X-Team. We scaled down the ropes and hit the ground. Once we were all down, Merrill ordered us to change into our old clothes, pack up our stuff, and get the bikes started. I moved towards the trees where we had left the bikes. The night was cooler now. Behind me, I heard the copters lift off and fade away in the distance, perhaps on the way to be booby-trapped or blown up somewhere.

A figure appeared in front of me from behind a tree. The white patch of E-1 was barely discernible on the black commando uniform. A woman's voice called out my name.

"How did you know it was me?" I asked.

"I guessed, but your face blends in with the dark."

I laughed. "I am the dark." I gazed into her mask, trying to find her eyes within. My tone softened. "I'm glad you made it."

She put her hand over my heart. "Me too."

Even in the darkness I could see her blink a few times before she turned away. "What is it with us?" I asked, grabbing one of her wrists as she moved away. She turned back to me, eyes slowly coming into mine. I could see her lips move, and then they quickly shut. I yanked down lightly on her wrist, hoping this might provoke a response, but she still didn't answer. She cozied up to me and put her free hand under my mask and over my cheek, cupping it for a second. Slowly, she slipped her hand out of the mask. Like a whip, she lifted it back, and slapped me across the face while breaking my grasp on her wrist. Then she disappeared into the starry darkness.

The teams split up, riding out in the thick of the night without head- or taillights. The whole operation had lasted only thirty-five minutes, yet it seemed as if a century had passed. We pushed along a dirt path for a while. The high hum of my bike rung in my ears. Wheels dug into the hard dusty road as we careened through the darkness. With the moonless sky and stars twinkling out in the vastness of the atmosphere, I thought of Kicking Bear under his tepee looking for light that would never come. I kept gazing up, searching for the spotlight of a chopper to swoop down upon us and strafe us with machinegun fire. But none came. Our hacked drone warriors had done the job, and I thought about the irony in that—how a weakness had become a strength.

We stopped at a clump of woods and Seee told me to follow him while Merrill and the rest of X-Team veered away. I wondered what this meant, but I wasn't given the opportunity to question it. We rode by the burned-out farmhouse and abandoned barn, but passed it, continuing until we hit the highway. There we stopped, hiding the bikes behind a patch of trees. Then something happened I didn't understand. A car approached slowly, lit up the brights once, and stopped. Seee stepped out onto the road while the driver rolled down the window. Something was passed, and then the car took off. Seee stepped back off the road and told me to get back on the bike. After another couple of minutes trailing down another rugged path, we came to a stop. We threw off our helmets, and for the first time since the old barn, I took off my mask. Seee made his way to a break in the woods and began stripping the camouflage webbing off a two-seater Cessna. "This is just to get us past any initial roadblocks. It's dangerous to take back roads as well within a certain circumference."

"Where are we going?" I asked.

"Don't ask."

"Can I ask what the purpose of that was back there on the highway?"

"It was a simulation."

"Simulating what?"

"A lie we might have to tell one day."

"A simulation of a lie makes it more the truth. Is that it?"

"That's why I did it."

"Should I be worried?"

"You're with me," he said. "I suppose so. I'm pretty hot right now."

We dragged the plane out into an open field. The blinking lights on the wings had been smashed out, but enough starlight gleamed on the runway's path. Within a couple of minutes, we climbed up in the plane and took off, altitude kept low.

"I know what you're thinking," Seee said. "Why me? What am I doing here?"

I sat silent, gazing out of the window listening to his voice over the high throb of the props. The red giant, Alpha Herculis, was out there beaming in the night, and now I stretched my neck to look for it.

"We've got one more mission to do, you and I. I also wanted to thank you personally for everything you've done." Words of praise rarely came from Seee's lips. In the moment, they captured me. "The Anthill has told me you are still holding some things back though."

"I am a man not trusted," I said. "I understand why. I haven't complained. But why should I put one-hundred percent of my faith in The Cause if The Cause doesn't trust me? I've already been used as a pawn for Stellar Wind."

"I have no disputes with that," Seee said. "It has been a challenge to convince others of your loyalty. I won't deny it."

"So you believe in me then?"

"I do," he said. "I have from the start."

"Did you know from the beginning? Before I even got to The Abattoir?"

"We knew about Pelletier. He knew something about us, but not enough. But what was he going to tell his superiors even if he knew more? These are political men. They think of containment. But now, we have forced their hand."

"You've fried us all," I said bitterly.

"Not the case. Some will go underground. Others have had elaborate alibis created for them. Beyond the electronic trail, we have people trails too."

"The Company will cut out the whole heart of operations now."

"We agree, but they will likely do it slowly."

"The Abattoir is blown," I said.

"We don't think so, but we have other locations if it's the case."

"Rose might have found out about it."

"How?" Seee asked.

"Well, they were dialed in to my machine when I was hacking into Rose. Certainly she caught that."

"She should have erased it from her memory. Isn't that the case? It's what I've been told by The Anthill."

"I think so," I said. "But it's difficult to tell. She has added complexity. We are dealing with a neuromorphic machine. The Rose at the test lab is not the Rose underground in Bluffdale."

"We will plan for that contingency," Seee said.

The interior of the plane was alight with the glow of instruments. The air speed indicator showed 80 MPH, the altimeter read 2000 feet; the directional gyro said we were flying southwest.

"So what's your opinion of tonight?" Seee asked.

"I'm still thinking about it. It's what you said you'd do, right? Rip out the heart of the financial oligarchy? Will it sway public opinion? Will they think it was just?"

"Justice has dissolved in this country. No longer is it the salt of the people. It is water—the liquid to the slippery slope of tyranny."

"You are saying that law is no longer equally distributed," I said.

"Do you think it is?"

"No, but will tonight really change the power structure?"

"True power lives dormant in the masses. In the police state we live in today, the only way to get it to wake is if there is simultaneous acceptance of the same idea and a willingness to fight for it. This is what we have accomplished today."

"Really?" I asked. "So many people—they believe in nothing but themselves. Ask the sheep for sacrifice and all you'll see are lambs running from the wolf."

"I'm not sure I agree. Isn't it our duty to protect the lambs? They are our people, are they not?"

"We must force a choice," I said. "The cliff or the wolf. The population cannot escape without blood being spilled."

"The angry heart beats louder than the arrhythmic one."

"A revolution does not burst into flame with dead coals. They must be lit and kept alive. Do you think this one event will change anything?"

He looked a bit forlorn when I said this. His eye twitched and for a moment I could see this was perhaps the first time he had contemplated the question: what if nothing changed?

Finally, he said, "I have to believe that it will. Further blood might have to be spilled, but for The Cause the ends justify the means. Not all revolutions turn into violent ones. Look at the Rose Revolution, the collapse of the Soviet Union; arguably the Iranian Revolution was fairly bloodless. The people were hungry for change."

"The common thread you speak about in these cases was a weak, unpopular control authority. That is not what we have today. While unpopular, they are still well within control."

"I know," Seee admitted. "But not as much today as

yesterday."

"You yourself have preached that anarchy is not the answer."

"It isn't," Seee said, "but it might be a necessary intermediary."

"What you did was dangerous," I said. "It exposes all of The Minutemen."

"It was a calculated risk. The people must see a real face. Someone who is willing to say *enough*."

"I don't believe it was the right move. The Cause doesn't end with today. It starts tomorrow."

He smiled at this, pleased with the words, his face aglow with the controls. "You don't see all of the angles yet. You don't have all of the information. But you will."

Seee flicked the nose lights on and off in a Morse code. A farmer on the ground turned on some lights and for a moment there was a landing strip in front of us before the lights disappeared. It was all Seee needed to guide the plane in for a landing. As we descended, he asked me to put on the mask again, saying he didn't want me compromised. He told me not to speak, unless I used the modulator.

We landed in an open field, a strip of land a hundred miles south of Salt Lake City. Once we were on the ground, we jumped out and Seee ran up to the man guiding us in and bound him up in a big bear hug.

After Seee let the man down, I had almost caught up to them. "We did it!" Seee said.

"You sure did," the man said. "We were watching it on the Internet until it went down."

"Your Internet went down?" Seee asked.

"It did," the man said. "I called around to a couple of neighbors, and it seems I'm not the only one."

The man stood burly and stout, a gray-bearded guy with rugged facial features, worker hands rough and callused. I silently took the scratched and scabby hand he offered, but no names passed between us. Although the man averted his eyes and an awkward silence crept between us, a certain politeness in him smoothed the situation.

"How much did you see before it cut out?" Seee asked.

The man cackled and said, "Enough to know the chairman is dead and at least one other."

"Things are moving fast, my friend," Seee said. "Let's get this plane inside."

We rolled the Cessna into the barn. Once inside, we didn't linger. A minute more for a further update and farewell, and we hopped up onto another set of motorcycles with a new set of gear already prepared for us. I slung a new backpack over my shoulders, started up the bike, and rode out of the barn following Seee. We stopped at the edge of the man's property, and Seee told me a rendezvous address in case we were split up.

"Why there?"

"No one knows we're coming," he said, "and where we're going no one will find us."

We wound our way to the 257, heading for Las Vegas.

Chapter 28

"For heroes have the whole earth for their tomb; and in lands far from their own, where the column with its epitaph declares it, there is enshrined in every breast a record unwritten with no monument to preserve it, except that of the heart. These take as your model, and judging happiness to be the fruit of freedom and freedom of valor, never decline the dangers of war."

-Pericles

The sun cracked the sky into a soft light dancing over a set of high arching clouds colored pink and maroon as we arrived in Las Vegas.

We ditched the bikes by the side of the road on the outskirts of the city and scaled a chain-link fence at an overpass before climbing down into a storm drain. The ten-yard sloping slab of concrete we stood on led to a ten-foot-high tunnel going underground. We stopped at the entrance. Seee unzipped his backpack and tossed me a headlamp, a flashlight, a poncho with a hoodie, and a Glock 19. He told me to put on the poncho and keep my head covered. He put on rubber boots and told me mine were in the backpack. After I had changed, I asked him if there was another Anthill in here. He laughed and told me no, saying the people inside held onto higher moral codes. But then he told me to blind anyone looking at us.

We crept into the tunnel with our headlamps underneath our hoodies. The air cooled as we stepped into the pitch black. A platoon of Tunnel People camped near the entrance hidden in makeshift shanties, each meager dwelling sectioned off by tarpaper, wallpaper, roof liner, or bedsheets. We heard the playful song of a child drifting from within the darkness. As we approached, the child went quiet, conditioned for this sort of disturbance, like a well-taught cheetah cub crouching low, slithering through tall grass while keeping its tail down. We moved past a shack where the little girl's voice had come from. The entrance had a shower curtain jerry-rigged to the ceiling. The curtain was pulled back, and inside the dim room a bug-eyed man stared out from behind a book, a candle burning behind him, a shotgun on his lap. The man had a long, stubbled chin reaching out and grabbing the darkness. Pinned-up hair was braided into cornrows and flowing over his shoulders. As we passed, he was in the midst of rolling one of the serpent strands up in a finger. He gazed at us from behind a pair of spectacles as if we were a pair of loitering predators. A hand moved quickly toward the weapon, but Seee blinded him with his flashlight and the other hand went to his eyes. We moved past. A daddy longlegs scurried up a wall as our head beams moved back over the exterior. I had been surprised looking inside. The whole room sat on top of wooden pallets, runoff flowing beneath. An old-timey icebox sat in there, a sofa, double bed, coffee table, sink, rolled up sleeping bags. Lines of cultivated moss soaked up the wash running between the pallets, and at one end of the room the man had sawed-up whiskey barrels with tomatoes growing out of them.

"Man's got a penthouse in there," Seee said once we were well past.

"Viva Las Vegas, right?"

"Exactly," Seee said.

"Better digs than my jungle mansion."

"You had free room and board," he snorted. "Nothing to sneeze at."

I laughed as we slogged through the running water streaming down the corridor. The hexagonal tunnel lit up with burning candle lights as we dove deeper inside. I looked back at the strip of sunlight thinning from the tunnel's entrance. We were exploring the hallway of a marooned spaceship which had lost power and drifted out in space, a *Battlestar Galactica* type of scene where the Cylons had invaded the decks and pulverized all of the humans, the survivors now stuck in the midst of the rubble.

As we moved past another village of Tunnel People, the stench of urine, feces, and mildew grew. The farther in you went, the less motivated you were to travel out. Seee turned on his flashlight. The middle was a no man's land. On its borders, the accommodations slipped to simple sleeping bags atop pallets. Duffle bags were stuffed and ready to move, most spots deserted. No man's land was a stew of garbage, legions of ants, cobwebs, dead rat carcasses.

We walked in deeper, past the garbage dump, took a left and kept going. The cockroaches kept us company on our march through the sludge, scurrying up walls and following. Perhaps we went another two hundred yards when we saw another glimmer of sunshine down the long corridor. We stopped at an air channel and sucked in the breeze.

We kept going. Another hamlet of Tunnel People emerged, but none to put an eye on. We hopped a wall of sandbags mounted to direct the wash through a funnel and moved into another no man's land.

"What's your real name?" I asked as we dipped back into the darkness.

"Why do you want to know that?" Seee asked.

"It's part of you, isn't it?"

"A dead part—sure—I suppose so. But here I am. My name is Seee. I exist in the here and now. Why do you need to know more?"

"I am not searching for your existence. I am searching for the truth."

"Truth cannot be found in a name or words alone. Some truths are self-evident."

We passed through a shallow lake in the middle of the corridor. The water was up to the top of our boots, stagnant and briny. Minnows darted in the water under the beam of my flashlight, and I thought about how the place had its own ecosystem. Separate rules of evolution reigned here in the catacombs different from the outside.

"You still don't trust me," I said.

"It is Cyril Tetsu," he said abruptly, his tone carrying an air of seriousness.

"Come on," I said. "That name I've found tumbling inside the QX. It's like a surfer caught in an undertow of Montgomery information waves."

"You profiled Montgomery?"

"Why wouldn't I? We need to know our enemy, don't we?"

Seee stopped, turned his flashlight on a wall of graffiti in competition with gray mold and green algae. The light beamed over the rainbow-colored words, *Viva la Revolution*. Directly below it was an airplane outlined in a circle—the peace sign, painted in black.

"So how about it?" I asked.

"You will never find a record of my existence."

"But yet, here you are," I said.

"Here I am."

We walked a while in silence. He seemed to know exactly where we were going, maneuvering throughout the labyrinth of underground tunnels expertly. My curiosity with his tie to this place was aroused. Was he just a rat that had come up through the sewer? A man from the true Underworld and not the virtual one? Perhaps he truly didn't have a name and was never part of the State apparatus. Maybe everything about his past coiled into a simple fabrication. Instead of being a deadly assassin working for The Company all of those years, perhaps he elevated himself to god of the conmen, juking anyone gullible enough to bloody their names in his quest for liberation. Perhaps he was simply a cult, a numen to The Cause instead of a solid man.

Finally, Seee said, "It is time we ditch your State name. I will now call you Cerberus. He has always been a part of you as Seee has been a part of me." He moved the light off the wall and on to me, pointing it at my chest. "Do you see him? He's a different man with a different name. He can see through six eyes instead of two, and you will need every one of them for the future that will sweep you up in its winds."

I walked silently behind him, the gun tucked behind my back in the crease of my jeans. He knew as well as I who had the strategic position. A lack of fear within him one could only equate to trust. I felt I had walked over a line, but the significance of the moment I wouldn't yet fully comprehend.

After another hundred yards of stepping through a stream of broken glass, we came upon another scattered collection of shanties. This time Seee went into one. When I entered through the slit in the tarpaulin, he was shaking hands with a man he introduced as Turner.

Turner had a reedy voice, stood tall and upright. A bald-headed man who spoke with an accent I couldn't quite place.

"You had any Noahs recently?" Seee asked.

"Bad one last summer," the man answered. "Worse yet since I been down here." He pointed up at the wall. A black strip of paint over the words *RIP Dorma May* was drawn above a spraypainted array of flowers amongst the other graffiti randomly splattered up there. "The place flooded up to that mark. Killed a hundred people. But I handcuffed myself to the pipe there."

He showed us the scar on his wrist, a ring of pink and wrinkled flesh. "Cut me up pretty bad. Dislocated my shoulder the current was so strong."

Seee nodded, patted the man on the shoulder. They talked about the floods, the new Tunnel People tenants surrounding Turner's dwelling. Then Seee said, "We've been on the road for quite some time. Mind if we take a rest?"

"My home is your home," the man said. "You can take that mattress there."

We crashed on a queen-size mattress on top of two wooden

pallets. I fell asleep within a couple of minutes, the sound of the stream lulling me to sleep. I woke an indeterminable amount of hours later. Seee whispered to Turner over a low candlelight, a mason jar in his hands, drinking something that smelled like rye. I kept my eyes closed, interloping on their conversation. It might have been Yoncalla, perhaps a Tunnel People argot, but their voices were low and muddled.

Finally, I stirred and sat up. Turner threw a miniature box of cereal at me.

"Breakfast?" I asked.

"That or lunch or dinner," the man laughed, elbowing Seee.

After a cup of coffee, Seee and I were on our feet again and moving through the dark tunnels, slogging through a sandy stream until we hit a patch of concrete. We walked through the middle of a long corridor absent of inlets or drains that might have provided a hint of sunlight. The roar of traffic came from overhead. Suddenly, Seee stopped and turned to me.

"Give me your flashlight," he ordered.

I did as I was told. My headlamp beamed over his face and he squinted in the light. "Turn that off as well," he said. Once I had done as he asked, he turned off the lights, and we were standing about two yards away from each other in the pitch black.

"It wasn't so long ago a pair of bars stood between us down in the darkness. Do you remember?" Seee asked.

"Of course I do."

"You had a thirst for light."

"I wasn't used to being blind."

"Eventually you realized you don't need light to see, didn't you? The darkness taught you something about instinct, Cerberus. Didn't it?"

"It did," I said, wary of what leash he strung me on. In the midst of the blackness, I sensed a change, and I felt like a rabbit in an open field freezing under a circling shadow. Everything had lead up to this moment—why we were down here, why his mood had been so strange. I sensed a subtle movement and a chill raced up my spine.

"I have a vision it will be you who will lead The Minutemen in the future," he said.

"Kumo is second in line," I said warily, "and you're not dead."

"Yes, and Kumo deserves the honor, but I don't think he'll last." A shadow seemed to pass before me, but I knew my imagination played tricks as the darkness was pure.

"Why don't you think so?"

"He's street smart, no doubt about it. But he doesn't see all of the angles."

"And I do?" I asked. "I don't understand the angle right now."

"But you know there is one."

"I figured."

"You are a man who can find his way out of the dark, and live in it at the same time. You can coexist in two worlds. Kumo is present in only one."

"Are you saying I can liaise with The Anthill more effectively?"

"Information is more important in the modern world than swords or guns. It is the NSA whom we must battle. You would be a great asset inside."

"This is all hypothetical talk," I said. "We will hide you away, won't we? You are Seee, alive in the here and now."

He ignored what I said. His voice turned inward, lethargic and tired, as if I were barely there. "They will follow my command, even if I am dead. Merrill has a recording of my wishes if things go badly. I buried something at The Abattoir. Remember the tree you scratched the date into?"

"Yes."

"It's buried in the ground around it in a small vial. It has the names and contacts of each of the cells. Kumo is the only other who has it."

I felt veered away from the words he didn't want to speak. He had a knack for steering conversations to the direction he wanted them to go. I tried to swerve it back and asked, "How am I going to get into the NSA? How am I going to explain that I'm here with you now? The Company will probably have my ass and…"

Something occurred to me that stopped my thought process. I stood there silent a moment. I could hear him breathe in the blackness. Like a ripple in a lake, a tiny wave of it rolled over me.

"You see the angle now," Seee said. He flicked on one of the flashlights from his waist, and the light streamed across his face. His eyes danced in the shadows, his gun pointing directly at my head.

"Pull your weapon out," he ordered.

I stood there frozen, looking him over. A crazy look buzzed in his eyes.

"I won't ask you again," he said.

I pulled out the gun tucked in my jeans from behind my back and held it down at my waist.

"Point it at me," he yelled.

My thumb touched the steel on the front of my belt buckle, the gun clenched tightly in my fist. His eyes creased and turned yellow in the light.

"The star that burns the brightest is the one closest to death. My spirit is on fire and you must be the one to snuff it out."

"I cannot," I said, my voice gritty and furious. "I will not!"

"You can and you will. Have I taught you nothing?"

"You have taught me everything."

"Then you know what you must do."

He tilted the flashlight to the scabby concrete floor, and his face went dark. Then I felt a sharp pain shoot through my shoulder. I flicked on my headlight and saw him with a hunting knife in his hands, the tip bloody and red. The same knife with the twine handle and nickel guard I had used in the jungle to carve up the tree.

I tilted my headlamp to my shoulder and saw blood seeping

through my shirt. The wound wasn't deep, but the blood kept flowing, dripping down on my boot.

"It should leave a nice trail," he said.

The light passed underneath him once more. He looked like a glassy reflection in a river eddy—me at the river the morning after I had drowned Burns, a man not entirely of this world, a man about to leap for the Lushing Tree, a man ready to climb Jacob's Ladder from the sandy Pit. I put my hand to the wound, and applied pressure, asking myself how I could pull the trigger on a man birthing an idea that might actually change the world.

"Are you fucking crazy?" I yelled out to him, reaching out and pushing his gun out of my face. "This is not a game!"

"The State needs a head. The media needs a hero. Let's not let them jackoff to a huge search where I'll end up dead anyway. Let's do this on our own terms. I will not be a prisoner to anyone." With his knife, he stroked each cheek, making streaks of red, a war-painted face. "I know this is no game, but this is game-over if it doesn't get done."

I waved my flashlight over his eyes to blind him from my expression. "Why did you let me live knowing my motivations coming into The Abattoir?"

"You came in with preconceived ideas. You knew nothing of The Cause. You were a traitor then, but you aren't one now. Everyone knows it. Everyone has seen it."

"You don't know that."

"I do know that."

Tires swished by on a road from the world above. Way off in the distance, some drunk howled at the wind. Down in the darkness of the sewer, the steady sound of the stream flowed through the pitch-black corridor.

His tone softened as he grabbed ahold of the barrel of my pistol and pointed it at his chest. "One of the hardest things in life is having to say goodbye to someone you love. In this score, we are brothers. I appreciate that it will be you if it makes any difference."

I thought of my father squirming on the ground after I shot him, after I had taken off his mask, after I had thrown my gun long and far across the parking lot. He asked the impossible. "This doesn't have to be done."

"If you look at it clearly, you'll see that not only does it have to be done, but it has to be you."

He pushed his chest against the barrel. "Pull the trigger. It's what you've wanted? Now is your chance."

"I've given up that chance. It's not what I want at all."

"It's not what we're going to make them believe."

With my gun against his chest, I felt his fingers over the trigger guard. Like his every move, reason and intent stood behind it—cold calculation, rational thought in the midst of stormy emotions. A memory of Drew Gareth being shot by the map man flashed in my mind, Seee standing there without even blinking an eye.

"How are we going to make them buy such a story?" I asked.

"We've left a trail for you. Messages to Pelletier. You are no longer at The Abattoir. You've been on my tail now for a while. You knew about Jackson Hole. You texted it to them a few minutes after it started happening."

He tilted his head back and laughed. "You, my friend, are a patriot."

Strained lines furrowed deep in his pallid face. He spoke with the voice of the earth, graveled and fading, light dimming in his eyes. A realization dawned in him that these were his last minutes, that they would be spent with me, that I was the man standing in front of him whom he was going to say goodbye to. His lips were void of color, a breathlessness rising to the surface. Flesh on his face thin, like snakeskin ready to peel away.

"Tonight is Second Sight," he said. "My leap of faith. I die either way. The only question is will you help me?"

I paused to think. He kept silent, running his flashlight

against the walls of graffiti. My mind tried to penetrate his, discover how time moved for martyrs, men lingering in the womb about to be birthed to another world. His facial features became more oblong as he yawned in the artificial light, as if casting a shadow upon himself. But I realized he wasn't stretching his jaw out of fatigue. My procrastination caused him anxiety, so finally I agreed, submitting to his final wish.

He explained how things would proceed, pouring it out in a stream of sentences. He told me my alibi, where I was and at what times, how it would be conclusive evidence of my patriotism. He gave me a phone and a key, told me what they were for. When he was about finished, I stopped him. Out of my backpack I dug out my photo of the Earth. I tilted my head and held it up so he could see it. Our headlamps illuminated it, brought it out of the darkness. There it was—the aqua-planet, suspended in space, a sky full of clouds whirling over a cerulean ocean. He remarked he had never seen anything so beautiful. I gave him the photo. He fingered it, felt the frayed white edges, the folds, the deep furrows within the glossy surface. As he took it, he said, "Sometimes it isn't easy being brave."

I squeezed his shoulder, and then we moved out of the double-barreled tunnel and into the starry night, the air weightless and misty. A strong breeze blew over my face, a Mojave wind torched with the desert heat. My feet seemed to be moving in slow motion, not really believing what was happening. A golf course on the right, we paused gazing out behind the concrete wall of a runoff drain for any groundskeeper in the area. On the other side of the fence, Las Vegas Boulevard bustled, two lanes of traffic to thread through to get to the other side.

He told me to give him a two-second head start, then he ran forward. The rattle of the chain-link fence rung in my ears as he scaled it. He was almost over when I sprinted forward. My heart thumped in my chest, a hammering force, a giant's footsteps. My fingers slipped into the parallelograms of the fence and I was climbing. Looking up at the sky, the world felt alien, the neon glow of Vegas clouding up Orion in a gas of carnival colors. At the top of the fence, I glassed the tunnel, the darkness inside deep and massive. Gravity pulled me back to it, but my feet hit the pavement, and I bolted across Las Vegas Boulevard afraid I would lose him. The Mandalay Bay towered to my left. Over the street the *Welcome to Fabulous Las Vegas* sign sparkled, the star atop of it blinking in raucous colors of orange and red. Yellow lights outlined the heart-shaped sign, an artery of bulbs racing around it and flowing into a ventricle. I heard the sound of jazz coming from across the street. A throng of tourists was out there for a free twenty-dollar giveaway, pulling on one-armed bandits, relics with the lever on the side.

Seee hurdled a small green fence, taking it in stride as I gained on him. A ribbon of dust whirled in the air, a tiny maelstrom of dry desert hardpan gobbled by the wind. I saw him pull his gun out of his pants—slowly, deliberately, as if he wanted to make every instant count. I hurdled the fence, yanked my Glock out of my jeans and fired two shots well clear of his shoulders.

Screams from the crowd.

Panic.

The future is Turbulence.

The smell of tar in the air, blowing all the way from the north Salt Lake City salt flats. The idling highwaymen in orange jumpers smoking cigarettes. Steel-toed boots hot on the asphalt, the highway bouncing up and down in my vision, the blinking lights of the Vegas sign bursting in my eyes.

Man. Machine. The real world. The Underworld.

All of them crashing down. The squeal of a horn passed behind me. The word asshole coming from the car, dragging in the wind in a rippled Doppler effect. Panting breath—hot, hot, hot under the beaming moon. Shadowy craters, scoops of rock and moon dust cut out of the crust, a face pocked by meteors over eons.

The crowd still scampering away, except for a man near the Vegas sign post. Planted there like a root. His phone out recording the incident. Behind one of the old slots, another head popped up recording the scene. Two eye-witnesses.

And then Seee was there, in the special spot we agreed upon, in the middle of the sign ten yards out. I stopped and leveled the Glock, closed an eye and peered down the sight, a palm under my shooting hand to keep the gun steady. He whirled around and fired a shot. I pulled the trigger, my finger still squeezing as the bullet yanked Seee backward. I shot twice more before he hit the ground.

Yelling. Stopped traffic. Blaring horns.

I kept the gun lowered to the ground and walked forward.

People out of their cars. The wail of a siren.

I moved above him to see if he was still alive, if my shots had failed to hit their mark. But he was dead, a wide stare in his eyes, one not of shock, but of expectation, a plutonic expression of stoicism that said he welcomed the other world, that he had done everything he could in this one. Crumpled in his open palm was the photo of the Earth. A strong urge came to pick it up and pocket it. I stood there biting my lip as the breeze took it. It rolled around the dust for a few feet before it stopped. I let my gun fall out of my hand, and it thudded to the ground. I dropped to my knees as the sirens got louder. My hands went up in the air as the breeze picked up the picture once more. I watched it dance its way back over Las Vegas Boulevard. I had done my duty for him, a patriot in his eyes, yet a traitor in my own. I was Cerberus, the three-headed hound from Hell—patriot, traitor, and the gray in between.

Acknowledgements

A heartfelt thanks has to go to Robert Barclay who has supported me throughout, giving me sage advice and suffering through the beginning years. Thanks to Charlie Boodman, who got me started in this game and helped me become a better writer. Martin Fletcher, for his developmental edit, another big thanks to my main editor, Elizabeth White, and finally a warm thanks to my copy editor, Dominic James who was very patient with me. Sarah Reckefuss encouraged me, became my number one fan, and broke out her limited rolodex to help. Then there was Margaret Harmer at ShiftingWaves.com, the dream maker helping out with my vision for a book trailer. Thanks to my other beta readers: Amanda Callendrier, Massimo Marino, Fraser Grant. There are numerous people to thank in the Geneva Writers Group. A special thanks to Susan Tiberghien who runs it. Thanks to the Geneva International Book Club (Andy, Mehran, Helen) and Goodreads friends Stacey, Linda, Jenny, Amber, Chris, among others.

About the Author

Roderick Vincent is the author of the *Minutemen* series about a dystopian America. He has lived in the United States, England, Switzerland, and the Marshall Islands. His reviews and short stories have been published in *Ploughshares* blog, *Straylight* (University of Wisconsin, Parkside) and *Offshoots* (a Geneva publication).

For more information, to sign up for the email list (email not shared, has "unsubscribe" feature), or to connect with him, check out roderickvincent.com or find him on Goodreads in his Fiction Threads Goodreads Group (formerly Trauma Novels). Other places to find him are:

Twitter (https://twitter.com/R_D_Vincent)
Facebook (www.facebook.com/roderick.d.vincent)
Neo World View (non-fiction blog) (www.neoworldview.com)
Writing blog: (www.roderickvincent.wordpress.com)
Author Interviews and book trailer at:
www.youtube.com/results?search_query=roderick+vincent

If you feel inclined, please do an Amazon or Goodreads review. Reviews are increasingly more important as the publishing industry undergoes a wave of change. The author would truly appreciate it.

Truth in The Cause

The CIA regularly subcontracts to consultants. For example, they contracted SERE (Survival, Evasion, Resistance, Escape) instructor Air Force Capt. Michael Kearns and Dr. John Bruce Jessen (whose handwritten notes described torture techniques). The two later formed Mitchell, Jessen & Associates which taught SERE courses (SV-91). According to truth-out.org, Jessen and Kearns worked on "a new course for special mission units (SMUs), which had as its goal individual resistance to terrorist exploitation." These special mission units fall under DoD clandestine Joint Special Operations Command. The Abattoir is not so different with its advertised mission, although quite different with its intended one. It is not a CIA black site, but rather one owned and operated by the contractors, and its location is kept secret even from its CIA employers. While the character Seee was not based on Kearns, there is the similarity that people graduating from Kearns' courses were sent around the world on secret, covert missions much like the type of agents bred at The Abattoir. Unlike Kearns and Jessen, who appear to have fallen out, the characters Hassani and Seee worked together intimately from the beginning for The Cause.

The term "battle lab" (used by Seee in the chapter with Tongueless Downs) was used by Guantanamo officials Maj. Gen. Mike Dunleavy and Maj. Gen. Geoffrey Miller. http://www.truth-out.org/news/item/205:exclusive-cia-psychologists-notes-reveal-true-purpose-behind-bushs-torture-program

NSA Terms—Stellar Wind has been associated with the NSA's Utah Data Center in Bluffdale, Utah (http://www.wired.com/2012/03/ff_nsadatacenter/all/). From Wikipedia, the NSA's Tailored Access Operations is "a cyber-warfare intelligence-gathering unit of the NSA" (http://en.wikipedia.org/wiki/Tailored_Access_Operations). Turbulence is a cyberwarfare program within the NSA started in 2005 and might or might not be ongoing (http://en.wikipedia.org/wiki/Turbulence _%28NSA%29). StormBrew is another Internet surveillance NSA program (http://en.wikipedia.org/wiki/STORMBREW). Its usage in *The Cause* by Montgomery is fictional, but one can imagine there are certain ways to "control" the Internet.

611 Folsom Street in San Francisco is the true location of the AT&T Building where fiber lines converge. According to "The Shadow Factory" by James Bamford, this is where the NSA has a little room off to the side called the SG3 Secure Room. For more information, see (http://en.wikipedia.org/wiki/Room_641A).

The DARPA BigDog is made by Boston Dynamics, which has subsequently been bought by Google. Google plans to honor the remainder of its DARPA contracts (whatever that means). One can find information on the BigDog here: (http://www.bostondynamics.com/robot_bigdog.html)

Author's Note

It is my hope that this book stirs the fingers of controversy until they become the fist of ideas. Only with sober ideas can we hope for the flint to spark a long overdue debate. That debate is that all other debates have been but hairs on the head of the true problem. That problem is the wheels of America have begun to grind to a halt requiring ideas bigger than those our feeble politicians are willing to stomach. The danger of doing nothing exceeds the boldness of doing something. America has grown drunk on the fumes of debt and now the price of the hangover must be paid.

The rot within America does not take a keen eye to see. With government largess at epic levels, it begs the question, how long can it last? The United States government has increased spending by 67% per median household in thirteen years. What one must ask is why they had to do that? And more importantly can it be sustained?

Now, the government depends on artificial interest rates from the banking cartel of the Federal Reserve (not part of the government) for its spending. The economy sputters along at stagnating growth rates. Unfunded future liabilities should be seen as criminal and will be paid only by broken promises or a diminished dollar. All of this will work for some time, until it doesn't. This novel has explored a world where an inflection point begins, a world where government overreaches for power and begins to make enemies with its own people. The characters in *The Cause* are unforgiving of the perpetual looting of the middleclass by an increasingly power-grabbing government and Federal Reserve who distort their livelihoods. We are quickly approaching a time when the vote will no longer matter.

I hope this novel has raised questions while at the same time has been entertaining. I certainly believe the NSA, CIA, and FBI must be vigilant in their duties to protect America from asymmetric threats, but where is the line drawn between having one-hundred percent safety and a full and over-reactive police state? Is it when the NSA lies to Congress? Is it when the NSA breaks the law? What is the government's penalty when caught? As with banks, moral hazard disappears when there are no repercussions for one's actions, when losses can be socialized.

Events of yet another whistleblower in the NSA have caused quite a storm amongst pro-government zealots. One must ask the question: What did Eric Snowden give up that was so pertinent to U.S. security? Since his revelations uncovered a corporate/government conspiracy against its people (PRISM), and the information exposed the totalitarian creep of where America is heading, shouldn't the citizen be made aware of this, especially since he/she funds the budget where money is then turned against liberty and breaks Constitutional rights? Recently, NBC did an interview with Eric Snowden. At the end of the interview, Brian Williams said, "A good number of Americans of course feel because of what they see as an act of treason, they sleep less soundly at night fearing this massive leak of secrets has endangered the country." Is it possible to pack a statement indoctrinating paranoia more than that one? Perhaps NBC and Brian Williams need to read Benjamin Franklin's quote from Chapter 27.

Many whistleblowers of the past have revealed similar embarrassments to the NSA (Echelon, for example). Why such a large reaction to this one? I hope *The Cause* explores the question: What is a traitor, and what is a patriot? The line to me is certainly blurred, as I hope it is in this book. I leave you with some quotes of Snowden's naysayers and ask—what are they so afraid of?

"America is now a less safe place. The world is a less safe place because of what Mr. Snowden unilaterally did. He deserves to be prosecuted. I hope they find him in the hole that he's hiding in in Hong Kong and

bring him home and try him." – **Karl Rove**

"I hope we follow Mr. Snowden to the ends of the earth to bring him to justice." – **Lindsey Graham**

"What he did was an act of treason." – **Diane Feinstein**

"He's a traitor." – **John Boehner**

"We do not see a tradeoff between security and liberty." – **Keith Alexander – NSA Director**

"The national security of the United States has been damaged as a result of those leaks. The safety of the American people and the safety of people who reside in allied nations have been put at risk as a result of these leaks." – **Eric Holder**

"And I hope that he is prosecuted to the fullest extent of the law." – **Mitch McConnell**

"Now you've got this 29-year-old high-school dropout whistle-blower making foreign policy for our country, our security policy. It's sad, Brian. We've made treason cool. Betraying your country is kind of a fashion statement. He wants to be the national security Kim Kardashian. He cites Bradley Manning as a hero. I mean, we need to get very, very serious about treason. And oh by the way, for treason — as in the case of Bradley Manning or Edwards Snowden — you bring back the death penalty." – **Fox and Friends**

"I think on three scores — that is leaking the Patriot Act section 215, FISA 702, and the President's classified cyber operations' directive — on the strength of leaking that, yes, that would be a prosecutable offense. I think that he should be prosecuted." – **Nancy Pelosi**

At Roundfire we publish great stories. We lean towards the spiritual and thought-provoking. But whether it's literary or popular, a gentle tale or a pulsating thriller, the connecting theme in all Roundfire fiction titles is that once you pick them up you won't want to put them down.